M. A. MADDOCK

# A Flutter on the Wind

Paperback ISBN: 978-1-7397449-6-0



**This novel was written by a human. Not an AI.**

Cover Design by Diana TC - Triumph Book Covers
Butterfly illustration by Tegan Sommers - Art by Tegan
Interior Design & Formatting by Platform House

M. A. MADDOCK

# A Flutter on the Wind

Book Three

*The Sixth Amulet Series*

*Dedicated to all writers.*

*"Let true artistry shine through the hands of creativity."*
M.A. Maddock

*For Sherlock*

*Forever with me.*
*This one is for you.*

Urquille
Skyraffin
Elboru Castle
Muir Forest
Paths of Lome
Affin Shire
Ardmanoth
The High Mountains of Ardmanoth
Ruins of Moyne

# Shaw

# FOREWARD

By

Gavin Gardiner –
Author of *For Rye, The Last Testament of Crighton Smythe &
Witchcraft on Rücken Ridge.*

"A tapestry of familiar mythology – and wholly original creations –
weaved through a world you'll happily get lost in.
A story that truly sings."

These are my words - words I'm honoured to have included on the back of *The Moon Chasers* - the follow-up to *The Sixth Amulet* and the second part in friend and fellow-author M.A. Maddock's compelling historical fantasy epic series.

Given my unfamiliarity with the genre, I predictably reach for titles such as *A Game of Thrones* or *The Lord of the Rings* when attempting to equate parallels to the world Miriam has created; but I don't band these names around without good reason. The ensemble cast of characters, interplay of diverging and converging arcs, and extraordinarily high stakes are some of the elements I most enjoy in the aforementioned classics, and Miriam's compelling series does Tolkien and Martin proud.

A worthy continuation to the first and second instalments and an intriguing set-up for Miriam's next offering.

G. Gardiner

## OTHER BOOKS IN THIS SERIES

***The Sixth Amulet***
***The Moon Chasers***

**An important note to you, the reader.**

Thank you so much for purchasing *A Flutter on the Wind.* I truly hope you enjoy it. But there is something I would like to ask of you when you finish it. Reviews are important to authors. Unfortunately, not many are aware of how important. They don't have to be long; a word, a sentence or a short paragraph is all we seek—and it only takes a couple of minutes. Honestly, it does! An acknowledgement (of our hard work, as well as our stories) means so much to us. So, please, make an author's day, and share your thoughts. (reviews can be posted on Amazon and Goodreads). Thank you, and happy reading! X

# Prologue

From within the sanctity of Elboru, it waits—the *Shenn*—the immense force created to give its bearer the power to be a formidable Ruler. It belongs to him—the Magus—Lord of all Warlocks—and he belongs to it. But two worlds lie threatened by an evil that wants to dominate and destroy them. And yet, all is still not lost; for the belief in its true worth remains strong, heightening the courage of those who have united to risk everything, to see it placed in the hands of the *Chosen One*—to see him quench the darkness.

# Chapter One

*Scotland: North-West – 1630*
*The Forest of Garve – Beyond the Cordhu Pass*

Her body flinched, reawakened by the sound of something scurrying about her.

Oblivious, the small mammal continued to go about its business, scavenging for food. Listening intently, she followed the sound of its quick labour, her eyes dancing wildly beneath their tightly closed lids, fighting to unlock the newfound sight which would astound her. Through no control of her own, they flew open, vibrant with new life.

Reluctant to move, Kara remained motionless and unsure. She then had a vague recollection of intense pain. Fearing its return, she kept still, her new—and heightened—senses taking over. Beyond the cave's shelter, she became aware of the outside world: the babbling brook, where she had tried to ease the agony of the blistering sun on her skin; the trees, their branches clicking loudly as the wind pushed them together, it hissing and sighing as it passed by; and the animated sounds of natures' residents, enhanced—so loud they almost crowded her thoughts.

Her newborn eyes travelled around the cave, its dank smell burning her nostrils. Despite the lack of daylight, she could make out its uneven dome-like shape, with its moss-covered roof—the flowerless, green plant, carpeting the surface. Within its *pile,* insects and spiders scattered frantically, disturbed by her presence. One thing was certain: she was not in Valhalla.

Though anxious, Kara felt an added resilience to her previous strength; her mind was clearer, sharper, and tenacious. Her thoughts returned to the images that had tortured her mind before she had fallen into darkness, now aware they had been nothing but a figment of her torturous end. *But this is not my end*, she realised. No, she felt alive—more than ever—and yet still feared the pain. *What if it comes back?*

There was only one way to find out …

Carefully, she extended her long fingers, feeling the knuckles crack. She flexed them. It felt good. Her eyes suddenly darted, reminding her she was not alone.

The little ground squirrel stopped abruptly and raised its head, its curious nose twitching, searching for the familiar scent of food to stockpile before the onslaught of the coming winter. It then became aware of the stranger, sharing the cave with it. It edged closer, stopping and starting, unsure.

Kara listened to its approach, hearing the tap of its tiny nails on the hard ground. In an unpredicted move, she snatched the little creature. It screeched in pain. She drew it closer, scrutinising it; it stared into her red eyes, frozen with fear, having sensed her malevolence. It felt soft between her thick fingers; she could feel its tiny heartbeat accelerate, pounding with distress as it wriggled in its pathetic attempt to escape from her clutch. Beneath its fur, she could feel its tiny bones—so fragile she knew she could crush them, without effort. *Just like that!* she thought.

As if reading her mind, the squirrel's survival instincts kicked in, and it bit down, hard. She winced, letting it go, and examined her hand, musing over her reaction; she had felt no pain, and yet the marks of its sharp teeth were visibly deep. She tilted her head, fascinated, when the blood began to seep, its sweet, fresh metallic smell enticing her rising senses; her nostrils flared as it continued to ooze from the puncture wounds. Watching it, she swallowed—the sudden dryness in her throat urging her to taste it. She let her tongue glide over the wounds, her taste buds heightening as the blood slid down her throat. As she closed her eyes to languish in its appeal, she remained alert; even after its hasty departure, she could still hear the squirrel's escape, in the distance, listening to the patter of its tiny paws as they faded away.

Reminded of its bite, and the sweet taste in her mouth, she returned her attention to her hand, then paused; the bite had already faded, leaving only two faint scars.

Kara was now aware of the influence of her mind over her new body. It made her detect an unfamiliar capability—one she no longer feared.

Free of pain and nightmares, she rose with a bearing grace, then looked down. Raising her arms, she examined herself: the muscles beneath her pale, porcelain-like skin were twitching, exuding strength, and the veins—almost blackened by the venom—pulsated and brimmed with life. Gone were her battle scars, where arrowheads had once left their permanent dents—the marks of past victories. She inspected the wound on her arm, where the Dhampir's blade had sliced the skin; it was almost gone, save for a dark, brownish-red line—the reminder of her transformation. She reached up, stretching and bending her body, like an accomplished athlete, aware of every muscle and sinew reawakening as her strength increased.

Glancing down, she eyed some moss-ridden stones, scattered on the ground. She picked up two, recoiling from their strong, mouldy stench. Clenching her fists, she squeezed, grinding them into fine powder. She gasped at the minimal effort it took, then laughed out. A sudden rush of mixed emotions overwhelmed her: she felt exhilarated, excited and aroused by her new body. *Why not?* she thought, admiring herself. *Am I not perfect, desirable?*

It was then she realised … she was naked; it seemed she had pulled away her armour and tunic, during her painful transformation, and yet had no recollection of doing so. She examined her impeccable torso with her probing hands, guiding them over her body: her breasts were full and high, her abdomen hard and toned, and her thighs lean and shapely.

Alerted, once more, to the outside world, she promptly clothed herself—the tunic now clinging to her firm body, where it had once hung loosely.

Without inviting him in, Magia Nera intruded on her thoughts as though he were inside her. It then occurred to her, that it was all *his* doing. *The blade was smeared with venom*, she thought. She was now cursed, just like him.

She shot a glance at the exit from the cave. Like a young child braving its first step, she took *one*—the thud of her foot breaking ground. She wanted to run, run for miles, without stopping. She made to exit, hesitating when a stream of sunlight managed to find its way in as though searching for her. Unsure, she stepped back. The threatening single ray, its tiny particles of dust dancing through its shimmering light, crept towards her. However, as it advanced, she sensed nothing—neither cold nor heat—yet still felt trapped within her confines. *It cannot be like this*, she thought, alerted to an unusual sense of fear seeping in. *Fear?*

She shook her head, staring at the ray of sunlight, challenging it.

'I fear nothing!' she snarled, her new voice strident and emotionless.

Resilient to the core, Kara threw her hand out into the path of the sunbeam.

Nothing happened.

Relieved, she smiled and, keeping her hand there, bathed her fingers in the light, letting it penetrate her luminescent skin—the glow of her deep, carmine blood, visible. She then noticed the palm of her hand, where the skin had been burned and melted away, when she had attempted to take the dark Warlock's amulet. The unsightly scar was now barely noticeable.

She gasped, in awe. 'Just like Wareestha!' she muttered, visualising what she could do, now. She paused for thought, her mind awash with endless possibilities. 'It could all be mine!'

Her eyes then fell on the Obsidian—the spear lying lazily on the ground, dormant. When she snatched it up, it failed to spark at her touch as though it no longer recognised her, and yet it *felt* the same. She caressed it with both hands, reacquainting it with its mistress, bonding with it again. Within moments, it sparked to life! Flashes of light danced wildly, highlighting the beauty of its deep-emerald glass, while its serrated, silver tip gleamed like new.

Reunited, once again.

Kara eyed the silver armour which once graced her body. She contemplated leaving it behind in the cave, along with the spirit of her former self but then changed her mind. She had always worn it with pride—the symbol of who she was and where she came from. As she put it on, it hugged her firm body, like the return of a long-lost lover, never wanting to leave again. She squirmed with discomfort, feeling something press against her, then checked beneath its girth, feeling the small dagger she had overlooked.

'You will be useful,' she told it.

Strewn on the ground, lay her double-edged longsword—her "back up weapon"—and returned it to its pride of place, attaching it to her bodice of armour, on her back.

Kara emerged from the cave, now fearless of all possible threats. She looked around, more alert to nature, its shades vibrant and new to her, and its distinctive sounds and movements now dominating her senses.

She jolted, reminded of the added weight on her back. Inhaling deeply, she arched her spine feeling their release, then looked over her shoulder. Kara's great wings expanded, larger and wider than before. Her eyes widened as she marvelled at their beauty—the sun enhancing their newness. Their colour—once white—now gleamed like polished onyx, like that of the precious stone in her gold headband, matching her blackened heart.

Prompted by a sudden instinct, she looked sharp, distracted by a distant, high-pitched sound. She turned and looked up, quickly locating the source. Without thought, she ran, her speed swift and exhilarating.

Kara stopped when she saw Nakia in the distance; the hawk was in its final descent towards the earth, its death-like screech echoing, then foundering until it fell into silence, beyond the mountains.

Where once she might have felt pity—and avenged the killing of her "pet" after years of companionship and loyalty—Kara now felt empty inside. The hawk had served its purpose.

She no longer needed it—or *anyone*, for that matter.

Turning away, from where the hawk had disappeared, her attention was diverted, once again, by the amplified sounds of *life!* It was the here and now that interested her, and it all made sense: the Dhampir's poisonous blade; the venom; her near-death; and the transformation. She inhaled deeply, drawing in the smell of her new heightened senses, and grinned. She finally had what Wareeshta had always denied her—the gift of long life, with added strength.

With the possibility of greater power—now there for the taking—Kara was lured back in the direction from whence she came … hell-bent on destruction.

As she turned, leaving her past behind to rot away in the little cave, she paused, on another instinct: aside from the hawk's death cry, she had heard another sound—that of a woman's voice, screaming.

A disturbing, sinister curl crept across her face ….

# Chapter Two

*The Ruins of Moyne – (North-West Scotland)*

'R*un!*'

But it was quiet … too quiet.

She was sure they were still out there; if so, they would see and hear her every movement. Nevertheless, she knew she had to go—had to get out.

It was her only chance.

*"Do you trust me?"*

Wareeshta's words echoed as she turned away, leaning against the cold, jagged wall of the sepulchre, her mind still churning. She closed her eyes, listening to her heart, it pounding in time with her racing thoughts as they screamed at her. But, for once, it seemed both head and heart were united, spurring her on.

*"You can do it, Eleanor!"*

Her eyes flashed open, hearing another voice in her head, and though she did not recognise it, it drove her determination.

Hidden inside the doorless entrance, Eleanor took a deep, nervous breath, it quivering when she slowly released it. She peeped out. *Just another step*, she thought, craning her neck forward, her chest still heaving with anxiousness. She let her eyes wander around the grounds of the ancient ruins; they were deserted. But for how long? She then caught a movement from the corner of her eye. She gasped, recoiling back into the dim light, concealing herself again from the unknown source. Maintaining a steady breath, she listened …

It was still quiet, save for the whispering sigh of the trees.

She waited a few moments before daring to look out again. She saw and heard nothing. Perhaps her mind was playing tricks on her, making her overthink and second-guess her planned escape.

*Go—Eleanor—now!* she told herself, keeping her thoughts to herself, fearing the dark Warlock might hear her. At that moment, Wareeshta's words rang through as though reminding her:

"His senses are weakened by sunlight."

This encouraged her. *It's now or never!*

"He is too preoccupied with L'Ordana."

Motivated by Wareeshta's enduring advice, Eleanor quickly surveyed the grounds again. And though her heart thumped with fear, her mind was determined and set on freedom. Taking another deep breath within her place of holding, she leapt forward …

Though tired and hungry, Eleanor somehow found the inner strength to run. Wareeshta's instructions had been clear: she had to get out of sight before the Dhampir soldiers returned; Wareeshta had lured them away to "feed", as a distraction, to give her time so they would not hear her escape. But time was limited. She threw a glance skywards. Wareeshta was right; the clouds were descending—and quickly, too. Regardless of the Dhampir's warning, she was more than familiar with the Scottish weather and its ability to change drastically, especially in the Highlands; it was not unusual to experience all four seasons in one day. Occasional rays of early sunlight darted through the gathering clouds, giving her time, but would block out the sun, soon enough. Then the dark Warlock would be free to roam again.

Knowing she was on the cusp of her escape, Eleanor put all negative thoughts aside and focused on her task, telling herself she could not—*would not*—let them take her alive. *No matter what!*

The Ruins of Moyne somehow seemed bigger and less sparse, now that she stood within their central core. She checked her surroundings, conscious of the wide-open space, it making her vulnerable—and easy prey. She had to get out of sight. Casting a glance towards the dark Warlock's holding, she caught the silhouette of a figure moving across its threshold. She halted and briefly held her breath, fearing they would look out. But when they stepped from view she spun, and ran in the opposite direction.

A feeling of unease came over her as she rushed across the clearing where the Dhampir soldiers had stood, only a short time ago. She could almost sense their presence, and glanced about, to make sure there was no hint of their return; by then they would be stimulated, after having had their fill of fresh blood.

*The burial ground with the twisted trees.* She reminded herself again of Wareeshta's instructions.

She looked up now seeing them, their thick, puzzle-like branches, creaking and bending in the breeze, through the thick foliage ahead of her. Once there, the trees would conceal her until she reached the other side of the kirkyard.

*At last!* she thought, throwing a glance over her shoulder before crashing through the foliage. However, in her desperate bid to get out of sight, she lost her balance and stumbled over the crumbled remains of a headstone—the name of its perished soul now covered with ivy and faded into obscurity. But as she threw her hands out to break her fall, she grazed her palms, re-opening the same wounds she had received from her fall in the castle of Balloch, while recoiling from the Valkyrie's threats.

Biting down on her pain, she picked herself up and paused, ears cocked.

Still nothing; nor was there any sign of nature's inhabitants. It was as though they *knew*, and chose to remain hidden from the evil hovering in the stagnant air.

She shuddered when the wind picked up, its sudden sharpness catching the nape of her neck, its presence evident by the trees' bare branches clicking hard against each other.

Now alert to everything around her, her survival instincts took over, guiding and protecting her, giving her the added confidence to do what she had to, otherwise … No—she could not dwell on that now.

Wiping her hands on her grubby skirt she pushed on, watching her step, trying not to look back; doing that would waste time. Every second counted. The strange puzzle trees grew thicker as she pressed on, eventually forcing her to slow as she veered through their overgrowth. The further she waded through the unusual burial ground, its ancient gravestones weathered with age and tilting low, the atmosphere grew dense and eerie. Monuments and crumbling vaults, containing the remains of ancient warriors who had fought great battles over the centuries, their legacies now lost and hidden within the forest, closed in on her. But she did not stop. If she were to think about the dead, below and around her, allow them to haunt her thoughts, her anxiety would prevent her from reaching the other side of the kirkyard.

*"Tis not the dead you should fear, Nori."*

Her grandmother, as usual, was right; it was the living she needed to be wary of, not the dead. But while there was truth in it, she knew her would-be pursuers were not quite of the "living". They were callous, with no regard for life—half-human, half— She shook it from her mind and focused on Onóir and their times together, to keep her mind occupied. She prayed her grandmother was safe and well. She missed her. She missed them all … desperately!

Eleanor stopped for several moments to get her bearings. The overgrown graveyard seemed never-ending, and with no visible path to guide her, its theatre of resting souls still played heavily on her thoughts. It unnerved her. She glanced up at intervals, still seeing occasional streams of sunlight filtering through. *Good,* she thought, nodding to herself; as long as they continued to do so it would widen the distance between her and her hunters—and give her more precious time.

Her stomach rumbled, for the want of something to eat. But food was not an option; there was none. She would just have to keep going.

Shaking the thought and image of sustenance from her mind, Eleanor battled on, visualising the reunion with her family and Asai, and the joy of being together again. Her mind focused, she looked ahead with fresh hope, then hesitated. There, in the distance, she saw the span of morning light pushing through and widening as the trees grew sparse, its brightness guiding her, like a beacon, towards its embrace.

She was almost there.

Smiling to herself, Eleanor quickened her pace with Wareeshta's words in her head.

*'Look for the path. Though faint, it is there. Follow it until it divides. Take the left one; it will bring you to a river. I will leave one of their horses there for you. Follow the river—but do not cross it. Keep to its course until you come to a valley; go through it, then travel north."*

Emerging from the kirkyard she paused, for a moment, and swallowed, her throat parched. *I need water*, she thought, then realised … *The river!* The water, coming down from the Highlands, would be cool, crisp and fresh. She swallowed again—the mere thought of it almost quenching her thirst … It kept her going. But first … she had to find the path.

Eleanor looked down, her eyes darting frantically for the faint outline that would mark the next leg of her escape. She tutted, frustrated at not being able to see the path.

'Look for it, Eleanor!' she muttered, blinking continuously, desperate to find it. Unable to, her doubts began to gnaw at her, wondering if Wareeshta had led her on a wild goose chase. 'No! I trust her.' She looked around again, her brows knitted tightly, determined. Still, she could not locate it. She panicked. 'Oh, no! I must have taken the wrong turn! What am I going to—' She then gasped, her eyes widening with sheer joy. 'There you are!'

Elated, and not wanting to lose her way to freedom for another second, Eleanor kept her eyes fixed on the path's faint outline. From time to time, it seemed to disappear, forcing her to stop to search for it again. More time wasted. But spurred by persistence and much concentration, her eyes gradually grew accustomed to its diminishing route.

Taunted by the increased rumbling of her empty stomach, she ignored it and pressed on, her eyes occasionally looking up, checking the clouds; they were gathering quickly now, and the early morning sunlight was slowly losing its battle to penetrate their thickness. It would not be long. When an image of Magia Nera being released from his holding entered her mind, Eleanor picked up her pace; she needed to maintain her distance from him—from *them*.

The farther she went, her surroundings seemed to crowd in on her again as the path narrowed. She had little sense of time, just a vague notion of how long she had been travelling, and surmised it to be an hour or so. Another glance skywards told her the clouds were taking charge, and she felt a biting nip in the air, it stealing the little warmth the sunlight had provided.

She slowed, then stopped, uncertain, and looked from left to right, where the path now divided, her mind a sudden blank. She gasped and threw her hands to her face, her eyes widening with alarm as she stared down.

'Oh, Wareeshta!' she exclaimed, wishing her friend was with her. 'I can't remember!'

Tiredness, hunger and thirst were taking their toll, affecting her ability to think, rationally, making her second-guess her decisions. Inside, she could feel the unwelcome return of panic creeping in on her; its unwanted presence would make matters worse if she were to let it take over.

Eleanor clasped the crown of her head with her hands, tapping her fingers against it as if to reawaken her memory. Again, she looked right, then left, then right again.

'*Right.* Aye. I'm sure it was—' She stomped the ground with her foot. '*Think*, Eleanor! Yes, it was—' She stopped dead and spun, hearing a noise, like branches, cracking beneath someone's feet.

For a moment she froze, her mouth gaping, her breath fast.

*Oh, no! They found me!*

She ran.

Eleanor's breath grew heavier with each exasperated step, it clouding her thoughts and hindering her hearing. The path she had chosen grew dark and gloomy. Something was not right; she felt surrounded—no longer alone. She stopped, swallowed, then leaned against a tree, trying to catch her breath. She hesitated, holding it, then flinched, hearing the same noise again; only now the footsteps were hasty and heavy—and coming towards her.

*I won't let them take me.*

Frantic, Eleanor glanced about, looking for somewhere to hide, pausing when she caught another swift movement. Then she saw it—the puff of smoke—spurting from the bushes. She stalled, her eyes lifting, staring at it until it dissolved into the sombre sky. She glanced around, staying alert. Who, or whatever it was, made her suspect it was not the Dhampir warriors; they would be upon her by now.

Curious, she lingered in the silence, biding her time, as precious as it was.

Convinced she saw another wisp of angry smoke, Eleanor, though anxious, braved a step forward, to get a closer look. But as soon as she moved it vanished again. She jolted when a wild rabbit leapt out from under a bushel, then drew back, throwing her hand over her wild-beating heart, somewhat relieved.

When the small mammal scurried away, Eleanor resumed her search for the path, but it was nowhere to be seen. Quickly, she gathered her thoughts, to calm herself. Now, with no knowledge of where she was, she felt her anxiety gnawing at her again. Agitated, she wrung her hands; though clammy, they were cold.

'Stay calm, Eleanor,' she told herself, trying to find her bearings. 'You can do this. You know you—' She froze, drawing a sharp breath.

What felt like hours passed in seconds as they stared at each other. Eleanor remained still, afraid to move as the little creature sat on its rock, tilting its head from side to side, each equally curious of the other.

Unable to take her eyes off the goblin-like creature, Eleanor regarded it. Small in stature, it had a wrinkled appearance, like an old man. Its body was covered in short, curly brown hair, except for its head. It had a long face and pointed ears and wore a goat-like beard, and its tattered clothing gave it the look of a vagrant. Her eyes then fell to its lower body; its legs were similar to that of a goat, and its feet were unusually thick and long with toe-like hoofs. But when she looked up again and into its face, its expression was somewhat friendly, almost humbling. Despite its unappealing appearance, she did not feel threatened by it. And though she could scarcely believe it, her eyes did not deceive her … because she knew what it was: a *Urisk*—the fabled *Rock Monster* or *Brownie* she had heard so much of, from tales relayed to her and Gill by their neighbour, Heckie Grant, when they were children.

Suddenly it smiled at her. It was a friendly, eager smile, and when it spoke to her, she gasped.

'You lost,' it said, nodding its head towards her, its voice timid and raspy. It had not been a question, and it was clear it had been following her.

For a moment, Eleanor could only stare at the little creature, such was her fascination; she never knew the *Urisk* could speak English, as broken as it was. When she moved, the creature shifted on its rock, carefully watching her, but without any threat.

She edged towards it and nodded.

'I … I think so,' she said, chewing her lip, unsure.

'You seek … *watter?*'

Eleanor frowned, leaning her head to the side before it registered what the *Urisk* was asking. 'Oh, you mean, *river?*' she said, unable to take her eyes off him.

He grinned and nodded back, repeating the word.

'*River!*'

Then, slowly lifting his hand, he pointed with his long, bony finger. She followed its line, turned, then sighed; she *had* gone the wrong way.

'I take you,' he said, smiling and patting his chest. 'You … my friend?'

Eleanor smiled, knowing what he meant. Anyone familiar with the folklore of these creatures knew how much they craved friendship, to keep them company in their humbling and, sometimes, lonely world. And though renowned for being mischievous and unpredictable, it was also widely known that they were harmless.

Feeling pity for him, but glad of his company, Eleanor smiled wildly and nodded, her blue eyes lighting up.

'Och! *Bonnie!*' he said, pointing to her—the wrinkles on his long, drawn face deepening as he beamed with delight for having found a new friend.

'Thank you!' she replied, moving closer.

The *Urisk*, still clinging to his rock, drew back. Eleanor raised her hand, reassuring him she meant no harm. He leaned his head sideways, unsure, then smiled, revealing his large, stained teeth.

'I am Eleanor,' she said, placing her hand on her chest, then pointed to him, nodding, urging him to speak again.

Excited, the *Urisk*, almost falling off his little pedestal, clapped his grubby hands together.

'Me … *Muk!*'

Eleanor, extending her hand of friendship and maintaining her broad smile, said, 'Well, Muk, I am happy and honoured to make your acquaintance.'

With the assurance of its new "friend" the *Urisk* hopped from the safety of its rock with a thud and, unexpectedly grasping Eleanor's hand, gently and quickly led her back from whence she came, to where the paths had crossed, and guided her safely along the proper route. Although its hand was coarse and hairy, Eleanor felt comforted by it as the little creature guided her; it reminded her of when Oran used to hold her hand when she was a child, and frightened.

Eventually, the *Urisk* stopped and, lifting his nose, sniffed the air. He then pointed.

'River!'

Eleanor gasped, her brows shooting up. 'Where?!' she exclaimed, looking, yet was unable to see it.

The creature grinned mischievously, then, with his index finger, tapped the side of his long, hook-like nose. Eleanor laughed. It had been so long since she had done that; until that moment, she had had no reason to. Charmed by her, the little creature clapped its scrawny hands again with delight.

Brightened by one another's company beneath a sky laden with heavy grey clouds, the two unlikely friends took each other's hand and made their way towards the river. As they approached the water, Eleanor pointed.

'There it is!' she cried out, almost euphoric, then released a long sigh of relief when she saw the horse Wareeshta had left for her. 'Just as she said.'

As promised, Wareeshta had taken one of the Dhampir's horses and led it to the river, where she had tied it to a large piece of driftwood, lying by the shore. Eleanor made to run towards it but stalled when she felt the tug of the creature's hand. She turned and looked down at the *Urisk*. Its little, old face fell, aware she would be leaving him. He held on to her hand tightly, not wanting to let go. Seeing the sadness in his eyes, she knelt before him.

'I must go,' she said, feeling an element of guilt. Still clutching her hand, he lowered his head. 'But I will never forget you, Muk. You saved me. And …' She felt the lump in her throat and swallowed. '… I can't thank you enough. One day, you will meet your soulmate. I promise.' With that, Eleanor leaned forward and hugged the little creature, inhaling his scent; it was like the forest, a combination of moss and wet tree trunks—earthy and woody—and pleasant to her senses.

In return, the *Urisk* patted her on the back.

'My … friend … *Nori*,' he said.

Stunned, Eleanor pulled away from the *Urisk*; Gill had always called her that. She drew her brows and shook her head, unable to comprehend it. 'How do you know that …?' The *Urisk* tapped his nose and grinned, then keeping his secret, turned and ran off, back into his world of Scottish myths and folklore.

The short time spent in the *Urisk's* company had been most pleasant, temporarily distracting her from her fears. However, the feeling quickly passed when it was overshadowed by a sense of foreboding and the urgency to press on. Behind her, the horse thumped the ground and whinnied; it was on edge. She could relate.

With her experience of horses—Oran had taught her how to ride Farrow—she approached the Dhampir's with caution, extending her hand towards it, uttering soft words of encouragement. The steed was larger than Farrow, but she knew she would be able to mount it, as long as she could win its trust. She stopped, her mouth opening when she noticed the deep gashes on its flank, where it had been abused, by its owner.

'Oh, you poor thing!' she said, carefully lifting her hand, then pausing when she saw how nervous the horse was; its ears were drawn back and eyes wide as it side-glanced her. But when her hand touched it, it seemed to know instinctively that she would do it no harm, her soft, kind touch reassuring it as she stroked it with tender loving care. Eleanor pressed her lips together and shook her head, her eyes welling as she studied its wounds—the diagonal lacerations now dry with thick scabs. They seemed to be healing. Still and all, she wished she had one of Blair Grant's honey-based balms; their neighbour's homemade remedies always worked wonders for humans and animals. She was glad to be rescuing it from its abuser.

'Time to go!' she promptly told the horse as though it understood. She was thankful it was saddled, her eyes then lighting up when she saw the large pouch attached to the side of the saddle. Eleanor untied it and looked inside. Wareeshta had packed a costrel for her—the leather container full of fresh water. There was also food—the small "feast" made up of berries, nuts, dried meat and biscuits. She had no idea where Wareeshta had acquired it; nor did she care, and quickly helped herself, making sure to save some food and re-fill the costrel, for the journey.

Feeling a bit more *human*, and revived, but sensing the brooding atmosphere close in around her, Eleanor promptly secured the saddlebags, eager to leave; she did not want to waste another moment there.

To reassure the horse she was its friend, before mounting, Eleanor continuously stroked and patted its flank to keep it calm, all the while being mindful of its wounds. However, aware she was not its master, the horse became edgy again, refusing to keep still.

'This is no time to be stubborn,' she said, now taking firm control of the reins. Still, it persisted, reluctant to follow her guidance.

'Keep still.' She frowned and tutted. 'What on earth is the matter with—'

'Going somewhere?'

# Chapter Three

*The Ruins of Moyne*

'Where is she?!'

The Sorceress stomped about the empty sepulchre, fists clenched as she hurled her demand at Wareeshta, her accusing eyes glaring at the Dhampir as she hovered in the doorless entrance. But the reverberated silence that followed only fuelled her rage, and when the Dhampir cautiously stepped down into the chamber, L'Ordana threw herself at Wareeshta.

Caught off-guard, Wareeshta jolted, then recoiled when two faces leapt out at her from inside L'Ordana's fury, revealing themselves in their frenzy of terror. They had a look of anguish etched on their features, like two tortured souls trying to escape the clutches of someone—*something*—unwilling to let them go.

L'Ordana drew back, momentarily unable to breathe—the overwhelming feeling of drowning taking hold of her, again. She grasped her throat, gulping for air as Wareeshta looked on—the Dhampir's mouth partially open, speechless, and taken aback by what she was seeing.

And then they were gone—the two faces hauled back to where they had come from.

As if snatched from a nightmare, Wareeshta flinched, hearing her mistress's raised voice, and stared at her.

'What are you gawping at?' snapped L'Ordana, then promptly turned away, tugging at her hood, fearing it might slip, conscious of her ageing flaws. Wareeshta wondered if the Sorceress realised what had just happened. It was difficult to know; she seemed unphased, unaware of it, and yet …

'Well?!'

'Nothing, my lady,' said Wareeshta, despite what she *had* seen; though brief, she did not doubt it for one second.

Nor was she the only one; Magia had witnessed it, too. He had been standing in the stepwell, all along, watching and listening with heightened interest. With the sunlight now hidden behind the blackening clouds, he was again savouring his freedom, despite his limited powers. But he was not concerned, knowing they would return, come nightfall.

A snide grin crept across his face; he suspected L'Ordana's servant was aware that her mistress's beauty and powers were gradually fading. But from what *he* had observed, however, it appeared the ancient spirit, he had placed inside the young woman he had once known as *Kristene*—almost sixty years earlier—was battling to get out. Or, perhaps, it was striving to take over its *host.* He wondered if the spirit was aware of where they were going. *It is possible*, he thought. Another likelihood entered his mind: the spirit of the ancient Sorceress could be seeking revenge on the Elliyan, for putting her to death, centuries before, for engaging in a forbidden love affair with a Warlock. It was a compelling notion and, with L'Ordana's diminishing powers … *Intriguing*, he mused. Though, unless she was renewed, and soon—he wondered about that—then "L'Ordana" would no longer exist and "Kristene" would die of old age. It was possible the ancient spirit could—and perhaps would—dominate, then. *Now that would be interesting*, he thought. The idea of it all tempted him to stay until the end, to witness the outcome—to see who would win the Shenn amulet. Not that it mattered; it belonged to another. No, the L'Ordana he knew, this Sorceress with her flaws and failings, could never own the Shenn. It would destroy her. He knew that. She did not. Until now, she had kept control of the spirit inside her, revelling in the power it had given her. But if the spirit were to take full possession of its host … there was a chance it could bond with the Shenn—should its true master fail to do so; after all, the spirit had, in its former life, been a part of the Elliyan and its *Council*—rare and equally as powerful.

Revenge was the likely motive.

'I asked you a question, Wareeshta.' L'Ordana slowly turned to address the Dhampir, trying—with little success—to maintain her composure. 'Or are you deaf?!' she then roared, her eyes blazing, their whites bloodshot. 'Where is the girl?!'

'I do not know, my lady,' Wareeshta lied, lifting her hands, feigning helplessness and shaking her head.

'Did I not tell you to watch over her?' L'Ordana leaned closer. 'Did you not administer the potion?'

Wareeshta casually nodded.

'As you instructed … my lady.'

L'Ordana's eyes, now burning with doubt, surveyed the sepulchre. The makeshift bed, where the girl had been kept in slumber, was empty—the blanket flung across the chamber. Her eyes studied it as her suspicions mounted. Then, with a single gesture of her hand, she silently commanded the blanket away; when it failed to move, she glowered down at it, pursing her lips. *Move!* she yelled, inside her head. Slowly, as if reluctant, it slid away, revealing the scarred area on the stone floor, where the potion had been poured.

'I think not,' she seethed, pointing to the blackened circle coating the rim of the hole, where it had scorched the surface before melting through the stone.

While her thoughts raced inside her head, Wareeshta maintained her outward control, aware of her company, aware she was being scrutinised. She could not risk giving herself away. Not now. She then shrugged and shook her head again.

'I thought she was … sleeping—at first,' she began, masquerading her surprise at Eleanor's escape. 'As I leaned over her, to inflict the potion, I was fooled. The girl was pretending. For a moment, I was caught unawares—when she struck out—causing the vial to slip from my hand.'

A deep-rooted grunt, filled with sarcasm, came from behind. L'Ordana looked over her shoulder and glared at the dark Warlock.

'And dare I suggest *you* are aware of this?' she sneered, pointing at the evidence.

Magia slowly lifted his hands and pulled a long face, pleading his ignorance in silence.

'I caught it before it fell to the ground,' Wareeshta continued. 'Some of the potion—what little remained—had already been lost before I could prevent it. I assure you, Sorceress … there were a few drops left—just enough. I forced it into her mouth, then waited for it to take effect before leaving.'

L'Ordana, lowering her head, scowled at the Dhampir.

'She *was* unconscious,' Wareeshta persisted, daring to challenge her. 'I swear it!'

Narrowing her eyes, L'Ordana held Wareeshta's defiant gaze; there was something different in her servant's demeanour—something nudging at her, and burning her suspicions. If Wareeshta was lying—which was likely—she was quite convincing. Eyes still locked on the Dhampir, she hoped Wareeshta's wilful look would shift from hers, and betray herself. But Wareeshta held her own. No, she would not be intimidated.

The silent, furtive stand-off between mistress and servant suddenly drew on Magia's reservations. Had Wareeshta lied to him, too—about the book? Her "performance" had been compelling, to say the least, when she explained how it was moved "from time to time to conceal it from prying eyes." She had him believe L'Ordana had the book. But he had his doubts now; he knew the Sorceress would do anything to keep him onside, knowing her powers were weakening. And yet, he could not be sure … and unless he had credible proof, then … *So frustrating!*

The Sorceress, throwing out a long-winded sigh, turned from

Wareeshta, her eyes returning to the empty makeshift bed.

'You fool!' she snapped. 'It was not enough!' She side-glanced the blackened hole in the sepulchre's stone floor. 'What was wasted gave the girl her escape.' She spun, glaring at the Dhampir, her face crimson. 'You should not have been so presumptuous!'

'I was distracted, my—' Wareeshta stopped when L'Ordana's face, distorted by anger again, displayed that of another; the deep-lined features of a grey-haired old woman leapt out at her. Wareeshta gasped at the familiar-looking face, though was unable to place it. And then it was gone.

When another low-grunted laugh came from behind her, L'Ordana turned her head, eyes burning into the dark Warlock as he remained in the doorway, arms casually folded, apparently finding it all quite amusing. Her tolerance of him was beginning to run its course, despite their so-called "allegiance". It was no secret he was revelling in her frustrations. She would just have to grit her teeth and ignore his revelry. She needed him. With time pressing on her, and the girl now missing … It was all taking its toll on her and— She stopped short.

'Distracted, you say?' she then queried Wareeshta, unconvinced by her "story" and also irked by her persistent gaze. She moaned. 'What *are* you staring—'

'By Kara's hawk, my lady,' Wareeshta cut in. 'Nakia.'

L'Ordana blinked, confused. 'What has that … *creature* got to do with this?' she said, rolling her eyes.

'It has been destroyed.'

L'Ordana lifted her brows, surprised by the revelation. '*Destroyed?*'

Wareeshta nodded.

'*Da!* It is true, Sorceress,' she proclaimed. 'I heard its death-cry, and took it upon myself to find it …' Her eyes darted towards Magia. '… *and* its mistress.'

'Where *is* Kara?' L'Ordana then pressed—the sudden hint of nervousness obvious, by her prompt reply, aware the Valkyrie was nowhere to be seen and could be lurking in the shadows, watching her. 'She should have returned by now—from the *Pass*,' she lied; in truth, she had no idea where the Valkyrie was. 'I had sent her to make sure *they* had not found a way across.' Despite this, and despite what they had to do to cross the Cordhu Pass, by battling the lake's condemned spirits, she could not underestimate Reece and Asai; they were clever, especially the Samurai. If anyone could find a way, it was he. A thought struck her: *Could they have killed the hawk?* It was possible they had. There was no denying that crossing the lake posed a great risk—she knew they were capable—but if they *had* succeeded, they too would be making their way towards Elboru. She would need the girl, then; Reece's granddaughter was a vital commodity until she was no longer required. Then she would simply … discard her.

'I cannot say, my lady. But I am certain Kara will return … soon.'

By now, Wareeshta was convinced Kara was dead. True, because of her making, she knew the venom would not have worked as swiftly on the Valkyrie, compared to a mortal, who would die within the hour. She had seen it for herself; the venom from the Dhampir's poisonous blade had made its way into the laceration inflicted on Kara and had been gradually working its way through her veins. The Valkyrie had to be dead. Regardless of it … she had no intention of telling the Sorceress *that*.

'And my warriors …?' L'Ordana continued, unable to hide the edge of panic in her voice. 'Where are *they?*'

'While I was certain the girl was sleeping,' said Wareeshta, maintaining her deceit, 'I had them accompany me, to search for Kara.'

L'Ordana snorted. 'You?! I find it difficult to believe that *you*, their creator, needed *their* help. Do you not think it strange that Kara has not returned?'

'It is my understanding that she will, Sorceress,' Wareeshta replied.

L'Ordana leaned towards the Dhampir's expressionless face. 'Well … *I* think not!' she hissed through gritted teeth. 'It is *my* under—'

'Be warned, *Bella*,' interrupted Magia, 'or your enemies shall outnumber your allies. Wareeshta tells the truth; I saw her leave with the Dhampir. Besides, they need to *feed*, to keep up their strength—should we need them to fight against our enemy.'

Wareeshta's eyes widened, then flashed towards him; had he seen her lead them away from the grounds? Worse still … As though he had read her mind, Magia threw her a subtle nod, away from L'Ordana's scrutiny and suspicions.

'And then …' he promptly continued, 'there is the girl. She is just a *mortal*—weak and of no consequence. She would only delay our task. Despite what you said, ask yourself this, Sorceress: do we *need* her?'

'I am touched, by your … *concern*,' L'Ordana returned, in a scathing tone. 'But, while what you desire is still in my possession, you will have to endure any further delay until the girl is returned to me.'

With that, the Sorceress strode towards him, then stopped; he was still blocking the entrance. Magia tilted his head and lowered his eyes to the side, listening.

'Panic over, *Bella!*' he said, smirking. Her eyes slid across, meeting his. 'Your … *warriors* have returned,' he stated.

L'Ordana looked over his shoulder and out onto the grounds of the ruins. At first, she saw nothing, then, one by one, the Dhampir warriors leapt from the shadows and into the clearing, brimming with energy.

'Good,' she said, her tone projecting an air of renewed confidence, though, inside, she was concerned, wondering where Kara had disappeared. It was likely the Valkyrie had absconded. If that were so, and with her notions of power, there was the fear Kara would secretly follow them to Elboru, and try to take what she herself desired. *Never!* she quietly vowed. *I would destroy her, rather than let that happen.* 'Now that they are back,' L'Ordana went on, 'they can easily trace the girl's scent. I imagine it will not take them long to find her,' she added, then stormed out from the sepulchre, forcing Magia to step aside. Shaking his head, the dark Warlock sighed, suppressing his frustration.

As Wareeshta moved to follow her mistress, Magia looked sharp and raised his hand.

'Wait!' he said, lowering his voice.

Wareeshta looked up at him and, seeing his eyes narrow, followed his suspicious gaze; L'Ordana was beckoning two of the Dhampir.

Turloch, his long, white mane, making him stand out from the rest, strode towards the Sorceress, closely followed by another—Dakkus—who was glancing around, surveying the grounds, his red eyes alert, hungry and glowing like beacons, slicing through the bleakness of the late morning—the darkness of his ashen skin emphasising them. Alert to this, Magia quickly drew Wareeshta away from the entrance—narrowly evading Dakkus' probing look—then waited, to listen to their unfolding conversation.

'You are my favourites, you know,' the Sorceress purred, working her powers of persuasion on the two Dhampir. 'There are few I trust,' she professed, continuing to spill her lies on them. 'But I know I can rely on *you*.'

'Where is the Valkyrie?' asked Turloch, his tone hard and insisting. He had noticed Kara's lengthy absence and the tension in the air, heightening his suspicions.

'Kara will be back, soon enough,' she snapped, initially caught unawares by the enquiry, though it came as no surprise; she had observed his "fondness" for the Valkyrie—for want of a better description—and Kara had been quite "attentive" towards him, just as she had been with the Highlander. She would have to be careful; the last thing she wanted was for these two Dhampir to know her concerns. For now, she needed to concentrate on the girl. Inhaling, she calmed herself. 'Kara is not the issue, here.'

'What would you have us do, then?' asked Turloch.

'Find the girl and'—she glanced over at the group of Dhampir;

they were growing agitated, pacing about, eager to hunt, eager to kill—'return her to me … *alive!*'

Turloch stared at her, sensing her inner discomfort.

'And make sure *they* do not harm her,' she added, aware of a young Dhampir's ability to kill without thought—and mercy.

'What do I—' He stopped to correct himself, knowing Dakkus was still hovering behind him, his craving lingering in the air. '—*we* get in return?'

Dakkus nodded with vehemence; he too was on edge, feeding off the other warriors' raised senses—the constant stroking of his hairless crown a sign of his restlessness.

L'Ordana lifted her head. There was a time she would have punished them for merely looking at her the wrong way, let alone question her. However, she knew she had to keep Turloch on her side; she needed him, too. It aggravated her, having to *need* anyone.

Trained by the Samurai, Turloch almost matched Asai in skill. Almost. And yet, she was confident of his capability to challenge—even overthrow—the Samurai.

'You *will* be rewarded,' she replied, tilting her head, her eyes drifting from one to the other, enticing them.

Turloch held her gaze with his striking, pale-blue eyes, his pan-faced stare making her feel uncomfortable as if he had intruded on her thoughts, dissecting them, one by one. His full lips twitched before a subtle smirk appeared on them.

'In what way?' came the broad accent from behind.

Her eyes darted back to Dakkus. She smiled wryly at him, holding her calm exterior. 'In more ways than you imagine, Dakkus. You will see … when *I* rule.'

'Then what?' said Turloch. For a moment, L'Ordana said nothing and stared up at him, his eyes mesmerising. 'The girl?' he prompted.

She flinched. 'I need her—for now—or at least until …' She hesitated. 'Reece and Asai will come looking for her—*that* I have no doubt of. You see, now that she is conscious, it seems she and Asai have a … *connection*; they can "sense" one another. Therefore, I want you to find her before they do. But should your paths cross again …'

Turloch lifted his head with keen interest—the smirk now broadening across his face, while behind him, Dakkus grinned, knowing exactly what she meant.

'Good,' she said. 'Now you understand.'

'What does she mean to do?' said Wareeshta, lowering her voice as she edged closer to Magia, peeping over his shoulder as they eyed the Sorceress, hoping she would not hear them. But L'Ordana seemed too engrossed in conversation with Turloch and Dakkus, to even consider the idea that anyone would eavesdrop on her.

Magia grunted, still musing over L'Ordana's words and obscure behaviour.

'I had wondered why she kept the girl alive …' he muttered, still surveying the Sorceress and the two Dhampir. 'At first, I thought it was to use her—for obvious reasons … But—'

'You saw them, too,' Wareeshta stated. 'Those faces—when she was angry.'

He nodded.

'It is clear her youth and powers are gradually diminishing, and yet …' He paused. 'She does not use the girl … like the others.'

'To renew herself?' said Wareeshta.

'Indeed. And there can only be one explanation for that.'

Wareeshta raised her head, staring at him from behind as he lifted his hand and rubbed his chin, his mind turning it over—the reason.

'*Sí!* She is missing—or has lost—something precious to her.'

Wareeshta held her poise, suddenly aware he was secretly scrutinising her from where she stood, behind him. And though he could not see her, she avoided reacting to his suspicions; she had already lied to him about the book—a lie she had to maintain, no matter what.

He nodded, then turned to face her again, continuing his study of her.

'But, of course!' he exclaimed, lifting his hands in his moment of *Eureka!* Wareeshta flinched. 'The dagger!' he voiced. 'Why—it is obvious! Otherwise, she would have used it on the girl by now. Without it—to use for her transformation—time will run out, and—'

'Asai stole it,' Wareeshta blurted. Anything to sway the dark Warlock from mentioning the book. She hoped Eleanor's father still had it. *Better with Oran, for now*, she thought, *than with you.* She stared at him, tempted to smirk, but refrained from doing so, otherwise, he would know she had lied to him.

He looked sharply at her. 'The *Strange One?* No!'

'*Da!* It seems he—'

'Spare me the details,' he interrupted, dismissing her with a flick of his hand when he noticed L'Ordana pointing to the restless Dhampir warriors, Turloch nodding, attentive, taking in her instructions.

'Look at her, *Piccolina!*' Magia threw back over his shoulder, from the corner of his mouth—the Dhampir hanging on his every word. 'No. I believe … she does not intend to barter the girl despite what she had said.' He shook his head, now convinced. 'No. She wants to lure the three who escaped—especially the girl's grandfather—back into her bond; they pose a threat to her plans. And if she succeeds, she will …' He stalled, suddenly conscious of Wareeshta's body pressing against him, her warmth penetrating his clothing, working its way through until it collided with the coldness of his skin. He closed his eyes for a moment, roused by it, then swallowed before continuing; '… punish them, by destroying the girl right in front of their eyes.' Wareeshta gasped. He turned and, letting his eyes glide over her, added; 'It will, also, be her payback.'

Stunned by this new revelation, Wareeshta found herself in a predicament. Her eyes passed him and stared out at the Sorceress, who was now finalising her instructions to the remaining Dhampir warriors. She now feared they would catch up with Eleanor. If so, the girl would stand no chance against them; she would be hauled back to her captor and used as bait before ... She could not even think of that. She hoped Eleanor had made her way to the river and found the horse she had stolen for her. She craned her neck forward, her eyes darting, surveying the hungry warriors; they were growing dangerously restless by the second. She then looked to where the remaining horses were still tied up, by the cemetery; keeping them there had made it easier for her to steal one, and she was certain its absence had gone unnoticed. Not yet, at least. She, however, did notice something: one of the Dhampir had not returned.

Inside, Wareeshta's thoughts ran riot with her concerns: *What if he found his horse?* No. The missing Dhampir would have returned by now … *With or without Eleanor.* She panicked. *What if he—*

Wareeshta's thoughts were then severed by L'Ordana's raised voice as she prepared to give the final command. The Dhampir, each armed with a single-edged backsword, promptly readied themselves to leave, their eyes burning and minds fevered with thoughts of the hunt, desperate to begin.

'Foolish child!' L'Ordana gloated to Turloch. 'Her escape will have been in vain. No matter. I believe they will be quick, now they are well-nourished. Then we can proceed on our journey.'

The Sorceress stood with a smirk on her face as she watched the Dhampir lift their heads, snatching the air, searching for Eleanor's scent of mortality. Suddenly their mood shifted, to one of exhilaration and expectancy. They looked sharp. Detecting the hint of a familiar, and enticing, aroma on a passing breeze, they unexpectedly turned their attention towards the ancient burial ground. With their senses heightened, they knew exactly what had distracted them: the sweet, scent of blood, where Eleanor had cut her hands when she fell, during her escape.

Led by Turloch and Dakkus, the hunt began.

As she watched the warriors attack the cemetery, hell-bent on hunting down their victim, Wareeshta realised she had made a terrible mistake, by encouraging the Dhampir to *feed*; with their speed now accelerated, and the irresistible scent of a mortal hanging on their senses, it was inevitable they would catch up with Eleanor. *What have I done? I have condemned her. Oh, Eleanor! Forgive me.*

When the hunters vanished from view, L'Ordana made to turn, then stalled, on an inkling. She looked back towards the cemetery, her eyes narrowing as she stared into its void. She turned and made her way towards it, stopping at its threshold, her brows furrowing when she noted the battered foliage, where the Dhampir had crashed through in their frenzied pursuit.

'West?' she muttered, tilting her head as she mused over their direction. 'Why are they going west, instead of—' She stopped when it registered, then nodded: 'Of course! The girl has gone *that* way! They must have—' With her mind quickly made up, L'Ordana spun on her heel. 'We are not wasting another moment here. Prepare to leave!' she called out as she marched towards her tent—the echo of her voice reaching Wareeshta and Magia.

'No!' muttered Wareeshta, through gritted teeth as she shoved by Magia. 'I will not let her.'

Desperate, Wareeshta left the sepulchre, eyes locked on L'Ordana as she made her way to her shelter. She would confront her mistress and threaten her if need be. Her hands reached down, her fingers twitching, prepared to remove the stiletto daggers hidden inside her boots. She envisaged their lethal, needle-like points entering L'Ordana's throat, deeply. If there was a time to strike it was now, while the Dhampir were gone. She could not allow her to kill Eleanor. She had to do something. But as her fingers touched the tips of the daggers' hilts, she felt a firm grip on her arm before being hauled away.

'Don't be a fool!' Magia hissed, dragging her back into the safety of the sepulchre.

Wareeshta spun, struggling, trying to break free.

'You heard her!' she hit back through gritted teeth, keeping her voice low. 'She plans to *kill* her.'

'So, it seems,' he said, his casual response inflaming her anger.

'I cannot let her,' Wareeshta insisted, still trying to shrug away from his firm hold.

He leaned towards her, his intimidating look registering with her. 'I know it was you … who helped the girl escape.'

Wareeshta halted her struggle and stared back at him, eyes wide. He *had* known, after all. There was no point in trying to hide it; her guilt was written all over her perfect features. Fearing his betrayal, she swallowed, her mind racing.

'Never mind me,' he said before adding his warning: 'If you act, even threaten L'Ordana in this way'—he glanced down at her boots, where her daggers were still concealed—'then she will know it was you who helped the mortal. Already she is suspicious.'

'Eleanor was the only one who showed me true kindness,' she finally admitted, purposely using the girl's name to add some "humanity" to her plea.

Magia, releasing her from his grip, nodded.

'As difficult as you may find this, Wareeshta … I understand.' She raised her brows, taken aback by this. 'However, I do not care if your little … *friend* lives or dies.'

Wareeshta's face hardened, her eyes now a pale, glow.

'But—' He lifted his hand, holding her attention, disregarding the look of hate she was giving him. 'It is clear you … *care* for the mortal. So …'

Wareeshta drew her brows, her eyes tapering as she let her hands fall to her side, then lifted her head, waiting …

'Therefore, *Piccolina* …' he continued, 'I will protect her'—he stroked her face and, gently caressing her chin with his finger, tilted her head to meet his gaze—'if you get me the book, that is.'

Wareeshta pulled away from him, stone-faced, then slowly shook her head.

'I give you my word,' he said, placing his hand across his chest, where his blackened heart resided, cold and lifeless. And as the wry smile appeared on his thin lips, he turned on his heel, leaving Wareeshta with no doubt in her mind …

He was lying.

# Chapter Four

*The Gap of Lome: Affinshire – (North-West Scotland)*

*"Brave are the ones who challenge this place—for it belongs to the dead."*

Amidst the Highlands of Scotland, where the vast mountain ranges are crowned in white quartzite, and their peaks sweep up to meet the heavens, a great and ancient clan once reigned, hidden within their rich valleys—now long gone. All that remained was the echo of their past … until the birth of a child, whose power would measure that of the universe—a power shared through a source bound to him … and only him. And it was in these fabled lands that the clan's ghosts were resurrected, by a great supremacy, to protect a sacred place, where no mortal belongs. And so, they lie in wait—the *Clan*—to challenge the unfortunate soul who happens upon it.

And it is here *he* must make a choice … if he is to survive.

The group came to a halt and dismounted, finding themselves in a wide-open clearing, shaped like a half-crescent, and cocooned by a cathedral of majestic trees. Old as time, and touched only by the breath of each season, their dense, leaf-bare branches spread out, touching each other in unity. Beneath them, the clearing's floor was carpeted with nature's foliage, its shades of yellow, copper and red, vivid and spectacular, in all its finery.

''Tis … beautiful!' gasped Rosalyn, her footfall silenced by its thick, bed of damp leaves as she walked over its surface, in awe of its splash of autumnal colours as though it had been painted by a higher being. She closed her eyes, inhaling the mid-morning air, and as she glorified in its sweet scent, a stillness settled on her like a soft veil. Suddenly she was overcome by a happiness she'd not felt for a while. It warmed her heart. She wanted to keep it there, stay wrapped within its embrace. Spurred by an uncontrollable urge, she opened her eyes and looked over at Daine. He was staring back at her; he had felt it, too.

They smiled at one another, momentarily lost in the aroma of its allure before the veil was wrenched away, by a sharp chill down their spines. Aware, and feeling exposed, the smile ran from her face and she looked away, leaving him equally exposed and vulnerable.

But, despite the clearing's enchanting beauty, there was something amiss.

''Tis too quiet,' Tam remarked to Reece and Asai, his voice low and cautious, his two colleagues nodding in agreement as they surveyed the area. 'No,' the Highlander went on, slowly shaking his head, 'I do not like it, one bit.'

He glanced over his shoulder back towards the trees. Only now did he notice the strangeness of it; no bird or animal stirred. It was known that deep within the remote parts of the Highlands, the terrain was brimming with wildlife. He recalled the times when he used to hunt, with his father, his brother, and other members of his clan. In that moment of reflection, his family came to mind, embracing his thoughts, their faces clear as if he had only seen them the day before. Then something struck him—something he had not felt until now: he missed them, and hoped to return when … But, no—now was not the time to think of *that*; he, too, had made the *vow*. *First things first*, he thought.

With his clan still in his thoughts, Tam patted his kilt, ever proud to be wearing the Brodie plaid. And though the wool was worn and its vivid shade of red fading, it represented who he once was … *And still am.*

He then looked from left to right, unamused at the surrounding wall of impenetrable trees, rising in a steep incline, their presence invading and menacing as though they were regarding them closely. Faced with the onslaught of yet another forest, he moaned.

But this was no ordinary forest.

Reece looked back towards the gorge where they had just exited, then let his eyes travel up; it was well-protected on each side by escarpments, their sheer ragged walls too treacherous to climb. It had been a challenge, navigating through its narrow, snake-like route, while trying to keep the horses calm as they guided them in single file along its lengthy passage. Nevertheless, they had made it. Another hurdle dealt with. But he knew this was not the end of it; there was only one way they could go now—and back was out of the question.

*They knew what they were doing, when they chose this place*, he thought.

'Auch! Sure, a man can barely fit through there!' Tam complained, approaching the edge of the forest, pulling Reece back to the matter at hand: their next obstacle.

'It appears so,' Asai replied, his brows knitting tightly in troubled thought as he, too, tried to contemplate their next course of action. Always quick to find a solution, the Samurai, however, found himself strangely at a loss, and unable to think rationally. It bothered him, prompting him to check his weapons—the katana and wakizashi securely in place. Again, he checked them—and again, snatching his hands away—the sudden compulsive need to constantly check his steel disturbing him; he knew, despite how many times he touched them, they were always there. He also knew it was irrational, and wondered why he felt compelled to do it. There had to be a logical explanation.

Surveying them closely, they noted how each tree stood in perfect alignment with the next, like silent sentries standing to attention, as though they'd been planted that way—and for a purpose.

'I mean, it would be difficult to make our way through,' Tam determined, trying to measure the narrow gaps with the wide head of his axe, then prodding their trunks, their bark fleeced with moss, thinking they would budge. At a push, it would be possible, though difficult. But he knew the horses would never fit, and besides, the unusual terrain seemed to soar to the heavens. 'Aye, 'tis too steep.' And with the close-knit trees hampering his vision, it was difficult to know how far the forest stretched from where they stood. It appeared they now found themselves in the cradle of a deep valley. He grunted and turned away, frustrated, then hesitated. 'And—what are *those*?' he added, now pointing his axe towards three separate openings, leading right into the forest's core. It was then they saw Gill, standing alone, staring directly at them in silence, with a far-off look in his eyes. They had failed to notice him—too caught up in their new and strange surroundings.

The rest of the group approached Gill, all six now staring blankly at the three unusual entrances, sceptical, and keeping their distance, at first. Each entrance was guarded by an ancient stone—four feet in height and two in width—the large, granite pillars standing in marked position—twelve feet apart. Their tops slanted towards the group and were not identical—each containing a plaque embedded onto their surface and outlined with a rim of pure gold. And when a ray of sunlight escaped the gathering clouds, slicing down through the gaps in the trees overhead, it momentarily highlighted the plaques and their reliefs, in all their splendour.

The three monoliths were immaculate, giving the group the impression they were well-maintained, on a regular basis. The pillar to the far left bore the relief of the sun, its disc gleaming, almost on fire: it was pure gold, carved deep into its plaque, on a surface of lapiz-lazuli. The one to the far right depicted the moon, its face made of white moonstone, and gleaming on a surface of black graphite. The centred pillar depicted a cloud of mother-of-pearl—a representation of the universe; it swirled continuously on a bed of black opal—the speckles of multi-coloured light in its stone, glinting like precious gems when the sunlight touched it.

'What are they for, do you think?' asked Rosalyn, moving carefully from one to the next, her hand hovering high over each surface, mesmerised by their beauty, and yet was afraid to touch them. When she felt a sudden surge of energy emanating from them, and pulsating through her palm, she snatched it away, unsure.

At her feet, Rave was lifting her snout, trying to catch a scent, and when a small breeze brushed by the hound, she raised it higher, sniffing the air; still, nothing toyed with her sharp sense of smell.

'Even the hound has her misgivings,' Tam remarked, scratching his deformed ear. He then eyed their horses, where they had left them tied, to a nearby boulder; they were anxious, their ears flicking back and forth and tails swishing, alert and nervous. 'Hmm … something is not right. I can *feel* it.'

They all could, each conscious of the energy rising from the pillars, strong and growing.

Reece look at Daine with expectancy. 'Well?'

The guide's eyes slowly travelled to the Dhampir, meeting his lucent green stare, it penetrating and intimidating.

Daine shrugged, confused.

'I've never seen anything like them,' he stated. 'How could I? I have never ventured beyond the *Pass*, therefore …' He slowly shook his head.

'And you, Tam?' said Reece, turning his attention to his colleague. 'Then surely, *you* must know. Are you not a Highlander?'

Tam slowly turned his head and raised a brow at Reece, for merely questioning his heritage.

'Aye, that I am,' he said, his tone determined and proud. 'But …' He hesitated, his eyes then narrowing as he surveyed their surroundings further. He shook his head. 'I have never been *here*, and I am familiar with these northern lands.'

'It appears Oran has failed to inform us of yet another "problem",' Reece muttered to Asai, his eyes flashing at Rosalyn, making sure his daughter was not within earshot of his remark—the reference clearly aimed at her husband. But Asai was looking towards the sky—the darkening clouds creeping down from the mountains, in their bid to take control of what little sunlight remained yet allowing it an occasional appearance.

'It will not be long, Reece-san.'

Hearing this, Rosalyn threw the Samurai a sharp look. '*What* will not be long?'

'The sun is losing its battle,' said Asai.

'There is very little of it—this far north,' she replied.

'And, once it has gone,' added Reece, '*they* will soon catch up with us.'

'Aye!' said Tam, nodding. 'And with Magia Nera roaming free, again …'

Rosalyn glanced around nervously, wringing her hands.

'Do you think … they are near?' she said, hugging her shawl tightly. As she did so, her hand touched the silver brooch her mother had given her, and as her finger caressed the sapphire within its centre, she felt Onóir's presence for a precious moment—along with the sudden, overwhelming feeling of her loss as it tugged on her heavy heart.

Then it left her.

'We cannot say,' said Reece, snatching his daughter from her thoughts. She gaped up at him, momentarily lost. 'But, no doubt, they will be aware by now that the Valkyrie's "pet" has been destroyed,' he went on, oblivious to her distraction.

'And Kara will be none-too-pleased, about that,' added Tam.

'Can one of you not scout, to see if they are gaining on us, or—' Daine stopped abruptly when Reece shot him another scathing look.

'We cannot take that risk,' he snapped.

'Why?' The guide's curiosity was resurfacing again; it was clear by his determined tone as he held the Dhampir's stare. He would challenge Reece for more answers. 'I have seen how quickly you move—and your skills … Surely, one of you can go?'

A deep-winded sigh caught everyone's attention when Tam approached Reece, rolling his eyes, his axe now resting on his shoulder.

'Just tell the lad, Reece, aye?' He was almost insistent. 'He is our ally. I think he deserves to know.' But before Reece could respond, Tam turned to Daine, taking it upon himself to divulge a little of what the guide had been itching to know since their first meeting, at the Ardgore Inn.

'We were once her—L'Ordana's—prisoners, bonded to her. Should we attempt to go within a few feet of her, now, we risk being drawn back into that bond, where she will punish us … perhaps worse.' He paused, shaking his head. 'And 'tis something I would not care to experience.'

Daine nodded in understanding, reminded of his encounter with the Sorceress and her cronies, especially *him*—the devilish one; Magia Nera's searing red eyes and threats would be ingrained in his mind for the rest of his life.

'Well … that explains *you,*' he said. 'But what about *him?*' he added, pointing to Gill with his chin.

Tam's eyes slid towards Reece, followed by a hardened stare. *He* could explain *that* one to the guide; after all, Gill was his grandson. But as he raised his brows and nodded towards Reece, silently indicating he had no intention of divulging the true purpose of their journey to Daine, his eye caught a movement, high up between the narrow gaps in the trees.

'You will know soon enough,' answered Gill, stepping into the fold. 'Now, there are more important things on hand, here,' he added, pointing at the three monoliths.

Daine pressed down on his lips and slowly shook his head, irked for being dismissed, yet again. *Damn you!* He then caught Rosalyn's eye; she was aware of his frustration and annoyance. She slowly lifted her shoulders, her face softening to a smile, giving him a look of pity but keeping her thoughts to herself; she knew her father was keeping a watchful eye on the guide, having sensed the unspoken energy between them, since the struggle at the Cordhu Pass.

They all gathered around, carefully scrutinising each of the three granite monoliths, looking up and beyond them. There, ahead, through the gaps of each "entrance" a path waited for the brave intruder, each disappearing into a dark tunnel, beyond its arch of trees. It seemed to the group, each pillar was a guardian of its passageway, leading into the bowels of the forest.

Tam sighed. 'As if the Cordhu Pass wasn't enough, we must now contend with another puzzle?' He turned to face them. 'Does anyone know what they mean or—' He stopped dead, feeling a sharpness down his back as if someone—or *something*—had drawn a fingernail along the length of his spine. He glanced at his colleagues—the hasty nod from Reece and Asai indicating, they had felt it, too.

The three Dhampir exchanged wary looks before returning their attention to the tree line. With a subtle nod to his two colleagues, Tam strode towards it first, removing his axe from his shoulder, his eyes slowly travelling upwards, then muttering words to himself; 'No … I do not like it at all.'

Reece and Asai joined their friend. Together, the three lingered, watching and listening.

'We are not alone,' Tam then stated from the side of his mouth, his narrowed eyes fixed high. Reece and Asai nodded, their keen eyes alert, too.

On hearing the Highlander's words, Rosalyn and Daine were by their side, within moments.

'Could they have caught up with us, already?' said Rosalyn, lowering her voice, her panic evident in how she edged closer to her father.

Tam shook his head.

'No, lass. 'Tis something else.' He craned his head, tilting it higher. 'Aye, 'tis something I've not—' He pointed, seeing *it*—the faint cloud of grey dust meandering its way through the trees, swirling and caressing them, like a lover's embrace.

'What's that?' Rosalyn whispered to her father, peeping over his shoulder while subconsciously holding on to the tail of his waistcoat, like a security blanket; despite the sentimentality attached to her gesture—and as much as it pleased him—Reece did not react. For a few moments, the unusual mist hovered about the trees. Suddenly, it altered direction and was now creeping down towards them.

Rosalyn and Daine shuffled nervously when the dust cloud began to spread out, taking over its territory, gradually enveloping the trees within its ghostly pall as it continued its slow, measured descent.

'What the—'

'Hush!' said Tam, stretching his arm wide across the guide, to stop him from doing something he might regret, his axe firmly grasped in his hand, his other ready to remove the claymore. Daine glanced down at the Highlander's deadly weapon; he was going nowhere.

Rosalyn gasped when a shape emerged from behind one of the ghostly trees, altering as it came into view. She slanted her eyes, then blinked, shaking her head, thinking her mind was deceiving her, distorting her thoughts. But when the figure of a man gradually appeared out of the murk, she drew back, severing the hold she had had on her father's clothing, and covered her mouth, her eyes widening, seeing the sinister look stamped on the man's face.

His stature and physique looked similar to Tam's, and his garb akin to that of a Highlander. She glanced up at Tam, then back at the unusual stranger; no, he was much taller and broader than Tam.

'I see another,' said Reece, tilting his head slightly.

'And I,' said Asai, slowly drawing his hands down, his fingertips touching the hilt of his two weapons again, preparing to fight.

'And there!' pointed Daine, his eyes darting as the trees seemed to part, revealing what looked like a small army.

Rosalyn threw a glance over her shoulder, looking for her son; Gill had been unusually silent. But Gill seemed oblivious to their new plight as he stood with his back to them in a trance, staring down at one of the monoliths. Rosalyn moved to call him, then stopped when she heard the heavy footfall of the sentries behind. Slowly she turned, her eyes travelling up, seeing their menacing approach—the knot of anxiousness in her stomach tightening as they gradually stomped down, towards them.

Her mouth gaped, speechless. Aware of her distress, Daine drew her back, shielding her close behind him and the three Dhampir. With every action comes a reaction, and Daine felt hers—the warmth of her body against his and the quickening of her breath caressing his neck as she kept her eyes wide and fixed, and when the sentries began to spread out, she gasped and touched his arm; when he flinched slightly at her anxious touch, she took it back.

Reece, too, looked back to where Gill was and realised something was wrong. The situation in which they now found themselves was unnerving; there was something desolate and profound about the presence of the unexpected and hostile company, giving him the feeling that they were trespassing—and, perhaps, on unhallowed ground.

'This is not good,' he whispered to Tam and Asai from the side of his mouth, his hand clenched over his broadsword, but despite his attempt to draw his weapon, he could not. From the corner of his eye, he could see the slight strain on the Samurai's face; Asai was incapable of drawing his, too. They glanced at one another, concern mounting. Without their weapons, the Dhampir knew they were in trouble.

Tam, however, was taking in the unlikely Highlanders with curiosity, his eyes studying their clothing; there was something different about it. Tall and lean, typical of Highland warriors, he noted, however, they were not wearing kilts. They wore no headgear but kept their hair tied back. Beneath the long, un-shaped cloak, pinned at the breast with a brooch—the style he could not determine—some wore a long shirt, a *leine*, to the knee, its distinct shade of yellow fading as they closed in. The woollen cloak was of a simple tartan—one he did not recognise, making it difficult to identify the clan attached to it. Beneath the long shirt, most wore *hosens*—the footed leggings worn beneath *braies*—long, loose-fitting shorts. All were armed, some with two-hand claymores similar to his own, and yet they were different; theirs had a distinctive cross-hilt and longer steel. Others held steel-tipped javelins and oval shields—the umbo protruding from their centre, to deflect bows. But what stood out on their stone-like features, were the facial tattoos worn by those at the forefront, making him believe they were Chieftains.

'Who—*what* are they?' asked Daine, his voice a murmur, trying to hide his nervousness, for Rosalyn's sake.

'They are Picts—I think,' said Tam, holding his gaze. 'Highlanders—but not like me.'

'Then say something, quickly!' Rosalyn hissed, her eyes darting, too aware of the uninvited company, and their threatening advance.

'No! 'Tis impossible!' he mumbled to himself.

'What is?' said Reece, sensing Tam's sudden shift in tone; he seemed disturbed.

Tam shook his head, unable to comprehend what was unfolding before his eyes.

'They should not be—' He faltered when the reality dawned on him: they were not living, breathing men, but ghosts, phantoms from another time—born centuries before him.

'The threat of an army of mortals we can deal with, Reece … But this …'

Gradually, the illusion of "life" drained from the ancient Highlanders, and as their true forms came to light, a wavering silence cloaked the group—a silence like no other, brooding and hostile.

The unearthly Highlanders glowered down at them through the hollow of their dead, grey eyes, their faces bold and defined, their hardened stare set like stone. These living corpses were here for one thing, and one thing only: to protect something—and Tam knew, without a doubt, the group was in mortal danger.

As the gravity of their situation unfolded, Rosalyn clasped her hand over her mouth, shocked as the truth emerged, revealing the clan's grim identity. 'Oh, God!' she mumbled—the muffled sound of her frightened voice still audible.

'Somehow, I don't think *God* exists in this place,' Daine threw back at her.

'Talk to them, Tam,' urged Asai, his hands still hovering over his weapons, still unable to draw them—the unknown atmosphere preventing it, its strange energy eddying around the onlookers, manipulating and confusing them.

Tam nodded, but as he moved to take a step towards the spectres, the eerie silence was shattered by the sudden, almost deafening, withdrawal of swords when the phantoms stopped dead, taking their stance as if readying themselves for battle.

'They are going to attack!' blurted Reece. Again, he reached for his broadsword but failed to draw it. Desperate, he tried again. Asai, too. Daine, reaching over his shoulder, his hand almost striking Rosalyn in the process, also tried to unravel his sword from its black, leather sheath, but without success.

Suddenly, the phantoms resumed in their advance, like an army possessed, their rhythmic march defined, their shields forward and weapons raised high, ready to strike down the intruders. The closer they drew, their footfall grew louder with every dying second, drowning out Rave's constant barking. The hound raised her hackles in defence, exposing her sharp teeth, and yet was too fearful to attack, while the horses stomped and neighed, distressed by the disturbing, unearthly presence.

Rosalyn and Daine jolted at the deafening noise and froze,

helpless.

Incapable of drawing their weapons, it now seemed an impossible situation for the small company. Daine looked back towards the pillars. Gill was still motionless and oblivious to what was happening behind him; the phantoms were closing in on him, too. 'Gill!' he cried out, but the young man failed to respond.

Now sensing their end was near, Daine, without thought, grasped Rosalyn's hand; she responded by gripping his, tightly. He looked down at her, feeling her breath on his mouth, their eyes meeting in the same wanting way as they had done at the Cordhu Pass, when she had stumbled. In a brave and bold move, his mouth found hers, quick, hard and passionate; she willingly responded. But when the sudden sharpness of an ice-cold chill crept across her heart, she shuddered and drew back with an unwavering fear that death was seconds away … and this was its prelude.

'If only …' she whispered to him, then broke away from his hold—the desperate look in her eyes alerting him to her intention: she was going to her son.

Daine shook his head, frantic.

'No, Rosalyn, don't do it!' But as he reached out to grab her, they both stopped and spun, upon hearing the heavy thud of something being dropped to the ground.

Tam lifted his arms as he stepped away from his weapon, in a desperate bid to converse with their attackers.

'Wait!' he called out, holding his hands up, in surrender.

Still, the phantoms advanced.

'*Can eil!*' he shouted, then threw down his axe. 'No!' he cried out. '*Feith!* Wait!'

Suddenly the Picts stopped, their vacant eyes set on Tam, his own now glowing. But deep inside, the Highlander had a sense of failure—for giving up—when he eyed his sword and axe as they lay strewn on the ground. But this, he knew, was no battle against mortals.

This was different.

*Desperate times,* he thought, looking up.

*"Thoir an t-iasg à spuir na h-iolaire. Smarach, na trèig idir!"*

He flinched, recalling the words his father had instilled in him when he was a boy.

*"Snatch victory from the jaws of defeat! Never give up, lad!"*

Tam's eyes shot down at his pride and joy, once again: the claymore made for him by his father, before his coming of age—the chief of their clan thinking, at the tender age of fifteen, he was worthy of the weapon.

Fuelled by his pride, and coupled with shame for even thinking of surrender, Tam grunted, then smirked at the phantom army, challenging and mocking them.

'*Athairich's ann agad a tha an fhìrinn,*' he muttered. 'You're right, Father.' He reached down.

'No, Tam!' screamed Rosalyn, her voice loud enough to wake the rest of the dead.

As the Highlander's hand grasped the familiar hilt of his claymore, it refused to budge. He looked down then jostled it, trying desperately to retrieve his sword, but when it still refused to budge, he looked up—the look of panic now etched on his face; the ghostly Picts were dangerously close. He then tried his axe, but his attempt to retrieve that also failed.

Still unable to draw their weapons, there was only one thing they could do: Reece, Asai and Tam shared quick, knowing glances and nodded to one another—the three comrades vowing to fight with their fists—if that were even possible—to the end.

'Ready yourself, lad,' Tam threw back at Daine.

Daine, conscious of the Highlander's meaning, stole one last look at Rosalyn, their eyes momentarily burning with their unspoken passion.

'*I know,*' he secretly mouthed to her, then turned to join the three Dhampir. But he was not alone; she was now by his side, ready to die alongside them all. And in the moments before the ghostly clan were upon them, Rosalyn took one last look back at her son before the onslaught of death, then turned. With Daine's passion still on her lips and her hand returned to his, together, they took their brave stance.

# Chapter Five

'*Stad!*'

The Picts halted, hearing the voice, its mediator's hand raised peacefully as they casually made their way through the group, heads turning quickly to see who it was.

Rosalyn gasped, letting go of Daine's hand as her son brushed by her; she had barely recognised Gill's voice when he called for the spectres to *Stop!* Wrenched from her shock, she made to go after Gill, reaching out to him … but was prevented.

'Have faith in your son.'

She hesitated when confronted by Asai, then looked to her father.

'He is right, Rosalyn,' Reece agreed. 'We must place our trust in Gill.'

Gill's companions watched as the Picts hovered, staring at the young man approaching them, his other hand subconsciously patting Rave's crown as he strode by her, silently asking his dog to "stay". Rave lowered her head obediently as she returned to Rosalyn's side.

When Gill stopped in front of the Picts, they stared at each other within the tense silence, which was then broken by Rosalyn's heavy breathing as she looked on, chewing her lip, fearing for her son's safety. With no concept of what would happen, all they could do was watch … and hope for a miracle.

Pulled back from the mystery of the monoliths, Gill had been woken to the plight of his colleagues when a voice in his head said;

*"Speak with them."*

With seconds to spare, Gill had found himself stepping in before the unfolding nightmare could become a dreadful reality for his companions. And when the phantoms halted in his presence, Gill, without thought, had fallen into the ancient dialect—one that had been lost, along with the Picts, centuries ago. But he did not have to explain who he was, or his purpose; they instinctively *knew*. It appeared they also shared a common bond.

In an unexpected move, Gill bowed towards the ancient clan, his hand drawn across his chest before rising, lifting his head with an air of righteousness, and yet instinct told him he had no authority here. Not yet.

Within moments, the group could hear his voice; it was steady and calm as though it belonged to someone else as he began to converse with the ancient Highlanders.

'What is he saying?' Reece muttered to Tam.

Tam shook his head.

'I … do … not … know,' came the slow response, his mouth gaping, eyes narrowing as he tried to translate the ancient Gaelic, in his head.

Then the unthinkable happened: the whole clan knelt before Gill with their heads lowered.

Rosalyn gasped in disbelief. 'Oh, my …'

It seemed to her, and the others, Gill had delayed, perhaps even saved them from a brutal end. The next few moments would decide their fate.

One of the Picts rose and approached Gill, his impressive height forcing the young man to lift his eyes. The phantom stopped and peered down at him, his dead eyes then lowering slightly again. He pointed, prompting Gill to look, too. When their eyes met again, the two nodded—the acknowledgement then leading them into a conversation, followed by several nods from Gill, when the phantom turned and pointed towards the three monoliths. The discussion then resumed, briefly—the Pict listening, shaking his head slowly. For a few moments Gill stared back at the monoliths, regarding them with steely eyes, his expression set in deep thought. He then nodded sharply, as though in acceptance of a challenge.

In a final gesture, the Pict placed a closed fist against his hollow chest—the sound of its emptiness reverberating—then bowed. Rising, to his full height once again, he accepted Gill with imperial bearing, then simply turned away.

Head lowered and eyes fixed, Gill waited until the ghostly clan returned from where they came, gradually fading back among the trees, and leaving no trace of their presence or existence.

'Gill?'

He spun to find himself surrounded by the others, his mother shaking her head and beaming up at him, her eyes welling with relief and immense pride.

'What just happened there?!' cried Daine, unable to take his wary eyes from the trees, expecting the clan's return.

'They will not be back,' Gill assured them.

'How do you know?' asked Reece, subtly checking his sword, relieved it was his to use again, his eyes then catching Asai nodding to himself—the Samurai pleased to have the use of his weapons, too.

'Because they know who I am.'

They stared at Gill, taken aback by his statement until Rosalyn broke the stunned silence.

'They do?'

'Aye, Maw. Or, at least, *who* I am destined to be.'

'Then we have you to be thankful for—for saving us,' she said, sighing with relief.'

'Aye, lad,' added Tam, glancing back and up through the trees as he cautiously picked up his axe and claymore. 'But how is it *you* could speak with them? This is my native country, *my* language yet I could not understand *their* Gaelic.'

Gill briefly described the conversation he had had with the clan chief while, at the same time, failing to understand *how* he could converse with the phantom, despite his limited knowledge of his own Gaelic.

'You spoke it naturally as if you have done so all your life,' said Tam. Rosalyn nodded in agreement; she knew how much he had tried to avoid learning it in school yet he had just had a full-scale conversation with an ancient Highlander, in their lost dialect. She, too, was stumped. And now it was Tam who was curious to know, wanting to confirm his suspicions.

'You were right, Tam,' said Gill, answering his unspoken question. 'They were—*are*—Picts.' He then tapped the brooch pinned to his cloak—the one his mother had given him in his father's absence. 'The chief recognised the similarities,' he continued, 'especially the *name.* They are of the Pictish clan—the *Shaws!*'

'Ancestors?' said Rosalyn, her brows lifting, marvelling at the thought of her son coming face to face with his forebears, had it been so.

Gill smiled and shrugged. 'Perhaps. Though, I had no intention of disputing otherwise. It seems they were resurrected by the Elliyan, to protect this gateway to Elboru. Because of their constant presence, they have full control over the passages and of those who happen to "stumble" across this place. It seems the "victim" is given a choice; to die by the Pict sword—for trespassing—or … to risk one of the passages. Unfortunately, none have succeeded.'

'Until now,' Asai maintained. Gill turned to the Samurai. Asai tilted his head towards him. 'I assume you now know *what* they are, Gill-san, and know their purpose?' he added, referring to the monoliths.

Gill nodded.

'They are called *The Paths of Lome.* And though I was not threatened, by their sword, *I* must, however, choose one. It is a … *test,* of sorts. And regardless of who I am,' he went on, 'it appears I have no authority over the Picts … until time dictates.'

'In other words … when you become Magus,' Reece commented.

'So, it seems,' said Gill, shrugging.

'A *test?!*' Rosalyn blurted—the feeling of uneasiness creeping over her again. 'I don't like the sound of this, Gill,' she went on, chewing the side of her lip as she side-glanced the monoliths, their ominous presence more intimidating, now that she knew they would be without the help of her son's new "friends".

Gill turned to his mother, his face strong and defined, like a true leader, and looked down at her. He seemed taller and broader as he stood over her, his presence marked by his striking new physique. In the short time since he discovered his true identity, worth and fate, and with the gradual acceptance of his new role, Gillis Shaw had changed into a man worthy of nobility.

Rosalyn could feel the new *life* instilled in him, his energy and power oozing from inside. She knew there and then, he was ready, though not yet fully prepared for what was to come. With this day, his final as a mortal, stretching out before them, they had more to accomplish. And despite what further challenges awaited them—inevitable ones—she and the others would do anything to make sure he reached Elboru, to take his place on the *Throne of Council.*

Inside, she wished Kai was with them, and wondered where he was—not to mention the whereabouts of her husband. It was then, at this point, something dawned on her; she could feel it in the air, see it all around, how summer's late visit had vanished as quickly as it had arrived. Had it only been a few days since they basked in the glory of its brief stay? And now, the chilly effect of autumn's lateness was suddenly evident, matching their growing mood, dull and weary. But it was the day in question—the last of the month—marking something special. It was a day she had never forgotten—one she was reluctant to face … but knew she had to.

Rosalyn, stretching up on her toes, embraced her son, then kissed him on the cheek.

'Happy Birth Day, Gill.'

Gill drew back at the sudden realisation. He had finally come of age! Despite the significance of it—marking the fine threshold between his mortality and longevity—he had completely forgotten. But now, the importance of it was all too real, alerting him to the time they had left: until the last light of the moon's waning crescent. If he did not reach his destination before it vanished, to claim what was rightfully his, it would be there for the taking from another powerful source. *Not as long as I'm around*, he silently vowed. From here on in, he could not let his past interfere with his task. Just then an image entered his mind—Meghan—the girl he had left behind, in Balloch; the girl he had promised to elope with; the girl he— Gill shook any thoughts of her away, dousing the last embers of love, and a shared life that would never be. He would leave their love to *yesterday*, their past gone—and to be forgotten. Nor would he let it cloud his thoughts or actions; too much was at stake. And yet, he knew she was still there, young and vibrant, and deserved a future of her own. But the secret world—his father's—which had protected the mortals, was under imminent threat as it competed for the item awaiting him in Elboru—the Shenn amulet.

Gill looked sharp at the others, then pointed at the monoliths, their eyes following him.

'I must solve their puzzle—if we are to reach Elboru,' he stated.

'Puzzle?' Rosalyn's face fell, realising the danger confronting her son—the danger staring them all in the eye. 'You mean—the Picts never told you *how*?'

Gill shook his head as he walked away from them, back towards his next hurdle, his eyes narrowed and brows drawn in deep concentration—the importance of his task, vital and immediate.

Tam released a long-winded groan and rolled his eyes. 'Well, that's just great!' he moaned, stabbing the ground with his claymore.

'But—how can he possibly know if—'

'A moment,' said Asai, gently raising his hand to Rosalyn,

prompting her to be patient. Trusting the Samurai and his lucid way of thinking, she stalled and watched her son.

Gill stood over the first monolith, on the left, and looked up towards the passage ahead, then hesitated. Despite it—and the unknown danger—there was the one person equally important to his destiny.

'Gill?' Reece prompted, eager for his grandson to make a start as he glanced up, his eyes scouring through the trees, convinced the Picts were still lurking within their gloomy shadows.

As though seeking assurance, Gill looked over his shoulder at Asai, their eyes engaging in unspoken thought. The Samurai smiled; he knew what Gill was silently asking him.

'*Hai!*' he said, nodding briefly. 'Eleanor is still alive, Gill-san,' he added, tenderly placing his hand over his heart.

Hearing her daughter's name spoken by the man who loved her, Rosalyn swallowed the lump in her throat, her heart swelling, thankful for Asai's presence. And though Eleanor and the Samurai had only known one another a few days, she knew the look of love when she saw it and did not doubt theirs, and despite his "affliction" she hoped they would find a way.

With a sharp nod, thanking the Samurai, Gill returned to the task, at hand, and gazed down at the first monolith.

He mused over its surface in quiet solitude, taking in the workmanship; it was an elaborate depiction of the sun, with its golden rays spreading out over the surface, their tips shaped like hands, still gleaming, even without sunlight. The plate itself was made of a semiprecious stone he did not recognise, its vivid colour matching that of a deep blue sky, and when he looked closer, tiny particles of gold glinted up at him, matching the flecks in his eyes. The plate shone, as though it had just been polished, in anticipation of his arrival. He marvelled at its beauty, squinting each time another splash of sunlight escaped the gathering clouds as it shone on its mirror image, briefly enhancing its glory.

Slowly, he lifted his hands.

'Be careful, Gill!' blurted Rosalyn. When he failed to acknowledge her, she stepped forward, then felt the gentle tug of Asai's reassuring hand, stopping her again.

'Remember,' he muttered, in her ear. 'Have faith.'

Rosalyn, now chewing on her lip again, nodded and clasped her hands together, anxious, her heart pounding.

Gill let his hands hover over the relief of the *Sun*. His fingers twitched as the outer rim expanded, exuding immense heat. He lifted his hands away, clenching them, its energy astounding.

'What is it?' said Reece.

Oblivious to his grandfather's voice, Gill then approached the monolith, to the right, repeating the process. This time, the *Moon* dazzled a brilliant white, its surface glazing over like ice, its little crystals sparkling like diamonds; he could feel the sharpness of its freezing breath rising to meet him, then promptly removed his hands, fearing they would freeze, should he linger.

Gill's eyes then moved to the central monolith. As he stepped towards it, he could feel the pull of its vast energy, its depiction of the *Universe* expanding by the second, and stronger than the other two. He stopped and looked down at its surface. Without touching it, he let his finger follow the shape of the relief—the swirling cloud of mother-of-pearl mimicking his movement as though he were controlling it.

Overwhelmed, he pulled away from it, letting out a long breath, then looked back at the others, who stood close behind him, apprehensive and increasingly restless. It seemed to him, the three monoliths were not having the same overwhelming effect on them.

As he stepped away from the monoliths, he felt their impact subside. Eyes set in concentration, he folded his arms, then raised his hand, cupping it over his chin, running his fingers through the softness of his beard as he contemplated their enigma.

*"You must choose the right one."*

He slowly nodded, agreeing with the voice in his mind—his grandmother's—as Onóir's spirit guided him.

'*Which* one, though?' he asked. When met with silence, Gill knew only *he* could decide that.

'Do you know what to do?' said Daine.

'I am trying to decide which—'

'Then I suggest you do so,' Reece broke in—the uneasiness in his tone evident and mounting.

Apprehensive, they gathered near Gill and, keeping their distance, eyed the three dominating monoliths, wondering which he would choose.

'Take care, son,' urged Rosalyn, clasping her hands together.

With his jaw set, ever determined, Gill held his hands over the moon-faced plaquette again, feeling the cold current of energy already rising. And at the moment of first contact, it forced his hands down, pinning them to the surface. Suddenly, his eyes locked shut.

Gill's eyes flickered uncontrollably when a vivid image appeared in his mind: a single path stretched out before him, with arch-like walls of dense forest lining its way. He caught his breath, shuddering, as a profound feeling of separation swept over him. He looked up, his eyes widening when he saw his outer body rising, while his physical one remained rooted at the monolith.

With little or no control over his grounded body, Gill, though conscious and physically aware of what was happening, had no option but to let fate decide as he watched his *spirit body* make its way through the path's entrance before being catapulted away from him. It left him with a deep sense of loneliness.

The Pict Chief's words then echoed in his mind.

*"Do not fight it, until you must. Only the true Magus can conquer the Paths."*

After several yards, Gill felt an icy chill on his face, like someone breathing on him, and realised he could feel everything his outer body could. The path began to twist and turn violently, meandering like a wild river. As his *spirit body* moved forward, he felt the breath on him again, only more prominent now. Gill then knew he was not alone. And yet, he felt strangely comforted by the presence.

Suddenly, from the corner of his eye, he caught a flash of red, its swift movement following him. When he looked its way, it seemed to vanish. He blinked, feeling droplets of water on his face and looked up. At first glance, it appeared to be raining, and yet there was something unnatural about it. Curious, he held out his hand and, turning his palm skywards tilted his head and drew his brows together, confused; the drops splashing on his palm were black. Flicking them away, like an unwanted sickness, he pressed on—the "rain" now taking momentum.

Again, another flash of red snatched his attention. He looked through the thicket of trees and the downpour, seeing the unfamiliar shape of a creature, its pale, grey skin blending with its surroundings. However, its one prominent feature, like a beacon within the gloom, was its cap. *No!* he thought. *It couldn't be!* Heckie Grant's words came back to haunt him.

*"These murderous creatures show no mercy for their victims, lad."*

*Redcaps!*

So, it was true—the story Heckie told him. He had heard it often enough—the gruesome myth had given him many sleepless nights—and now, here he was, faced with its grim reality.

Similar to goblins, Redcaps were small and crouched like old men, with long, white beards and fiery-red eyes, matching the colour of their infamous trademark; after slaying their prey, the creatures soaked their caps in their victim's blood, then sported them on their heads, hence the name: *Redcap.* On their feet, they wore boots of iron, but these did not hamper their speed.

*"Once a Redcap sets his sights on its victim, Gill, there is no outrunning it."*

Again, he could hear Heckie's voice, as though their family friend was there, reminding him of his warning.

It was well known—the story of these creatures—that they needed to kill frequently, to stay alive; if—or when—their blood-soaked caps turned brown, as the fresh blood decayed, then they would die. In their desperation to survive they thrived on the blood of the slain.

Armed with a sickle in their left hand, these murderous creatures used their clawed hands to kill; their nails were so lethal, it enabled them to stab their victims to death.

The creature, its large fiery-red eyes, clear and menacing, stomped closer, its appearance emerging through the black volley. It wore little clothing, save for its long, sleeveless black coat, tied with a belt about its waist. Grasped within its long talon-shaped hands, was its weapon: a pikestaff, its long, black, metal tip serrated and sharp … and lethal.

Suddenly, Gill was aware the creature was not alone; there were now more of them, crawling out from every nook and cranny, drooling and grinning wildly at him as they began to pursue him along the lonely path. The closer they loomed, the clearer he could see their grotesque features and sharp teeth. Now it seemed there were hundreds of them; large speckles of red banding together, quickening their pace, to overthrow their victim.

Seeing the fire in their eyes, it blazing in a frenzy of doom, Gill pushed himself on—the black rain thrashing against his face; if he stopped, he knew they would be upon him in seconds. But as he ran, he was drawn to the ground, it crunching beneath his feet. He looked down, his eyes widening, seeing the scattered remains of human bones—remains of the unfortunate travellers who had made the wrong *choice* when challenged by the Picts, with no knowledge of what awaited them. As the path meandered into sharp bends, he was forced to slow, fully conscious of the army of creatures closing in from behind—the heavy, thunderous stomp of their boots, splashing through the mud. And just as it seemed to continue on its persistent journey, the path began to intermingle within itself, taking him in circles until it dawned on him: he was in a never-ending maze, and being pursued in a relentless chase. With no end of it in sight, and aware of them closing in on him, something made him stop. Breathless, he turned to face the creatures, then jolted—the force of energy wrenching him from his trance-like state and back into his physical body.

Gill recoiled from the monolith, shaking his head, exasperated.

'This'—he clutched his wild, beating heart—'is *not* the way,' he stated, to the others, waiting patiently behind him.

'Are you sure?' said Asai.

Gill nodded slowly, assured.

'Trust me, we would never find our way out through *there*,' he said, '… nor would we survive it,' he added. The others eyed one another, thinking it best not to question why, hearing the bleakness in Gill's voice. They had to trust his judgement.

As he moved towards the next monolith, on the right, Gill glanced up at the sky. The clouds were growing thicker, and with them, the sense of a dark mass, its energy gathering momentum, finally blocking out the sun, in its entirety. He hoped it would not manipulate the Paths or intrude on his ability to choose the right one.

Gill cautiously placed his hands on the next plaquette. Now, with his mind opened, not knowing what awaited him along the next lonely—he hoped it would be—path, he closed his eyes and watched his *spirit body* glide towards its waiting arch and into the expanse of its unknown route.

Once again, he was taken the same distance as the first, going deeper into the anomalous terrain, with no sign of any threat—*so far so good*, he told his *spirit body*—in the safe knowledge this could be his chosen route. But as soon as the thought entered his mind, he was abruptly plunged into blackness, so black and oppressive it gripped him, taking control. He was now struggling to breathe. Unable to find his way back to the light, he let the darkness take him farther, steadying his breathing in the process; to panic could be his failing.

Still, the gloom continued to pull him down … deeper. Feeling his lungs tighten, he grasped for air. With a sense of drowning, he stretched his body, clutching his chest as the air slowly left his lungs. He drew himself up, arms out-stretched, fighting against it until his hand broke the surface. Finally, he hauled himself into the light, mouth gaping, gulping the air as it gradually returned to the heaving lungs of his physical body again.

'This …' He paused, his breathing slow and heavy, welcoming back the breath of life, '… is not the way.'

Released from the monolith's hold, he now eyed the central pillar, apprehensive.

'Right, so,' said Tam, wedging his axe into his belt before returning his claymore to its sheath. 'Then this *has* to be the—'

'No, Tam! Wait!' The Highlander stared at Gill as he grasped his arm. Tam felt the strength in his grip; it was stronger than his own. 'We cannot presume it is.'

Gill briefly explained what had happened before advancing towards the third, and final, monolith. However, when Rave joined her master, Gill smiled down at the hound; she was relaxed, her tail wagging, eager to follow him anywhere. It lifted his confidence.

'Only one way to find out, Rave, eh?'

The dog barked, as if in agreement.

Gill stared down at the depiction of the universe, then looked up towards the final path as it waited to embrace him. Despite the weight of its energy, no impending danger seemed to lurk in its shadows. The feeling he felt was amiable, and when a smile appeared on his strong features, it seemed to indicate to the others that, at last, he had found their safe passage.

'I saw it!' he then exclaimed as Tam retrieved their horses, for what he hoped would be the final leg of their journey.

'What did you see, Gill-san?'

Gill smiled at the Samurai. 'Elboru! I saw Elboru.'

'Then, let us not waste another moment,' said Reece, confident it was within their reach. He looked up, quickly assessing the sky; the clouds were now dominating it, throwing down tiny droplets of rain to taunt them.

Relieved, they prepared to mount their horses, Gill volunteering to take the lead. But as he took the reins, he was drawn back to the three monoliths, his instincts urging him to do so. He stalled, narrowing his eyes as he regarded them.

'Something is not right!' he called out, stopping the others in their tracks.

'What's wrong?' His mother's voice was anxious. She then glanced at Daine, still feeling the touch of his mouth and hand when he looked at her. He shook his head and shrugged, also confused.

The group shared wary looks as Gill cautiously returned to the monoliths. For a moment, he stood transfixed, frowning at the structures before it registered …

Gill recoiled in horror, lifting his hands to his face, in disbelief, his head moving from left to right.

'I—I—don't understand!'

In an instant, they were around him, taken aback by what they, too, were seeing, sharing in his disillusion.

'Impossible!' exclaimed Tam.

'But how?!' cried Rosalyn, looking around her, feeling vulnerable again, expecting their enemy to show at any moment.

Reece and Asai surveyed the scene before them, exchanging looks, equally confounded.

Like a child, who had suddenly lost its way, Gill cradled his head, eyes wide with astonishment, trying to make sense of it all. 'How could they have ...? He was stumped.

The Samurai nodded.

'They have changed!' he stated.

As their eyes fell upon each monolith, it seemed that what was depicted on the surface of each plaquette had now altered; no longer did the *Sun* shine, on the far left, the *Moon* glow, on the right, or the *Universe* revolve between them. All three surfaces had swapped places with each other, throwing the group into chaos.

Asai then took a step closer, his dark, almond-shaped eyes, darting towards Gill, who stood rigid with shock. The great Samurai studied the monoliths, with a little help from Rave—the hound sniffing back and forth along the base of each, then lifting her nose, she equally thrown by it.

'Now what do we do?!' shouted Daine. 'Which one do we—'

'You thought it was this one?' said Asai, interrupting the guide, and rousing Gill from his shock as he pointed at the middle monolith.

The young man slowly nodded.

'Then it still must be that one,' said Rosalyn, joining the Samurai. 'Mustn't it?'

'I do not know, Maw,' said Gill. 'Have their passages stayed the same, or …?'

'… have *they* also changed?' added Tam.

'Either way,' said Reece, breaking in, agitated, 'you *must* choose one, Gill.'

'Aye, you're right,' he said, trying to feel less anxious yet reluctant to repeat the process.

Determined, he advanced towards the monoliths, but as he loomed over his "choice", it changed again. He drew back, hesitated, and then looked to the one on the far right; that, too, had altered. Now, each time he looked upon their surfaces, they changed, continuing to do so with each approach.

Gill spun and stared at the group, shaking his head, helpless.

'I—I can't do it! They keep—'

'Try!' yelled Reece.

Appalled by her father's abrupt and aggressive response, Rosalyn marched towards him.

'Leave him alone!'

'He is not a child, Rosalyn!' hissed Reece, his eyes glowing pale red as he glared down into his daughter's face. Eyes wide, with fury, Rosalyn pressed down on her lips and raised her hand; she winced when Reece snatched her wrist within an inch of his face, his eyes locked with hers. While he admired the love she had for her son, it frustrated him to see how much she showered him with it—the element of jealousy burning inside him for the unique bond she shared with Gill. However, his anger grew deeper, rising from the pit of his stomach; he was aware of what had passed between his daughter and the guide, in the moments before Gill had halted the Picts' attack on them.

'Stop it!' shouted Gill.

Exasperated, Rosalyn wrenched her arm away from Reece and held her stance. It was the first time her father had displayed any bitterness towards her. No, she would not be intimidated by him, or another man, for that matter. Gritting her teeth, she lifted her head, and yelled back;

'I *know* he's not a child!'

Reece, now conscious of the two individuals by his side—Tam and Asai always ready to intervene, when needed—took a step back, his hands clenching as he lowered his head, his eyes sliding towards Daine, his antagonistic look reminding—*warning*—the guide of his place among them. Feeling the threat of the Dhampir's stare, Daine glared back, challenging him, with no thought of the outcome, should he find himself in physical conflict with a *creature* he had no hope of defeating.

'Can you not feel it?' said Asai—the constant mediator when things went sour—as he observed his colleagues, sensing their mixed emotions already in early conflict. They would have more than the monoliths to contend with if he did not intervene.

'Feel what?' muttered Reece, through clenched teeth.

'The atmosphere in this place,' the Samurai continued. 'It is oppressive. Can you not feel the weight of its hostility? I believe it is affecting our emotions.' He shook his head, then cast a brief non-judgemental glance at Rosalyn, then back to his friend. 'And we cannot let that happen, Reece-san, otherwise'—he looked at the guide, Daine's eyes now meeting his—'things *will* get out of control.'

# Chapter Six

*Lein River – (North-West Scotland)*
*Near the Ardmanoth Mountains*

On hearing its owner's voice, the horse jolted against Eleanor, knocking her to the ground.

Though aching from the fall, she quickly forgot her pain when she found herself looking up into the pale red eyes of one of L'Ordana's Dhampir soldiers, mere feet from her.

When he stepped towards her, she scrambled back, then stopped, clasping her hand over her mouth in disbelief.

'Ma—Marcas?'

The young Dhampir halted and tilted his head as he looked down at her.

''Tis me,' she said, raising her hands in defence. 'Eleanor—Eleanor Shaw?'

Something—a memory, perhaps—stirred in his mind. But when his eyes darted, lured by the dry blood on her palm, he took another step towards her.

Eleanor promptly closed her hand as if snatching the air and slowly rose to her feet, ignoring her aching body. Seeing him again—the young man she had known from Balloch—shook her to the core as he stood before her with the familiar lucid want in his eyes. She wondered how she had failed to notice him before this. But she had chosen *not* to; each time one of the Dhampir leered at her, she had been forced to avoid their stare, knowing, through their frenzied look, she was nothing more than "fresh blood" to them.

Despite his altered appearance, Eleanor did not doubt this Dhampir's identity. She recalled the young man, Marcas Logan—once, a friend of Gill's—and how he used to be: slender and lean, he had been regarded as a "catch" among the young women in Balloch. Where his fair, straight, shoulder-length hair had once gleamed, it was now dark and slicked back from his face, exaggerating his sharp, pale features. And where his dark-brown eyes once smouldered, they now stared back, lifeless, behind the pale red.

They had known each other since they were children. It was thought, at first, that he and another, Athol Keir, had run away to become soldiers to *The Crown*. But when it came to light that they had not taken their belongings with them, the villagers quickly discovered the young men had disappeared without a trace.

Another proof of his identity was the birthmark on his left earlobe; she noticed it. From a few feet away, it looked like a piece of his ear was missing. When Gill mocked him for it, Marcas used to reply, while winking at her; "Sure, the wee lassies love it, do they not, Ellie?"

'*Ellie!*' she blurted when he moved closer. Again, he stopped. He frowned slightly, this time narrowing his eyes. She swore she saw a glint of recognition in them. 'Try to remember, Marcas,' she persisted, using his name, hoping it would jog his memory. 'Ellie? Gill's sister?'

Then something registered. He drew back, sword gripped in hand. She lowered her eyes, regarding it.

*"Be sure to stay clear of the Dhampir's blade."*

Wareeshta's words of warning came back, reminding her that their swords were coated with a deadly venom. Her eyes widened as she stared at the weapon, seeing the dark stain of the poison smeared on its steel. She edged away from it, swallowing. Marcas lowered his eyes to see what she was staring at. He grinned when he saw her peering at the blade, and relished in her fear, seeing it written on her face.

'You *know*,' he said, tapping his long fingernail on its steel. His voice was slow, deep and thick, unlike the one she had known before, upbeat and alluring. Just seeing him with the sword in his hand was unnatural in itself; the Marcas *she* had known, would have never harmed a soul. But he was no longer that person; he was now a Dhampir—a *creature*—and capable of killing her … without mercy.

Eleanor stood staunch, but with caution, keeping her eyes on him.

'I—I know you would never harm me, Marcas,' she said, struggling to keep her voice calm.

Again, he tilted his head, his eyes tapered. He was still unsure. Suddenly, he lowered the sword until the tip of the blade touched the ground, her eyes following his every move. Had she gotten through to him? *Only one way to find out*, she thought. Smiling through her anxiousness, she dared to take a step back. He remained still, statuesque-like. She took another step, now sensing the horse close behind her.

'Where are you going?' he said, his tone devoid of emotion.

'Home, Marcas … to Balloch,' she replied, maintaining her ploy, to jar his memory.

He drew his head back, lips parting.

'We were worried,' she continued. 'Your parents, Anny and Robert, and your brothers, Duncan and Adam.'

Marcas flinched, hearing the names.

*It's worked!* she thought. 'They miss you—and want you home.' By now, she could feel the horse and reached behind, groping for the saddle, still watching him. His eyes were now darting over the ground as if searching for the memory.

Frustrated, he grunted, unable to recall, and yet the names the girl mentioned, though vague, sounded familiar. He lifted his eyes to her with a lost look, as though seeking her help.

Taking a bold risk, Eleanor held out her hand.

'Come with me, Marcas.'

Suddenly his whole expression changed—the deadpan look returning, followed by a subtle dark one, threatening and menacing. 'Now why would I do that?' he sneered.

Eleanor's eyes widened, alerted to the sudden and impassive

change in his demeanour. She panicked. She would have to do something—and fast!

'Let me go, Marcas,' she said, in a firm voice.

His eyes then shifted, looking over her shoulder.

'That is *my* horse,' he stated, pointing with his chin.

Snatching the reins, she held them out. 'Take him! Just—let me go—please!'

The seconds dragged as they stared at one another, undecided. Slowly, Marcas lifted his hand. Thinking he was taking his horse back, Eleanor extended hers.

The movement had been quick and sharp. She cried out in pain when he gripped her wrist, squeezing it so tightly she thought it would snap. The pain was excruciating, and as his grip tightened, she was forced to her knees, her face distorted in agony.

Eleanor shook her head, trying desperately to free herself, but the more she struggled the pain intensified. Despite her attempts to lure him back to the happy life he had once shared with them as friends, Eleanor knew Marcas was dead inside—a warrior trained to kill, without remorse.

Marcas was now sneering down at her. 'Think you can escape … *mortal?*' He lifted his sword, brandishing it over her. She tried to recoil as he drew it dangerously near—so close she could smell the venom on its steel, its sharp tang making her flinch. 'I can dispatch you, right here, right now,' he boasted.

'No, Marcas! Please! Don't kill—'

Eleanor suddenly fell back, freed from his grip. It had happened so swiftly, she did not see them coming. Clambering to her feet she stared, taken aback as she watched Marcas being dragged away by a group of Urisks. What the little creatures lacked in stature, was made up by their abnormal strength.

Nine in total she counted as they hauled the Dhampir towards the thicket of trees; and as Marcas screeched and writhed, trying to escape their clutches, Eleanor stood dumbfounded, watching until they disappeared. From where she stood, she could hear the heavy, busy rustling of bushes, mixed with muffled sounds of continuous struggles; the Urisks were masking the sounds of their actions, to avoid alerting the enemy.

Unsure, she glanced back at the horse; the steed was drinking from the river as if nothing had happened. What was she to do? Should she go, or wait?

*Wait for what?* she thought. Did she want to know?

Then all went quiet, save for the river burbling behind her. Eleanor held her breath. What if Marcas had butchered them all? She knew he was capable. 'Time to leave,' she muttered, turning, then stalled, seeing a movement among the trees. She stepped back, ready to mount the horse—whether he liked it or not—to make her getaway. But her eyes were diverted to the low ground as the bushes gradually parted. She smiled with relief.

Out into the clearing, the group of Urisks re-emerged. She could see them clearly now; some were different in size and shape. They all smiled up at her, then at one other, nodding, looking pleased with themselves.

Eleanor's eyes passed over the Urisks, searching, as they chattered away in their ancient tongue, pointing at her, then back at the trees.

'Where is Muk?' she asked them, moving closer.

The Urisks glanced from one to the other, smiling, then clapped, skipping and jumping around each other.

'*Nori!*'

She beamed, hearing Muk's voice call out to her from the bushes, followed by the heavy thump of his big feet as he made his way out into the clearing, eager to see his new friend again. The Urisks, still applauding, parted as he came into view.

Eleanor's face then dropped with horror; Muk was running towards her, brandishing the very weapon Marcas had tried to kill her with—the Dhampir's sword now drenched with his own deep-red blood. Eleanor's heart almost stopped. Then panic struck.

'No, Muk!' she cried, waving at him. 'Put it down! Please, put it—'

It was too late. By now, Muk had raised the sword for all to see, proud to show them what he had done—the *Victor!*—then clasped the blade with his free hand.

In that moment of dreaded fear, Eleanor's world seemed to slow as she ran towards her little friend. She gasped when the sword fell from his hand to the ground—the impact splashing Marcas' blood everywhere.

'Oh, no!' she cried when Muk stared into the palm of his hand, where the blade had made its fatal cut. Confused, he looked up at her, then dropped to the ground.

Frantic, Eleanor fell to her knees in a bid to help him. Feeding off her dismay, the other Urisks were thrown into utter panic, prompting them to rush to her aid.

But Eleanor was at a loss as she stared down at Muk. She simply did not know what to do. Fraught, she looked to his friends for help.

'We must do something!' she cried, her hands raised, searching for an intervention she knew would never come. But the Urisks just stood and stared back at her as though they had already accepted Muk's demise. She had to try something—*anything!*—but as she reached out to touch her friend, she jolted, recoiling in horror, seeing the black venom pumping through his veins at an alarming rate. His small body convulsed into spasms, desperate to fight off its fatal attack.

Then, it was over.

Though swift, it had been a dreadful and painful death. Eleanor shook her head, her mouth partially open, shocked into a despairing silence after what she had just witnessed. The sound of slow, shuffling feet roused her from her dismay. She looked up through the well of tears, seeing the Urisks surrounding her as they stared down bewildered at their friend's body. And though they could not converse with her, Eleanor knew, by the sombre look on their faces, they understood. Placing a hand over her heart, she slowly shook her head in silent apology for their loss, and hers. But when the look on the Urisks' faces suddenly altered to that of revulsion, their eyes now fixed on Muk's body, Eleanor drew her brows together. Even before she looked, she could smell it, drawing her hand over her nose and mouth from the overpowering stench. Muk's body was rotting—the venom already eating away at his corpse. She rose, backing away, sick to the pit of her stomach, feeling immense guilt.

'It's my fault,' she mumbled, shaking her head. 'It's all my fault.'

The group of Urisks looked up at her and shared confused glances. She could not help but notice how strangely calm they were. Was it something in their making that made them see death from a different perspective? She failed to understand—failed to understand anything at this time. One approached her and, reaching up, tugged her sleeve. She looked down at him, her eyes red and swollen, heartbroken, blaming herself. He slowly shook his head, then pointed to the horse.

"*Greas!* Hurry, Nori! Go!'

She gasped when he called her by her pet name. Muk must have told them about her. She shook her head, in protest.

'*Greas ort!*' he urged, now taking her hand. 'You must go.'

The Urisk, watched by the rest of his group, led Eleanor to the horse. Nodding, he pointed up. As much as she wanted to stay, Eleanor knew the Urisk was right; she had to leave.

With help from the little creature, she hoisted herself up into the saddle and looked down at the Urisk.

'Thank you!' she said, wiping away the tears. 'Take care of Muk,' she added, patting her heart, then pointing to where his body still lay. With a nod, the Urisk turned and left her, to tend to his dead friend. And with a heavy heart, Eleanor guided the horse away. This time, it did not resist; it seemed to sense her pain and kindness now, causing her no more trouble.

Before she left, she turned to look back to where the Urisks had stood, mourning their friend. They were gone. The only proof of what happened still lay on the ground: the sword Marcas had almost killed her with—the Marcas she once knew, who no longer existed; nor did she care.

After checking that all was secure on the saddle, Eleanor re-adjusted the stirrups, then looked up, taking in her surroundings. In the distance, she saw a ray of sunlight appear, over the Ardmanoth mountains, its light then consumed by the clouds. It would not be long before her absence was discovered—if not already—then *they* would come looking for her.

'Go west, through the valley, then north,' she muttered, outwardly repeating Wareeshta's directions. The Dhampir had suspected that was where her friends were, and where the Valkyrie's black hawk, Nakia, had been slain by one of them.

*"Elboru."*

The name appeared in her mind, as though someone had placed it there, to prompt her.

'But, of course!' She recalled her conversation with Asai, the night they "discovered" one another. It seemed like years ago yet it had only been days, since. '*Elboru.*' She nodded to herself; he had subconsciously let it slip, even though they had wanted to keep it from her, to stop her following them.

With the dawn of a new confidence growing inside her, Eleanor lifted her head. 'North it is, then.'

Eleanor squeezed her legs tightly, reminding the steed of who its new owner was. Still, it gave no resistance. Urging it on, the horse took off on her command, letting her steer it along the river. From there they headed straight into the valley—Eleanor, bringing with her the memory of the little creature that had saved her, and the stark and brutal reality of the new world she had been subjected to, it hardening her heart with every step.

# Chapter Seven

*The Paths of Lome*

'What are we going to do?'

When he received no response, Daine turned and glared at the three Dhampir; but they were ignoring him, their interests resting on Gill as the young man, now desperate, randomly made his way towards one of the monoliths. *Right, that's it!* he thought, infuriated by their disregard of him. Yet again! For a moment, he regretted joining them on their journey and, despite his relentless need to know the truth behind it, they still avoided answering all his questions. If they were going to persist in flouting him—just because he was "mortal"—then he would have to make his voice stronger, make them respect him. Therefore, he would take it upon himself to go to the source …

Gill.

As Daine turned away from them, his eyes fell on Rosalyn, but she was too caught up in the confusion to notice him, at that point. He sighed, reminded of the reason he chose to stay: the spark he had felt from the first moment their eyes met. *"If only …"* He needed to be sure what she had meant by it. Or had it been a spur-of-the-moment thing, thinking they were about to die at the hands of the Picts? But it had been the look in her eyes—one of regret—when she said it. He *was* sure of it. Yes, he would do that—when he found a moment to be alone with her. That, however, would be difficult—he slid his eyes towards her father—for obvious reasons. Regardless of Reece's underlying threats, and suspicions, he *would* find a way. In the meantime, he would not be cast aside by the others. He looked at Gill, confident he would get the truth out of *him*.

But as he stomped towards the young man, Rosalyn gasped, stopping him in his tracks.

'They've changed again!' she cried out, pointing at the monoliths. 'What on earth is—'

'It is this one! I'm—I'm certain of it.'

They stared at Gill as he stood over the monolith—to the right—where now the *Universe* swirled in perpetual motion. He was holding his trembling hands over its surface, thinking, hoping he could keep it there, suspending it in time until he was sure of his choice.

'Are you sure, son?'

Gill nodded in response to his mother's voice, afraid to take his eyes from the plaquette, fearing it would alter again.

'I … *feel* it,' he said, convinced he was right, and yet was trying to disregard the doubt niggling away inside him. With no one, not even his grandmother's voice in his mind, to guide him, he would have to rely on his intuition.

'Then we must trust his instincts,' said Asai, as though he had read Gill's thoughts.

'A moment!' prompted Reece, raising his hand, his keen eyes darting from Gill to the central monolith.

'What is it?' said Rosalyn, approaching her father and setting aside their altercation—the others now close behind her. Silence gripped them as they stayed focused on the three monoliths, watching them, intently, Reece still fixed on the central one, his eyes tapering, scrutinising it.

Her father then lowered his hand slowly, placing it on the hilt of his broadsword, still checking he could unsheathe the weapon, sensing his need to. With a slight gesture, he cautioned Rosalyn to keep her distance—the guide, too.

With Tam and Asai by his side again, the three Dhampir stood rigid, staring into the abyss of the dark passage, beyond the central monolith. In the distance, their keen sense of hearing caught the sound of emptiness, like a reflection of the non-existence of *life*: quiet … dead … nothing.

And then …

'I hear it,' said Asai, tilting his head, his voice calm and steady.

'Aye,' added Tam, slowly nodding, his face hardened and jaw set, grasping the axe and claymore in each hand.

'Hear what?' asked Daine, his anger subsiding when his eyes moved to Rosalyn. She shrugged, then diverted her look, still reminded of what had passed between them—and the words she had whispered—in the moments before she thought were their last, feeling the pang of guilt. But still …

'Something—no—*someone*—is coming towards us … and at great speed, too,' said Reece.

''Tis one thing after another,' Tam moaned, raising his weapons.

'I know,' muttered Reece, narrowing his eyes. 'Could they have returned, do you think? The Picts?' He looked sharp when he caught a glimpse of it—the form on its approach.

It then stopped, hovering in the distance, staying concealed.

Daine moved closer, his eyes searching. 'I don't see any—'

'Trust me,' Reece snapped, sliding his eyes towards him. 'It is there; nor am I waiting to see *what* it is,' he stated, gripping his sword, prepared to go into the unknown, to confront it. He looked at his two colleagues. 'Ready?'

Asai and Tam nodded, only too willing to oblige.

'No!' cried Daine, reaching for Reece's arm; the Dhampir recoiled, glaring at him, eyes paling to red. 'You cannot leave us here!'

'Stay!' Reece snarled, exposing the sharpness of his teeth.

'I will not!' Daine protested. Ignoring the warning in the Dhampir's tone, he quickly reached over his shoulder, feeling the hilt of his sword beneath its sheath, itching to use it, tempted to.

'Don't be foolish, lad!' Tam cautioned, shoving him away from Reece, for his own protection—the strength of the Highlander's push, forcing the guide to the ground.

'Stop it!' yelled Rosalyn, rushing towards Daine, having seen the contorted look of anger on her father's face, unable to predict his next move.

But as Asai and Tam moved to drag their colleague away from the guide—Reece dangerously looming over Daine—the sudden shift in Rosalyn's voice stopped them.

'Oh, my—look!' she cried as the figure emerged from the shrouded gloom, their appearance a sight for sore eyes, and enough to warm a cold heart.

'Kai!' Rosalyn's face lit up when she saw the familiar, ghostly being approaching them.

Daine's mouth gaped as he slowly dragged himself to his feet. *What the hell is that?* he thought, then drew back, stunned, when the Servitor transformed from its ghostly form to its earthly one.

Daine could not take his eyes off the "man" who now approached them: tall and lean, with his neatly-tied dark hair, and perfectly-groomed beard, his stride and clothes, he thought, were becoming of someone of nobility. Kai's warm, brown eyes lit up when he beamed at Rosalyn, his infectious smile lifting her soul. Daine was then taken aback when Rosalyn threw her arms around the great man. Tam grinned, having noticed the guide's reaction, finding it amusing. Amid the reunion, Rave joined in, leaping about, nuzzling everyone with excitement as she tried to voice her joy at their unexpected—and most welcomed—visitor.

'Oh, Kai!' said Rosalyn, then pulled away from him. 'It is so good to see you.'

Gill, hearing the commotion, and familiar name, looked up. Overwhelmed and relieved to see their family friend again, he subconsciously tore himself away from the monolith, then halted, his eyes wide when he realised what he had done. He glanced back, his shoulders slumping with a sense of failure when he saw its surface had changed again. But when a flicker of hope ignited inside him Gill nodded to himself.

*Aye, Kai will know what to do.*

'I wondered what had happened to you, after—' Rosalyn stopped herself.

'Onóir?' he whispered. She glanced at Gill, aware he was now beside her.

'I know, Maw,' he informed her.

'You do?'

He nodded.

'But you said nothing,' she returned.

'I thought it best, because …' His words trailed off, unsure what to say, not wanting to upset his mother. 'It's just—we have so much to do, now. But we can mourn and celebrate Onóir, later. And, we will—in a way most worthy of her, when all this is over.'

Rosalyn bit down on her quivering lip, trying to contain her tears; she was immensely proud of her son, especially now. *"When all this is over."* His words resonated, and she hoped with all her heart it would be soon, and *he* the victor.

'And, what is more,' he went on, to ease his mother's heartache, 'I know she is with us—in mind and spirit.'

Rosalyn stared up at her son, then looked at Kai, her friend smiling and nodding, reassuring her. At that moment, she felt the soft brush of a breeze kiss her cheek, then remembered the last words she had spoken to her mother before she died:

*"Wait for me."*

'Thank you.'

The group, hearing his voice, turned to look at Reece, who, for the first time, displayed a faint smile on his face at the Servitor as he approached him. It had been no secret—Reece's dislike of Kai; it was evident from their first meeting at the Ferryman Inn, in Balloch. He had been jealous of the unique bond his wife and the Servitor had shared during his long years of absence.

'Onóir regretted nothing, and was thankful for everything,' Kai told him. Then, in a gesture they thought they would never witness, Reece extended his hand towards Kai; the Servitor graciously accepted it, followed by a respectful bow.

Nothing more needed to be said between the two; they now understood one another—Reece, ever grateful to Kai for comforting his wife, in her final moments.

Overwhelmed, Rosalyn could no longer keep her tears and, burying her head in her hands, finally let them flow, weighed down by a sense of guilt, coupled with the loss of her mother and her daughter's abduction. Feeling her pain, Daine went to her side, wanting to place a comforting arm around her shoulder; though tempted, he resisted, aware of Reece's penetrating stare.

'Gill,' began Reece, dragging his scornful look away from the guide. 'Be proud of your grandmother. She was the one who protected you, in your father's absence.'

Gill grunted. *My so-called father*, he thought.

'Nothing could have saved her,' said Kai, 'or prevented the purpose of your journey, here.'

The Servitor, now mindful of the stranger in their company, eyed Daine with a spirit of enquiry but was then distracted when Gill removed his sister's dagger to show him, cradling the weapon in both hands, feeling her energy in its steel.

'We still have not found her,' he said, his saddened eyes meeting Kai's.

'I should imagine your sister will need that back—*when* we do.'

The group spun, hearing the booming voice behind them. Gill's eyes flickered in disbelief, at the same moment his mother's hands dropped from her face, hearing the word "sister" fall from the lips of the prominent voice they knew so well yet had not heard for three long years.

Father and son stared at one another, momentarily stunned. Oran, at first, neglected to notice the company with Gill as he slowly dismounted Nepthys—the realisation of seeing his son, now grown into a strong, handsome young man, rendering him oblivious to those around him. Gill's notable aura, alone, engulfed him with pride.

Silenced by the shock, the group could do nothing but watch as father and son continued to gape at one another, thoughts churning in their minds, unsure of what to say or do. Abandoned by words at the unannounced reunion, time took a deep breath, allowing them to become aware. But the savoured moment was abruptly interrupted.

The sting of the unexpected blow forced Oran's hand to his cheek to soothe the pain.

'And I would willingly accept the next one,' he responded, with reluctance, as he looked down at his wife.

Rosalyn, her face red with fury, clenched her fist again.

'Gladly!' she scorned, repeating the action, making a point of delivering it harder.

Behind her, the others looked on; Tam snorted, entertained by Rosalyn's feisty reaction at seeing her husband again, while Reece nodded, impressed by his daughter's strength. However, Daine was cautious, wondering who this newcomer was.

'Maw!' cried Gill, unexpectedly coming to his father's defence. Rave, reacting to her master's sudden outburst, barked non-stop, giving voice to the stranger.

'Quiet, dog!' Rosalyn snapped, her eyes still boring into her husband.

'And who is this?' said Oran, trying to take the onus from his wife's confrontation.

'Never mind *her*,' growled Rosalyn, pointing her finger sternly at her husband. 'Three years! That's how long it has been. Three years of our lives altered, without even a—'

'Rosalyn,' said Reece, deciding to intervene. 'Oran had no choice. Remember? I explained all that to you when—'

Rosalyn spun and glared at her father, silencing him.

'Are you defending *him?*' She grunted. 'Typical! Thank you for—'

Before she could finish her lecture, Rosalyn was swept off her feet back into the sturdy arms of her husband.

'And still, you do not listen, woman, aye?' he mocked, embracing her.

Rosalyn tried hard not to respond but then found herself surrendering to the re-awakened warmth of her husband's loving hold. She closed her eyes and, for an instant, lost herself in the sentiment of it, then broke away in self-reproach, glimpsing the dejected look on Daine's face; it was evident, in the way he was staring at her, his brow knitting tightly, he knew precisely who this "stranger" was, now. But when her husband tried to embrace her again, Rosalyn shrugged away from Oran, feeling the sudden awkwardness and guilt borne out of a growing situation, her mixed emotions confusing her.

'Be mindful of who you are.'

Daine looked sharp, hearing the soft, melodic voice in his ear, drawing back when Kai lowered his head, casting him a subtle look of warning.

'I was compelled to leave you, on *their* instructions,' said Oran, pleading his case. 'The Elliyan are … quite persuasive. Believe me, Rosalyn'—she almost swooned when he spoke her name—the way he always did when attempting to soften her mood—'I *tried* to leave, but …' His words trailed, followed by a subtle shrug.

'You could have sent word, a sign—anything at all—just to let us know,' she argued back. 'We thought you were—' She stopped herself, unable to say it. 'We had just begun to accept it … until Reece, Asai and Tam found us.'

Oran turned to find the familiar green eyes looking back at him. 'Ah! The new-found family member,' he remarked, approaching the three Dhampir. Oran threw out his hand and shook Tam and Asai's first, pleased to see them again, then turned to Reece. 'Thank you,' he added, nodding. 'You have done me a great service, protecting them.'

'To the death,' Reece stated.

Oran nodded, though was still dumbfounded by the knowledge that Reece was his wife's father. He cast a curious look between the two, and then saw the resemblance; her eyes—one blue, one green—the green matching his. He had never made the connection. Why would he? He had no reason to at the time—not even during the long hours spent in Reece's company, in the citadel, while they planned their escape. No, he never saw it.

Oran looked down when he felt a tap on his leg. He smiled and leaned over to stroke Rave. 'And who are you?' he asked, letting the hound satisfy her curiosity as she cautiously sniffed his scent.

'Another addition to the family,' Tam answered, moving to pet Rave on the head—the dog bowing to his strong touch—the Highlander having now disregarded the moment when she almost attacked him, on their first introduction.

Oran eyed the Dhampir. *Family?* he thought, bemused by Tam's casual usage of the word. It appeared—during their time together—the three Dhampir had made themselves comfortable within his family unit. But who was he to deny them the right? After all, he was in no position to criticise.

'Aye, and he's a fine addition, too,' was all he could say.

'*She!*' stressed Rosalyn, tilting her head, making a point of declaring the dog's sex to her husband, it typical of a man to presume otherwise.

Oran winced, feeling the sharpness of his wife's tongue and blank stare, and realised it would be some time before he was forgiven. *Change the subject, Oran*, he told himself. 'Aye! I can see it now,' he began, rising, looking from Reece to his wife. Rosalyn frowned. 'The resemblance?' he stated, pointing from one to the other.

'Though I have not caught up with time,' said Reece.

Then, in an unexpected move, taking them off-guard, Oran embraced the Dhampir, patting him on the back, stating how proud he was to have him as his father-in-law, while Reece stood rigid, unsure how to respond. It, however, was the gesture that broke the ice; Rosalyn finally gave in, by laughing at her husband's affection towards her father.

'But—how?' said Oran. 'How did you know you were … related?'

Reece turned and pointed to the item in Gill's hand.

'Eleanor's dagger?' said Oran, amazed by the unusual connection.

'Aye!' added Tam, snorting, as he recalled their first encounter with the young woman in the woods, near her home. 'The lass was brave, Oran, by wielding it at Reece, and threatening him when we first met.'

Rolling his eyes, Reece held out his hand—palm opened—silently asking Gill for the dirk. Gill handed it to him.

'See?' he started, running his finger gently over each initial engraved on the blade. 'I recognised it, instantly. Onóir used to threaten me with it, too. Also … Eleanor was holding it with her *left* hand.'

'Ah, yes!' Oran exclaimed. 'Rosalyn and Onóir—they, too, are—' He stopped, then sighed. 'I am … sorry … for your loss, Reece'—he turned to Rosalyn—'and yours.'

She slowly met his sympathetic look, seeing regret in his eyes. 'How did you know?'

Oran pressed down hard on his lips, suppressing his anger, recalling the moment in the Great Hall of Eminence, in Elboru—when he overheard the conversation between Kai and Tuan, and the disparaging manner in which the Great Warlock had casually mentioned Onóir's demise, as though he had almost forgotten her name. But even in death, Onóir rightfully deserved respect and honour, after everything she had done for the Elliyan—and his family. He sighed, his eyes travelling to Kai.

'It does not matter how I know,' said Oran, briefly returning his attention to the weapon before handing it back to Gill. For a moment, father and son looked at one another, feeling the weight of Onóir's untimely death. 'But the important thing is … I do.'

Silence held the group together for several moments as their eyes stared down at the dirk—the energy of its predecessors prominent—

even in the grip of a man.

'Nori's initials are there, too,' said Gill, breaking the stillness.

Oran opened his mouth, silently gasping, seeing "E.M.S" engraved on the blade. It filled him with pride. 'Daughter, and Granddaughter,' he whispered, regretting he had not been there to oversee the engraving himself. He looked up at his son.

'Kai saw to it,' Gill informed him.

Oran flashed a smile and a nod of gratitude to the Servitor, it returned with a graceful bow.

'Your daughter is truly a strong individual,' the voice behind them then stated.

Oran turned to acknowledge the Samurai—the one he held with great esteem, the one who played the prominent role in helping him, helping them all to escape. Asai bowed before they gripped one another's arms in a show of strength and unity.

'A "strong individual," you say?' said Oran.

Asai nodded sharply.

'*Hai*, Oran-san!'

'Aye, and a daring lass with it,' Tam remarked.

It was hard to believe. Oran had held an image in his mind of a young, nervous girl, who had been plagued by anxiety most of her youth. He could almost feel her little hand in his, holding on for dear life, knowing he would do anything to protect her. He turned to Rosalyn.

'Is he talking about *our* Eleanor?'

She nodded.

''Tis true. She has become a beautiful woman, since …' Her words trickled away.

Oran's face hardened. 'We *will* get her back,' he promised—the stern determination evident in his tone.

'Then you know who keeps her prisoner?' said Gill.

'I do, and what is more … I *know* L'Ordana will not harm her.'

'How can you be so—'

'I just know,' he snapped back at his wife.

Rosalyn, throwing her hands on her hips, drew back her head and slowly raised a brow. 'I hope you are right, Oran Shaw,' she began, then, pointing her finger, added; 'Or I will hold *you* accountable, should any harm come to her … or worse.'

Oran moved swiftly to her side, growling—the tension in the air growing thick and confrontational again. He glared down at her. 'Do you not think I—'

'Stop it!' cried Gill. 'We *know* she is safe,' he stated, throwing his father a disgruntled look as he pointed towards Asai. 'Because … *he* knows.'

Oran glanced at the Samurai and frowned, bemused. 'What has *he* got to do with Eleanor?'

Gill grunted. 'I will explain, later. But, right now, we need to be united in this. We have to get my sister back.'

'Lest you forget, son,' Oran returned. 'It is also—' He stopped, then took a step back, slowly nodding—the look of pride spreading across his face when his eyes fell on the silver brooch displaying their *Shaw* family crest. So, Rosalyn had given it to him. He was grateful for that—when the *Picts* came to mind. But then something occurred to him: for Rosalyn to give the brooch to their son, she would have had to rummage through his personal belongings—rummage through the coffer of his past life. He hoped she had not stumbled upon anything else. If so … well, he would cross that bridge ... His eyes, still resting on the heirloom, noted where it was pinned. 'Aye, lad,' he muttered, seeing his damask cloak gracing his son's broad shoulders; it still looked like new—the luxurious fabric—its deep, rich shade of noir, weaved with a subtle silk garnet thread was still vibrant. 'It suits you, indeed.'

'*Lad?*' Gill returned, looking his father in the eye. 'Lest *you* forget, I'm no—'

'I know, son. I—it has been too long. The only image I had of you in my mind, while incarcerated, was when I left Balloch; you were so young, then, just a wee …' He sighed. ''Tis only now, when I see you, I can hardly believe my eyes.' He stepped towards him again, nodding. 'Aye, you'll make a fine Magus—one I shall be proud to serve.'

'Well, there will be no Magus if we do not reach Elboru on time,' stated Reece. 'And with L'Ordana and Magia Nera on our trail …'

Oran looked sharp. 'Do you know where they are?'

'Making ground, I should imagine,' said Asai, looking up at the heavy, grey sky.

'Which is why we must get you to the *Egress*, Gill—before the last light of the moon disappears.'

'*Egress?*' Reece echoed.

'The Portal,' said Kai. 'When you failed to show at the meeting point,' he continued, addressing the Dhampir, 'we knew something was wrong.'

Reece then proceeded to explain what had happened: the attack made on them by the Valkyrie's hawk, Nakia; how they had killed it; and how they had to change their plans, realising the Sorceress and Magia Nera would soon be on their trail. And now, they faced yet another predicament: the *Paths of Lome*; his eyes glared at Oran for failing to inform them of this vital information, too. As Reece continued to relay more details, Daine and Rosalyn, in a moment of weakness, shared a knowing glance, feeling somewhat detached from the conversation. When it stopped, Daine quickly diverted his gaze. It did not go unnoticed.

'I'm afraid we have not met,' said Oran, lifting his voice and rising to his full stature as he approached the guide and Rosalyn, purposely separating them, his aim to intimidate the mortal.

'This is Daine,' she casually stated. 'And, had it not been for his help, we may never have come this far.'

'Let alone, cross the loch,' snipped Reece, casting the Warlock another grating look. 'Something else you neglected to tell me.'

Daine looked away, hiding the smirk on his face. Oran ignored Reece's remark, having caught the guide's snide look. When he moved to confront him, Rosalyn intervened.

'He has been a great help, Oran,' she insisted. 'He chose to continue this dangerous journey with us when he could have turned back.'

*I wonder why?* the Warlock thought, his eyes surveying the guide; though slight, he had sensed a connection between the stranger and his wife—and did not like it.

'Oran!' The Warlock spun, hearing his son's voice. It was evident Gill had sensed the jealousy in his father; it was plain to see, by the look of envy in his hazel eyes and the stiffness in his body. Gill was no fool, either; he had been aware of the attraction between his mother and Daine, even though nothing had happened, nothing he was aware of … yet. And, if his father continued to display the *Green-Eyed Monster*, he would run the risk of driving Rosalyn away. For now, he knew his father would be wise to pay heed and hold his anger.

In the meantime, Oran was staring at his son, feeling a little put out. He turned to his wife, his brow furrowed. 'Did he just call me …?'

'He calls me, Rosalyn,' she calmly admitted, easing the tension again.

Oran glanced at her, then back at his son. Gill was even taller than himself. He shook his head. The *boy* had grown into a *man* and he had failed to see it … until now. This, their chosen ruler, would soon become his Magus—his Overlord—and he the acolyte. It was hard to take in. *"By seeing what you look at, it is then, you will know its truth."* 'Never a truer word was spoken,' he muttered.

'What?' said Gill, scrunching his face.

'Oh, something my father once said to me,' Oran replied.

'Nor is he too old to take a clipping from his maw,' Rosalyn added, mocking Gill. Her son embraced her, not realising it would be the last time her comfort and warmth would envelop him.

Finally, the weight of ill-feeling gradually dissolved, leaving a still atmosphere. But with so many questions, Oran felt the time was not right; there was the pressing matter of the *Paths*. When he exchanged a look of apprehension with Kai, the Servitor nodded in understanding and approached Gill.

'Which did you choose?'

'They keep altering, Kai,' said Gill, eyeing the monoliths. 'The harder I try the quicker they change places. I—I can't ...' He shook his head.

'You can, and you will—because you *must*, Gill.'

'But why do they keep changing?' he implored.

'Because … they are reacting to all your emotions,' Kai revealed.

'Do *you* know which one it is?' Reece asked the Servitor.

Gill turned to Kai—the glint of hope returning in his eyes. He nodded, his enthusiasm mounting.

'Of course! Which one is it, Kai?'

'I am not at liberty to tell you, Gill,' he replied. 'Only *you* can choose.'

Gill, shifting his head to the side, regarded the Servitor. 'That may be

so … but you cannot lie to me.' He lifted a brow as a silent gesture of reminder to the Servitor—not that Kai needed it; it had been part of their "bargain" when the Elliyan released him from Purgatory. For several seconds Kai said nothing, trying to assess the predicament being placed upon him. He looked at Oran for any welcomed assistance, but all the Warlock could do was shrug.

'Is it this one?'

Kai looked to where Gill was standing, pointing to the monolith in the centre, his determined eyes sparkling—the flecks of gold glinting at him, waiting …

Still, Kai did not flinch.

Gill then marched to the monolith on the right, its plaquette changing when he glanced down at it.

'This one?'

A muscle twitched in Kai's cheek. It had been slight but obvious in his stillness. Had he remained in his true, ghostly form, he would have never betrayed himself—and they would have never seen his reaction. But perhaps Kai had purposely chosen to stay in his human state, to "flout the rules".

When a grin spread across Gill's face, he nodded; the group were now certain it was the right monolith. But when they looked down at its surface, it had changed, again.

'But—' Feeling his anger rise out of frustration, Gill clenched his fist and raised it high, ready to strike the plaquette.

'Remember …' voiced Kai, lifting his finger, silently asking the young man to stop. 'Control your emotions. Only then it will come to you.'

With the help of the Servitor, Gill faced the monolith once more, Kai's presence calming him. Behind them, however, the tension was building as the others waited, unable to help in this vital process. But the three Dhampir, their senses suddenly shifting, were taking no chances when Reece, on a hunch, promptly acknowledged Tam towards the valley's entrance; a sudden ominous awareness had lured Reece's instincts to it, alerting him—the growing feeling of expectation gnawing on his senses.

'Guard it. Your eyes and ears are sharper than ours,' he remarked to the Highlander, taking advantage of his youth. With the oppressive atmosphere beginning to bear its weight as it closed in on them, they had to take precautions.

'This place is aggravating our emotions,' said Asai, eyeing Tam as the Highlander discreetly sauntered towards the valley door. 'I am feeling … *confused*,' he quietly admitted to Reece, fighting the impulse to re-check his weapons, disliking the idea of not being in control. If there was one individual Reece relied on—when it came to logic—it was Asai, and without that …

'I know, my friend,' he said, then turned to see if Gill had progressed with his puzzling task. 'The sooner we move on from here, the—' His words and thoughts were severed when he saw

Rosalyn, his daughter detached from the group, her body frozen, eyes wide open, staring beyond him. Slowly, as though time had briefly altered, her mouth fell open.

Then it came …

# Chapter Eight

*Elboru: The Hall of Eminence – (North-West Scotland)*

'What have you done with her?'

The boy spun—thrown off-guard—the fear quickly appearing on his face.

'Well?'

Though trembling inside, the boy remained motionless as the eyes of blame glared down at him, their piercing blue colour dancing wildly, judging him. He shrugged.

'I—I do not know what you are—'

'Do not play me for a fool, Lorne. You know what I mean …' Greer paused, waiting, then snarled, his eyes glaring. 'Nepthys—my horse—where is she?!'

Lorne shook his head while trying to return to his true form—the young Servitor finding it difficult when caught unawares.

'I do not know, my lord.'

Greer leaned forward, penetrating Lorne's grey eyes, searching. He then drew back.

'Mmm … perhaps not *where* … but you know *who* has taken her.'

Lorne swallowed. Of course, he knew; nor was he under any illusion the High Warlock would find out. Regardless. Therefore, he had no option but to tell the truth—even if he tried to bend it a little. But no, not even *he* could escape Greer's insistence. He never could; the High Warlock had a manipulative way of extracting the information he required from him. And as for his threats … Greer meant every one of them.

'Mark my word, Lorne,' Greer continued, imprisoning him with his enquiry. 'Or do I need to remind you of the consequences—should you attempt to sway from the truth …?'

'I would not dare,' Lorne promptly returned, shaking his head.

'As long as you remember *that*'—he drew back from him—'then you shall remain here.' Greer then lowered his head, his face darkening with his ominous threat. 'After all, Lorne … a permanent existence in the pits of Purgatory is something I do not wish to enforce on you. However—'

'It was Kai!' Lorne blurted when an image of his time in *that* place—the so-called state of limbo after one's death, where it was alleged, they would undergo some form of *purification*—came back to haunt him. He had been told, by his mother, before the plague took both his parents, that it was a peaceful place before entering the "Gates of Heaven." He would never forgive her, for lying to him—even in death.

Greer lifted his head, his brows knitting tightly.

'Kai? What would a Servitor need with a horse? You are equally as swift as—' He stopped and turned away from Lorne, thinking it over, then slowly nodded to himself when it dawned on him: 'But of course!'

Lorne jolted when Greer spun to face him again, his eyes fixed with fear when they met with the Warlock's—the realisation peering back at him as Greer's danced wildly with insight. *He knows!*

Greer stared him down, sneering. He nodded.

'I see it'—he pointed at Lorne—'right there—in your eyes—as plain as day. Oran Shaw has my horse!'

Lorne pressed his lips together, reluctant to confess. He had seen Kai at the stables, preparing the mare while murmuring in her ear, to accept her new rider.

*"What a beauty you are, Nepthys! I am sure your master will not mind me borrowing you, for a spell. Be gentle with Lord Oran when he mounts you; he is the kinder of the two. He will treat you with the respect you truly deserve."*

Now there was no avoiding Greer's intimidation. He would have to admit it. As things stood, he was treading on eggshells with the High Warlock. No. He never wanted to go back *there* again; the mere idea of wandering through Purgatory, alongside other lost souls in never-ending limbo between the world of the living and the dead, terrified him. Life as a Servitor was challenging enough, having to abide by Elliyan rules. But it was better than *there*. At least, *here*, among living breathing people, he could communicate, and come and go with an element of freedom, despite some restrictions.

*I am never going back there!* he decided, looking Greer in the eye. 'Yes, my lord. It was Kai who took Nepthys … for Lord Oran.'

Greer nodded—the menacing look in his eyes now fixed as the grin of satisfaction spread across his face. 'That is more like it. It is in your best interest to be agreeable with me … as you well know.'

Lorne lowered his eyes, then scratched his arm—the flecks of dry skin falling away from the scars, caused by the infection of the disease that had taken him shortly after his parents. He could feel Greer's disgust as the High Warlock looked him up and down, his dishevelled state the same as when he left the world of the living: his dark locks no longer shone like they used to; his mother used to say how the *Almighty* had blessed him with strands of red gold. And as for his clothes … His shirt was grubby and hung loosely over his loose-fitting breeches; he could still detect a hint of the plague, its putrid stench lingering, leaving him with the grim memory of the remaining days of his life. And though he could not feel the cold beneath his bare feet, he had always been aware of not having shoes; someone stole them from his rotting body afterwards.

'Yes,' he finally replied, his voice barely audible.

'What was that?' said Greer, turning his head sideways, to make the boy repeat what he had said, and for him to know where he stood in the light of things.

Lorne lifted his head, and, as he did so, gradually transformed back to his true state—Greer narrowing his eyes from his luminescence.

'Yes … my lord,' he said, his voice now slow and steady.

'Good. So—you say, you do not know where they have gone? I assume Kai went with Oran, as I have not seen him this day?'

'No, my lord. I know not where.'

Greer knew there was no need to question him further; he knew the young Servitor was telling the truth. He would not dare lie to him now. Lorne knew his place—and he would not hesitate in returning him to Purgatory, despite what Lothian might have to say about it; having pitied the "child", the Great Warlock had plucked Lorne from his state of "limbo". But where, once, Lothian had a soft spot for Lorne, Greer disputed it now. He was certain he had heard Lothian scold the young Servitor, earlier—the old Warlock's raised voice drawing his attention, with Lorne's name carrying on its echo. Initially, he had disregarded it, but now … it niggled at him.

'Do the Elliyan know?' Greer persisted, side-glancing him, then inwardly wondered if his peers knew more than they should.

'I cannot say,' said Lorne.

'Cannot or *will* not?'

'Cannot … my lord.'

'Then tell me—why did Lord Lothian scold you?'

Lorne's black eyes widened. He did not reply.

'I heard his voice raised at you earlier yet took no interest, at the time. But while it seems you have nothing to say … I am even more curious …'

Still, Lorne remained silent.

'You see, it is the first time I have heard him do this—and to you his … *favourite*. I find it strange … It is seldom Lord Lothian lifts his voice to anyone.

'He …' Lorne struggled to bend the truth as he tried to delay his reply.

'Out with it!'

'He thought I had overheard a conversation between himself and Lord Oran. But I—'

'And did you?' Greer casually interrupted while carefully straightening the sapphire-studded gold band on his head before stroking his beard, with added interest.

Once again, Lorne knew he was being surveyed—the High Warlock's gift of insight constantly reading him like an open book, eager to study every page. What could he do? He had to tell him. There was no way to avoid Greer's questioning—albeit he … No, to lie was forbidden. Greer would see right through him.

Lorne nodded once.

Greer smirked. 'Well? I am waiting.'

Even without looking at him, Lorne could sense the High Warlock was revelling in his power over him. He had no choice.

'Lord Lothian'—he sighed and lowered his head, feeling shame—'gave—'

'Ah! There you are, Lorne!'

The Servitor and Greer looked to where the voice had come from before its owner appeared from behind one of the Great Hall's columns, where the ashes of past Warlocks were interred. Together, they watched as Lothian made his way towards them—the soft rustle of his silver tunic, like constant sighs as he shuffled closer, his eyes glancing at the columns at intervals. And though the weight of his age was evident in his slow but steady approach, neither was fooled by this ancient Warlock; where the once great warrior was concerned, looks were deceiving.

The Servitor quietly sighed with relief.

''Tis all right, Lorne,' said Lothian. 'You may go. I would speak with Lord Greer.'

Diverting his eyes from Greer, Lorne bowed, then left, his glow fading behind the columns.

'Must you taunt him so?' said Lothian.

'I do not trust him.'

'Oh?' said Lothian, raising a brow. 'Would this be why you were … keeping a watchful eye on him? Perhaps—Lorne has something to hide, Lord Greer?'

Greer threw a disgruntled glance at Lothian, then snorted.

'After all,' Lothian continued, 'we all have our secrets … Do we not, Lord—'

'What is it you would speak to me about?' Greer cut in abruptly, side-stepping his superior's remark.

'If you have come looking for it'—Lothian glanced down at the sealed, crypt, kept free of death to protect items of importance—'the *Book* is not there.'

Greer tilted his head, narrowing his eyes. 'Why not? I thought it was returned after I had deciphered it.'

'It is in safe hands.'

Greer drew back, suspicious, regarding the Great Warlock, his gift of insight working hard to unravel Lothian's meaning. But the old Warlock was wise to it, and returned his gaze, holding it, refusing to look away from Greer's eyes as they danced, probing.

'And whose "hands" would that be?' he was then forced to ask.

'Oh, it is no secret,' said Lothian, slowly clasping his hands together. 'I gave the book to Lord Oran.'

'*Oran?!*'

'Indeed.'

'Why would you do that?'

'For good purpose,' Lothian continued. 'Lord Oran needs it, if we are to succeed in protecting our future Magus. His son is en route here, and I am confident our fellow Warlock will overthrow the threat that hangs in the air, with the book's use.'

'Is Lord Tuan aware of this?'

Lothian regarded Greer with scepticism. 'He is … none-too-pleased, however, there is nothing he can do about it, now. Lord Oran has been gone these past few hours. And while his presence is of great importance here, it is of equal importance he is with his son, to guide him safely to Elboru.'

'And stealing my horse in the process,' Greer mumbled.

'Why would you deny him?' Lothian questioned. 'What has Lord Oran ever done to you? If anything, you should be more than willing to offer your services. After all, you are part of this *Council*, and I—' Lothian stopped short, hearing the roar of footsteps, in the background. They looked down the Great Hall of Eminence towards the entrance—the light emanating from the torches, throwing constant moving shadows across its great doors as the Bullwark made their way to the grounds to surround the fortress, in order to defend it.

'Good,' he said, as their forceful march faded. 'All, who are required to be here, for the transformation, have arrived. Preparations are almost complete.'

'And the Shenn?'

'The sacred amulet resides in the *Naoi*, where it will remain under the Ushabti's protection until the time has arrived. Let us hope Lord Oran successfully retrieves Magia Nera's missing amulet, to complete the process.' He threw his hands out as if dismissing any doubts. 'But I am confident of it.'

'And what of *him?*'

'Him?'

Greer rolled his eyes. 'Nera! He is still alive.'

'As we are fully aware,' said Lothian—the tone of condemnation in his reply, reminding Greer who was at fault for *that*. Inside the High Warlock was seething; he had failed to perform the final act in destroying Vlad Tepés, his negligence leading to Magia Nera's sadistic existence. It was something he did not want to dwell on, it, at times, proving difficult, with occasional prodding from certain quarters—namely Tuan—of his careless oversight. But some of the blame had to fall on Oran; he had fled the battlefield of Wallachia, leaving Magia at the mercy of the *Devil* himself.

'How can we be certain he will not show?' he said, avoiding another of Lothian's remarks while casting aside another of his failings.

Lothian looked Greer in the eye. 'Magia knows what would happen should he—' He stopped, then stepped back, drawing a deep breath.

'Are you unwell, Lord Lothian?' said Greer, regarding his peer with interest, and less concern.

Lothian then jolted, as if woken from a nightmare, his eyes momentarily fixated on the High Warlock. 'No,' he blurted. 'I am … quite well. Thank you!'

They held one another's gaze, one trying to outdo the other, with ill effect. Greer grunted with frustration, knowing he had met his match. Though no longer the great warrior he once was, there was no disputing Lothian's intelligence; it was there in his amethyst eyes, brimming with life, and more dominating with his advancing years, it compensating for his fragility.

'Then I shall ready myself for their arrival.'

With a prompt, and obligated, bow to the Great Warlock, Greer turned on his heel, his heavy stride marked with an arrogance Lothian had not noticed before. The Great Warlock glanced down at the sealed, empty tomb; no one had been or attempted to enter it. And yet … He looked sharp.

'Lord Greer!' he called out after the High Warlock. Greer stalled, then hesitated before turning. He lifted his head and eyed Lothian, without speaking. 'I am curious,' Lothian continued.

'About?' Greer replied.

'Why did you come looking for the book?'

The seconds passed as the two Warlocks regarded one another again. Suddenly, the flame from one of the huge lanterns, hanging from the rafters directly above Greer, died, cloaking him in a ray of darkness. Lothian's eyes shot up, briefly distracted by it. When he looked down, Greer was gone.

# Chapter Nine

*The Paths of Lome*

Rosalyn's high-pitched scream resonated through every one of them, echoing across the clearing where they stood, its residual effect then travelling out into the forest, alarming nature, its residents scurrying between the trees before disappearing again. The horses, too, reacted, jolting and rearing in response to the sudden, unnerving sound, while birds, who had kept their silence, took flight from their hidden places before their escape, beyond the treetops.

A brief, unsettling silence then seized Rosalyn before the rest of the group spun to see the look of terror on her face. But as they followed her fixed gaze, the sinister resonance of a female's gravelly voice, laughing, woke them to the identity of their unexpected guest as they stepped out into the clearing, in full view of their audience—the sight of them, sending the group into a rage of defence.

Within seconds, Rosalyn found herself thrown behind the protection of her son; Gill quickly reached for his sister's dagger as the others promptly joined him, with Oran signalling to Tam to safeguard Daine, while they shielded Rosalyn—all the while, the unwanted figure regarding them, finding it all amusing.

Kara had swooped down in a deathly sigh unlike before, when she had taken Eleanor, in Balloch. No one had heard her, not even the Dhampir, with their heightened senses. Reece was taken aback by it. Yes, he had sensed a presence looming, not thinking for one moment it would be the Valkyrie. He—they—assumed she had been killed, when there had been no reprisal for her hawk's demise; they had expected it when Nakia fell to earth after Asai's dagger had found and destroyed its target.

*How foolish we were,* he thought, *to assume it. She*— His thoughts were cut short by his grandson's voice.

'Leave it!' Gill snapped at Rave, fearful for his dog's life; the hound was crouched low, snarling and displaying her sharp teeth, preparing to leap. Obedient, she ceased at her master's command—the deep, blood-curdling sound reverberating from inside the hound as she remained still yet ready to pounce when told—the scent of evil prominent on her sensitive nose.

Emerging from the full glory of her re-birth, Kara casually sashayed towards the group, her eyes catching Rosalyn's through her protection, forcing her to recoil. Kara smirked at her, now aware that Rosalyn had been the voice she heard when her "pet" was destroyed, after her transformation. Also, she was sure one of her "protectors" had despatched the black hawk—not that it mattered, anymore; Nakia had served her purpose.

Alarmed by her new, hostile appearance, they all gaped at the Valkyrie, still thrown by her unforeseen arrival. Kara shot a look at Daine; the guide looked dwarfed beside Tam—the Highlander armed and staying close by his side. When their eyes briefly met, Daine recalled his encounter with the Valkyrie—the prominent lump inside his lower lip a stark, constant reminder of her attempt to lure the *creatures* with the scent of his blood. He shuddered as he drew his hand across his mouth, trying to wipe the memory of her hardened lips against his. His hand then twitched, desperately wanting to remove his sword now. He had had no time to do so after Rosalyn screamed; everything had happened so quickly.

'Leave it, lad,' Tam uttered beneath his breath. But when Daine shifted, his eyes dropping when he subtly moved his right foot, the Highlander knew what he was about. 'And that, too,' he added, casting his eyes down, aware the guide concealed a small weapon inside his boot. ''Tis not worth—'

'Missed me, Highlander?' Kara teased as she sauntered by Tam. Though he tried, the Dhampir, at first, was unable to divert his eyes from the Valkyrie; even with his great stature, he was forced to tilt his head up as she stomped by, her crimson eyes toying with him, new and inviting. Where, once, he had found her disturbingly alluring, despite her badness, this, he knew, was something entirely different—and unpleasant. A look of horror spread across his face, filling him with disgust and regret for indulging her. He shook the thoughts and images from his mind. If she was intimidating back then, when they were bonded to the Sorceress, it was evident now, by her new bearing, she was borne of a different evil—one they did not want to contend with. From where he stood, it oozed from her, prominent and foul.

Nor was he alone in his thinking; Kai had seen it, too, though differently. Through his Servitor's eyes, he could see the black mist of her aura shrouding her, its stain clinging to the Valkyrie as though protecting her. He stole a glance at the three monoliths; they were now in constant turmoil—the Valkyrie's unexpected presence causing a resurgence of emotions within the group as their surfaces changed erratically, reacting to the heightened strain of each individual's inner state of mind. And, even if he could, Kai knew Gill would be unable to choose one, at this moment. If something was not done to restore calm to the Paths of Lome, time would pass, and all would be lost.

Steady as a prowler, Kara circled the group, eyeing them, one by one, while regarding them with curious insight. She then caught Reece, his eyes darting around.

'I am quite alone, Reece,' she stated, then stabbed the Obsidian into the ground, making her mark; it sparked to life on impact, lighting up its deep-emerald glass and serrated silver tip. Such was her narcissistic conduct, Kara left her longsword in its sheath, on her back, confident she would not need it, should they … *I would like to see them try*, she thought.

Reece shot her a vengeful glance, infuriated by her arrogance; he wanted to attack and drive his broadsword through her poisoned heart, but he knew she was not the Valkyrie of old. His nostrils flared from her new scent; it was rancid, a far cry from the sickly, sweet lemon oil that used to waft from her. Tam and Asai had caught it, too. Everything about her had changed. She was like them, but stained by something else … something deeper … something monstrous, it marking their differences.

This—*she*—was pure, rooted evil.

Behind her father, Rosalyn clenched her fists, her breath now heaving with hatred for the creature that took her daughter—the image of Eleanor struggling within the Valkyrie's grip with a dagger held across her throat still ingrained in her mind.

'Tell her to be still,' Kara advised Reece. 'She makes me'—she grunted, turning her eyes to the heavens—'nervous!'

Gill and Oran edged closer to Rosalyn, in a bid to ease her anger.

Kara inhaled deeply—the stench of the oncoming winter, in the air, its dampness filling her nostrils. 'They think me dead,' she continued, returning to Reece. 'The fools!'

Reece frowned, sharing a confused glance with Asai. When an unexpected ray of sunlight escaped through a small gap in the passing clouds, slicing through the bleak, grey sky, it touched her skin. Kara drew her head back, eyes closed. She smiled wryly in self-indulgence, allowing it to caress her. If there were a time to strike, it was now, while she was distracted. But something, a wavering uncertainty, prevented them.

Asai looked at Tam. The Highlander appeared to be struggling to keep his eyes from her; they were fixed, mesmerised yet burning with hate. It was as if she still kept a hold over him. The Samurai's concern grew for the Highlander; if Kara maintained the slightest hold over their colleague, there was no knowing what would happen. It was a disturbing and worrying thought.

The instant the clouds snatched the light back into their gloom, the Valkyrie resumed her conversation.

'What is *his* misfortune, has now become my virtue,' she boasted, her eyes coveting the dark, brownish-red line on her right arm—drawing on the groups' attention. It was from this revelation, and seeing the scar left by the poisonous blade, the three Dhampir knew to whom she was referring: Magia Nera. Oran glanced at Asai, trying to grasp the Valkyrie's meaning. Then it dawned on him, what they were now witnessing—the transformation that had come about in her: her eyes were blazing, transfixed, her porcelain skin flawless, and her strength … there would be no denying it; it was emanating from every fibre of her new physique. Her body armour, once silver, had now altered; it gleamed like onyx, matching the stone embedded in the gold band around her forehead, to keep her long braids in place; and her hair, once golden, now shone like silver. Her features had been enhanced, by the mutation. She was utterly imposing, utterly unpredictable … and utterly toxic. Now, she stood in their way, threatening and unthreatened.

'If it had not been for the Sorceress,' she teased, her eyes darting between Reece and Asai, 'I would have despatched the girl, long before this.' A glint appeared in her eye. 'Then again …' She let the sentence die, meeting their look; they both knew what she meant.

'You sick, evil—'

'No, Gill!' warned Asai, moving closer to the young man. 'Do not give her what she wants.'

But Kara, pre-empting Gill's motive, had summoned the Obsidian from the ground, hoping he would compete against her. She was itching for it. A twisted curl appeared at the side of her mouth.

'Ah, yes!' she exclaimed, her eyes flashing to Rosalyn, then back to Gill, before pointing the Obsidian at him. 'I remember *you!*' She tilted her head. 'Though you have changed, somewhat.' Her eyes then slid towards Asai and, maintaining the smirk on her face, she taunted them. 'It appears … *Strange One* … that you have competition for the girl's heart.' She grunted a deep-rooted laugh from the pit of her stomach.

Gill was seething. 'How dare you disrespect my sister!' he snarled, stepping closer, with Rave crouched by his side.

'*Sister?*' She gasped, lifting her brows. 'Of course! I had forgotten. Quite the family gathering,' she remarked, glancing back at Rosalyn, briefly disregarding Oran; it was clear she was unaware of the connection. 'Such a pity,' she said, continuing her taunts, '*her* absence—and a shame she will not enjoy the pleasures of …' She paused, her eyes sliding back to Oran; she now recognised the Warlock. But as she opened her mouth to speak, her head turned sharply, alerted to the swift approach of steps from behind. Devoid of thought and regard for all living things, Kara commanded the Obsidian—the lethal weapon quickly finding its victim.

They did not see it coming; her movements had been swift and skilled, more than ever.

Rosalyn threw her hands over her face, horrified, unable to let the words of her distress out, while her companions stood dumbfounded.

The Valkyrie turned her head to discover the fatality; they stared back at her, their features frozen in shock as they grasped the lance, now pierced clean through their abdomen. The Obsidian glowed on contact.

'Too slow, Highlander,' she hissed, then edged closer, whispering; 'See it as punishment for your betrayal.'

Stunned into silence, and momentarily rooted, the others gaped, incapable of tearing their eyes from Kara as she stood over her fallen victim like a prized trophy, her foot now resting on Tam's body.

'He was only good for one thing,' she said, her voice emotionless. 'However, I did … "miss" him, for a spell. But'—she cast her eyes at Reece and shrugged—'no one is indispensable. Not even *you!*'

With a sudden, sharp movement, she wrenched the Obsidian clean from Tam's body, its inner sparks flashing like fireworks as she promptly stepped away.

'I do love this part,' she remarked, letting her eyes slide towards the shocked spectators.

Woken to the reality of her assault on the Highlander, Asai, Reece and Oran moved to attack the Valkyrie, prompting Kara to instinctively throw out her hand. But as they tried to push forward, they found themselves unable to; it was as if the world had slowed, delaying everything, while the Valkyrie glorified in their dismay and feeble attempt to reach her.

There was no disputing the victor, here.

Struggling to breathe, Tam writhed beneath her, feeling the inner effects of the spear's impact. He cried out in pain when Kara leaned over him.

'Stop moving,' she hissed, treating his struggle as an inconvenience. 'It will only hurt more … not that I care.' She threw her head back in laughter, then at the group as they struggled to get to their colleague. She slowly shook her head, fascinated by this, knowing they could not. Time, it seemed, had slowed for them, and she, somehow, was controlling it.

Tam's body began to convulse as his organs swelled before combusting inside him. Sparks ignited, turning to flames. As the Highlander's torso burned, shock turned to trauma as his friends were subjected to the Valkyrie's disturbing and grotesque form of "entertainment", knowing they were powerless against her—Kara revelling in their horror while indulging in the role of spectator. There was no denying her motive: she was forcing them to watch their friend's execution.

Repulsed by the sight and smell of burning flesh, Rosalyn heaved. It was all too much. Not knowing how much more she could take, she desperately wanted to look away yet could not. Overcome with nausea, she felt dizzy. But as she felt her body sway, she heard Gill's voice erupt, breaking the "spell" they had been under.

'Tam!' Gill's agonising cry was filled with anger and grief. But grieving would have to wait.

All hell broke loose.

'Tam!' echoed Rosalyn.

The group lunged towards the Valkyrie. This would be their moment. But their delayed reactions only gave Kara the advantage, by mere seconds, allowing her to escape. Timing was now of the essence for Tam's avengers. However, it failed them; as Kara wrenched the Obsidian from its victim, before leaping skywards, her huge black wings spread wide, lifting her higher, narrowly escaping Asai's hand as it brushed off her foot. As the Samurai swiftly removed the wakizashi dagger, he stopped dead. Craning his neck, his eagle-sharp eyes searched the trees and escarpments. Kara had disappeared. Such was her speed, that it had taken her mere moments, leaving the Dhampir behind, unable to keep up.

With all eyes locked skywards, they watched fiercely, weapons in hand, expecting the Valkyrie's return yet were still baffled by their inability to attack her.

The seconds rolled by, with no sight nor sound of Kara.

Oran shook his head.

'She was too—' He stopped, aware the others had now turned their attention to their fallen comrade.

The Highlander was dead.

As Tam's charred remains lay smouldering, Rosalyn and Daine covered their noses from the foul stench of his corpse, and just stared, while Rave crouched by the Highlander's body whimpering, in a touching moment. With tears cascading down her face, Rosalyn wanted to reach out, and touch him, but could not bring herself to do so. Repelled, she turned away—and into the arms of another.

'Oh, Daine, why Tam, why did he have to—'

''Tis the way of it—in our world.'

She broke away from the guide and turned to face her husband; Oran was standing, staring at them both, suspicions invading his thoughts. His tone had been flat, almost unsympathetic.

'In *your* world, perhaps!' she snapped, her cheeks flushed between grief and anger. Oran placed a hand on his wife's shoulder. She shrugged it off, his condescending touch, disgusting her. 'But not in *mine*, Oran!'

Reece closed his eyes, feeling his daughter's pain. Unlike he and Asai, the Highlander had not been "chosen" for this life. No—Tam had simply been in the wrong place at the wrong time. He did not deserve to die like this. But Oran had a point; they were more accepting of death, having been surrounded by it for so long, learning to detach themselves from the emotions that came with it. But now, he felt an inner pain—one of loss—similar to the one he had felt at Onóir's passing, though not as prominent. But it was there, inside him, and he was unsure how to deal with it.

'He looks so … peaceful!'

They all turned to see Daine standing over Tam, looking bewildered. The Highlander had been transformed back into his mortal body. Reece and Asai looked at each other and nodded, sensing their wave of relief; had their colleague's body not been afflicted by fire, they would have had the macabre task of removing his head, to prevent him from living. And had he "lived", he would not have been the same; he would have returned to them stronger, wilder and insatiable, with only death at the forefront of his mind.

They joined Rosalyn when they saw her kneel beside the fallen warrior. The Highlander's transformation had been a notable and miraculous one: his skin, once paled by his affliction, had a hue of "life" about it, its tone now warm. Almost afraid to disturb him, Rosalyn bravely reached out, then paused, when she noticed something else about Tam: his left ear was still deformed—the mark of his mortality having stayed with him since he was a young, eager child—a child who had simply been too ambitious with his father's over-sized sword. But it was the *curse* forced upon him, by Wareeshta, that was now gone. Daine was right; Tam did look peaceful. Tears slowly building again, Rosalyn placed her hand tenderly on his forehead, then flinched, snatching it away. It was warm.

'Maw?' whispered Gill.

'It's as though—' She flexed her hand, then cautiously placed it on his forehead, once more—the warmth now slowly fading, along with the last flicker of life. Staring down, seeing the passive look on Tam's face, Rosalyn recalled their first meeting: she had not trusted him, wary of his company, thinking he would bring harm to her family. But in the few days of their acquaintance, she had come to see his true worth; he was loyal to the core, and she had grown fond of him. A Highlander like Tam, she knew, would have ordinarily enjoyed a "good" death, earned in combat or war, and celebrated in togetherness. Stories and memories of his life would have been shared joyfully. But this had been a "bad" death, unwanted. Now, there would be no food or drink offerings to those guests who would have travelled from afar for his funeral; no celebration by his clan to host the repast; there would be no washing of his body or wrapping it in special burial cloth; nor would he rest in a tomb so befitting of him; nor would the Great Highland bagpipe play a lament for his loss. Therefore, taking the place of the Highlander's clan, Rosalyn kissed Tam's brow, her tears dropping onto his paling skin.

'*Fois shìorraidh gun robh aig d'anam!*' she whispered to him. 'May your soul have eternal peace!' She watched as her tears dried, leaving the faint outlines of her sorrow, then smiled, as though a piece of her was going with him on his journey. 'Tell Onóir …' She sighed.

Asai, joining Rosalyn, nodded and smiled.

'He is at peace, now,' he said. 'Our friend is finally free. His curse has been broken. He can now sleep forever in solitude.' For a moment the Samurai felt an element of hidden envy, but when a feeling inside him took over, he dismissed it; it was as though Eleanor, in that instant, was reminding him of her.

Oran stepped away from the group, eyes raised.

'We must leave … in case she returns,' he advised.

Still on her knees, Rosalyn stared up at her husband, aghast. '*What?!* We can't just … leave him here,' she pleaded, rising. 'Whatever it is *you* may—or may not—believe, Tam deserves to be buried, with respect.' She turned her attention to Kai—the Servitor quietly contemplating the Highlander. Kai looked at Rosalyn, seeing the appeal in her eyes. 'You see how it is … please, do this for me—for *him* … before it's too late.'

Kai looked to Oran. Inside, the Warlock knew he had no choice but to go along with his wife's wishes; to refuse her would be unwise. It was the least he could do. Besides, the Highlander had played an important role in their escape. He owed him this much.

'Of course, forgive me,' he said, bowing out of respect.

Before the Servitor took over, Rosalyn took Tam's claymore—the weapon he had cherished—from the hand that still clutched it, hoping it would, one day, be returned to his clan. But the axe he had so proudly wielded, if only to threaten, would stay with him.

Urging the group to give him space, Kai took on his true form—the transformation briefly catching Daine off-guard, again. The ghostly Servitor knelt beside the Highlander's remains and began his work. Just as he had done with Onóir, Kai then lifted Tam effortlessly into his embrace.

Kai closed his eyes, enveloping Tam in his gentle hold as he searched for the ember of life he hoped remained. He smiled, warmly. 'Ah! There you are,' he whispered, clinging on as though the Highlander had been waiting. Then Kai inhaled deeply, slowly withdrawing Tam's precious soul until it found its place inside him. The Servitor's aura glowed from its presence as he held on, bonding with it until it was time. Lifting his face to the dreary sky, laden with grey clouds, Kai finally released the Highlander's spirit, to join those gone before him.

Now silently chanting words over the empty vessel that was once their great friend, Kai brushed away some leaves, grasped a handful of fine clay from the ground on which he lay, and held it over Tam's remains. Leaning forward, the Servitor softly blew it over the corpse, and as the wind caught it, Tam's body returned to dust, it following the breeze as it took it on its journey back into the universe.

All that remained of the Highlander was his imprint, soon to be snatched away by *Mother Nature*.

'Thank you!' said Rosalyn, forcing a smile, then looked down at the great claymore weighing heavily in her hands. Her lip quivered. 'I can still feel his energy holding on to it,' she remarked, nodding. 'I can … *feel* his strength.'

'*Hai!* And it will continue to do so,' added Asai.

'The sword represented him and his honour.' It was the first time Reece had spoken, since. Rosalyn looked up at her father, seeing a hint of sadness in his eyes, but kept her silence. And when Reece held out his hand, she passed the claymore over to him. Carefully, he took it from her, feeling the Highlander's presence as though he remained; and in a way he did, and always would. Then, in a moving, and unforeseen, gesture, he turned to Gill and held out the treasured weapon with both hands, offering it to the young man.

Speechless, Gill stared down at the claymore, unsure, unworthy.

'Take it!' Reece urged him. 'Tam would be proud for you to have it.'

'But—'

'You are a worthy candidate, Gill-san,' said Asai, promptly adding his support.

Gill sighed then slowly took the sword in his hand. For a moment he closed his eyes, secretly seeking the Highlander's approval. Sensing nothing at first, he moved to hand it back when he suddenly felt the warmth of Tam's energy flowing through its steel and into him. Nodding in understanding, Gill smiled and opened his eyes, proudly accepting the responsibility of taking great care of the Highlander's sword.

'I am honoured,' he said. 'And when this is all over,' he added, looking up at Tam's comrades, 'I will have it returned to his clan, where it belongs.'

'And where it will eventually stay,' added Reece. 'But, for now, it remains with you, Gill. Use it well.'

'For Tam!' said Gill, grasping it tightly.

Asai bowed. 'Now, it remains to be seen who—' The Samurai looked sharp, his dark, almond-shaped eyes, staring into the crowded woods.

'Oh, no!' Daine's voice said it all.

Alert, they promptly re-grouped, preparing for another attack from the Valkyrie, watching above and beyond, ready to avenge the death of their comrade.

'This time,' said Gill, through gritted teeth as he wielded Tam's sword. 'we will not—'

'Where is Asai?'

Gill jolted—the others, too, when they heard Oran.

'He's deserted us!'

Confused at first, they stood transfixed and speechless by Oran's statement. And when they looked, the Samurai was nowhere to be seen, his sudden departure leaving behind their bewildered faces, and a sense of abandonment.

'No!' cried Rosalyn, defending the Samurai, 'Asai would never …' She stalled, her mind filled with confusing thoughts. *He wouldn't. He couldn't!* Still overwhelmed by Tam's loss, she began to doubt herself, struggling to deal with the notion of it all. She then dismissed it. 'No!' she said, her voice determined and fierce. 'Asai would *never* do this to us—or Eleanor.'

Oran narrowed his eyes and cast his wife a sideward glance; there *was* something they were neglecting to tell him. 'That is the second reference I have heard, relating to Asai and Elean—'

'They love each other!' Gill blurted.

Oran second-glanced his son, in disbelief. 'They'—he drew back, then, realising what Gill had revealed, frowned, the anger gradually appearing on his face—'*love* each other, you say?! How could they possibly—' He spun to face his wife, waiting, expecting a logical explanation.

'*She*—your daughter—is no longer the "girl" you left behind, three years ago, Oran,' she snapped.

Yet again, the Warlock felt the stab of sarcasm in his wife's tone as the remark was hurdled back at him. Still and all, he was finding it hard to take in—the mere idea of such a relationship between his daughter and a … *Unthinkable!*

He shook his head in complete denial, ready to confront his wife and son. Daine looked about him with a sense of awkwardness as another family debate erupted, wondering if it had always been that way. And yet, it seemed they were justified in their anger.

'You should know what it is like to fall for someone, Oran—when you cannot deny yourself.' Rosalyn caught her breath, conscious of what she had just said.

Still shaking his head, Oran continued to protest.

'Impossible! He's a—'

'I am well aware of *what* he is, and the outcome, should they choose a life together.'

Oran stepped away from Rosalyn's determination; it was evident whose side his wife was on. He saw her support for the two "lovers" etched in her face, and then glanced down at her hands, clenched by her side—the whites of the knuckles visible. He *had* been away for too long—and she was right: you cannot help who you fall in love with. He felt like a hypocrite; after all, Rosalyn still married *him*, despite his true semblance.

Oran sighed deeply, signalling his defeat, and glanced up at Reece. 'Accept my apology for insulting you in your …' He struggled for the right words.

'State of immortality?' said Reece. By now, the Dhampir was immune to insult, his thoughts on more pressing matters; he, too, had no idea where the Samurai had disappeared to but knew Asai would never desert them. His friend was too loyal and always had been. But *where* had he gone? *Surely, not after the Valkyrie.* Perhaps he *had* sensed Kara's return and, in a moment of uncontrolled madness, took it upon himself to hunt her down.

Oran raised his hands in dispute. 'But I cannot allow it. They have no future to—'

'We must survive all this, first,' interrupted Gill. 'Or, have you forgotten the predicament we find ourselves in? Right now, my concerns are not with affairs of the heart … no matter *whom* they involve.' A subtle glance passed between Daine and Rosalyn. But in her grief for Tam's loss, she momentarily forgot herself and held his gaze a moment longer, making no attempt to conceal it. Oran could not help but notice and wonder … What other secrets had been suppressed?

Now, Reece felt the insult, after everything he and his two colleagues had done for the Warlock—while losing Tam in the process. Furious, he turned on his heel to follow Asai, intent on leaving the bickering behind.

'A moment, Reece,' came the soft voice among the madness.

The Dhampir stalled, to find the Servitor by his side, his large black eyes looking at him with sympathy.

'You must forgive their heightened emotions,' he said. 'There is much for them to digest, after so long, and being here in this place has only hampered those feelings. It is unhealthy.'

Reece turned directly to face him. 'So, it seems. But they need reminding of what—no—*who*—is important at this time,' he snarled.

'They are more than aware of it,' Kai returned. 'Like any parent, they do not want to lose their offspring. But time is running out, and Gill is right, in that we must get on with this.'

'And what of *him?*' Reece added, tipping his head towards Daine, who had discreetly stepped away from the mounting family feud and was attending to his horse.

Kai nodded.

'It has not gone unnoticed. It came to my attention the moment they met. However, my feeling is …'

Reece lifted his brow.

'… nothing will come of it.'

Reece grunted, his eyes darting around. 'It had better not,' he mumbled.

'You know Asai has not deserted you,' stated Kai, trying to deflect from further confrontation.

'It never touched my mind. But I must find him'—he scowled at the three family members, still embroiled in their argument—'before *this* gets out of hand.' He grunted, eyeing Rave. 'Even the dog keeps her distance.'

'I will assist you,' said Kai. 'And, trust me,' he added, joining in the Dhampir's judgement, 'the moment we are gone, the bickering will quickly cease.' He looked over at the turbulent monoliths with concern. 'They know it must, otherwise …'

Reece threw another glance at the others, his eyes paling to crimson as his face hardened with resentment and determination. 'There is just one thing …' he said.

Kai gave Reece his full attention.

'When the time comes, the Valkyrie's demise belongs to me … or Asai.'

The Servitor nodded in agreement then, matching the Dhampir's speed, followed him—the two disappearing into the trees and leaving behind a dumbfounded silence.

# Chapter Ten

Asai had discreetly stepped away when he had suddenly sensed Eleanor—like before, after her abduction in Balloch, when he had felt the same surge of energy deep inside him. But it grieved him, knowing he was leaving behind the passing of his fallen colleague. But Tam was gone now. Nothing would bring him back. *We will avenge your death, my friend*, he silently vowed. But it was the living he needed to think about now if they—*she*—were to survive. And though he felt the loss and emptiness of the Highlander's untimely death, his slow-beating heart swelled with anticipation, feeling Eleanor inside him—the sound of her familiar heartbeat rapid, coming and going—and near. It was possible, she had escaped.

With hope in his heart, it spurred him on. But as he ran, back through the narrow gorge between the escarpments, his instincts guiding him, he battled the encroachment of other obstacles trying to interfere with his thoughts.

He stopped abruptly, his eyes quick and alert, remaining attentive to the sounds revolving about him—the fusion of good and evil, determined to sway him. He could feel it in the air, it growing closer the nearer they drew to Elboru. There was no doubt the Sorceress was gaining on them; he could almost smell—*taste*—her malevolence wafting through the sullen atmosphere.

But the Samurai was not deterred.

Removing his katana, Asai knelt on the damp ground. Placing the sacred weapon before him, he closed his eyes, then inhaled … slowly … and deeply … gradually slipping into his thoughts, to search for

Eleanor.

Soon the sounds of nature receded, leaving him alone in his private world of rumination. Then he heard it—again—her anxious heart, its erratic beating convincing him she *had* escaped. However, Asai could not rid himself of other interfering and unwanted sounds—sounds all too familiar, and worrying. And yet, he did not want to discard them; he sensed other heartbeats—three more, slow and controlled—crowding his thoughts. They seemed to be everywhere.

*Not good*, he thought.

*"Run!"*

Wareeshta's words still resounded in her mind, urging her on. But Eleanor felt exhaustion seeping in, and dragging her down. She had no idea how long she had been travelling. Occasionally, she glanced back, fearing Marcas would follow, despite knowing the Urisks had killed—no—*destroyed*—him. But *had* he deserved it? A moment of self-doubt pinched her, but when the image of Muk's body flashed across her mind, along with the putrid effect Marcas' poisoned blade had had on the little Urisk, she promptly dismissed it.

She grunted. 'Of course, you deserved it.'

Eleanor forced Marcas' horse on through the overgrowth, trying to avoid open spaces, fearing she would be seen—not that it would make any difference, should *they* be hunting her. Still and all, it was better than travelling in the wide-open terrain.

Bare branches hampered her advance as she pressed on, their sharp thorns catching her clothes and scratching her skin as she tried to push them aside. She looked at her hands; the cuts were long and deep. She winced, seeing the blood, then gasped when the terrifying thought gripped her: *Oh, God! Fresh blood! What if they…?*

Panic set in.

Sensing its nervousness—the horse was growing edgy in response to its rider's anxiousness—Eleanor tried to control the beast while being conscious of her bloody hands. In a vain attempt to wipe them on her clothes, she momentarily let go of the reins. Instantly, the horse took control and bolted. But as she reached out to retrieve the reins, the agitated beast lifted itself high onto its hind legs. Feeling herself slip from the horse's flank, Eleanor desperately tried to grip its mane, then let go—the darting pain in her hands forcing her to release her hold.

She fell to the ground with a hard *thud!* Her mouth gaped as she watched the horse gallop towards the trees, as though being chased by the *Devil.* She took a deep breath, cupping her hands over her mouth, ready to call it back, then stopped herself; aside from not knowing the stubborn beast's name, she could not risk being heard.

Aching, she dragged herself to her feet, checking herself over, thankful she had not been seriously hurt. *Nothing broken*, she thought, relieved. Thrown, many times before, when Oran had taught her to ride, she had learned how to "fall" without serious injury.

Eleanor took note of her cuts again; they were still seeping—the sight of them alarming her. *I have to cover them!* Tearing strips of material from the length of her skirt, she promptly wrapped the makeshift bandages around her hands, to stem the flow, while staying alert; *they* would catch her scent if the wind carried it in their direction. A sense of urgency took over when she looked around, unaware of where she was, or where she was going. Then, she felt them—the signs of her anxiety homing in on her: her irregular breathing, the sweating of her palms, and shaking inside. She knew she had to do something before they would drown and imprison her in her dark thoughts.

Again, she looked back to where the horse had now disappeared; it was likely it had gone in search of its master. Horses had a way of finding their way back. And, if it did, she knew it would not be long before the others realised Marcas was missing, and would catch up with her—if they were not already on her trail. And, with no means of travel, she would be easy to track. *No! I cannot let them take me back there*, she vowed. *No matter what!*

Recalling what Asai had told her about his parents' demise, Eleanor decided she—if given no choice—would also take fate into her own hands, rather than being at her pursuers' mercy. But this time, she knew, none would be shown; it was most likely they had been sent to kill her. The mere thought of that drove her on.

She formed an image of Asai in her mind, to comfort her. His features were vague. She contemplated speaking his name, hoping he might hear her, then discarded the idea. *Too dangerous!* So, instead, she gathered it strongly in her thoughts; seeing him there, she inwardly called out to him.

*Asai! Hear me! Please, help me!*

His eyes flew open.

Retrieving the katana, Asai swiftly removed the wakizashi dagger from his sash, then fled in her direction, repeating her name. Compelled by the faintness of her voice inside his head, knowing she was calling out to him, the Samurai persisted in his search, hoping she would sense him.

Eleanor turned to run in the opposite direction the horse had gone, then hesitated, her intuition telling her, *"No!"* It seemed to make no sense, it pulling her back from her logical path, to run *from* the enemy. But something was beckoning, urging her to do so.

And so, she ran …

Her heart swelled, to the point where she felt it would burst. With no time to question her irrational decision, she pressed on, obeying her instincts, her fear dissolving with each step. Then there he was, inside her mind, guiding her towards him.

Eleanor focused her gaze ahead, her thoughts solely on Asai, casting all other notions aside; the pain in her muscles and the stinging cuts on her bloody hands. Through it all, though, she forced a smile, feeling him inside her, her heart almost skipping a beat. She could now sense his nearness. The thought of seeing him again, and feeling his touch … She imagined them entwined in a clinch, so tight she thought she would die if they were to part. And though they had only known one another a few days, she knew, without a doubt, she had to be with him. Whatever the risks.

Wrapped up in notions of love, Eleanor momentarily forgot herself, its possibilities briefly distracting her. But it was all it took—those few idle seconds—for the smile to slip from her face; and as she felt it drop away, along with hope, her thoughts were, once again, hindered by a combination of dread and anxiety, their unwanted presence battling to take control. This, she could not allow.

Eleanor looked down to check her improvised dressings, then gasped; the blood had soaked through. She glanced up, hearing a noise; it was clear—the sound of heavy scurrying through the thicket around her. Unable to identify it, she pushed herself on. But her throat was parched, and she was hungry again. However, the two most precious sources of life were still attached to the horse's saddle. While she could survive a little longer without food, water was her priority, if she were to keep up the fight—and without that …

*"Eleanor! Eleanor!"*

She flinched, hearing his voice inside her head. Like fuel for life, it re-ignited her.

Eleanor glanced back over her shoulder, her eyes widening when she caught a swift movement. There was no mistaking it … she *was* being followed. She halted, seeing it again. No—Asai would never tease or frighten her like that; he would come for her. Unable to determine the source, she strained to listen for the comforting sound of Asai's voice again. Nothing.

Whatever—or whomever—it was, they were gaining momentum, and heading her way.

Inside, she was screaming: *They found me! Oh, Asai, where are you?* She wished she had her precious dirk. With hope and its motivation fading, Eleanor ran, knowing her life depended on it. Her legs were now tiring; she could feel them trembling beneath her weight. She heard the sound again. This time it was louder. They were getting closer.

With time running out and fatigue weighing on her, Eleanor knew she could never outrun her predators, despite her fool-hardy attempt; they would be upon her at any moment. And, even if she had her dirk, *they* would not let her take her own life. No, they would toy with her first, perhaps even … The thought of them tearing at her clothes, their cold clammy hands on her skin, and their talon-like nails puncturing her flesh so they could … It sickened her. She had seen it in their eyes when they used to leer at her. She had seen it in Marcas, too, that time—his disturbing look—it animal, raw and wild. They would never stop in their frenzied desire for her human flesh.

As her strength began to wane, and her body slow, Eleanor concluded she had only imagined Asai, in her desperate attempt to believe he would rescue her.

In a moment of despair, and with a sense that she was drowning in defeat, she chose to stop, resolved to face her end. But she would not go without a fight. She would take control, here and now. But then another heart-wrenching thought dawned on her: she had no weapon to perform the *act*.

She had nothing.

Hearing their advance and, devoid of energy and drive, she slowly turned her weary body towards her on-coming assailants, trying to obliterate the images in her mind of what they would do to her. She swallowed hard, preparing herself. With the little strength she had left, Eleanor forced herself to straighten her aching body, to fight to the end … for what it was worth.

As she felt the weight of exhaustion finally taking its toll, tired and disoriented, Eleanor slumped. And as her body gave way, she imagined herself tumbling into the comforting hold of another.

'Eleanor!'

Her body jolted.

'Eleanor!'

The young woman found herself seated against a large boulder, as she roused herself after hearing their voice. Opening her eyes, she drew back, almost hitting her head on the rock. She gasped.

''Tis you!' she whispered, seeing the family resemblance staring down at her, their brow knitted together mixed with thought and concern. 'Just like before,' she added, managing a smile.

Satisfied his granddaughter was all right, Reece smiled back at Eleanor, then turned to Kai—the Servitor smiling and nodding at her. 'Protect my granddaughter,' said the Dhampir, his voice firm and dominant.

Kai, placing his hand over his heart, bowed to Reece—the Servitor's silent promise, assuring the Dhampir she would come to no harm.

In an instant, Reece was gone.

Kai returned his attention to Eleanor.

'We have been most concerned for your welfare,' he stated.

Eleanor stared up at the Servitor, still mesmerised by his ghostly form. Aware of this, Kai then transformed into the man she had been more acquainted with, thinking it best; it was clear she was distressed after her ordeal, and yet he sensed an enormous change in the young woman since her abduction, a few days earlier. She seemed to have grown, from caterpillar to chrysalis, ready to emerge into flight, to display her newfound character and strength.

Rubbing her eyes, Eleanor beamed at her friend as he helped her to her feet. Gradually she gathered her thoughts, and as her breath eased, she finally found her words as the tears welled.

'Oh, Kai!' Overjoyed, she flung her arms around him. 'Thank you! Thank you!'

As she drew away from him, she winced. The thrashing her body had endured since her escape from the Ruins of Moyne was prominent. But it had been worth it—the escape—and to be finally reunited with those she loved, after her failed attempt at the Cordhu Pass.

Suddenly the sound of clashing metal drew her head up sharply, distracting her from her pain. She stepped closer to Kai, unsure, her eyes flashing about, wondering where it was coming from.

'Where is Reece?' she said.

Kai turned and, transforming himself back to his true form, silently motioned her to follow him. 'Be wary, Eleanor,' he warned, hearing the noise escalate on their approach. 'Do not venture away from me.'

Eleanor had no intention of leaving the Servitor's side, as she was unarmed. Staying within his "protection", she focused her attention through a large gap between the trees, where he was pointing. Her mouth fell.

'Do not be concerned,' said Kai, reassuring her. 'They are no match for your *Heroes!*'

*Heroes?* It then dawned on her, his meaning, as *they* came into view: the long, jet-black silky hair flowed in harmony with its master as he moved with the gracefulness and skill of a marked warrior. Striking in his long kimono, his chest half-covered, the Samurai's presence was unmistakable as he fought alongside his colleague. Eleanor's heart skipped a beat when her eyes fell on him—the mere sight of him elevating her heart and spirits.

'Asai!' she whispered, cupping her hands over her mouth, in shock. Wanting to run, to be in his arms again, she subconsciously moved forward.

'No!' warned Kai, raising a hand.

They watched intently as Reece and Asai leapt effortlessly around three Dhampir—the creatures occasionally glancing at her, their eyes flaring. She glanced down at her hands. *They can smell my blood!* she realised—even though it had dried into her makeshift bandages. Quickly, she crossed them behind her back, hoping to thwart the scent.

'Do not even think it!' Reece snarled at them, catching their hungry, roving eyes. 'Not as long as we are here to protect her.'

A chill ran down Eleanor's spine, hearing them sneer and hiss at her grandfather. However, she knew Reece was right; the young Dhampir warriors, despite their agility, were no match against the skill of their peers. She watched Asai, recalling how he described the bond he shared with his prized weapons, still amazed at how he mastered them when united. She was in awe of it. She was in awe of him. His movements, compared to Reece's, were precise and graceful while her grandfather fought with a skill befitting a knight, strong and bold.

Suddenly, the three creatures stopped and leapt back from their opponents, leaving Reece and Asai in their centre, each, eyeing the other as if silently planning their next move.

Keeping his broadsword high and his eyes fixed, Reece edged towards Asai.

'What are they doing?' said Reece. 'This is unlike them.'

'They are … *thinking!*' stated Asai, narrowing his eyes.

'Impossible! They cannot—they are too—'

'Look at them!' interrupted Asai. 'It is like they are reading each other's—'

With only a second to spare, Asai quickly raised his weapons, drawing them across each other when one of the creatures rushed him, without warning. Instantly, the young Dhampir met with the Samurai's crossed swords, their lethal blades swiftly removing his head.

Eleanor gasped as she watched the severed head catapult into the air; its dark blood splattered everywhere, painting *Mother Nature's* abode with the creature's death, then burning it with its toxic stain before the head fell back to earth with a heavy *thump!*

With little regard for their fallen comrade, or sparing a glance, the remaining two lunged at Reece.

'Their blades!' Eleanor blurted.

'What do you mean?'

'They are smeared with deadly venom, Kai. That's how Kara was killed.'

The Servitor stared down at her as she nodded at him; it was clear Eleanor was unaware the Valkyrie was still alive. He then looked back at Reece and Asai, who were now in the height of it with the two creatures, his eyes focused on their deadly blades. Now he knew the reason for Kara's transformation. Should Reece and Asai be inflicted with the same, how would it affect them? Would they be like *her?*

'I have to warn them, Kai!' she said, stepping out from her protection. But as Eleanor opened her mouth to call out, she could not find her voice—the Servitor preventing her as he held his hand to her mouth, stopping her words.

'You will only distract them, increasing the risk,' he warned.

Her eyes, wide with fear and desperation, silently pleaded with Kai.

'Do not call out,' he urged her.

Though it was killing her inside, she nodded.

Kai regarded her as he cautiously removed his hand, fearing she would alert them.

'Then,' she started, swallowing hard, 'if I cannot warn them, there is something I *can* do.'

Kai followed her gaze as she looked down, showing him her blood-stained hands.

'Do what you must,' he said, stepping aside, roused to her meaning.

With no time to lose, and seeing the battle between the four Dhampir take momentum, Eleanor quickly removed the dressings from her hands, wincing, then bravely held them out. What had been her affliction, she hoped, would be the cause of the creatures' demise.

As was her intention, the two remaining Dhampir looked sharp in her direction, staring at her with their frenzied, hungry look, it chilling her to the bone. But when they unexpectedly vaulted over Reece and Asai—and straight for her—she recoiled and promptly stepped back into Kai's protection.

'Divert your eyes, Eleanor,' warned Kai—the Servitor wanting to spare his friend from witnessing what was about to happen ...

# Chapter Eleven

'No!' she insisted, clenching her fists. 'I'll not look away.'

Eleanor watched with horror as her grandfather and Asai wasted no time in their desperate pursuit to reach her assailants, trying to win back those precious seconds of hesitation when the two creatures had caught them off-guard.

The attackers suddenly halted, within inches of her; having pre-empted their move, the Servitor had thrown out his aura, stopping them in their tracks, and forcing them to their knees; as it shrouded them, Kai could see it—the vibrancy of his blue aura changed to that of cloudy black—diseased and impassive, marking the assailants' true characteristics.

It was at that moment, when they dropped to the ground, letting go of their swords, their hungry eyes still fixed on her, Eleanor's mouth gaped in recognition, before crying out;

*'Athol?'*

Swayed by her outburst, Kai had flinched, dropping his guard—the momentary diversion creating an opening, allowing the other Dhampir to escape. In seconds, he was gone, fleeing into the cauldron of trees.

Before she could utter another word, realising what she had done, Reece had gripped the remaining creature by the hair, wrenching his head back for Asai; the Samurai held his katana across his throat, leaning the edge of the lethal blade against his pale skin.

'Wait, Reece!'

He looked sharp at his granddaughter. *Wait? For what?*

'I—I *know* him!' she stated as if reading his thoughts. Reece shared a confused glance with Asai. ''Tis true,' she added, biting her lip. And yet, how could she *not* have noticed him, that he, too, had been part of this madness? But now, seeing him up close, she *knew* it was him.

Athol Keir had been Marcas' best friend—the other who had mysteriously disappeared from Balloch when it was thought they had secretly left for Eddin, to become soldiers. And now here he was, before her, on his knees, barely recognisable: his hair, once blessed with a mane of thick, black curls, was now drab and straight; his skin, once sallow, now looked drained, bloodless, except for the black veins pulsating beneath his pallid flesh; and his eyes, once deep blue, now flared red, their whites yellowed. The only distinguishable feature that remained was his slight cleft lip. She could see it now—she could see *him*. And then the gruesome reality struck; like Marcas, Athol's only thought was to *kill*.

Struggling in his fevered rage to escape Reece and Asai's hold, Athol strained to retrieve his sword. But when Reece stooped to snatch it away from his reach, Eleanor called out;

'Do not touch his blade! It is stained with venom!'

'Is it now?' snarled Reece, leaning in, so closely Athol could see his reflection in his incarcerator's eyes. Infuriated, he writhed and screeched—the high-pitched sound of his inhuman wail deafening, forcing Eleanor to cover her ears. Wanting to divert her gaze from the horror that was, she resisted and stood her ground, staring down at him with disgust and loathing. Given the chance, she knew he would attack and …

'Where is she?' demanded Reece, his eyes flaring, burning into Athol's as he pulled his head back, to emphasise his *Adam's Apple*, silently warning him of his fate. 'Well?' he snapped. 'Where is the Sorceress?'

Athol rolled his eyes back to meet Reece's and snorted.

As Reece forced his head back further, they could hear the crunch of the Dhampir's cervical vertebra. Adding pressure to the katana across Athol's throat, Asai then placed the wakizashi dagger behind his neck, marking the spot where the *Atlas* bone keeps the head attached to it, ready to separate them in one effortless move. And, though fully aware of her presence, the Samurai knew he could not look at Eleanor, fearing error; to give this unreasonable Dhampir leeway would be fatal, bearing in mind, the other could return at any moment.

'You will know, soon enough,' he hissed, then spat up at Reece into his face, grinning wildly before lowering his ravenous eyes to look at Eleanor again, his breathing quick and anxious. Athol drew his tongue across his lower lip—the scent of her bloody hands driving him to the point of madness; so near, and yet unattainable. Promptly, she hid them behind her back again.

Reece grunted. 'Like to "dispatch" her, would you?' he teased, using the Valkyrie's familiar, and descriptive, method of killing her victims while boasting of her "artistic" style. Then, seeing the feverish look, and sensing his rising heartbeat, he growled into Athol's ear; 'Do you think I care whether she knows you or not?'

Athol leered at Eleanor. She swallowed, wanting to say something, but nothing came. A spark of recognition flashed in his mind. For a second, his eyes narrowed. She gasped, seeing it, then recoiled when it disappeared, his crimson eyes burning once more—burning for her.

Baring his sharp teeth, Athol slowly lifted his gaze to Reece. 'And do you think *I* care?' came the strained, raspy response.

Reece looked up at his granddaughter, his intense stare warning her of his next move. Undaunted, yet unsure of how she would react, Eleanor took her stance and braced herself. She then nodded—the briefness of it telling him she was ready.

As with Marcas, she no longer saw the Athol she once knew. She no longer cared.

With no regard or sympathy for him, Reece lunged his blade into Athol's spine, holding it there as the Dhampir's body twitched and spasmed with the broadsword embedded inside him. Asai stepped back, both weapons still in hand, watching, ready to perform the final deed. Eleanor gasped when Athol's eyes sprung open and looked directly at her, their red pupils dilated. She drew a sharp breath when his eyes clung to hers—the ever-constant hunger evident.

Shifting his weight onto the balls of his feet, Reece steadied himself. With all his strength, he drove the blade further through, forcing the Dhampir to arch his body back as he twisted it, severing the spinal cord—and his ferocious look at his granddaughter. In seconds it would be over.

The moment Athol Keir's limp body dropped to the ground, down came the katana, slicing through his neck, clean and quick—the severed head then rolling away, to join that of the other.

Eleanor could not divert her look from Athol as his dead eyes—still wide open—continued to stare at her. But through it all, she had forced herself to watch, with no thought or respect for the *creatures* who would have destroyed her, given the opportunity. *No remorse*, she told herself, intent on stomping her fear. She shot a glance skywards, distracted; already the crows were hovering low, waiting to descend, to feast on those vacant eyes that seemed to be glaring at her, even in death. *They are welcome to them*, she thought.

Her attention was stolen again by her grandfather's voice, calling the Samurai's name, when Reece saw his comrade sprinting towards the trees, his weapons raised high.

Within moments, Asai was battling with the third Dhampir, who had been waiting in the wings, choosing to strike when their backs had been turned. He was quick and strong, and Asai was finding the battle relentless, but not without its awareness. Suddenly, the young Dhampir flicked his sword—the clever technique used to bend the blade, to strike back. Asai leapt, barely deflecting it. Behind them, all the others could do was watch, with Reece itching to join his friend—the broadsword gripped in his hand, should he be called upon.

'Do not!' warned Kai, quickly reminding Reece of the poisoned blade, then promptly revealed what Eleanor had told him about Kara. Reece threw a look of shock at the Servitor, then back at his colleague now fully aware. Should he intervene—even the slightest distraction—it could prove fatal for his friend. Sensing her anxiousness, he glanced down at Eleanor, seeing the intensity on her face as she looked on, helpless. Suddenly, without any indication, his granddaughter lifted her hands, repeating the same motion, to entrap the rogue Dhampir.

The creature flinched, catching her scent. Thrown into another blind rage, he swung his sword, briefly catching Asai's clothing.

Thinking the Samurai had been struck, Eleanor screamed—the unexpected disruption disorienting the three Dhampir; they jolted, hearing her high-pitched voice, it almost deafening to their sensitive ears. But in those seconds of disruption, it gave warning to the rogue Dhampir, telling him the other—Reece—would now join the fight. He had to think quickly. He could run or ... Realising he was now outnumbered—and knowing the bleak outcome—he took his chance and fled.

'Where is he?' said Reece, spinning, still brandishing his broadsword. But the creature had already escaped them.

Leaving her "protection", Eleanor ran to Asai—the Samurai grunting, seeing the small tear in his silk kimono.

'Are you all right?' she cried, looking him over, searching, terrified he had been cut. But all Asai could do was stare down at her, relishing in her touch as she frantically checked him over.

'I have not been hurt, Eleanor,' he said, smiling, feeling the harmony of their beating hearts, despite their difference.

The sound of his voice, speaking her name, dissolved her concern for him as she stopped and looked up into his dark, almond-shaped eyes, they meeting together in recognition and complete understanding of one another.

Behind the reunited lovers, Reece moved cautiously around the two Dhampirs' bodies, watching for any movement. And though their heads had been removed, he was taking no chances; any hint of *life*, and they would have to burn the remains. But deep down, he knew they had been dispatched.

Eleanor felt elated when Asai reassured her he had not been harmed—the animated rush of energy and passion enlivening her, aware of their closeness. Her throat tightened as she tried to swallow, wondering what next to say. Kai nodded at Reece—the two, conscious of the bond between the lovers; it was unbreakable. But the Servitor himself could see it in their aura as it swirled, its vivid hue, of emerald-green enveloping them, uniting them in strength.

*How could they not be together?* he thought.

Eleanor gazed up at Asai. Nothing was out of place. After what she had just witnessed, he remained calm; his breathing was light and controlled, and his mane of long, hair hung gracefully over his broad shoulders, resting on his bare chest. She blinked, diverting her eyes; awkward and aware of her dishevelled appearance, she tried fixing her hair.

He smiled at her. 'You are more beautiful now than the first moment when my eyes touched you,' he whispered, sensing her embarrassment.

Momentarily consigned to obliviousness, she placed a bruised and scratched hand where his heart was, feeling its slow beat, disregarding the faint, horizontal line across it. Gently, he covered hers with his own. It was immediate—the energy they both felt—and intensifying with every second, joining their bodies in love, pure and unique. Eleanor closed her eyes, letting it restore her soul.

They watched as she gradually regained her strength, eliminating the fatigue and strain which had consumed her exhausted body.

'My granddaughter's valour makes up for what she lacks in stature,' Reece stated, with pride.

The Servitor nodded.

'I think their bond is stronger than we anticipated,' Kai remarked. 'It has … revitalised her in a most compelling and … unique way.'

'She has her brother to thank for that,' said Reece, smirking, keeping his voice low.

'Gill?' she exclaimed, suddenly reawakened. She looked at her grandfather. 'Thank him for what?'

'If Gill had not—'

'Enough, Reece-san,' snarled Asai. The last thing the Samurai wanted was for her to know about *that* incident—when her brother had stabbed him with her dagger, by accident.

Eleanor, scrunching her face, looked from one to the other. 'Tell me, please?' she begged.

Asai slid his eyes towards Reece, then discreetly bared his teeth as a silent threat, warning his colleague not to pursue it. Reece retaliated in jest, by holding his hands up, feigning his surrender; he knew best to keep his silence. However, Eleanor, ever more suspicious, took it upon herself to intervene, intent on extracting what was, evidently, a secret between the two friends. It was then, it occurred to her … someone was missing.

She glanced around.

'Where's Tam?'

Silence loomed over them, overshadowing their moment of joy as Reece and Asai exchanged a mournful look, reminded of the absence of their fallen comrade. Sensing the awkwardness of the moment as Eleanor's face slowly fell—woken to the fact that something dreadful must have happened—Kai volunteered to inform her of the Highlander's untimely and heartbreaking demise. Eleanor lifted her hands to her face as the shock of Tam's death hit her, her eyes tearing—the feeling of his loss, overwhelming her.

She shook her head.

'I—I can't believe—'

But she was cut short when Reece spun on his heel, his gaze fixed to the left of where they stood, in the clearing. His eyes narrowed as he took a few cautious steps; something had stirred in the trees, beyond. Snatching his basilard dagger from inside his boot, he hurdled it—the weapon lodging deep in the bole of a tree, missing its target by inches. He grunted loudly, his face contorting in anger, his eyes flaring, inwardly cursing his failings.

'How could we have missed that?'

Gracefully, and without effort, she glided above the tips of the trees, still smirking to herself, before lowering to a secluded spot. The instant her feet touched the ground, nature's surrounding residents recoiled, scurrying from her presence. She never noticed.

The Highlander was dead—no more. And it pleased her, so much so, that she found it intriguing—how unexpectant it had been. Nevertheless, he *had* betrayed her—and after she favouring him among the others … well, he had, at least, been her second; the other one, Reece, had been her preference. But *he* had never succumbed to her advances, his constant rejection of her initially making the challenge more interesting, driving her determination to *have* him. But after hearing of his alleged encounter with the Sorceress, she finally gave up on the one with the intense green eyes. It was then she had turned her attention to the Highlander, realising how easy it would be to lure and manipulate *him*; after all, he was relatively *young*. She grunted. *Had been young.* A brief memory of one of their rendezvous flickered in her narcissistic mind. She rolled her eyes and shook her head. *What's done is done!* she thought. *What a pity!* In a twisted sort of way, she would miss him. But then again …

'One less to contend with,' she muttered before dismissing Tam from her memory.

Taking note of her position, she looked up. The light would start to fade in the next few hours. Then dusk would creep in, and then … time would run out.

Kara strode with the poise and magnificence of an unequalled rival as she prepared herself for her next move. She had devised a plan and was intent on carrying it through. Self-assured of a favourable outcome, she conjured images in her mind—victorious ones, no less—of her fallen enemy, begging to be spared. But she would spare no one an honourable death unless they were worthy of *her*, and a place in *Valhalla*, where they would wait on her and serve her every whim. She would win. Failure was not an option. It never was, in her eyes.

A distant, familiar sound brought her to yield. She raised her head, listening, searching for its location. Alert and calculated, Kara followed the sound until she found it. With her keen, new vision, she was able to observe from a safe distance, though, aware of the risk; she knew *they* would be out to avenge the Highlander.

Her eyes glowed red with excitement at the sight of her two foes in combat with three others—no doubt, these young Dhampir obeying the orders of the Sorceress. But she knew their time was limited, regardless of their youth and agility; arrogance would be their downfall. She could not dispute it. Reece and the *Strange One* would overthrow them. Their skills were far superior. No, the three warriors had no notion of what was yet to come … And it excited her. Feeling a rush down her spine, she slowly ran her tongue over the tip of her lip, and dared to stay, until their end.

There was no doubt in Kara's mind who the victors would be—and what a glorious victory it would be, too. She had always loved watching the Samurai and how he dispatched the enemy, his unique style, flawless. She grinned. *Spectacular!* she thought. *Some things are worth the—*

She looked sharp when a light breeze shifted, passing under her nostrils, sensing the presence of another mortal. But this one was different. Their sweet, succulent scent of *youth* was enticing, almost unbearable; Kara swallowed, parched by it, then followed their scent, treading carefully until she found the source.

*Well, well*, she thought, seeing Eleanor. *So, you escaped.* But aware of the young woman's company, she drew back, concealing herself, unwilling to risk being caught up in combat with two warriors such as Reece and Asai, their skills unmatched; also, they would be on alert, wanting to avenge the death of their comrade. Besides, she wanted to observe them, in their clash of steel.

Eyeing the girl, she recalled, while under the Sorceress' rule, how she had been determined to destroy her—against L'Ordana's wishes—the constant urge frustrating.

*"L'Ordana!"*

Suddenly, the name seemed to announce her presence. Kara glanced about her, listening, imagining she was near. But there was no sight nor sound of the Sorceress—or Magia Nera, for that matter, their whereabouts heightening her curiosity. She knew L'Ordana's militia was rapidly declining; she had lost quite a number of her young warriors, at the Cordhu Pass. She still marvelled at how the black wave engulfed so many of them—*and so quickly!*—before swallowing them up, leaving them to the mercy of the loch's spirits, especially *her*—the one who had almost succeeded in taking her down. At times, she could still feel the residual effect of Spectre's ice-cold touch on her foot. A near miss, but a near one, nonetheless—something she would not let happen again. And now, another three would soon be dispatched—Asai and Reece were about to do her a favour—leaving the Sorceress with only a handful. *All the better*, she thought. And the *mortals?* They did not count, meaning the girl was of no threat. Besides, even if she desired to do away with her, the girl was well-protected now.

Kara glared at Reece—the underlying resentment for him still gnawing at her. But not the Samurai; he was different: quiet and strange in his ways, perhaps, but unique and highly skilled as a Master of combat—more so than his colleague. It surprised her to know she admired and respected him. He was loyal, too. She recalled how he had bravely tried to take his own life, to be with his loved ones, after they had taken siege of his castle, in the Realm of Saó. His young wife had been pretty, though weak—and why she "encouraged" her over the cliff. It was this loyalty she had secretly envied, for a time, spurring her desire to have a mate. But that was then. Things had changed now—that yearning, long vanished, along with her past life.

No more would another command her to do their bidding. *I would like to see them try*, she thought. She now had free will to do as she pleased. She would find the Shenn amulet, possess it, and then rule with it. She would rule them all.

The amplified, heavy clash of blades brought Kara out of her wandering thoughts, and she almost gasped in wonder when Asai swiftly dispatched the first opponent. *Glorious!* Her eyes darted to Eleanor, observing her with intrigue as she stood within the protection of the ghostly creature beside her; it was clear who the young woman favoured as she watched the Samurai … *Her lover!*

Kara's ice-cold, grey eyes then widened when Eleanor unexpectedly exposed her bloody hands—the intoxicating smell of their opened wounds maintaining the Valkyrie's undivided attention. She swallowed.

*Oh, how clever of you*, she thought. *Distracting them like that.*

Then something occurred to her—about the girl: a change of sorts, had come about in her. *Perhaps, a potential threat?* But Kara's curiosity was cut short when the battle between the Dhampir elevated. It was simply thrilling—the anticipation of their deaths—watching as the two remaining warriors struggled under the ghostly figure's invisible hold. And when one escaped, she held her breath, engrossed in the remaining Dhampir's final moments as he thrashed out under Reece's grip before his head was spectacularly separated by the Samurai, to join his fallen comrade.

The fighting had ceased. It was over.

She inhaled deeply, then flinched—the austere, heady scent of the dead warrior's blood, making her restless. She looked sharp when the third suddenly reappeared, engaging in surprise combat with the *Strange One.* Her body tensed when the young Dhampir's poisoned blade struck out at the Samurai.

*Losing your touch, Asai*, she thought, then jolted when the girl screamed—the brief disturbance allowing a window of opportunity for the third Dhampir to escape, yet again.

Seeing the Samurai and the girl together, she mused over the relationship and its unexpected advantage. *It appears love has become your weakness, Strange One.*

Still and all, Kara commended how the Samurai had fought. *If only he were my ally.*

*Ally!*

When the thought struck her, she realised they had left their other companions alone—where she had dispatched the Highlander. She then made an assumption: two were *mortal* … perhaps, three? She was unsure about one; his scent was unusual. Then there was the Warlock. It would amuse her to finally have her battle with *him* after he had been under the protection of the Sorceress for so long. *Not any more, Oran.*

A glance back saw the ongoing tenderness between the Samurai and the girl. Now was her opportunity, while both were caught up in their little reunion.

*Make the most of it, "lovers!"*, she sneered inside, grateful for the underlying weakness of man, despite *their* affliction. She then regarded Reece; he was preoccupied, checking over the bodies of the warriors as the "ghost" looked on. She grunted. *Beautifully dispatched, Reece!*

Kara looked in the direction where the vulnerable group was most likely still waiting for their colleagues to return and envisaged *their* demise, when she caught Eleanor's scent again. Her throat burned; she was thirsty and craved relief. She licked her lips, imagining their warm blood slowly trickling down her throat, satisfying her growing needs. She could almost smell them from where she stood, craved by the young woman's intoxicating scent. Glorifying in its sweetness, she could no longer resist. It prompted her into action. However, in her eagerness to go, overwhelmed by the desire to "feed", her swift departure exposed her presence.

# Chapter Twelve

The wind had shifted, alerting Reece to the bold, sinister presence.

'You were watching us, *whore!*' he snarled, beneath his breath.

Having heard Reece, Asai looked down at Eleanor and, forcing a smile, said, 'Wait here with Kai.'

She frowned, her lips parting to protest, not wanting to be separated from him again. 'But—'

'You are safe now,' he insisted, his voice calm as he placed a tender kiss on her forehead. 'Please, stay here.'

She nodded, and as he left her side, she touched where his delicate kiss lingered, it reassuring her.

'It is all right,' said Kai, distracting her; she turned to face him. 'They are making sure there is no other threat.'

'Where?' Asai's hand grasped the hilt of the katana. Too consumed by the reunion with Eleanor, he had failed to notice the Valkyrie's presence. It concerned him—the distraction.

'Just beyond it … *there!*' said Reece, pointing with his chin to where his dagger was still embedded in the tree.

'We will hunt her down, then,' he stated, his hand removing the katana as he made to pursue the Valkyrie, hell-bent on avenging more than one score.

'Wait!' said Reece, following swiftly at his friend's heel. But Asai had already stopped at the place where Kara had been spying on them, his eyes moving over the ground where the heavy imprint of her presence still marked the spot. Together, the friends sniffed the air, then looked up, catching it—the unearthly smell as it lingered, mingling with the dampness, emphasising its stench.

'No wonder we could not detect her,' said Reece, retrieving his basilard dagger from the tree, its bark snapping, disturbing the insects behind it, then falling away as he wrenched the blade from it. 'We had been too familiar with her scent for so long, we overlooked its change,' he noted. 'We had … *forgotten!*' he added, turning his head, still catching the remnants of Kara's new odour, its sour and offensive smell meandering after its owner. He pointed up in its direction.

Asai nodded.

'What also concerns me, Reece-san … is *why* we missed it. We should have sensed her presence, without fail. This concerns me.' He looked back at Eleanor. 'I fear, being in the company of mortals, once more … it is clouding our thoughts and emotions. While I do not regret it'—he tore his look from her back to Reece—'it has already proven fatal, and may do so, again.'

Reece knew Asai was right. He was *always* right, and though it irked him at times, he, too, was troubled by what he said; as long as Kara was roaming free—and with her new powers adding to the threat already hanging over them—they would have to try to detach what little emotion they felt away from the others if they were to protect them. *Easier said than done*, he thought, conscious of the Samurai's bond with his granddaughter.

Reece glanced over his shoulder at Eleanor and Kai, who were in conversation. He was sure the Servitor was also aware of what had occurred and was distracting Eleanor, who was clearly oblivious. He sighed.

'How do we tell her, Asai? She thinks Kara is dead.'

Eleanor roused herself at Asai's sudden departure from her. And though she could see him nearby with her grandfather, she felt his absence but knew to stay where she was—under the Servitor's protection. Kai stood over her, doing his duty while watching the two

Dhampir in deep discussion; he was aware of what had transpired, having sensed the Valkyrie, too, after.

With Kai's attention briefly on Reece and Asai, Eleanor looked up at him, still fascinated by his ghostly form. It was mesmerising. Always curious, she boldly raised her left hand, tempted to touch him. For a moment she wavered, unsure, then reached out …

To her astonishment, her hand passed through him. Instantly, she felt the icy chill of the Servitor's true presence biting at her fingers, making her shiver.

Kai smiled to himself then closed his eyes briefly, feeling the warmth of her hand as it moved inside him; it felt like Onóir's. He turned to meet her bewildered face. Like a child, caught up to mischief, she gasped, her eyes widening before wrenching her hand away, then cradling it with her other, trying to return a little warmth to it. In a loving gesture, Kai leaned over and, blowing softly, melted away the cold, restoring the warmth to her hand.

The Servitor's smile then faded reminded of his purpose in the mortal's world. '"A slave for eternity," or rather a "Servant to eternity," as *they* would have me call it,' he stated, outwardly speaking his thoughts.

'*They*?'

'The Elliyan,' he replied, looking down at her through the blackness of his eyes. 'The ones who cruelly forced your father from you—and the ones who control the Servitor. We are the remnants of torn souls, trapped in a world between life and death.'

'*Purgatory!*' she said. 'I remember. Where they save your lives, only to rule them.'

He nodded.

'However, I would rather live the life of a slave among mortals,' he admitted, 'than be kept in torturous limbo.'

'But at least you have *us*, Kai. And Onóir adores you.'

The Servitor held her gaze at the mention of his dear friend's name, realising Eleanor was unaware of her grandmother's death. *Oh, you poor child*, he thought, feeling a tug on his heart as he looked into her innocent face, it glowing with youth, and in the early blooms of love. 'Perhaps,' he said, tilting his head. 'But only for a time; you shall all eventually return to the universe when your circle of life is complete. Then I will be forced to return to Purgatory.'

Eleanor's mouth gaped, her eyes widening. Her friend was right; he would live on, thrown back to that hellish life for eternity, while having to endure the immensity of their loss. It was a cruel thought, that he should be forced to do so, rather than being allowed to join his loved ones in everlasting, restful peace.

'You see, I have gone against their wishes, Eleanor,' he stated.

'What do you mean?'

'I betrayed them,' he confessed. 'And, because of that, it is most likely—'

'You mean—no one here can save you?' Tears began to form in Eleanor's pale blue eyes at the thought of never seeing their friend again when their own lives were done. But Kai had been more than a friend to them, his father-like figure watching over the family, especially Gill, when their own had disappeared.

'It is the way of it,' he lamented. 'But do not waste your tears on me, Eleanor. You are …' He hesitated, sensing Reece and Asai's agitated return—the two still engrossed in low conversation—Asai subtly sheathing the katana and Reece outwardly venting his frustration as they approached.

'I cannot believe the Valkyrie was here, watching—' He broke off, aware of what he had just said. He closed his eyes and shook his head, irked by his stupidity.

Eleanor jolted.

'*Kara?!*' she cried, looking about in a state of shock and fear. 'I—I thought she was *dead!*'

Reece groaned, then looked to Asai who scowled at him. Still, she had to find out sooner or later.

'Why did you *think* this?' said Asai, approaching her. It was clear by her stunned reaction, she had been convinced of the Valkyrie's demise. Still looking around, Eleanor clasped her hands together, wringing them, her eyes darting back and forth. Inside, Asai could feel her pain, and the torment she had been subjected to, by the Valkyrie. He vowed to return the "favour".

'I was assured of it,' she said, her voice now trembling, fearing Kara's return.

'By whom, Eleanor?' said Kai—the softness of his voice, calming her.

'Wareeshta.'

They stared at her—the one name they did not expect to hear, burning their ears. Reece, his eyes beginning to flare, moved towards his granddaughter.

'*Wareeshta?!* And you believed her?!' He was not angry at Eleanor, but at the notion that she had, perhaps, been used as a pawn in their games.

Eleanor nodded with certainty, and yet was prepared to shield her friend.

'Aye! I did—and … *still* do. She had plotted Kara's death with the help of another.'

'And … her accomplice?' asked Reece, giving her a sideward glance.

'The other Warlock.'

'Magia Nera,' stated Asai, slowly nodding.

'Truly!' she insisted. 'I had no reason to doubt Wareeshta's word.'

Still, they stared at her, perplexed, finding it difficult to accept that she would defend the very one who had damned them to a long life of depravity.

'Eleanor,' whispered Asai. She lifted her eyes to meet his, a faint blush returning to her cheeks, giving him back her undivided attention. 'Why would you accept the word of the creature who did *this* to us?' he asked, placing his hand where his heart beat slowly.

'Have you forgotten it was *she* who changed—*stole*—our lives?' Reece added—the bitterness evident in his hardened tone. 'And that it was *she* who condemned us to a lifetime of misery, for her mistress's pleasure?'

Eleanor chewed on her lip, conscious of the resentment in her grandfather's voice yet she was torn; if it had not been for Wareeshta … She lifted her hands, in self-defence. 'I know,' she said, wanting to state her plea, to justify her loyalty to her loved ones' enemy. She knew they were right to hate Wareeshta. *They have every right.* 'I know …' she whimpered, her voice trailing to silent thought, her eyes straying from her grandfather's persistent glare.

'But?' Reece was adamant.

She slowly lifted her eyes. 'Wareeshta was … *kind* to me.'

Reece threw his head back, letting out a loud grunt. '*Kind?!*' Now he was furious, by his granddaughter's betrayal. Did she not know where her loyalties lay? She would have to choose. Regardless. Lowering his head, he met with Eleanor's pleading eyes, his intention to show her the error of her decision. 'You were nothing but a pawn—used as a go-between in their games,' he snarled. 'It is our … *vocation*, our intention, to rid this world of Wareeshta. Do not doubt me when I say this, Eleanor'—he leaned closer, holding her with his determined stare—'we *will* destroy her, and take back what is rightfully ours … our freedom *and* mortality.'

Eleanor's mouth fell, hearing this, then turned to Kai for support; however, the Servitor only nodded, confirming Reece's words. And when she looked to Asai—the one she had hoped would understand, who would side with her—he inclined his head in agreement, too. It was torturous, being torn between two different loyalties—one for her loved ones, the other, for the vow she had made, to their enemy—her friend.

*"Do not let them kill me."* In her mind, Eleanor could still see the dread in Wareeshta's eyes when she spoke those words to her before

her escape. But she was determined to do what was right. Eleanor pressed her lips together and shook her head, defiant.

'No! Wareeshta saved my life!' she hit back, continuing to mark her name, to justify her defence of her friend. 'And for that, I cannot—*will not*—let you.' Now, she was insistent.

Reece slid his eyes towards her. 'You have no say in—'

'Listen to her.'

Reece and Asai looked at Kai.

'Eleanor has been through a lot,' the Servitor went on, 'and it is clear she knows more than we do. She is also quite adamant,' he added, with an underlying warning to the two Dhampir.

'Please … Grandfather,' she begged, her face solemn as she tilted her head forward, her pleading eyes then lifting to meet the hardness in Reece's.

Reece second-glanced her, caught unawares; it was the first time she had called him that. *"Grandfather"*. It echoed in his stubborn head. Conscious of her motives, Kai smiled as he watched her display the actions of a female when looking for something from the opposite sex. The Servitor looked at Reece, attentive to the Dhampir's reaction.

Reece drew back, his face relaxing, warming to the young woman who reminded him of his wife. He sighed, rolling his eyes. *Just like Onóir*, he thought, then suddenly realised Eleanor did not know her grandmother was …

'I'm not lying to you,' Eleanor persisted. 'It *was* Wareeshta who took me under her protective wing. It was *she* who kept the predator from my door. Had she not, Kara would have had her way, then, and I would be—' She stopped short, and turned to Asai. 'The Sorceress kept me sedated—by using a potion—so I could not communicate with you. But Wareeshta destroyed it, right in front of my eyes. *She* was the one who helped me escape.' Eleanor chewed on her lip again as she watched her *Heroes* share dubious glances. She had to convince them. 'We spoke, often,' she then maintained, trying to justify her unusual friendship with their foe. 'I even learned about her past and goals. There's a side to her you do not—'

'*Goals?*' Reece interrupted, lifting a brow.

She nodded.

'To free herself from L'Ordana. She has been biding her time. Like you, she was—is still—a slave. So, do not blame her for her wrong-doings. Wareeshta simply wishes to—' She stopped herself, and looked away, briefly.

Reece leaned his head to the side with added interest; his granddaughter was withholding something from them. 'Well? She wishes to …'

She shrugged, stretching her face, feigning innocence. 'Oh, nothing.'

'No, please, do enlighten us,' he persisted, his tone sarcastic, still unconvinced.

'As I said … she wants her freedom … just like you.' As she held her grandfather's gaze, she was also mindful of Kai and Asai. *Do not look away*, she told herself, *otherwise, they will know. Say something else.* 'The games have long since commenced between L'Ordana and that Warlock,' she blurted. 'He believes she has something belonging to him, and she would have him think it—because she needs him, to win over the Elliyan and to claim the Shenn.'

'A true game of *Cat and Mouse*,' stated Kai, inwardly impressed by Eleanor. 'And what of Magia Nera—the Warlock? Is this not *his* goal?'

'No. He only wants one thing: a book, and …' She paused, recalling Wareeshta's heartfelt story: her traumatic past before being rescued by the Sorceress, and her love for Magia Nera—though she would rather see him dead than own something that was rightfully hers, and part of her legacy. And yet, she aimed to destroy it—because of its evil attachment. 'That's all he wants,' she then added. 'Nothing else.'

Reece glanced at Asai. They were both wondering the same thing:

was it the same book Oran had used to help them escape the citadel? Most likely.

Reece groaned at the difficulty of their new dilemma. 'And there lies the problem,' he said. '*Our* problem; if we kill Wareeshta, we are given back our freedom and mortality.'

'But at a price,' said Asai.

Reece nodded.

'What do you mean?' asked Eleanor, her brow knitting tightly.

'Reece and Asai would lose their … *gifts*,' said Kai.

'Though, I would not call them that,' added Reece, returning his dagger to his boot.

'At this time, we cannot afford to lose them,' Asai explained to her. 'They are vital to this cause, and yet …' His voice trailed. Eleanor lowered her head, saddened by their predicament, it prompting her to ask herself: *what future do we have?* Asai would lose her to the cruelty of time. It was inevitable; while he continued to live on, for an age, she would wither and eventually … *Die!* The mere notion of it—the mere thought of being parted from him forever—terrified her.

Sensing Eleanor's hopelessness, Kai put forward a compromise: 'Should Reece and Asai vow to take no part in Wareeshta's demise …' he began. The two Dhampir shot the Servitor a wary glance. '… allowing it to fall to another,' he went on. 'Would you *then* accept her death?' Eleanor regarded the Servitor, unsure. 'True to say, you would mourn her loss, but without the blame falling on Reece and Asai,' he stated.

Thoughts churned in her mind as she mused over Kai's words; they made sense. She turned to Reece and Asai. 'Promise me—you will not participate in Wareeshta's death, should you meet this night?'

The seconds passed in uncertain silence as the Dhampir considered the Servitor's compromise.

'*Promise me!*' she insisted.

The two Dhampir shared a brief, knowing glance before looking back to Eleanor. Then, with a simple gesture—a nod from Reece, and a sweeping bow from Asai—the agreement was struck.

'I think it is time we made our way back,' said Kai, breaking the uncertainty, still hanging in the air. 'The others will be wondering where we are, thinking we have deserted—'

'*Others?*' Eleanor echoed, her spirits lifting—the urgency in her brightening tone now obvious.

'Enough of your questions!' said Asai, mocking her as he swept her off her feet. She gasped at the unanticipated move, then relished in the safety of his hold, it strong and natural.

As Eleanor wrapped her arms around Asai for support, a distinct scent of jasmine billowed around the lovers. As it swirled, enveloping them with its pungent aroma, the Samurai stalled, feeling the presence of his forebears, bestowing their love and consent upon them. But there was only *one* approval he longed for …

A butterfly suddenly emerged; it hovered about the couple, its delicate wings with their unusual tint of gold and silver fluttering, vying for the Samurai's attention. Asai watched its movements carefully, his eyes focused as it drifted away towards something—towards *someone.*

He then knew.

When the image of his beloved Ayumi materialised before the couple, Asai drew a sharp breath, seeing her; gone was the look of the once tortured soul that had been cruelly—and prematurely—snatched from him, during the siege of Odani, so long ago. Her features were now replaced with the warmth and serenity of someone at peace, and it simply emanated from her. Her hands were drawn together as though in prayer. She still looked beautiful—just as he remembered. He watched as the butterfly approached her, her small hand extended, luring it back to her. It hovered a moment before resting on her open palm. She smiled down at the insect, letting it nestle before lifting her hand. It then settled back on her jet-black hair, where it belonged, its gold and silver wings now prominent, reminding him of the piece of jewellery he had commissioned for her to celebrate their engagement.

'Asai? What is the—'

'Shh!' Kai lifted his hand, asking for Reece's patience; the Dhampir frowned at the Servitor, then glanced back at Asai. 'Wait,' Kai whispered.

Asai hesitated and stared at his late wife as she held his look, noting an element of guilt in his eyes; he tensed, knowing she was aware of it. Conscious of his tightening hold, Eleanor stared at him, concerned; his gaze was fixed ahead, distant. And though wrapped within his embrace, she felt detached from him.

No longer saddened by their separation, Ayumi's eyes smiled when she moved her look to the young woman in her husband's arms.

'What is it?' whispered Eleanor. He failed to hear her. Then she felt it—the ghostly presence. She knew who it was without asking, wishing she could see her, speak to her. But instead—and respecting their private moment—Eleanor held her silence.

'*She* approves,' whispered Kai—the Servitor enthralled by the spirit's presence; Ayumi smiled at him with kindness in her eyes, then acknowledged him with a subtle nod. Kai returned it yet kept his distance, mindful of the kindred bond between the Samurai, his late wife and Eleanor, not wanting to interfere.

Ayumi, now returning her attention to her husband, smiled at him with requited love and bowed, as was their custom, sealing her approval of his new love. Her eyes lifted to where the butterfly had returned to its rightful place, then back to him.

*"I shall always be with you, Koibito!"*

Asai closed his eyes, silently returning the endearment in his mind, his guilt now melting away as they held each other's gaze for the last time, his arms then gradually loosening their anxious grip on Eleanor; she squeezed him gently, letting him know she was still there. He needed no reminding of it.

Having finally accepted their fate, husband and wife bowed to one another, with respect, before Ayumi returned to her spirit world, content—while Asai remained temporarily lost in the world of mortals.

With nothing left to say, the four swiftly departed—back to the Paths of Lome.

# Chapter Thirteen

'Tis too quiet for my liking,' said Oran, pacing back and forth, his rising concern making Rosalyn and Daine increasingly nervous. ''Tis like a prelude to something—'

'Trust me, Oran,' interrupted Gill, 'the others will be back. I promise.' His father paused, raising a curious brow as he stared back at his son then threw a look at his wife, still silently questioning their son's ongoing casual usage of his name. Rosalyn shrugged, casting her eyes to the heavens.

A small movement snatched the Warlock's attentive eye. From inside its burrow, a wild hare's small head and twitching nose peeped out, sniffing the foul air. It contemplated leaving, to forage for food, then decided against it, swiftly scurrying back to its haven.

Oran grunted. 'Even the forests' residents are wary of the evil attached to this place.' He nodded to himself. 'Aye, they *feel* it, too.'

Daine, conscious of Rosalyn standing beside him, her infectious energy keeping him all too aware of her, discreetly stepped away.

Oran grinned, catching him. 'And you?'

Daine flinched.

'Do *you* fear it, too?' he mocked, turning to address the guide. Caught unawares, Daine stumbled over the words in his mind, unable to speak. 'And *fear* it you shall,' Oran persisted. But when he caught Daine glancing at Rosalyn for a moment—too long for his liking—Oran moved towards the guide, his eyes glowering at him before whispering in his ear; 'Be mindful of your place in our world … *mortal!*' he warned, emphasising the word. 'It has not gone unnoticed—the way you look at my wife.'

Feeling his anger soar, Daine slid Oran a side-long glance; he had had enough threats throughout this journey to last him a lifetime and was not prepared to take more. He bravely turned to meet Oran face to face but was forced to look up, to match his challenging stare.

'And what is it *you* fear … *Warlock?*' he hit back, through gritted teeth—the anger prominent in his voice.

Surprised by the guide's retaliation, Oran raised a brow and drew his head back, sensing the challenge, then hesitated when something struck, rendering him silent.

Daine snorted. 'And now you stare at me … *Warlock!* So, what is it *you* see?' he goaded.

Dismissing the remark, Oran stepped closer with growing interest. Daine recoiled, unnerved, then frowned. *Too close for comfort*, he thought, taking another step back.

In an unexpected move, Oran clutched Daine, with such force the guide found himself elevated, his eyes wide open, glaring down into the Warlock's intense stare.

'Stop it!' cried Rosalyn, aware of her husband's capabilities. 'What the hell do you think you're doing, Oran Shaw?'

Ignoring his wife's pleas, Oran narrowed his eyes and tilted his head from side to side as he studied the struggling guide. Refusing to be overlooked, Rosalyn ran to Farrow—the steed shifting as she retrieved the item from his saddle while, inside, disgruntled her husband had failed to notice his own horse.

'Leave him!' begged Gill, staring up at Daine; the guide was now gripping Oran's hands in his feeble attempt to release himself.

'There!' Oran pointed with his chin. 'I see it—in your eyes. Aye! You remind me of—' He broke off, hearing Rosalyn yell out, then lowered his head sideways to find himself staring down the blade of a great sword—his own.

'As old as it is,' she threatened, struggling to hold the weapon in her hands, her lips pressed hard as she concentrated—the strain of its weight now visible on her face, 'it still carries the strength and power to claim another victim.'

Releasing a long-winded sigh at the empty threat, he finally unshackled Daine from his grip.

When the guide landed hard on his feet, Daine scrambled away, lifting his hands in defeat and shaking his head in protest; he wanted no part in the husband and wife's dispute, even if it did include him. He glanced over at Nahla; the Friesian was stomping the ground with her hoof, wanting his attention, her white mane and tail making her stand out among the other horses. He knew by her behaviour she longed to go home—as did he, feeling the tightness in his chest as the dampness in the air grew thick with the withering of the day. And yet, he knew why he *still* could not go—the residual effect of *that* kiss, preventing him.

Oran continued to hide his grin as the weight of the sword gradually slipped from Rosalyn's hold, its tip stabbing the ground. He reached down. 'Ha!' he mocked, taking it effortlessly from her aching hands. 'Reunited!'

Oran turned and raised the great sword to the level of his eye, admiring, as always, the ancient workmanship of its hilt and blade. He then slowly ran his hand down the length of its polished metal, caressing it as the others looked on.

*If only he looked at his wife the same way*, thought Daine, keeping his distance.

Rosalyn's face turned crimson, furious at her husband's arrogance, while he continued to let his eyes wander over his "precious" sword.

'The blade is still sharp as if cast for the first time,' he remarked, ogling it like a long-lost lover. 'It never blunts!' he boasted, unable to help himself. He turned to Daine, holding it up, bent on showing it off yet maintaining his underlying threat to the guide for being a little "over-friendly" with his wife. 'Isn't it … *glorious?!*' But Daine had already turned away, uninterested; as long as the Warlock's intentions were not to use it on him …

'Enough!' demanded Rosalyn, then threw a double-glance at her son—the smile of "betrayal" on Gill's face, telling her he was clearly enjoying his father's humour. 'We are here as allies—not enemies,' she scorned at them. 'Need I remind you of why we—'

'I leave you bickering,' a familiar voice boomed, 'and *still* I return to it.'

'Reece!' Daine called out, relieved, for the first time, to see the Dhampir—and relieved for the welcome distraction of his return.

Reece strode out from the passage between the escarpments and into the clearing, his eyes darting towards the pillars; they had changed again, and continued to do so—the blame falling on the heightened emotions and the ongoing bickering. *Will they ever stop?* he thought, shaking his head.

Seeing her father, Rosalyn's anger melted into a smile; it then dropped at the sight following close behind him.

'Oh, my—*Eleanor!*' she cried, when Asai emerged, carrying her daughter. Behind them, Kai silently followed—the Servitor keeping alert.

On hearing Rosalyn call out the name of the one person they had longed to see again, the bickering instantly stopped. At the same time, Rave, who had grown bored of the relentless and meaningless conversations surrounding her, now roused herself—the heightened sound of her mistress's voice calling out the name she recognised. The hound leapt and pounded towards them.

The group stared, speechless, as the Samurai carefully released Eleanor from his hold; at first, she was reluctant to leave the comfort of his protective arms. However, on seeing her mother, the unwillingness slipped away, launching Eleanor into Rosalyn's waiting embrace while almost losing her breath as they reconnected.

'I knew you would come back to us,' Rosalyn sobbed, fighting back her tears of joy as she held on to her daughter, stroking her hair. Eleanor burrowed herself in her mother's warm embrace, absorbing all the love being lavished on her—the true maternal love she had so dreadfully missed. It seemed like years since they last touched, spoke, or laughed, and yet it had only been days. But so much had happened in that short space of time. At their feet, overjoyed to see her again, Rave barked and danced about. Eleanor broke from her mother and looked down, grinning at the hound.

'If you wag your tail any harder, Rave, it will fall off!' she laughed, then knelt, receiving the dog into her open arms, letting her lick her face, Rave whimpering, her vocal display of sheer joy overwhelming Eleanor, and almost reducing her to tears.

Rosalyn stood back, taking in her daughter's sorry state; she looked as though she'd been in the "wars". And, in a way, knew she had been; her clothes were stained from her ordeal, and hung loose, where she had lost some weight. And yet, her daughter seemed unphased. She knew the reason why, glancing up at Asai. The way the Samurai was looking at Eleanor, his gaze protective and filled with devotion, told Rosalyn she need not worry as long as he was by her side. She was indebted to him, and it gave her comfort to know he would remain, despite the hurdles the two lovers faced. *They'll find a way*, she thought, her heart bursting with pride at the match. There was always a way when two people truly loved one another. Rosalyn then shifted her gaze to her husband, her thoughts mixed with emotions of uncertainty—but with the guide's lips still lingering on hers—and embedded in her mind—she looked away.

Oran patiently waited, feeling the lump in his throat as he watched the reunion. Inside, he was struck by the change in his daughter; Eleanor had matured so much, he hardly recognised her. She was no longer the girl of thirteen. *No, fourteen, or was it fifteen?* He felt ashamed, unable to recall her age. He should have known. He should have remembered it. But now, as he watched his family reunite, he felt like an outsider—and it was clear she had not seen him, yet. He wondered how she would react …

His wait was over.

*'Paw!'*

He looked sharp, her voice jolting him from his thoughts and fears.

*"Paw."* The word had fallen naturally from her mouth.

Eleanor beamed up at her father, then rose, leaving Rave nudging her for more attention while, in the background, Daine looked on with enquiry; he saw no resemblance between father and daughter, secretly prompting him to question it.

As Eleanor approached him, Oran threw a double glance between his daughter and Reece, who stood quietly beside Asai and Kai. He could see it now—the uncanny likeness between the two. They had the same shaped eyes, and when Eleanor drew nearer, he detected the taint of peridot, stumped that he had never noticed it before—blue being their prominent colour.

Drawn and pale yet brimming with life and her newfound confidence, Eleanor stopped and looked up at Oran. He felt vulnerable, searching for the words he had stored away, especially for this day—when they would be reunited. And yet, he could not recall any of them; they had dissolved into a distant memory. He opened his mouth to speak, hoping the right words would not fail him.

'Forgive me, Eleanor,' he whispered—the arrogance he had been displaying now dismantled by her presence. It was all he could say. It was enough.

'Oh, Paw, there is nothing to forgive,' she blurted, reaching up and throwing her arms around him. 'I understand, and am so happy to have you back.'

Humbled—and with his sword still in hand—Oran returned her embrace, enveloping himself in her hold as she gripped him, not wanting to let go. A glance at his wife saw Rosalyn's face soften as she looked on, their emotions finally finding their place, returning to calm. Lost in the moment, Oran closed his eyes, swallowing the lump in his throat, his heart melting.

A prominent cough then came from behind.

'And what about me?'

Breaking away from Oran, Eleanor turned and looked up at Gill.

Her eyes widened, taken aback by the physical change in her brother since she had last seen him, a few days ago.

*Is it possible?* she asked herself. She glanced at her father, her mouth gaping.

Oran nodded.

'He will make a fine Magus,' he said, in answer to the look of disbelief on her face.

Brother and sister embraced. Like her mother, Eleanor also felt the enormity of Gill's inner power and strength. It was incredibly transcendent. Her father was right: he was going to be a great ruler of this other world she had been subjected to. Regardless of how she felt, she knew she could no longer fight the inevitability of having to let her sibling go. Her heart swelled with pride.

'I think it is time to return *this* to you,' he said, pulling away from her.

Eleanor gasped with delight at the sight of her dagger, while Gill was relieved to finally return the dirk to his sister, wanting to forget a certain "incident".

Reaching out, she took it. The moment her left hand grasped the ornate hilt, she clenched it with all her might, her thumb subconsciously rubbing over the sapphire embedded in the pommel. This time, though, it felt different. She frowned, unsure.

The others shared wary looks as they regarded the dagger's unusual influence on Eleanor; they knew why … and hoped she would never find out.

Eleanor stood back, lifting it to her eye, regarding the polished weapon—the intensity of its steel rising with fervour. As she felt its potency enter her body, she smiled, recognising it, welcoming it back as part of her. Her face then fell. Her mouth gaped as she slowly turned her attention to her brother, then across to the Samurai, narrowing her eyes as the truth hit. Her eyes flashed back to Gill.

'You drove my dagger through Asai's heart?!' she yelled, glaring at him.

Stunned by his sister's unexpected outburst, Gill recoiled when she pointed the dirk at him, threatening to drive it through *his* heart.

'No, Eleanor.'

The Samurai's voice was calm and collected as he took the place of her brother. She jumped, snatching back the dirk, aware of whom she was now pointing it at.

'Forgive me, Nori,' pleaded Gill, peeping over the Samurai's shoulder. 'I swear, it was a mistake—I—'

'Gill!' Reece broke in, holding his gaze. 'It was an *error*—on Asai's part.' He turned to Eleanor. 'Your brother simply … got in the way,' he lied, to ease the blow.

Eleanor looked from one to the next, a hint of doubt niggling at her.

'It's true!' Rosalyn jumped in, sensing it.

'*What* is going on?!' Oran demanded, confused.

Then something occurred to Eleanor: *I know*, she thought, turning her attention to Kai. The Servitor would tell her the truth; he had no choice, but to.

'How did you escape?' The urgency in Rosalyn's voice distracted them all, silencing them. Rosalyn approached her daughter, smiling. 'You must tell us,' she added, her tone steady and encouraging. 'How?'

Eleanor gasped, clasping her hand over her mouth. Her eyes then lowered to the weapon still clutched in her hand, realising what she had just tried to do. She could barely take it in. How could she even think it? She raised her teary eyes—the guilt visible as she watched Gill step out from behind Asai, her brother now smiling at her.

'Oh, Gill, I'm sorry.'

''Tis forgotten, Nori, aye?' he said, briefly pulling her into his hold before releasing her, eager to hear of the escape—and to distract her from *that* incident; after all, no harm had been done to her beloved. 'Tell us … *how?*'

With the welcome return of water and food—Eleanor's eyes lit up when her mother gave her a bannock, stuffed with cured meat—a brief description of her escape was then relayed, with the occasional interruption:

Oran shook his head, stunned.

'*Wareeshta* helped you?!' he cried, trying to piece everything together, only to be hushed by Rosalyn, insisting their daughter continue, while encouraging her to eat more. Eleanor went on to tell them about the Urisks, Marcas and Athol, her family shocked to hear the fate of the two young men from their village. But when she unexpectedly mentioned the *Book*, Oran stared at his daughter—the stunned look on his face, prompting her to say;

'Wareeshta *knows* you have it.'

Oran had no idea how long he had stood staring back at Eleanor, hardly believing what she had said, it echoing in his mind, and the potential danger associated with this unwelcomed revelation—despite the Dhampir saving her life.

*"Wareeshta knows you have the book."*

*This is bad*, he thought, glancing over at Nephtys as she playfully nudged the other horses by her side. Whether Greer's horse was teasing or trying to master them, he could not say. He was sure the other High Warlock was missing her by now. *Greer is the least of my worries.* It was then he saw Farrow, his beloved horse a vision of health, where he had been well looked after. A momentary smile appeared on his face, then slipped when his eyes were lured back to Nepthys, and to the leather satchel tied to her saddle where the book was hidden. He would still have to destroy the item, but not until he rid both worlds of the evil spirit inside L'Ordana. *Then* he would gladly discard it.

'The Sorceress is growing weak,' Eleanor went on to reveal.

Oran looked sharp at her. 'Weak, you say?' he replied, with invested interest.

'This is good news,' said Reece, nodding.

'It appears her endless supply of youth has … run out,' Eleanor added. 'Another reason for my escape.'

Reminded of his servant, Lucia, when they lived in Triora, and what L'Ordana had done to her—the image of the young, woman's charred remains seared in his mind—Oran stepped closer to Eleanor. 'You mean … *You?*'

She slowly nodded.

'It seems … *I* was to be her next.'

'But as long as she is without the book … *and* the dagger,' Asai commented, 'her powers are limited.'

'Book? Dagger?' asked Rosalyn, adding her piece, wanting some clarity to their discussion.

'She needs both,' Reece stated, 'if she is to—'

'Do not concern yourself, Rosalyn-san,' said Asai, cutting in. Eleanor's mother did not need to know the horrific details of L'Ordana's methods, to maintain her youthful appearance.

'He is right, Rosalyn,' said Oran. 'The dagger is safely hidden away from its counterpart.'

'You mean this … *book?*' she insisted.

'Aye—and that, too, is quite safe,' he said, winking back.

'From what I understand, she has not mastered it,' Eleanor then stated.

Oran side-glanced his daughter. 'Are you sure?'

She nodded.

'I assumed she would have done so, by now,' he remarked. 'It had been in her "care" for long enough.'

'Not according to Wareeshta,' she said. 'She maintains the Sorceress is desperate, now that she no longer has the book.'

Oran mused over this, for a moment, rubbing his hand over his chin, then scratching it. 'With Magia by her side'—he shook his head, unconvinced—'somehow, I doubt it,' he sneered, casting another watchful eye towards Nepthys.

'She *needs* him,' Eleanor revealed. 'Which is why she fills him with endless lies—to keep him on her side—until he gives her what she wants.'

Oran groaned, knowing what *that* was. 'The Shenn,' he stated, looking at his son.

'She'll not have it,' Gill determined.

'Nor will she have the book,' said Oran, smirking and nodding in agreement with his son. He then took Eleanor with a hardened stare. 'Nor will Wareeshta'—he shook his head, resolved, sealing his statement—'not while it is in *my* possession.'

'But—it is neither yours *nor* theirs to keep,' Eleanor informed them, '… or to destroy, for that matter.'

Everyone stared down at the young woman in bleak silence until Oran, determined not to part with the cursed item just yet, stepped in. 'Then … *who* has that right, Eleanor?'

Defiant, she shook her head in protest.

'I promised I would not betray them,' she hit back, stepping away from him.

Adamant, Oran moved towards his daughter to confront her, only to be stopped by Asai—the Samurai politely lifting his hand, asking for the Warlock's patience; when he bowed, Oran seemed to understand and trust him, as he had done before. With a single nod, the Warlock stepped back.

The great Samurai smiled warmly down into her anxious face. 'Eleanor, my love,' he began—Oran did a double-take on hearing the term of endearment, ignorant of the profound bond between the two—'Time is short for us, here,' he said, casting a glance at the pylons, noting how their shifting had slowed. 'We cannot keep secrets with so much at stake. Therefore, I vow to you, here and now: whomever the task of destroying the book belongs to, I assure you it *will* be so; the honour shall be theirs.'

Placing all her faith in Asai's promise, Eleanor, still carrying an element of guilt, feeling she was betraying her friend, reluctantly turned to Oran, whose eyes flashed between her and the Samurai with enquiry. 'Then … that honour will be … Wareeshta's,' she revealed.

'*What?!*' cried Oran, his face turning crimson, and setting aside Asai's endearment, for now.

'You heard me,' she spat back, her fists clenching and her face set, refusing to be intimidated.

'This cannot be happening,' he moaned, clamping his hand across his forehead. Turning away, his mind provoked by disturbing thoughts, Oran stomped back and forth across their path while casting intermittent looks of disapproval at his daughter.

Angered by her husband's reaction and behaviour towards Eleanor, Rosalyn marched towards Oran, then hesitated, casting a quick eye at the three monoliths. *Stay calm, Rosalyn*, she told herself, reminded of the profound effect their emotions were having on the structures. She took a deep breath.

'We need to listen to her,' she urged, placing her hand on his arm. Oran spun and stared at his wife, for a moment, then glanced at Eleanor. 'Please, Oran,' she quietly added, conscious of how much time had dwindled.

Aware of the insistence in his wife's voice, and the worry in her eyes, Oran nodded.

As Eleanor quickly divulged Wareeshta's fate—and her plans—the group listened intently, then eagerly explained to her the purpose and reasoning behind the monoliths. She looked over at them, gasping when they changed.

'I can't choose until they stop,' said Gill, 'which is why we must remain calm; they are reacting to our emotions, Nori.'

When Eleanor moved to inspect them, she stalled when the eye of a stranger, who had initially gone unnoticed to her, caught her curiosity. When he gave her a faint, awkward smile, she kept glancing at him until it came to Rosalyn's attention, her eye following her daughter's sudden interest.

'Eleanor …'

She turned, hearing her mother's voice.

'This is Daine,' Rosalyn continued, reaching out her hand and inviting the guide back into the group; as he stepped forward, Daine momentarily forgot himself and lifted his hand to take hers, then promptly lowered it again, sensing Oran's *Green-Eyed Monster* watching him.

'We, too, would not be here if it had not been for his help.' Daine and Rosalyn looked at one another—their look lingering again, longer than it should have. Eleanor noticed it. And when he approached her, smiling—his hand extended—it became evident when he drew closer … There was something conspicuous about the stranger.

Titling her head slightly, a frozen expression crept across Eleanor's face when an image entered her mind, taking her back to the horror of the Cordhu Pass. In it, she saw the *Whispering Waters*, where she had been trapped between friend and foe. She saw the hand stretched out to her—L'Ordana's—and looked up into her eyes … and then …

The image faded.

Daine stopped, his uneasy hesitation alerting the others; it was apparent they, too, were conscious of Eleanor's sudden, irrational behaviour. Her striking, steely blue eyes then travelled to meet the guide's anxious look. Lowering her head, eyes fixed, she slowly stepped forward, her intimidating move now causing concern; she was still clutching her dagger, and running her thumb over the sapphire on its pommel again, thinking …

'Eleanor?' As Rosalyn stepped towards her daughter, Eleanor moved away, paying no heed.

She stopped again.

All eyes flicked nervously from one face to another, wondering what Eleanor might do … if anything. And yet, it was inconceivable to suggest or imagine the young woman could cause harm to another soul. But as she held her stance, Daine found himself rooted, unable to take his eyes from her as she maintained her stare, her threatening-like manner similar to that of her grandfather's—only Reece's threats were all too real.

Wrenched from her troubling thoughts, Eleanor jolted, her face displaying a startled look as if she'd seen a ghost. She looked sharply back at Oran, then edged towards him. But when the Warlock moved to meet his daughter, she avoided him, holding her hand up, silently telling him to "halt!"

Frustrated, Oran looked at Rosalyn and Gill; his wife and son shrugged, equally baffled. Eleanor then turned abruptly to face Daine, again—the line between her furrowed brow deep with concentration as she studied him—the dirk still in her grip.

*What is she doing?*

Feeling somewhat threatened, Daine backed off, his nervousness prompting Gill to intervene.

'Nori?' he said, approaching his sister. She failed to hear him. Gill then hesitated, seeing Kai hover between the three pylons, assessing each one. The Servitor looked back at him, and nodded; they had stopped changing.

Mindful of how they would need to press on, and soon, Gill knew he had to break his sister from the unnatural trance-like stare she was holding on Daine.

'Eleanor—we really must—'

When he touched her, she shrugged him off, moving closer to Daine—the guide still backing away from her advance, towards his horse. If only he could …

Oran grunted, watching them, then turned to observe his wife's reaction, only to be met by her steely glare. Inside, Rosalyn was reeling; her husband seemed to be getting too much enjoyment from watching their daughter threaten the guide. But Oran could not help himself and smirked when Eleanor pinpointed her dagger at Daine, nodding to herself. But the Warlock's amusement was short-lived when something flew by Eleanor.

It came from nowhere, catching them unawares—Eleanor taking

the brunt of the brief and unexpected collision.

'On your Guard!' yelled Reece, removing his broadsword, wise to the sound he and Asai had been all too acquainted with. Instantly, the two Dhampir leapt forward, caught up in an unforeseen pursuit.

'Eleanor!' cried Gill.

By the time the others reached her, Eleanor had collapsed.

# Chapter Fourteen

*The Ruins of Moyne*

"I *release you from your bond."*

The long-awaited words spoken to her by her mistress had thrilled Wareeshta, at first. Already, she felt *different*—unleashed. And, with each word still playing out in her mind, it filled her with hope, and the prospects of a happy future—even if it meant living a solitary one; anything was better than the miserable existence she had been forced to endure, as well as the unspeakable unhappiness she had been "required" to enforce on others—innocent victims of L'Ordana's selfish ambitions. And for what? For the want of a power, she was unlikely to gain.

*"But … do not fail me,"* she had then been warned, tarnishing her hopes.

*"I will not fail—"* Her reply had purposely omitted the one word she could not—and would not—vow to the Sorceress:

*"You."*

Things had changed, though—the reasoning, Wareeshta assumed, being the possible loss of more Dhampir; the three L'Ordana had sent to hunt for the girl had failed to return, their failure to do so now causing her great concern for Eleanor's welfare. When frenzy takes over, and coupled with desire …

There was no way of knowing what became of the missing

warriors. However, they were still bonded to the Sorceress, therefore, they *had* to return. Regardless. It still begged the question, though: where were they?

*Could they have been destroyed?* she wondered.

A spark of hope ignited inside Wareeshta. And yet, she dared not think of the likelihood, though had hoped it to be true. But there was still that small, niggling possibility they *would* return—and with Eleanor—*her* "prize" as Turloch so crudely put it.

L'Ordana's patience and desperation were slowly diminishing. The disappearance of more Dhampir warriors had knocked her confidence—and Wareeshta knew this, keeping it to herself, to avoid further suspicion. But trying to maintain some form of decorum was becoming difficult. Also, she had to be careful of what she said—and to whom. With L'Ordana and Magia Nera still constantly playing mind games with one another, she could not risk one slip of the tongue. No, it would create havoc. Still and all, L'Ordana's inner fear had been the key to her freedom. Well, almost; she was not quite out-of-the-woods, yet. But it was the freedom she had yearned for and, finally, it had been granted. And, with the Valkyrie out of the way, it would make things easier.

*"Take these three with you,"* the Sorceress had instructed her. *"I am sure the others will return … eventually,"* she had then added, trying to convince herself, they would.

The newly-appointed warriors waited for their orders, eyes flaring as their adrenaline pumped inside them, throwing eager glances at L'Ordana, their impatience slowly getting the better of them, driving them towards an unstoppable frenzy.

'Look at them, Wareeshta!' she said, smirking, trying to hold her poise, though finding it increasingly challenging. 'Like starving hounds, ready to hunt the fox.' She turned to face her servant. 'Do not allow them to'—she pursed her lips, then glanced back at the three warriors with distaste—'well—you understand my meaning …

Just make sure you return the girl to me … *Alive!*'

'But of course, my lady,' Wareeshta replied, making L'Ordana believe she still had her loyalty.

'And though I have released you,' she went on, 'be mindful of your duty to me, Wareeshta; remember, it was *me,* who protected you from *them.* With Reece and his two companions still out there—*somewhere!*—you are more vulnerable than ever.'

Having heard the underlying threat, Wareeshta's "freedom" now felt short-lived. She felt trapped again. Her only hope now was that Eleanor had found her friends and relayed what had happened. She also hoped the girl would keep her vow, and stick by her. If not … That was something she would deal with, should the worst happen. Despite the underlying doubt nibbling away, she truly believed Eleanor would keep her promise.

She had given her a good head start—at least an hour—and if she had found the horse, she had left for her … A dreadful thought crossed her mind: perhaps that Dhampir … She tried to remember his name: *Marcas?* What if he *had* followed, looking for his horse? What if he *had* found it—worse still—found *her?* All she could do right now was—no—not *pray.* She had never done that; all reference to religion had been long destroyed and banished by her father, Vlad Tepés, long before she had been born. He had renounced all things *good* and *holy,* after the tragic death of his first wife when she had been falsely informed of her beloved's death—the cruel deed a ploy, to bring down his empire. The heartbroken woman fell into a state of deep despair, driving her to the point where she could no longer exist without him. Therefore, believing he had been killed in battle, she drowned herself. So, with no knowledge of the thing created by man—religion—all Wareeshta could do was … *hope.*

'Reece and his companions will gladly destroy you, to take back their petty, little lives,' L'Ordana added, digging her heel further, to maintain her hold on her servant. 'Remember that, too.'

Wareeshta looked straight into L'Ordana's preying eyes and, for a split second, swore she detected a sneer behind them, it then making its way to her thinning lips. Despite the risk of "bumping into" Reece and his two colleagues again, she was willing to take it. Also, there was still a chance the Sorceress would claim the Shenn Amulet; if so, her "services", she knew, would no longer be required, with death following. Either way, her fate was sealed. Her only choice, now, was to choose which one.

Her suspicions had also been roused, by a change in plan: Magia had suddenly announced that there was "another way!"

*"It is a much quicker route,"* he had assured them.

Now they had to back-track towards the west, then go north to Affinshire. She was suspicious of his sudden change in direction, it constantly gnawing away at her. But, for now, she would obey L'Ordana's orders … until she and the three Dhampir were out of sight, where she would then do her best to distract them. It would be challenging; they were young, eager, with a good nose—and quick, too. They would also pick up on the girl's scent, easily. And once that touched, there would be no stopping their fevered chase.

*"Like starving hounds, ready to hunt the fox."*

Disregarding almost everything L'Ordana had said to her—bearing in mind her own vulnerability—Wareeshta's plan was set: the "hunters" chosen to accompany her would, hopefully, become the hunted—assuming Eleanor had found Reece and his companions, and warned them. She hoped, for her sake, her friend had.

She had worked it out as soon as it was suggested the three Dhampir "escort" her. She had intended to choose them herself—preferably the weakest; she had been observing them, with a keen eye, and it soon became clear who they were. After much persuasion, she had eventually convinced the Sorceress to let them go with her, until Turloch—the clever one—intervened, insisting *he* make the choice. And when he had suggested leading the "hunt", as he so brutally stated, followed by a sinister look towards her, it had made her anxious. L'Ordana had teased her by contemplating Turloch's suggestion, however, in the end, the Sorceress had made her decision: Dakkus would go instead, and Turloch would stay, along with the remaining six Dhampir and Magia Nera. She needed to surround herself with her strongest. And now that Magia was free to roam beneath the shadowy sky, his powers were renewed and strong enough to match the remaining Dhampir, combined. But something was amiss; she had sensed it in L'Ordana's secretiveness.

Without a word, Wareeshta turned on her heel, fleeing into the forest's dark domain—with the hungry Dhampir hot on her tail.

The farther they distanced themselves from the Ruins of Moyne, the three Dhampir gradually picked up pace—Wareeshta watching them intensely as they ran through the foliage, ducking and diving, avoiding obstacles without effort. Despite their speed, she had the edge on them though, always keeping one step ahead. But when a shift in the wind crossed their path, carrying with it a familiar scent—*mortal!*—the Dhampir stopped dead. Lifting their noses to meet it, they drew it in deeply, languishing in its sweetness.

Inside, Wareeshta panicked: *Eleanor!* Though faint, she knew the scent was hers. She knew it well; it had clung to her after their many conversations.

The three Dhampir looked sharp—to their left—finding the direction from whence it came. The predators bolted, aroused by the lure of their potential victim—and the succulent bouquet of human blood.

With their senses heightened and speed increasing, by the second, Wareeshta knew she had to act.

Dakkus—the shrewd one—made his move first, followed closely by the other two, who saw him as a leader.

The third—and slowest—stopped briefly for several moments. He raised his head, looking from left to right. He seemed confused. She knew why: another shift in the breeze had distracted him. She sensed it, too—the natural scent of wintergreen, it toying with his nose. She looked ahead of him, while he was distracted, seeing Dakkus and the second one pressing on. *Good,* she thought, aware they had not detected it. Out of range. *Do it now, Wareeshta.* She would have to be swift if she were to catch up with the others, after. Her timing could not have been more precise; just as the lone Dhampir moved to chase after his comrades, she pounced on her unsuspecting victim, catching him unawares. In seconds, it was over. He felt nothing.

Conscious of time, Wareeshta quickly wiped the stain of the Dhampir's death on his clothing before returning her stiletto daggers to the inside of her boots. Then, in a spur-of-the-moment gesture, she leaned over the corpse and carefully placed the Dhampir's decapitated head where it used to be.

'In peace may you repose,' she whispered. She thought it fitting; after all, he was once mortal before being forced into an immoral life of brutality. And though his body would rot, his soul would now rest.

The deed had taken moments, but precious ones she had to retrieve. On she pushed herself, like never before, eventually catching up with the other two. Neither had noticed her absence, failing to glance back to check, too consumed by the enticing scents urging them on, driving their insatiable hunger.

Dakkus still kept the lead. This concerned her. Lately, she had become conscious of a notable change in his behaviour, prompting her to observe *him* more closely. She had also seen it in his eyes; they were bright and alert with intelligence. It appeared the black-skinned Dhampir had become aware of his *place* and was "thinking" for himself, bringing confusion and making him question his origins. She had felt his resentment each time he looked at her—a sure sign of his awareness. Dakkus would be difficult to destroy.

Another sharp breeze shifted, forcing them to stop, much to her relief, giving her back those wasted moments. The two stood like statues, waiting for it to settle. Time was of the essence now; if she hesitated, she would miss her opportunity. Two at the same time would be a challenge, but achievable.

Removing her daggers, she prepared to pounce when Dakkus jolted and turned to face her. She stalled, unsure. *Take him now!* He inhaled deeply, his eyes widening when he found it again—the scent. It was stronger.

'We are near,' he stated, addressing her in his deep, rough voice, and drowning with thirst. It caught her off-guard, that he had "spoken" to her; until now, Dakkus had little to say yet always watched with suspicion. His eyes then dropped, seeing the daggers in her hand. Wareeshta glanced at the other Dhampir; young, irrational and oblivious, his nose was still in the air, drunk on human scent.

'I am ready,' she stated, sauntering towards him, making a point of wielding her daggers, to thwart his suspicions. His eyes then darted about, searching for the third Dhampir. She expected him to question his absence, but, instead, Dakkus did something that unnerved her. Tilting his head, he looked at her, his deadpan stare provoking. Then, rolling his tongue across his upper lip, his eyes lifted and looked over her shoulder back towards the direction the Sorceress would be waiting, perhaps even following them by now. He smirked and grunted—the deep-rooted laugh clouding her reservations. *What are you up to, Dakkus?* But when his eyes dropped, meeting hers again, she saw a purpose in them, alerting her to something else—something altered … and she realised what it was; it was evident, in those hateful eyes as he stared at her—the retaliation for a stolen life—*his*—and the resentment, fuelling the hostile look of revenge … and betraying his intentions. Dakkus wanted payback for his affliction. He spun and ran.

*He's going to kill her!*

Dakkus' speed accelerated as he made his way towards his intended victim. Dread turned to survival instinct as Wareeshta turned on the second Dhampir. With no time to contemplate her actions, she lunged at him, destroying him as quickly and cleanly as the other.

Wasting no time on words, she wiped her blades on the Dhampir's clothing before leaping over him, in her desperate chase to catch Dakkus, scolding herself for not seeing the signs, sooner. If she were not careful, the human weakness in her making would be her downfall.

As she pounded through the forest—her hunter's eyes frantically searching for Dakkus—Wareeshta sensed she was not alone; she felt a black emptiness seeping in as though it were watching her. It seemed to be everywhere, almost suffocating the closer they drew to their target. Nothing stirred, not even a whisper of nature's residents, they having the sense to hide from the unearthly influence lurking in the air.

She then had a sense of height, as though crossing over a hill or mountain, but was unable to see, her vision obstructed by the mass of trees, their towering height over-whelming and dominating.

Wareeshta's nose flared, now catching a mix of odours. Some, she recognised. *Reece and Asai*, she thought, and yet she could not detect the Highlander's scent. But there were others, too; *More humans!* These, mixed with the others, confused her senses. However, there was no mistaking Eleanor's overpowering and alluring scent; it stood out, from the rest.

A flash of steel stole her attention. It seemed to come and go. And when she caught a swift dark movement, she instantly knew what Dakkus was doing.

As he descended the steep incline, Dakkus, with sword in hand, darted from side to side, moving effortlessly through the narrow spaces, between the trees; he had observed Asai using this technique many times to confuse the enemy and avoid being seen. But, despite the trick to "fool the eye", he knew the Samurai would see him.

*He knows where they are*, she realised. Dakkus had also caught their scent. It was the only explanation for his sudden, erratic movements.

Spurred by the desperate need to save her friend, Wareeshta pressed on. Making her way down the steep slope, darting effortlessly between the battalion of trees, she caught sight of the wide clearing in the distance, ahead of her rival.

Disregarding the fact he was outnumbered—and driven by the intoxicating cauldron of odours swarming his senses—Dakkus heightened his pace, planning his moment to strike.

As the seconds dashed by as the clearing rushed towards them, Wareeshta felt the pressure of keeping up with Dakkus as she mimicked his movements. She had never seen speed like it before. It was new and worrying.

Dakkus glanced over his shoulder—the whites of his pale-brown eyes, fiery red. He had seen her. He shifted his direction, narrowly avoiding a tree. But Wareeshta, her heart pounding like never before, persisted, disregarding the danger ahead.

When Dakkus leapt into the clearing, his accelerated speed initially went unnoticed by the group, except for his pursuer. With no thought for her safety—and mere inches away from him now—Wareeshta flung herself into the wide-open space, her eyes firmly locked on the attacker as he prepared to strike his victim. She then hissed—the subtle sound distracting Dakkus, prompting him to make a self-inflicted error: he looked back, catching her resolute stare. But in his misconception, he brushed off Eleanor, unbalancing her; Wareeshta contemplated catching her friend, but kept going, her mind set on killing Dakkus.

'On your guard!' yelled Reece.

Having heard the distinctive hissing sound, Reece and Asai had sprung into action, after catching a glimpse of Dakkus—the Dhampir's unexpected presence throwing the whole ensemble into chaos.

Caught up in the scenario—and one she would never have predicted—Wareeshta found herself in Reece and Asai's company again—the three now united in stopping Eleanor's would-be attacker.

Dakkus became disoriented when he was suddenly faced with the *Paths of Lome* … And yet, he could not stop. That would be suicidal; he would be forced to fight his pursuers, then—especially the Samurai. Now resumed in their puzzling game, the three monoliths bid him *welcome,* daring him to enter one. The Dhampir halted, for a moment, his eyes darting over each one, conscious he was now the hunted—conscious of the grave error he had made—yet heedless of the other he was about to make.

On seeing this, Reece subconsciously reached out, hauling Wareeshta back.

'What are you doing?' she hissed, trying to free herself from his grasp.

'Wait!' he snapped, eyeing Dakkus.

In his error of judgment, Dakkus leapt forward beyond one of the monoliths and disappeared into its tunnel of trees.

Gill and Oran rushed to their sides.

'Oh, no!' cried Gill. 'What if he—'

'It is unlikely he chose the right one,' said Oran.

Gill stared at his father. 'How can you be sure?'

'Have faith Gill,' said Kai, joining them. 'Besides, he is not the *Chosen One*.'

Satisfied, and keeping his grip on Wareeshta, Reece dragged her away from the monoliths.

'Why did you let him go?' she demanded, still struggling within his unyielding grip, glancing back to where Dakkus had disappeared. She then stopped, her eyes wide and eager, glimpsing Eleanor on the ground.

Reece, his anger building, jostled Wareeshta into the reality of the situation she now found herself, refusing to release her. 'Your Sorceress is not here to protect you now,' he sneered, glaring down into the face of the one who had *cursed* him. 'Nor is my granddaughter,' he added through gritted teeth when her desperate eyes glanced at Eleanor again. 'Do not even attempt to speak with her.'

Wareeshta froze, her mouth gaping and eyes wide, woken to Reece's meaning. Unable to break from his hold, she was trapped, vulnerable—and completely at his mercy. She could see revenge in his fevered eyes, knowing he had every right to it, and knowing what he might—*would*—do.

For Reece, this was the opportunity he had waited for. To destroy Wareeshta. And as she stood locked in his grip—with the fear of death in her eyes—it took him all his might to resist the temptation. But he—*they*—had made a vow not to kill her, by their hand. However, he knew there was another way …

'Be my guest,' he said, removing his hold, then extending his arm towards the *Paths*. 'Go on! Follow him …' he urged, smirking from the side of his mouth.

Confused, at first, she frowned at him then looked towards the path Dakkus had "chosen", flinching when she heard it—the chilling, curdling faint cry as it echoed back to her from the void.

'… if you dare,' he added, dragging his look from her as he walked away.

She mulled over his words as her startled eyes flashed to the monoliths again, deciding against the pursuit.

'Dakkus is no longer our concern …' said a voice behind her. 'He is gone.' Wareeshta jolted, then spun to see Oran glaring down at her. 'So—we meet again, *Wareeshta!*'

Unsure of her fate, Wareeshta cowered from the High Warlock. He slowly shook his head. 'Whereas *You* …' he said, towering over her, 'are going nowhere.'

Oran, Gillis and Asai remained on guarded alert, Oran keeping a watchful eye between Wareeshta, Rosalyn and Daine—the guide anxious, expecting an attack from the Sorceress and the dark Warlock. He had been the first to rush to Eleanor's aid when the Dhampir clashed with her, catching her just before she hit the ground. But the young woman was already in the capable loving hands of her mother.

Daine's eyes then wandered to the newcomer, who had driven the creature into the passage towards his demise. There was something familiar about her; perhaps she reminded him of someone else. It was clear she knew Reece though no friendship existed between them, judging by their heated discussion. He frowned, frustrated, it niggling on his memory, and yet, for some reason, it disturbed him. His brows shot up when her eyes found his. Wareeshta held him with a knowing stare—the look then thwarted by a voice.

'Thank you, Daine!' said Rosalyn, luring him from the Wareeshta's gaze.

He shrugged, throwing a cautious glance at Oran, then back to her, and smiled, it slipping from his face, feeling her husband's jealousy burning into him. *Is it that obvious?* he asked himself, trying, with great difficulty, not to look at Rosalyn in "that" way as she tended to her daughter—the reluctance on his face making it more obvious.

'I was the closest to her,' he casually returned. 'Is she … all right?'

Their eyes rested on each other for several long seconds—the tender moment witnessed by Oran, and when Rosalyn smiled back at Daine, there was something in it that made the Warlock's heart sink; it was clear the shared look between his wife and the guide revealed something he did not want to envisage—like an unspoken passion. He wondered if they had … He dismissed the idea. *No. Rosalyn would never betray me—not like that.* Though he could not blame her if she had. He felt envious of them—the envy turning to guilt and self-blame for his absence. He now regretted disobeying the Elliyan, back then. And yet, on reflection … *I was forced. I had no choice.* But he was determined not to lose his wife to another man, and as much as he wanted to take his anger out on the guide and run him through with his sword—he relaxed his grip on the hilt—he realised it would achieve nothing. No, it would only drive her away, further into his arms. *What have you done, Oran Shaw?*

Seeing Eleanor on the ground, Asai remained rooted, though was torn between love and duty; constant in his observations of their surroundings, and how vulnerable they were, he cast, at intervals, a concerned look at Eleanor, sighing with relief when she found her footing. She looked up at him, smiled and nodded, silently assuring him she was "fine."

'Are you hurt?' Rosalyn asked, checking her over.

Eleanor smiled. 'I am all right, Maw, don't fuss,' she returned, dismissing the incident, though unaware of what had made her stumble—Dakkus' presence going undetected, at first. She then turned to Daine, her cheeks flushed with embarrassment, and thanked him. The guide nodded in return but was also relieved the incident had distracted the girl from her intense scrutiny of him earlier—at least, for the time being.

Conscious of his ongoing concern, Eleanor's eyes flashed to Asai. She smiled again, reassuring the Samurai she *was* unharmed. But as she moved to be with him, she hesitated and slowly turned, now aware of the familiar yet unexpected presence of another.

Eleanor's face lit up when she saw Wareeshta smiling awkwardly back at her—the Dhampir continuously conscious of the intimidating company she was in now, her eyes sweeping nervously from one to the other. It made her uneasy, not knowing what their plans for her were—if any. But when her eyes met with Asai's, the Samurai's deadpan look said it all: he would gladly kill her, to have a normal life with Eleanor. At first, she failed to understand why he or Reece had not followed through with their vengeance. A glance at Eleanor then answered her question when her friend nodded at her, her look soft yet confident. Wareeshta then knew …

*She made them promise!*

Despite the urge, Asai remembered his vow, and looked at

Reece—the two thinking the same thing while finding it difficult to fight the temptation. Asai grunted to himself. *If it were not for Eleanor…*

It was evident by their glowering that Wareeshta knew what they were thinking, despite her friend's promise. She wanted to run—she contemplated the risk—then stalled when Eleanor's voice finally called out, thrilled to see her new-found friend again, while letting the others know of their unlikely friendship.

'*Wareeshta!*'

The Dhampir's face lit up, hearing the only voice that spoke her name with genuine warmth, her expression then altering when her eyes met the warning in Asai's.

To everyone's surprise, Eleanor ran to her friend, throwing her arms around her, making the Dhampir uncomfortable at the sudden outpouring of emotion being showered upon her. She drew back, holding Wareeshta at arms-length.

'How are you here? *How* did you—'

'She released me—from her bond.'

Eleanor gasped. 'You mean—you are *free?*'

Momentarily forgetting the inquisitive and suspicious eyes on her, Wareeshta nodded with enthusiasm. She grinned, lavishing in Eleanor's warmth, and happy to be reunited with the young woman, for more than one reason.

'You know what this means?' said Eleanor.

'*Da!* I—' Wareeshta stopped short and narrowed her eyes.

'Don't worry, my friend,' said Eleanor, 'You *are* safe, here. They'll not harm you.' She smiled and winked.

But the Dhampir remained quiet, regarding her friend; she had detected something deep within Eleanor's dilating pupils, her perception telling her she had seen it before. Her nose twitched. Gradually, the smile faded to a look of grave concern.

'Why do you look at me like that?' asked Eleanor, drawing her head back, frowning.

Wareeshta stepped back, bringing further attention to her curious conduct. Then, circling her friend, the Dhampir scrutinised her clothing. She hesitated, noticing a small tear in Eleanor's skirt, at the base of her thigh, just above her knee.

Wareeshta looked up, sharp. Though Eleanor's face was still flushed, her cheeks were now inflamed.

'*Eleanor?*' There was an urgency in the Dhampir's tone.

The tension was mounting as the others moved towards Wareeshta, suspicious of her unsettling behaviour as she studied the tear in Eleanor's skirt, her lips slightly parting, in deep concentration. Eleanor leaned over, noticing it. Slowly inching the fabric above her friend's knee, Wareeshta's expression changed; she stiffened when she saw where the dark blood had stained the underskirt. In an unexpected move, she grabbed Eleanor's hand; it was cold—like ice—beneath the redness of her skin.

The group rushed towards Eleanor when Wareeshta tore the piece of clothing away, tossing it aside. They stopped when the Dhampir recoiled, staring wildly at Eleanor's leg. A laceration—no more than an inch long—was visible, and already swelling with inflammation.

'I must have caught it on a branch,' Eleanor remarked, shrugging.

However, Wareeshta had a clear recollection of something similar—something ominous. Panic set in, and though she tried to contain it, her tone betrayed her distress.

'His blade!' she stated, looking up at Reece—the look of terror in her eyes now visible when they darted between Asai and Oran.

Their eyes widened. They knew.

'The—the what?' said Gill, feeding off their mounting stress as they stared down at his sister with a look of dread.

Rosalyn drew closer. 'What do you mean?'

Wareeshta stared into their bewildered faces, searching for the right words … but they would not come.

'Tell me!' Rosalyn pressed, glaring at the Dhampir. When Wareeshta lowered her eyes, holding her silence, Rosalyn looked at her daughter, her mouth gaping in disbelief as she observed the progressive change in Eleanor's outward appearance: her skin was losing the rush of youth as a waxy hue spread its sickness over it—the darkening veins beneath its pallor pulsating as beads of fevered perspiration began to trickle down her forehead.

'Maw …' said Eleanor, her voice slow and notably hoarse. 'I … don't feel—'

Suddenly, Eleanor was surrounded by her loved ones. Something was wrong—desperately wrong—the strain of worry etched on their faces.

Wareeshta lifted her hands as though admitting defeat, then shook her head, her unspoken display of helplessness warning the others.

A hand grasped her shoulder, pulling her away. Oran stared at his daughter, then, turning his attention back to Wareeshta, growled at her.

'Tell me it's not true!' he snapped.

Wareeshta parted her lips to speak, but nothing came out. All she could do was stare back at the Warlock. It was enough.

'Oran?' begged Rosalyn, her lip quivering, not wanting to believe what her intuition was trying to tell her—warn her.

Asai stepped in. '*Dakkus!* His blade was coated with venom.'

Daine and Rosalyn threw a second glance, shocked by what they were hearing.

'*Who? What?*' asked Daine.

'Magia coated their swords with his venom,' said Reece. 'Eleanor has been struck.'

'Wha—what does that mean?' said Rosalyn, her instincts confirming what she already knew, deep down. Oran looked at his wife and son. He could not say it, let alone think of the outcome. Rosalyn shook her head. 'Don't!' she whispered, feeling the lump rise in her throat. But as he opened his mouth to speak, to comfort her, she raised her hand, stopping him. 'Don't say it!'

Eleanor stared back at her friend, her eyes widening, seeing the distress in Wareeshta's deep brown eyes—then in all their faces as everyone stared at her, speechless.

She shook her head, fraught with concern.

'Tell me—what—' Eleanor flinched and reached for her throat, her sharp intakes of breath alarming the group as she gulped for air, struggling to breathe.

'Do something!' yelled Rosalyn.

Behind her, Wareeshta could now feel the weight of their concern pressing down on her. She jerked when Asai grabbed her—the Samurai then releasing his hold when Oran intervened, gripping her by the throat. 'You mean to tell me'—he swallowed, his chest heaving—'my daughter will become one of *you?!*' he shouted, his face flaring.

Wareeshta, struggling under the Warlock's hold, shook her head, then pulled away from him. '*Nu!*'

'Then *what* will happen to her?!' Gill pleaded, his panic taking over.

Wareeshta hung her head in remorse.

It was all they needed to know.

# Chapter Fifteen

*The Ruins of Moyne*

He observed her every movement while she paced about, checking and re-checking all was in order before they left, while occasionally glancing over her shoulder towards the ancient cemetery. She was agitated—eager to go—yet he sensed her reluctance until she knew Wareeshta and the three Dhampir had returned with the girl.

Magia's eyes remained transfixed by her, accompanying her movements, trying to read her thoughts. He could barely make out her features as she kept her head low, her mind in deep reverie while constantly tugging at her hood. This obsessive behaviour had truly exposed her weakness. He mused over it until it finally dawned on him: *she knows her time is running out.*

Hovering about near the sepulchre, he maintained his surveillance of her, pondering what to do … when their first meeting came back to him. How different she was now, compared to then. An innocence ruined. And who was to blame for it …?

She had been a young girl—a child—full of goodness and vitality as she held on to her mother's protective hand. It was the first time he had seen her smile, capturing him instantly before her mother drew her away. But that brief smile from his memory of her suddenly morphed into one of distraught when, years later, she had witnessed the wrongful execution of her mother, at the stake.

*"Witchcraft!" they* had said—the allegation—once voiced—leading to only one outcome.

*No!* he inwardly argued, as though he were still defending her mother's honour to the accusers. *She had simply been gifted—and it had been a true "gift"—a precious one she had handed down to her daughter.*

But those voices from the past were long gone—as was their victim.

A fragment of guilt then brought with it an element of regret, leading him to acknowledge his wrongdoing.

*I am to blame. I should have saved her mother.*

But what was done was done. Regrets were of no benefit to him now. They would only expose a weakness—one he refused to bow to.

It was not long after that when she herself had suffered the same accusations, *they* sentencing her to a watery grave. However, it had been a master stroke—his rival sending the creature to save the girl before fleeing with her—the two then disappearing into the night. He grunted. *But you were always good at that, Oran—running away*. Even now, he still resented his rival for taking her; he had wanted her for himself.

For a long time, he had searched for them, with no results, mourning over the lost years and the precious time he could have had with her … until one day—when something lured him back to Triora, Italy—back to his home—the Realm of Meddian. And it was there, by mere chance, their paths crossed, again—seven years later …

The woman he had known as *Kristene*, had grown bored with her life. Triora no longer held her interest as Oran whiled away his time with other interests, in his vain attempt to live a normal existence among those who would accept and humour him with their lavish and wily ways.

Magia smiled, recalling their first encounter in Triora: she had stumbled on a dark, cobbled street, after looking over her shoulder; she must have perceived someone was following her. Regarded as the *Village of Witches*, the little town of Triora had its superstitions, and the local women were wary.

He had taken her by surprise when she stumbled, falling into the safety of his arms. She had thanked him gracefully and smiled, holding his look. For an instant, he thought she had recognised him, from when she was a child, but realised she had been taken in by his unusual eyes when they glowed back at her. He had then insisted on taking her to a small *Taverna* for a refreshment after her little "stumble", to recover—and to distract her from her boredom.

They had sat, eating *bruzzo* cheese with *focaccia* bread, and drinking wine from the *Cirque Terre* coastal region. He indulged her with compliments. Her long, dark hair fell naturally and gleamed, complimenting her hazel eyes. It was evident, she took pride in her appearance; her skin was like alabaster—flawless—and her lips … every time she had parted them to sip her wine, their moistness enticed him in.

He remembered it well. He had never forgotten her.

As well as her beauty, the talented "gift" she had inherited from her mother emanated through every pore, it resulting in an unwavering passion to take her under his wing. She was bored, craving some distraction—and he had been more than willing to give it.

That first meeting then led to another. He had watched her from a distance, carefully timing and planning their second encounter. Over time—and while Oran was otherwise occupied with his wealthy cronies—their secret meetings became frequent, taking place under the veil of darkness and, at times, stretching out into the dead of night.

Secretive and wary, at first, she eventually warmed to him as he listened to her with interest—she, lavishing in the attention, he growing conscious of it with each rendezvous. Gradually it had become no effort to him as she eased herself into his confidence and trust. He had seen it in her smouldering eyes when she shared her deepest thoughts; they danced when her pupils dilated—no longer staring at him with suspicion. At last, she had dropped her guard. That was when he knew he had her—and would finally *own* her.

He had begun by showing her simple tricks of magic and, in return, she amused him by mimicking them without effort. But through obsession, the simplicity of his conjuring soon metamorphosed into something sinister, inviting her further into his dark world. And she welcomed it.

Throughout their time together, he had vowed never to reveal his true identity. No, he wanted her completely, therefore, avoiding the risk. Besides, she had never questioned it, or the timing of their secret meetings—the blanket of night serving them well, for their own reasons.

He then recalled, with distaste, the moment he told her he *wanted* her: she had stared at him with disgust, repelled by the mere thought of it—while he had regretted it the moment the words fell from his mouth, his insatiable thirst for her exposing his flaws.

"There is another!" she had hurdled back at him before disappearing again into the dark, winding streets.

It was deplorable—*a fiasco!* How could he imagine that someone as beautiful as she would have ever contemplated it? And when she ran from him, he had watched, silently begging her to look back—"just once!"—as she faded from view. But the request had been denied. And, although she had offended him, he still longed for her return.

Days passed after her disappearance, with the certainty he had lost her, forever. At first, he was concerned; the rumours had escalated in the town and he feared for her safety. Once in the clutches of those who believed in the sinister goings-on, there would be no reprieve. And yet, something told him he would have known it, had she been incarcerated. He had almost resolved himself to the fact that she had gone—left Triora—or worse, returned to the arms of the "other one".

But the appetite for more knowledge of the *Black Arts* eventually lured her back to him. She could not help herself. But when she returned, something in her demeanour had changed dramatically; something distinctive—almost offensive.

She had sent word to him for a meeting. He recalled her entrance, when she sauntered into the little *Taverna*: a worrying silence had come over the place. Those present had noticed it, too; it impelled them to pause and stare when she entered, her mere presence intimidating, commanding a reluctant, and unwanted, audience. He then knew he would have to be careful. They both would.

She had sat before him with a new look of arrogance in her eyes, fingering the rim of the glass of *Grappa* brandy he had ordered for her. No words had passed between them, at first. And while he scrutinised her face, she raised the glass to her mouth, letting it linger there before throwing it back, in one. Then, placing the empty glass on the table—her eyes penetrating his—she slowly lifted her chin as if allowing him to admire her. It was then he had sensed the underlying malevolence stirring within her soul, it overwhelming him when she leaned across the table, moving closer, before insisting:

"Teach me more!"

Despite it, though, he had been pleased to have her back and eventually bowed to her request; besides, he knew—had he refused—she would have persisted. But *he* was the one to decide when the time was right, to show her the true art of *Black Magic.* And so, the agreement had been made.

"They are truly exquisite!" she had later remarked when he finally produced the *Book* and the *Dagger*—the two items, when brought together, powerful … and fatal.

There had been a wanting in her; he had seen it in the way her hand delicately touched the dagger's onyx grip and how she had handled the weapon, by lifting it slowly to inspect it further, her eyes taking in every inch of its curious make.

"What do they mean?" she had enquired—almost breathless—while staring at the long blade, admiring the deep engravings: the unorthodox cross and *Order of the Dragon*—both symbols united, by the tip of the dragon's tail touching the cross.

"Together, they are *one*," he had explained.

But when she turned her attention to the book—she had gasped when her eyes fell on its ox-blood, leather-bound cover—a worrying doubt came over him. He had watched how she touched it, letting her fingers delicately trace over the surface where the same dragon had been seared into the hard leather. He had told her—should she stare at it long enough—its tail would move. And like a child, who had been given its first toy, her eyes had widened, anticipating the thrill of *seeing* it, and discovering what it could do. With each touch, each caress, it created a new possibility, and as her eyes feasted on its devilish cover, it exposed her craving to have it, warning him of the mistake he had made. But, by then, it was too late; from the moment her eyes had met with the book, she was obsessed.

And though the dragon had never moved for her, she indulged herself in the book's pages, turning them over and over, trying to unlock its sinister secrets, imagining the powers she could never comprehend. As each word rose from the page to greet her, she consumed them one by one, but with little understanding of them. At times, he had been reluctant to reveal what *he* knew, but her incessant powers of persuasion had played on his weakness for her. Even then—and at such a young age—she knew what she was doing. Yes, she had taken advantage—by preying on *him*.

"Tell me—what is the secret of immortality?" she had coaxed with her charm. But he had resisted. "Show me … and I shall never leave you, Magia."

He recalled how she smirked at his eager response to her empty promise. Her powers had grown such, he denied her nothing.

Almost.

She had been thrilled at the thought of prolonging her youth, showing no remorse for the consequences: the price of another life.

"You must remember, *Bella*, the dagger is only for the *purpose*, not the pleasure. And the book—only your guide, should you—"

"Only for my *immortality*?" she had interrupted, disregarding his warning.

"That is all. Nothing more," he had persisted, wary of her.

"But why do I feel incomplete? Something is amiss … inside me. I feel *its* absence."

That was when he knew the tables had turned … to *his* advantage, realising he had to act upon it. He had wanted to erase the thoughts and images of the "other one" from her mind. He had wanted her to forget—to forget Oran Shaw. It was a certainty, and she had been the willing candidate, it igniting his plan.

It had been the perfect plan, too.

He had called upon the dormant spirit of a great Sorceress, Eryian, a true witch whose immoral wrongdoings—caused by the influence of necromancy, and a forbidden love affair—led her to be executed by the Elliyan. If it had not been for the request made on him by her *lover*, to intervene, the great Sorceress would have been no more. An agreement, therefore, was struck between himself and the *lover*: he would save Eryian's spirit, so she and her *lover* could be together again in the future—when it was deemed safe. And so, in her dying moments, before the pyre consumed her melting flesh, he had called on the book's influence to retrieve her flailing soul—without the Elliyan's knowledge. But, when envy set in, he went back on his word—the evil inside prompting him to steal her spirit, for his own purpose.

Hidden away from the world, until such time, he had waited, then seized the opportunity when Kristene came back into his life. *She was the perfect host*, he recalled, thinking at the time. Then, with her consent, he proceeded with his plan, locking away the young woman, *Kristene*, banishing her to the doldrums of her mind—and re-awakening the stolen spirit into the heart and body of its new vessel. The transition had been successful, and the ease with which *Kristene's* young body had accepted its new host, stimulated his motivation.

'*Magnifica!*' he had described the transformation, revelling in his sinister motive.

But there had been one little matter to consider: her name. No—he could no longer call her Kristene; nor could he call her Eryian. That would have aroused suspicion—had the Elliyan gotten wind of it.

'I shall call you … L'Ordana … after my *Madre!* She would have been proud.'

She had finally become *his* … or so he had thought; spurred by the bounds of her own prudence, L'Ordana quietly drew her plan against him.

He had admired her shrewdness and ability to sustain herself, and imagined the faces of the Elliyan, should they meet again—which was likely, for she had an agenda. Despite it, he had been captivated by his creation, clinging to her every word, her enduring charm then ultimately leading him to her bed. But it had been a ploy, to learn more about the book, and he—the fool—had given in to her wants and needs.

He had trusted her to use it—to a degree—and she, in return, convinced him she would never abuse its power. And when she had expressed interest in it, he showed her his Warlock's amulet, suppressing the urge to reveal the enigma behind its true purpose. When her powers had strengthened, her time with him grew less, making him suspect the "relationship" had almost ended. He had served his purpose.

His suspicions had finally come to the fore, the night he took it upon himself to follow her back to the great house she had shared with the "other one". He had watched over it, witnessing the evil envelop its foundations, and throwing it into chaos after the murder of the young, servant girl.

That was the last time he saw her. She had fled into the night, along with his amulet, the dagger and his precious book, leaving behind her trail of destruction—and Oran. Her motives had become evident: to preside with animosity over their world—and the world of mortals, while his agenda was to retrieve his possessions—then destroy what he had created.

Years went by before they met again. As her small army of warriors accumulated, traces of her presence had become prominent, by the trail of ruin they had left behind, his senses detecting the familiar aroma of death. From all appearances, in her determination to triumph, he had come to recognise her "mark of ruin", following it—with discretion being his priority.

*"Distance yourself from mortals."*

He had tried to live by his own advice after his experience with her; despite it, however, it had been the one thing he could not avoid—not since the battle of Wallachia when Tepés changed all that, forcing him into his deprived world of the *undead*. No. He could never distance himself from mortals, his unquenchable thirst tempting him into their company, for the few moments it took to satisfy his needs, then isolating himself once more.

Always a *need*—not a *want*.

It had been one of those "occasions" where he had not "fed" in days. The terrain he had found himself in had been that of a wilderness, and it repulsed him to feed on wild animals; their blood made him ill. But it had been by good fortune he happened upon a small cottage, in an isolated part of the land.

At first, he had taken it to be unoccupied, but when he turned to leave, he had caught the scent of a young female on his nose; subtle yet evident. He had mused over the mortal's choice of abode; it had been a bleak and desolate place. All the better for him. And when her scent grew stronger, enticing him, it had driven him to an unavoidable frenzy.

He had taken himself to the shadows of the trees, surrounding the run-down cottage, waiting patiently for dusk. Some livestock roamed freely in the yard. He knew they had sensed him, by their restlessness. He had watched his impending victim with wanton eyes, assuming her to be alone, after a quick perusal of her lodgings, perhaps to see what had disturbed the animals. But when he had detected the faint hint of another female—a mother? Daughter? Sister?—it heightened his vigilance of the mortal.

While the young woman had pottered about, oblivious to his presence, he determined when to strike; when she had ventured out from the yard and into the woods, to retrieve some firewood, his insatiable thirst impelled him to. When he prepared to leap, something had forced him to stop: a threatening stillness, compelling him to look around. But he had been unable to ignore his craving, and when he turned his attention back to the mortal, she had disappeared.

He had stepped forward, daring to risk being seen, his hungry, red eyes darting, looking for her. He thought she had retreated to her cottage, then stirred when he had caught her scent again, it barely detectable. Something else had stirred his senses: that of the other female, their distinct odour mingling with the woman's, confusing him. He had perceived a threat of danger, it encroaching on his space. When his perception had not betrayed him, he turned to flee; but his escape was prevented, by his unexpected imprisonment.

He had raised his head in an attempt to call upon his powers, to destroy the creatures circling him. But his powers had weakened, due to his lack of nourishment. He had been rendered defenceless, by the familiar and dominant presence when they came into view.

*She* had found *him*.

"Kristene!"

He recalled how she hesitated when she stepped out from the

sanctum of the surrounding forest and stared at him, bewildered by his address of her—it then followed by her shaking her head, and the stark reply as she sauntered towards him:

"I am L'Ordana, Magia Nera. And this shall be the last time your path will cross with *Kristene*."

How long she had imprisoned him, at the time, he could not recall. She had toyed, punished and almost starved him, letting him feed off the rats that had regularly visited his holding, deep within the bowels of a citadel—below her chambers. But not once did he recoil.

It was when she had stumbled on the other Warlock, Oran—sent by the Elliyan to search for, and destroy her—she thought herself victorious, having two Warlocks under her rule.

She had preyed on the life she had once shared with Oran, trying to charm him, by lavishing him with extravagant things, tempting him, hoping he would bow to her wants: to extract the information she needed, regarding their amulets. But he never succumbed. No. Oran was clever. He had always known that, despite their hostility towards each other. In his shrewdness, Oran had befriended three of her prized warriors, playing on their resentment of her until he persuaded them to help him escape. It had been another cunning move by his rival—and she had undeniably underestimated him.

Yes, L'Ordana's error of judgment had been the key to what he knew would lead to her downfall.

L'Ordana's continuous shuffling, as she paced back and forth, snatched Magia back to the present. She was alone now—no loyal servants by her side. And she was agitated, wringing her hands together—on edge. He saw her glance over to where the Dhampir were being briefed, by Turloch. She was becoming more reliant on them, and soon she would rely on him. Completely. The growing signs of uncertainty and self-doubt were evident in her whole demeanour. He could smell her vulnerability from where he stood. A part of him resented everything about her, and yet another part pitied her state; after all, he did love her—once. And, although he would never openly admit it, he was to blame. He quickly shrugged it away, thinking it was time *he* preyed on her weaknesses.

Magia regarded the six remaining Dhampir; he knew they were restless, now that they were conscious of their missing counterparts. If the others failed to return, too … He mused over that; they were still bonded to her. *They may have been destroyed.* It was the only logical explanation and, if so … by whom?

Magia looked sharp when Turloch strode by his place of survey. The most prominent one—with his long, white hair and dull, amber skin—had taken it upon himself to take charge of the remaining Dhampir. He was not to be trusted.

L'Ordana approached the edge of the cemetery, staring into its far reaches, still anxiously watching and waiting for the return of Wareeshta and the other three.

*What is taking you so long, Wareeshta?* she thought. They would have to move quickly—if they were to reach the place Magia Nera suggested: the Gap of Lome. *It had better be the quicker route.* Everything was ready now. They were prepared to leave.

As he regarded her, Magia realised he had three choices: One: to lend a hand in her lust for power. He had the means to do so. Just a small matter of reclaiming his amulet from her—an effortless task; she kept it on her person, at all times. At least he knew where *that* was. His book, on the other hand, was another matter. Two: he could render her powerless and destroy her. But not while the six Dhampir remained nearby. *Too risky.* His third—and final—choice was more appealing: he could abandon her. She would not survive without him. He knew that. It would be the simplest solution—to let her be the cause of her destruction. Time was pressing on him to choose …

In his mind he tossed the dice; *Uno … Due … Tre …*

It was decided.

Staring at her, from behind, he grinned.

She failed to hear his approach.

# Chapter Sixteen

*The Paths of Lome*

'This is all *your* doing!' yelled Rosalyn as she clung to Eleanor, her daughter weakening with the dwindling of every precious moment.

Oran turned to discover his wife's words had been catapulted at *him,* with pure indignation. And as she stood glaring at him, her tears of hate married with dread, fearing she was about to lose her daughter, the Warlock could see something deeper in her look: resentment, it stabbing him in the heart.

'Aye! *Your* fault, Oran Shaw. You have brought all this upon your family—along with all this … *death!*' Stunned, he stared at her, his mouth partially open, unable to respond. 'Aye, Oran!' she persisted as if he had failed to hear her the first time. 'It is because of *you* … I stand to lose both my children.'

The High Warlock stood helpless, his eyes then lowering, staring at the young, innocent soul being cradled in her mother's arms, looking wretched and defenceless. He was torn. Emotions were running high on a wave of tension as it continued to mount, ready to crash down on them all.

*Damn this place!* he thought.

'Save her,' spoke a calm but firm voice, its owner's mind restless as they toiled over a desperate—but possible—solution.

The company turned at once to see Asai approach Wareeshta. The Dhampir stepped back from the Samurai's advance, shaking her head, her eyes pleading mercy, knowing what he was asking her to do.

'*Save* her!' This time, he was adamant, his overbearing presence pressing down on Wareeshta; she flinched when he placed his hand over the hilt of his katana.

'I—I do not think I can—'

'You can—and you *will!*' he demanded, gritting his teeth, his eyes burning as he gripped the hilt, his knuckles white and his hand shaking from the tension of his hold on the weapon. 'Or I shall "dispatch" you,' he added, his callous usage of the Valkyrie's term for "kill" letting Wareeshta know he would do so, regardless of the consequences.

Reece moved to Asai's side in support of his colleague's demand, followed by Gill and Oran as the Samurai prepared to draw both his weapons.

Wareeshta gasped. 'Destroy me, Asai—and Eleanor will surely die!' she retorted, purposely using her friend's name to play on the Samurai's ripening emotions. '*Then* what shall you do? True—your "life" will be restored to you—but for what? To live it without her?'

Asai recoiled as Wareeshta's words struck him to the core. She was right; he could not live without Eleanor. The Samurai turned to Reece for guidance, but was met with a look of confusion; his colleague was also at a loss. Asai then glanced around at the other faces staring back at him, equally confounded. Regarded as the "logical" one—the one with the solution—Asai knew he was going about it the wrong way, his heightened emotions and feelings for Eleanor, dulling his senses. He looked down at the woman he would now die for; it was tormenting him to watch her struggle in her fight against the venom, fully aware of what it was doing to her, its lethal poison ravaging her body.

Perceiving the inevitable, Asai turned back to meet Wareeshta's anxious stare.

'It seems death is to be the victor, here,' he said, trying to maintain his decorum. 'Only to be dragged out, delayed by this cruel twist of fate.' He stepped closer to the Dhampir, returning his weapons to their place, then held out his hands, in a pleading gesture. 'Then I ask you, with whatever goodness remains in my heart'—he stopped, then bowed—'no, I *implore* you, to *try* and save her. She cannot survive for much—'

'No!' Oran broke in, stepping between them. 'I will not let you touch her! I'll not have my daughter become one of *you!* I won't allow it! She is—'

'Not *your* daughter!'

A harrowing silence shrouded the group as they prepared themselves for the Warlock's reprisal against the Samurai's heart-wrenching remark. The usually calm and private warrior was determined they would try any means to save his Eleanor—with or without the consent of those equipped to do so.

Oran's eyes glazed over, stunned, as reality was hurdled at him yet again. He knew he was not Eleanor's father; her real father had died in a mortal battle when she was a few months old. But he had willingly taken her under his wing, loved her as his own. His heart swelled each time she called him "Paw." It was *he* who had held her hand when she was frightened, *he* who had trained her to use her dirk. Filled with guilt and shame, his heart sank. The solemn expression on his face now told a different story; he felt defeated by those around him. Even the guide, he knew, without the measure of a glance, was judging him, too. His eyes travelled to Kai for support, but the Servitor shook his head, unable to intervene.

*Even you know I am at fault here*, Oran thought.

'Forgive me, Oran-san,' said Asai, lowering his head out of respect. 'I spoke too harshly. It is not my custom to offend.'

'There is nothing to forgive,' he returned, glancing over at Rosalyn. 'Nor did you—'

'You have *my* consent, Wareeshta,' Rosalyn broke in, her face stern, throwing her husband a harsh look, warning him not to go against her. He had no intention of doing so.

'Aye! And mine,' added Gill. 'Do it! Do whatever it takes.'

Wareeshta moved cautiously towards Eleanor—the young woman now falling in and out of consciousness—while her mother murmured words of encouragement in her daughter's ear, to keep her focused, and awake.

Rosalyn pressed her lips together, fighting off the tears as she looked down at Eleanor's dishevelled state: her skin was translucent and waxen; her veins pulsed and writhed as they turned a deep shade of purple beneath her skin, where the poison was manipulating her blood. Heavy beads of sweat now appeared on her brow, trickling down her face as the fever took hold; in her vain attempt to keep her cool, Rosalyn blew softly on her daughter's brow while dabbing them away with the corner of her shawl. Beside her, Rave crouched on all fours, whimpering—the hound's sixth sense working overtime, aware of something sinister happening inside her mistress.

'I can … but try,' Wareeshta appealed to her gathering audience. What they were asking of her held a great risk. But she had to try—for her friend's sake. And should Eleanor die …?

*"Save her!"* The Samurai's heart-felt plea rang in her mind. *I must,* she thought, glancing at the anxious faces staring at her. *If not for me, then … for them.*

Wareeshta forced a smile at Eleanor, then lifted her shoulders slightly, in silent appeal to her friend. Unable to speak, though conscious of what was happening, Eleanor blinked her approval.

Beneath her skin, the venom was now taking momentum; it coursed through Eleanor's veins, meandering like a snake as it worked its way with purpose—the coming of death, its solemn overture announcing the beginning of its imminent arrival—and alerting Wareeshta of the impact of what she was about to do, despite her reluctance. And yet, she knew she had to … no matter what.

As the heat of her blood intensified, Eleanor could feel the slow progression of pain making itself known, affecting her muscles, making them spasm. She arched her body within her mother's hold as it gripped. She tried to speak, but her throat had swelled, making it difficult for her to swallow. Her eyes widened, her struggle now visible, causing her great distress.

'Be on your guard!' warned Reece, imagining what was to come. 'We must give them room. And remain alert—there could be another attack.' His eyes then met Wareeshta's. With a subtle yet determined nod, he gave his approval, too, in the hope that the "creature" who had done him wrong could redeem herself, by saving his granddaughter's life. Yes, he would gladly sacrifice his chance of having his mortality restored, as long as Eleanor survived. And despite his scepticism, where the dead resided, Reece made a despairing plea to his wife: *Do not let our granddaughter die, Onóir.*

Everyone, except Rosalyn and Asai, readied themselves, protecting Eleanor while Wareeshta worked up the courage to battle against the lethal enemy ravaging her friend.

Before he left her side, Eleanor slowly edged the dirk towards Gill. He took it, his eyes firmly fixed on hers. A solemn moment passed between the siblings—one of hidden dread, and the fear that they would never see one another again.

'I'll mind it for you, Nori. You will need it … after.' He smiled, attempting to keep her spirits alive. Then kneeling beside her, he placed a tender kiss on her cheek; it was burning with fever. 'Fight, Nori. *Fight it!*' he said, his teeth gritted with purpose, spurring her on, before leaving her to mark his defence. As she watched him walk away, through the blur of her failing vision, Eleanor could already feel her brother's absence. It terrified her.

When Asai motioned to Rosalyn to move aside from her daughter, she glared at him, reluctant to leave Eleanor's side. She wanted—*needed*—to be with her—even if it meant to the end.

'Trust me, Rosalyn-dono!' he said, with urgency.

Putting her faith in the Samurai—and the Dhampir who had cursed him and Reece—Rosalyn let go of Eleanor and released her into Asai's protective hold, knowing he would give his life for her daughter.

Whispering in her ear, Asai instructed Eleanor to hold him as tight as her waning strength would allow. He held her arms firmly; and though she felt the agony of his loving grip, she did not cry out.

Before giving his consent to Wareeshta, to proceed, the Samurai leaned over Eleanor and quietly whispered something to her. Reece glanced over his shoulder and smiled, hearing him.

'*Itsumo aishiteru!*' he promised, telling her he would "always love her!"

Unable to reply, Eleanor simply smiled, then slumped in his arms.

With a sharp nod, Asai urged Wareeshta to begin.

The Dhampir leaned forward, her eyes darting, assessing Eleanor's state; the venom was working swiftly now and beginning to dominate her body. When Wareeshta gently took her friend's hand, she could feel the fever working beneath her fingers, its movement manipulating, marking its foul presence. Her sharp eyes constantly trailed over Eleanor's body, studying its hostile course. Wanting to avoid too much blood-loss, and to keep her blood pressure low, she would have to be sure of her actions. Therefore, instead of choosing an artery—and avoiding the risk of accelerating death—she felt for the jugular vein, at the base of Eleanor's throat. It was not prominent, like the others; the venom had not yet worked its way there. *Good*, she thought. However, she knew it was only a matter of time. Again, Wareeshta looked down at Eleanor's weakened body, her eyes then shooting up, meeting Asai—the Samurai silently letting her know, through the calmness behind his dark, almond-shaped eyes, that he trusted her.

Wareeshta carefully pulled at Eleanor's bodice, loosening it, then narrowed her eyes, studying her breathing; it was short and erratic, and her heartbeat was accelerating. The venom was spreading out, like a map, weaving its way up towards her chest. She would have to be careful and work quickly. Taking a deep, nervous breath, Wareeshta leaned over and whispered in Eleanor's ear; 'Forgive me, my friend, for the pain I am about to inflict on you.'

# Chapter Seventeen

*The Ruins of Moyne*

'I *know.*'

L'Ordana remained with her back to Magia, ignoring him as she lingered at the edge of the ancient cemetery, staring into its obscurity. She squinted, searching between the leaning headstones and swaying trees, thinking she saw some movement, then cast it away, certain her mind was playing tricks on her. Her head thumped again with a sudden ache; she closed her eyes, waiting for it to pass. When it subsided, she sighed with relief, her eyes then opening wide with alarm. *He knows? What does he know?*

'I know you no longer have it,' he revealed as though he had read her thoughts.

She spun to face him, jolting when she saw he was within inches of her; his voice had sounded distant.

'*My* book,' he then stated, his dead-pan eyes boring into her with purpose.

At first, she glowered at him for his insolence. But when his eyes flared, his anger directed at her, it made her nervous. She flinched when he drew uncomfortably closer; she stepped back, swallowing—the startled look of discomfort briefly marking her features.

Magia smirked, then grunted with satisfaction. He was right; it was written all over her face. As he parted his lips to speak and challenge her about the book, he blinked and drew his head back sharply when a woman's face leapt out at him; it was creased with pain and strained by effort as if trying to escape from inside L'Ordana. Though old in features, the woman's face looked familiar. Without thought, he mouthed the word, releasing her name:

*'Kristene?'*

Then she was gone.

'What did you say?' snapped L'Ordana.

In the blink of an eye, the beautiful but fading face of L'Ordana glared back at him again, her eyes tapering with suspicion. He doubted she was aware of what had just happened. It drove his suspicions further; aside from the fact, the book—*his* book—was no longer in her possession, he suspected the dagger was gone, too. They had been her only means of preserving her youth, strength and immortality. *Another reason for keeping the girl,* he maintained, otherwise, she would have used and discarded her by now. And now, the very thing threatening her demise—the scourge of ageing—was beginning to take its toll on her mind and body, right in front of his eyes.

Despite his curiosity, Magia was sure he knew the identity of the woman who leapt out at him. He spoke it again.

'Kristene?'

She stared at him with a blank expression, her mind distracted in endless turmoil as she attempted to make sense of things. And though her thoughts were clouded by confusion, the name, however, echoed in her head:

*"Kristene!"*

He uttered it again. 'Kristene!' His brows shot up, convinced he had noticed a flicker in her eye; a glint of recognition? But no, it was a reaction—one of unrest—coming from the mind's eye for a tortured past that was about to resurface.

Trying desperately to hold on to her train of thoughts and doubts as her imagination tormented her, L'Ordana closed her eyes, pressed down on her lips and breathed deeply, in a vain attempt to take back control. But inside she struggled, sensing her life was in disarray and on a downward spiral towards disaster.

She shook her head.

*No!* she thought. *This cannot be happening!*

A hint of pity appeared on Magia's face, his smugness faded as his expression took on a look of concern as he witnessed the clash between her past and present unfold.

'I will help you, *Bella!*' he said. It was unexpected.

Her eyes flew open, and when he nodded, she narrowed them. '*You?*'

'*Sí!*'

As she slowly tilted her head to the side, she subconsciously rubbed the raised scar beneath her left ear, then winced from its sharp sting. She disregarded it.

'Why would *you*, of your own free will, help *me*, when I know of your capabilities, Magia?'

'Because … I am convinced Wareeshta has lied to us.'

'What?' L'Ordana shook her head, refusing to believe him. 'She would *never* lie to me!' she hit back.

Magia lifted his hands and shrugged.

'Then … where is she, your … "loyal" servant?'

L'Ordana looked around, her "search" then pausing when her eyes fell on the six remaining Dhampir, engrossed in conversation with Turloch; occasionally, he would glance over, eye her, then resume discussions with the warriors. It made her uneasy. *What are they up to?* she thought, hoping they were not plotting against her. She looked up at the sky; the grey clouds seemed to be lifting, making it easier to determine the time of day. She harboured a guess, concluding it to be late afternoon. She suspected Magia was right; Wareeshta had been gone awhile. *Too long.* As for the Valkyrie? *Where is Kara?* She wrung her hands, feeling vulnerable and exposed. *They would never …*

Shrugging off any notion that her "loyal" servants would abandon her—*and after everything I have done for them*—she returned her attention to Magia, feigning her self-assurance as she looked down her nose at him. 'Oh, do not worry, Wareeshta will soon—'

'I *assure* you,' he insisted, 'she will not be back. And as for the warriors you sent to assist her?' He grunted. 'Their fate was sealed the moment you released her from her bond. I have no doubt the beautiful Wareeshta—your "devoted" servant,' he added, with an edge of sarcasm, 'has deserted us, and is no longer our ally. It is my belief, she has been your—*our*—antagonist, for some time.'

L'Ordana stared at him, horrified, her brows drawn tight, her mouth gaping, speechless. As her eyes flashed to the waiting Dhampir, her face creased with concern; she had also released some of *them* from their bond, believing in their allegiance. *No!* She then realised … *I released them all, thinking…*

She nodded to herself, aware of the magnitude of her mistake, now certain she would be unable to recapture the warriors, her weakening powers preventing her. Her thoughts trailed back to Wareeshta—*my favourite!* Had she not been good to her? After all, she had saved the wretched soul from madness, gave her shelter, gave her … She shook her head, vehemently.

'I *saw* it—in her eyes,' Magia persisted, 'when I questioned her about the book's location, and what is more … I believe she was the instigator—the *traitor*—behind the girl's escape.'

'Wareeshta would never betray me,' she snapped, rejecting any claims of deception on the Dhampir's part.

'Why not? She was nothing but a slave to you—just like *them!*' he said, lowering his voice as he threw a look at the Dhampir warriors. He hesitated. 'You must question their allegiance, L'Ordana,' he then suggested in a whisper, planting another seed, adding it to her anxiousness.

'Kara!' she then blurted—the Valkyrie's lengthy absence, also, brought to mind.

He shrugged, pulling a long face, stifling all knowledge of her disappearance.

'And what of *her?*' she wondered, with a hint of panic in her voice. 'Surely, they—' She stopped short, rubbing the scar again; he noticed the constant attention she was giving the little trophy the Samurai had left below her ear, on their first meeting. Though it was some time ago, it now looked fresh and angry, its sudden, noticeable presence, adding to the signs of her deterioration.

Again, she shook her head, trying to dismiss it; the mere idea of her two servants uniting was absurd. *They hate one another.* And yet, there was an element of doubt in her mind when she lingered on the thought, her eyes thinking, second-guessing herself.

Magia pondered on her self-doubt for several moments before adding to it, letting her think the unlikely alliance between her servants was probable. He slowly raised his shoulders, stretching his face again. 'I—*we*—can only presume Kara and Wareeshta could be …'

She glowered at him, her face distorting in anger, insistent. 'But they despise one another!'

'Then, if this is so … we must assume the Valkyrie is working alone and could be somewhere nearby—perhaps … even lying in wait, or …' His voice trailed again as he watched her glance nervously around, almost expecting Kara to show her face.

L'Ordana now felt defenceless and bare; and though reluctant to admit it to herself, she knew she desperately needed the dark Warlock now. *Without him* … She shuddered at the idea of having to depend on him, knowing she could not trust him.

By now, it was clear to Magia that she relied on him. Completely. It was obvious—by the way her eyes darted back and forth at the remaining Dhampir—that she was beginning to doubt their loyalty, too. He was sure they would do as *he* asked. However, Turloch—the cunning one—would be difficult, his confidence rising so, he would soon disregard any demands made on him, given leeway.

'You understand my reasons for keeping the truth from you—about the book,' she stated.

'Where is it?' he asked, his voice calm and composed while, inside, his patience was wearing thin—along with the time remaining. His eyes scanned the sky with suspicion; it appeared to be brightening a little. *As long as the sun stays hidden*, he thought. Come nightfall, he would part the clouds again—if need be—to check the moon; its last sliver of light would start to fade in less than two days, along with Elboru, if the new Magus was not bonded with the Shenn, before the next new moon. Another possibility occurred to him: he suspected the Valkyrie was still alive and making her way there, too, despite the poison inflicted on her. He had seen it himself—the abrasion on her arm, caused by one of the Dhampir's blades. But, because of her making—she was not mortal—he questioned the venom's effect on her. *It is possible.* Also, she had the advantage of flight. *Sí!* For all he knew … she could be in Elboru by now, causing havoc. He snorted at the idea. *Now that is something I would love to see.*

'I do not know where the book is,' L'Ordana stated.

And there it was—*finally!*—her admission.

'I'—she stopped abruptly, lifting her hand to her head, rubbing the temple of her eye, to ease the throbbing pain—'I fear it is … with the Elliyan.' She looked at Magia, seeing him through a moment of blurred vision, his outline distorted, making her light-headed. Her face paled, then flushed red again as it contorted into another unruly outburst of anger.

'No!' she cried out.

"*I am the one in control!*" the voice of another hit back, in retaliation. "*Not you!*"

The six Dhampir and Turloch turned, hearing the unfamiliar voice—the power in its tone prominent and commanding. Magia regarded L'Ordana after hearing it, too—lashing out from inside her. He shot a glance at the Dhampir, narrowing his suspicious eyes. *Maledetto!* he cursed inside. *She has drawn their attention to us.* He reached out to touch her, but she recoiled before his hand met hers, and when he looked her in the eye, the *face* jumped out at him, again. He flinched, taken aback, now seeing it clearly; it was *Kristene!* But not the young, beautiful Kristene he had fallen for, so long ago. Her features were now colourless, haggard, like that of someone who had struggled all their life—the lines of stress etched deep into her sagging skin.

Then she was gone again.

It seemed the true Kristene was trying to emerge through L'Ordana's weakness, in a vain attempt to win back the body that once belonged to her. And yet, the voice had not been hers; it had been that of another—domineering—and he knew precisely to whom it belonged: the spirit of the ancient Sorceress, Eryian—the one he had stolen for her despairing *lover.* Was it battling against its host, Kristene, to own it—to own *her*—in order to be the victor?

Magia began to fear the worst; should the *spirit* take control of Kristene's body, then *Eryian* would be capable of taking the Shenn amulet and destroying everyone—and everything—in her path. She had once been part of the Elliyan, therefore, privy to the Shenn's history, and what it entailed. But *would* she take it for herself? Regardless of her motives, he was in no doubt that—first and foremost—Eryian would be out to seek revenge on the Elliyan, for putting her to death, for an act of love—a natural *need*—that did not warrant her demise.

*This changes everything,* he thought, accepting some responsibility. He now deemed L'Ordana unstable and unpredictable. Time was paramount, and if he were to help her, they would have to move—and soon. They could no longer afford to wait around. Wareeshta was not coming back.

As the pain in her head subsided, L'Ordana strived to compose her thoughts, though she was deeply troubled by her strange behaviour. *Am I losing control?* The side effects of being without the book and the dagger weighed on her mind and soul. But it was the suddenness that had thrown her—not to mention the fear—the one thing she could not comprehend. She had not felt anything like it before, not since—

An image assaulted her thoughts: she saw a young woman, bound, naked and crushed, her fate dragging her down to a slow and painful death. Again, her breathing became tight and restricted, giving her a sense of drowning beneath a murky surface, forcing her to struggle for air.

The faint sound of someone calling her roused her back, their voice repeating itself. *Who?* she thought as the name became clear. She gasped, shocked by the realisation; it was *her* name being repeatedly spoken by Magia as he vied for her attention. For an instant, she had forgotten who she was.

She stared at him, baffled—the colour of her eyes paling to grey as the words finally poured from her gaping mouth:

'I—I fear I am—losing control, Magia,' she said, in a breathless whisper.

Until now, they had taunted one another with their mind games. But the tide had turned, altering everything—the onset of her unpredictable and erratic behaviour, forcing him to ask himself; *Can I play with this madness?* But when the hood of her cloak slipped from her head, fully exposing the obvious signs of her diminishing beauty—she was now ageing quickly—he drew back, momentarily stunned; even her scent—the familiar sweet almond oil that had once teased his senses—had diminished. It was then he realised … their "games" were over. She truly needed him.

His eyes flashed to the Dhampir; though maintaining their distance, he sensed they were secretly watching them. But something was wrong—something in their demeanour that troubled him. Something was afoot.

Magia pulled L'Ordana closer and, lifting her hood to conceal her face again, whispered through gritted teeth as he stared into her eyes; 'Keep your thoughts and concerns to yourself,' he warned, tipping his head towards the Dhampir. 'Or *they* might—' He stopped. For the first time since their reacquaintance, Magia now witnessed the profound fear in L'Ordana's eyes, like the marked prey of a predator. It prompted him to act.

He abruptly led her back to her holding, away from the Dhampirs' prying eyes and ears. She glanced around her makeshift abode, her expression vacant, momentarily oblivious to where they were, then turned to him, her mouth quivering, like a child lost in the wilderness.

'I *am* losing control,' she then admitted, suddenly taking hold of his hands as if her life depended on their support, her nails digging into his flesh; he snatched them away from her, fearing they would break his flawless skin and release the intoxicating scent of his blood into the air. No, the Dhampir, especially Turloch, could never indulge in the potency of his *Blue Blood.*

L'Ordana stepped back. 'It is as though … there are two beings inside me, in constant battle with one another, trying to take over my body. I can feel their tug-of-war. It is like a weakness that has been reawakened, fighting to reach the surface. I fear it shall soon dominate what little strength and power I have left. I cannot let this happen, Magia, or I will surely die—and then it will have all been for nothing.' She shook her head frantically as panic gripped her. 'I—'

'Then *let* me help you,' he urged, cautiously extending a hand, in a bid to reach her mind. She recoiled, glaring at it as though he were wielding a knife at her.

'*Per favore, Bella!*' he said, with genuine appeal, all the while conscious of the passing of time. 'My amulet?' he then asked, his hand still open, wanting the item returned to him.

Reluctant, at first, to part with it, she took a hesitant step towards him, searching his eyes for the slightest sign of betrayal, only to be met by the warmth of their amber glow smiling back at her, it temporarily calming her.

She reached inside her cloak, where she kept it, in its satin pouch. She fumbled to open it. When her pale, long fingertips finally touched the amulet's precious stone, she winced in agony, quickly withdrawing her hand without it; she had forgotten to put on her gloves to protect her against its burning influence.

'It is like hot coal, to the touch!' she exclaimed, staring at the blisters appearing on the palm of her hand, where the amulet's metal had seared her fragile skin. Magia's nose flared from the acrid smell of burning flesh.

'May I?' he asked, indicating her cloak. He smiled, waiting, itching for her approval.

On her consent, he moved swiftly, then reached inside, retrieving what had always been *his*. He eyed the entrance of her tent, then moved towards it, taking care to look out. Turloch and the warriors were out of their eye-line, though still present. He could hear their murmured conversation: it was talk of war, boasting of great things to come for them. *Delusional fools!* he thought. But as long as their conversation held, it would distract them from their own. *Good.*

Stealing the opportunity, while the Dhampir were preoccupied, Magia lifted his amulet to the daylight, to catch its true magnificence. Reunited with its rightful owner, the amulet sprung to life, its centred diamond gleaming back at him, its intense reflection like the sun on his face.

*Ah … The Light of Life*, he reminded himself as it emanated in his hand, alerting him to the ongoing urgency of their venture.

Magia raised the amulet higher, scrutinising its vibrancy; the light radiating from its yellow stone expanded as it reached out, displaying its magnificence to the universe. Behind him, L'Ordana averted her eyes from its glare, such was its force, while he remained focused on its centre. He had waited a long time for this—for the amulet to reveal itself in its entirety—having never witnessed it before. As the light dimmed, he turned to her, drawing her attention to its beauty. It was breathtaking.

'Now do you see it?' he said, displaying the precious gem in front of her pale eyes.

She nodded.

'I do,' she replied, astounded by its clarity yet still ignorant of its true purpose.

Mindful of her uncertainty, he answered her imminent question. '*That* …' he began, pointing to the centre, '… is the *Egress*—the portal through which you shall receive your true fate and glory.'

'The *Shenn!*' she whispered, in awe—the mere thought of it renewing her passion, and taking her mind from the turmoil inside her. For a moment he saw a taint of youth return to her features.

'*Si!* It will now guide us to the very place. I perceive, by taking the new route I suggested, we could arrive before our "friends" do. He grinned when her eyes found his, brimming with life, and wild with excitement. 'You see, my *Bella*, there are two paths to choose: the long and arduous one; and then there is the other, permitted to those who possess a trinket, such as mine. *This!*' he added, caressing the amulet, 'will allow us to enter the *Egress* … which will take us directly inside the walls of Elboru.'

She reached out her hand, wanting to touch it again, then hesitated—the stinging in her palm, reminding her of its power; she could feel the heat of its energy coming from its centre, and yet she could not resist its lure.

'What is it like?' she begged, her hand twitching as she continued to stare at Magia's amulet, imagining the magnitude of its unrivalled counterpart. She was desperate to know, desperate to have the *true* amulet.

'I have no words to describe the great Shenn,' he began, 'for I have never laid eyes upon it. But I am conscious of the extent of its power. Truly, a worthy prize bestowed on the—' He stopped to correct himself. 'On *whoever* shall take ownership of it.'

'And *I* shall be that—' She stopped as pain gripped her once more, and as she cradled her head in her hands, she shook it, mumbling madness to herself. Releasing her hands, she clenched her fists and screamed. 'No! *Never!*'

As he watched the Sorceress battle against the entity inside her, Magia was resolute in his decision to leave the ancient Ruins of Moyne, as soon as possible. Again, he glanced out from her shelter, drawing back when he discovered the Dhampir had moved closer, within earshot of them. Now he was under no illusion … They were being watched. He contemplated destroying them, then changed his mind; they could serve him well as a decoy of destruction—should he need them. *A mere precaution*, he casually thought.

They would now have to veer back a few leagues if they were to reach the *Egress*—deep in the forest of Muir—then go north through Affinshire, and on to the Gap of Lome. The horses had been well-rested, and he knew the way—thanks to his amulet—it firing his confidence as he held it in his hand. There would be no delays now. He calculated the distance—a few hours, no more—speculating that they would arrive by early evening. It would then give him time to decide what to do. For now, any plan to desert her was out of the question. And though she no longer had the book, he suspected where it was, and by that, he would have to enter Elboru.

'Give it back to me!'

The sound of her demanding voice made him start. He peered into her fevered eyes, ignoring her stiff, open hand as she gestured for him to return his amulet. He saw an unpredictable madness in her features—that of a woman possessed, her lined face red and crooked with anger. It was clear to him she was finding it increasingly difficult to maintain control. The weakness inside her was no longer docile as it strived to resurface.

L'Ordana reached out to grab the amulet but lacked the strength and speed to do so.

In one swift movement, Magia slipped the heavy gold chain over his head, welcoming its return, its presence charging his strength. He felt the weight of its power and the influence of the Shenn when the precious stone touched his pale skin, its new and overwhelming effect, throwing him into a moment of ecstasy.

L'Ordana recoiled, feeling betrayed as the light disappeared beneath his garb. 'I should *never* have trusted you,' she snarled through her teeth—the ugliness of her hate visible in her face, like a wild animal ravenous with hunger.

He looked sharp.

'Listen to me!' he hissed, seizing her hand. 'You can and *must* trust me.'

'Give it back!' she yelled, blocking the entrance, disregarding the Dhampir outside, who were now invested in the raised voices coming from her tent.

Aware of their "eavesdroppers", Magia dragged L'Ordana back out of their sight and gripped her by the shoulders.

'My amulet is of no use to you,' he said, keeping his voice to a firm whisper. 'And my intentions—despite what you think—are not to delude you, but to assist. Call it'—he paused, rolling his eyes, shaking his head—'a *debt* owed.'

She drew back from him, frowning, her lips parted, staring at him, trying to grasp his meaning. She then lowered her head, thinking she had caught a hint of guilt in his eyes. But the confusion swirling in her mind was taking its toll, again, as she felt the pain return.

He could see it, too. 'We must go. Now!' he urged. 'The Shenn awaits you, *Bella*. It will restore you, and grant you your—' He broke off and looked up, listening, certain he had heard the beating sound of nature; he was aware of it now after it had ceased when they first arrived at the ruins.

'A *what* owed?' she snapped.

He flinched, snatched back by her anger, and sighed.

Her face relaxed as she slowly nodded, hanging on every word, while he explained, her eyes widening each time he mentioned the Shenn. She knew she had to trust him, now. Forcing a smile through her pain, she placed her vulnerability, and trust, in his hands.

'It *all* waits for you, *Bella!*'

Having already wasted too much time, Magia coaxed her back out, and into the clearing. He looked around for the Dhampir warriors, ready to give them orders. His eyes flickered from side to side, searching for them among the ruins. But all that remained was the trace of their insatiable scent …

# Chapter Eighteen

*The Paths of Lome*

An immense force of excruciating pain erupted inside Eleanor when Wareeshta—in a desperate bid to save her friend—attacked the vital area, where she needed to administer her venom, timing being the key.

Eleanor cried out—but only once—the initial shock throwing her body into spasm as Wareeshta worked on her with controlled precision. Such was her concentration that the Dhampir blanked out the faces of those who surrounded her as they watched and waited, their anxiousness prevalent by their unnerving silence.

Eleanor's sharp, broken nails tore at Asai's flesh while he held her. Trails of blood seeped from his open wounds yet he remained unperturbed, feeling no pain, only hers; he knew the wounds would heal, soon enough. He then regarded Wareeshta with a wary and attentive eye, still wondering whether he could trust her. He had to. They all did. And should she fail …? He would cross that bridge, if or when ….

Rosalyn's eyes filled with tears as she looked on, helpless yet thankful the Samurai had taken her place; it was unlikely she would have been able to cope with the stress of having to maintain her hold on Eleanor while Wareeshta tried to save her daughter.

Eleanor's legs began to convulse as the venom took hold, making its way through the complex route linking every vein in her fragile body.

Feeling the need to help—to do *something*—Daine rushed forward and dropped to his knees, locking his hands around Eleanor's ankles, in an attempt to steady her infected body. Seeing this, Oran moved to intervene, only to be obstructed by Reece.

'Put an end to this jealousy you vent inside,' he hissed in the Warlock's ear, as a warning. 'There is no time for it—not here.'

Oran glared at Reece when the Dhampir held his stance against him. But, knowing he was right in what he had said—though not wanting to admit his failings openly—Oran stepped away. He needed to stamp out the jealousy raging inside him. *Not here*, he thought, echoing Reece's words as he looked down at his daughter, running his hands through his hair, trying to understand the full extent of what was happening to her, all the while feeling powerless and shameful.

Satisfied with Oran's "retreat", Reece returned to his post, to keep a watchful eye out for their enemy. Besides, he had no desire to witness the visible pain his granddaughter was experiencing. He knew only too well what her body was going through as the fiery heat consumed it. It was unendurable, but a pain she had to bear if she were to survive. And it was ironic in that the individual who had caused the same affliction on himself and his colleagues—against their will—was now doing the same to his granddaughter. But it was different for Eleanor, hers being a torturous necessity. And for her to live—he grunted at the irony of it; *live?*—it was likely he would never return to a mortal life. But with Onóir gone it was a worthy sacrifice, and he was prepared to accept the consequences. The intent to destroy Wareeshta was no longer theirs … unless Eleanor died. It was a waiting game …

Vigilant, while protecting his sister, Gill tried, with great difficulty, to remain calm, his eyes occasionally scouting through the trees for signs of another attack. He gripped Eleanor's dagger, so tight it ached. *If Nori dies, I—* He shook the thought from his mind. *No, she is strong.* Every few moments he stole a glance to see her progress, his blood running cold each time he saw her. She looked nothing like the vibrant girl he had grown up with—the big sister who had always looked out for him. She was now frail, and her skin, which once glowed with the flush of youth, was now pale and translucent while, beneath it, her veins flowed the colour of deep purple and pulsated from the sinister virus that was poisoning her body. For a moment, his thoughts were thrown, reminded of his fate. He still knew nothing of what was to come. None of this had been expected. He felt tested, questioning his ability again, to rule over a world he never knew existed—until a few days ago. The time was almost upon him and he was tired—unusually tired. He began to second-guess everything—the effects of the journey and the dilemma at hand, clouding his judgement, despite what *they* had said. *I'm not ready! I can't—I can't do it!*

He stopped, dismissing his self-pity—*stop thinking of yourself, Gill*—while his sister lay on the ground in the arms of the *one* she loved, fighting for her life. Again, he glanced at Eleanor, then quickly diverted his eyes when he saw her writhing in pain in Asai's arms; the Samurai and Daine were struggling to hold her down. *Don't let her die, Onóir!* he silently pleaded to his grandmother, wishing he could bear the brunt of his sister's agony. But he was powerless.

No one save the Servitor saw the fear in Gill's eyes as he struggled to look at his sister, knowing her life was out of his hands, in spite of *who* he was. Kai also wished he could remove Eleanor's pain. But this, he knew, was something he had no control over. As it stood, Eleanor's life was in Wareeshta's hands.

As if sensing his agony, the one true companion Gill had known, since his father's disappearance and the death of his best friend, Will, came to her master's side. Rave nudged him, letting him know she was there. Gill reached down to pet the familiar head—the hound's presence having a calming effect on him. He then felt his grandmother's presence, certain she had sent Rave to be with him, in his time of crisis.

With time pressing on her, Wareeshta became aware of the crucial moment, where the fine line between life and death was making its approach. Her pace gradually steadied in time with Eleanor's slowing heartbeat, her concentration deepening as she continued to work on her. Too much—and her friend would surely die. Too little—she was unsure. However, it was not her intention to find out; her life, also, hung in the balance, should Eleanor die. She had seen it in the eyes of those who regarded her, particularly the Samurai. When Asai made a threat, he meant it; he was a man of honour, who kept his word. And like his colleague, Reece, was more than prepared to destroy her, should things go wrong. That was a certainty.

As the fever took hold of Eleanor's body, Wareeshta could feel its torrid effect, it almost burning her mouth as she continued to inject her venom into the jugular vein, at the base of her friend's neck. Then came more convulsions, forcing Asai and Daine to tighten their grip, their hands shaking, trying to steady her, so as not to break the blood's rhythm as it journeyed through her veins.

When the crucial moment came—and not wanting to risk another second—Wareeshta recoiled, releasing her hold on Eleanor. She then turned away, spitting a thick mouthful of poison from her mouth, her brow furrowing in disgust when it turned autumn's glorious amber leaves to black, burning them until they turned to dust. She hoped she had removed it all.

With the feeling that *life* was being drained from her body, Eleanor, aware of it, and aware of *him*, tensed within Asai's hold. Life was fading—too far gone beyond her reach—and it was taking something precious with it: her soul. She fought hard, feeling its tug, not wanting to let it go.

Her body jerked, then stopped dead. She then felt a slow gradual pull as it began to move again, giving her a sense of detachment; she was looking down at herself, witnessing the chaos: she could see Asai and the guide holding her to the ground as the others looked on, frantic. And yet, she could not feel them … or *him*. *Am I …?* The mere thought of never seeing her Samurai again …

*Fight, Eleanor! fight it!* her silent voice yelled out, her eyes widening as she watched the mark of death meander through her veins—the speed of its progress taking precedence as her friend—*quick, Wareeshta!*—tried desperately to stop it. In her state of unrest, she saw Kai, her panic then turning to hysteria when an image of *Purgatory* flashed through her mind; she recalled the Servitor's grim description of the world—the "prison"—he had eventually been plucked from, by the Elliyan, after being kept in a state of limbo for years, after his murder. She could not end up *there. Please, Wareeshta, try harder!* Though aware they could not hear her, she cried out again to her friend. *Save me!* But when she saw Wareeshta draw back from her body, thinking the Dhampir had given up, she persisted; *No, Wareeshta, you cannot stop—not now!* As the scene below her faded, their misty silhouettes morphed into shadows, unrecognisable. They would soon be gone—for good—leaving her with only a memory of what was.

*Tell him, Eleanor, before …*

Eleanor's eyes flickered open; she was no longer looking down at herself. Through her deteriorating vision, she saw Asai leaning over her. She sensed his inner restlessness, by the tightening of his grip—the pain of it excruciating as his eyes darted between her and Wareeshta. It seemed to her, the Dhampir, having worked tirelessly to save her, *had* given up. Eleanor was now conscious of the last ebb of life drifting away, gradually taking her from everyone she loved. Through the strain and fear of its slow departure, she looked up, wanting to get the words out—to tell him—her mouth barely opening and closing.

But nothing came.

As Wareeshta kept her eyes fixed on her friend, she was wary of Asai's watchful eye and mindful of everyone's anticipation. She placed her hand on Eleanor's chest, then leaned close to listen to her heart. She could hear nothing. She shot up and stared down at her friend, unsure.

'What—what is it?' blurted Daine, his anxious voice drawing the others closer when he no longer felt Eleanor's struggle beneath his aching hands.

Eleanor's body suddenly slumped in Asai's sturdy arms, her features pale and gaunt as she lay lifeless on the damp ground. Wareeshta could feel the tension in the air, it quickly turning to panic when Rosalyn rushed to her side and looked down, seeing her daughter motionless.

She shook her head, unable to fathom the unthinkable, realising the Dhampir had failed.

'Oh, no! She cannot be—' She stopped herself from saying *it*, her dread then soaring to the brink of overwhelming grief as she drew her hands over her mouth, to prevent its release.

Daine slowly let go of Eleanor's feet—the imprint of his warm hands still visible on her pallid skin. He slumped back, shaking his head, speechless. Aware of Rosalyn's heartache, he stole a look, wanting to reach out, to console her, then promptly discarded the thought when she lashed out, dropping to her knees in despair.

Still cradled in the arms of the Samurai, Rosalyn held Eleanor's face in her hands, it devoid of all expression. All she could do was stare. Then they came—the tears—falling on her daughter's deathly white face. Feeling the heaviness of her heart as it broke, Rosalyn leaned forward and kissed her child's brow; she shuddered from its icy touch. And yet, she held on, her warm tears flowing down Eleanor's cheeks, refusing to let her go … refusing to say goodbye.

'This is not how it should be,' she whimpered, her outpouring of grief there for them to witness as she sobbed her heart out; she could not bear the pain of having to accept the loss of her child.

Behind her, the others stood dumbfounded, unable to fathom

what had happened.

Wanting to console his wife, but felt incapable, Oran turned his attention to Wareeshta. Thoughts of betrayal weighed on him as he glared at her with contempt. Then, in a moment of unquenchable rage, he attacked the unsuspecting Dhampir.

Weary from her efforts, Wareeshta was caught off-guard, and found herself in the Warlock's clutches, staring up into his enraged eyes—the whites red with anger and grief.

'You've killed her!' he snarled, his face contorting between hate and sadness.

'Nori?' Gill's heartache was unmistakable as he fell to his knees, beside his mother—the tears beginning to stream down his face. He reached out his hand, letting it hover over his sister's body, still holding her precious dagger in his other, unable to bring himself to touch her. He was convinced she would pull through. It was inconceivable—the thought of her … *gone?* And though surrounded by friends and family, he felt utterly isolated without his sister. 'She can't be—' He stopped short; like his mother, he could not bring himself to say what he refused to believe. 'Try again!' he blurted, wiping away his tears with the back of his hand.

Everyone looked at Gill, hearing his plea, but his eyes were fixed only on Wareeshta. Still trapped in Oran's grip, the Dhampir stared down at the young man. Seeing the storm of emotions behind his hardened stare, she swallowed, fearful for what would come. 'I—I …' she stammered, taken aback by what he suggested.

'Let her go, Oran!' demanded Gill, rising. Oran did a double-take when his son marched towards him, then promptly released Wareeshta, shoving her towards Gill.

'What are you saying, Gill?' asked Reece.

'Please, Wareeshta?' he said, ignoring his grandfather. 'I don't know why but—you *have* to.' Gill's face, though marked with despair, softened as he sought a solution from the Dhampir—the uncertainty in her eyes then evident when she slowly lifted her shoulders and shook her head. 'I am begging you,' he whispered.

Wareeshta was fully aware of the outcome, should she refuse his request, knowing she could not escape Reece and Asai, not to mention the Warlock. She felt trapped and defenceless. Her time was running out. But as the face of her friend's brother stared at her, she could only see purpose and hope in his eyes—with no underlying threat. Her brows lifted when flecks of gold glinted back at her through their unexpected warmth.

'You must *try!*'

She looked sharp at Asai; the Samurai's voice—now brightened with hope—gripped her with renewed energy. *Is it possible?* she asked herself, glancing at Eleanor, still cradled between his arms, with Rosalyn gently stroking her daughter's hair.

*I must try*, she thought. Spurred by Gill's insistence, Wareeshta reached out and placed her hand gently on Rosalyn's shoulder, who, so caught up in her sorrow, neglected to notice the Dhampir's touch.

'Please?' Wareeshta begged. Rosalyn, her face sodden with tears, looked up at her. 'Let me try—one more time?' she urged.

Rosalyn caught her breath, momentarily taken away, by the flicker of renewed hope. With faith in her heart, she quickly moved aside for Wareeshta.

As the Dhampir moved towards her friend, trying to detach herself from the nuance of doubt still taunting her, she flinched when a hand gripped her shoulder. Her eyes met with the Samurai's. Asai nodded once, then clung to his beloved, to let Wareeshta try again.

As Rosalyn rose, Oran moved to comfort his wife but was cast aside by his son when Gill stepped in, throwing a protective arm around his mother's shoulders, her pitiful sobs waning as she looked on, with the others by her side, waiting anxiously. The thought of losing one of her children—perhaps both, and in one day—was too much to bear; there was also no certainty Gill would survive the ordeal *he* had yet to face. But it was the here and now that mattered. She had to concentrate on Eleanor. An icy chill suddenly crossed her heart. She pulled her shawl, wrapping it around her, and as she did so, her hand brushed off the brooch her mother had given her—Onóir's wedding gift from Reece. *I would gladly take her place, Maw*, she quietly told Onóir as she stared down at Eleanor.

The chill then left her.

'Go to the source,' Asai suggested, his voice steady.

Casting all doubts aside, Wareeshta did not delay, deciding her only chance would be to change tactics. Folding back the piece of clothing, concealing the wound Eleanor received on her leg from the warrior's poisonous blade, Wareeshta regarded the laceration; it was still raw and raised, the rim, stained purple by the venom.

Pre-empting Wareeshta's next move, Reece now took Daine's place—the guide happy to step away from the drama; Oran watched when he moved closer to Rosalyn, biting his tongue each time Daine stole a glance at her as she watched over their daughter. But Rosalyn was oblivious, her eyes only fixed on Wareeshta and Eleanor, silently spurring the Dhampir on, and willing her daughter to live. Though compelled to join her, Oran still felt unable to, knowing nothing *he* could do—or say—would make it better. *At least she is being comforted by Gill and not—* No, he had to stop thinking like that, stop letting his jealousy influence his thoughts, otherwise, he risked losing Rosalyn; already, he felt a part of her had died inside him. Still, he could not help it. His eyes flashed to Daine again, but the guide failed to notice, his concern for Rosalyn now obvious to him, by the way he was looking at her, his eyes displaying more than just concern. It was then Oran knew … Daine wanted to be with her.

'When you are ready,' snapped Reece, alerting Oran to Wareeshta's second attempt, and conscious of the Warlock's ongoing resentment. Reece held Eleanor's ankles, his strength pinning them to the ground, while Asai resumed his position. 'Do it!' he said—the underlying threat still evident. 'Now, Wareeshta! Or else!'

# Chapter Nineteen

Hearing her name spoken by Reece for the first time fired Wareeshta to act on it. With all hope riding on her last—and desperate—attempt to save her friend, the Dhampir launched herself at the laceration on Eleanor's leg, forcing her venom directly into the wound itself.

Her blood was of *his*, their venom alike. However, *she* had been born of it; hers was pure, unlike Magia Nera's, his having been polluted by her father's blood. Therefore, she would force Magia's out with her own—the dominant one.

Once again, Wareeshta worked carefully and methodically. Now she could taste the poison—*his*—its bitter-sweetness foul in her mouth. *Do not swallow*, she told herself, wanting no part of it … or *him*. The seconds passed …

Still, no sign of life.

'Keep going, Wareeshta!' Rosalyn urged, her hands clasped together, against her chest.

The softness in the woman's voice when she, too, spoke her name, gave Wareeshta some belief in humanity. A new sense of comradery now enveloped the Dhampir, giving her the strength to carry on until she no longer could. A wave of fatigue washed over her as she pumped her venom into Eleanor's veins again. But she persisted.

She then paused, feeling something, her mouth still latched onto the wound.

Asai looked sharp. He stared at Eleanor for a moment. His eyes, now alive with hope, flashed to Wareeshta. 'I felt it, too,' he whispered, his voice quiet yet urgent and confident.

The single heartbeat reignited Wareeshta's determination. Despite her exhaustion, she carried on—that precious sign of life they so desperately needed, renewing her hope, and dismantling her doubts. As long as there was a flicker of life ...

The heartbeat—though faint—brought with it a sense of euphoria within Wareeshta and Asai, when they looked at one another after Wareeshta drew back from Eleanor, satisfied that Magia Nera's venom had lost its battle and would soon depart her friend's body. The Samurai and Dhampir shared a brief and rare smile as the young woman's body began to react as it was slowly pumped with *new life*, it gradually finding her again. Asai looked across at Reece and nodded, feeling Eleanor's heart as it beat in unison with his, her gradual return soaking up the tension that had saturated the air. His warm, almond-shaped eyes then found Rosalyn's, hers lighting up when he smiled and bowed to her, confirming her hopes and dreams; her daughter was *alive!*

Wareeshta jolted when she found herself caught within Oran's grasp again—the Warlock now dragging her away from Eleanor. The Dhampir's eyes widened with fear as she struggled to speak. But Oran's deadly intentions were short-lived, by the sudden and unexpected intervention of another, jumping to her defence. The Warlock, refusing to let go, glowered into their threatening eyes.

'Would you betray your family, Reece?' he hit back, his stature overbearing on Wareeshta's small physique as he tightened his grip, his hands now clasped around her throat. She struggled to break free, but with each failed attempt she could feel the squeeze of his hands around her throat.

'Release her!' Reece yelled, his eyes flaring, his voice drowning out the chorus of cries behind him, to let the Dhampir go.

Oran grunted. 'She is nothing to you.'

'Perhaps,' stated Reece. 'But we made a vow to Eleanor. This Dhampir is not *ours* to destroy—not anymore!' he insisted, then pushed him away, shielding Wareeshta in the process—the force of his anger taking the Warlock by surprise. Fists clenched, Oran turned his resentful look to a stunned Wareeshta and pointed.

'You protect this … *creature* … even though she condemned you to … *this!*' he said, casting his eyes up and down Reece. 'And now she has claimed the life of—' He stopped and glanced back at the state of his daughter, then back to Reece, who stood his ground. 'This vow was *yours* to make'—he shook his head, the sinister curl now appearing at the side of his mouth—'not mine! Therefore, the *creature* is mine to dispose of, as I see—'

'Eleanor lives, Oran,' Reece hit back.

'"*Lives!*" you say?' He shook his head, his eyes sliding to Wareeshta, who stood beside Reece. 'Not in my eyes.'

'No, Oran! I forbid it!'

The Warlock stopped dead, hearing the command in the voice of authority, and spun, rendered speechless by the order instilled on him by his son before being reminded of Gill's true identity; should their journey—their task—end in triumph, he would be duty-bound to serve him as the new ruling Magus.

'Wareeshta is no *creature!*' Gill began, lest you forget her lineage. If it was not for the human blood that mingles with her father's, it is unlikely she could have assisted us in our time of need.'

'The vow was made to Eleanor,' added Reece, 'after Wareeshta helped her to escape, and, in return, Eleanor pledged to defend her *friend*.'

'Now you see how it is,' said Gill.

Oran glared at Wareeshta, with distaste, his resentment of her—and the others—evident, by the way she was now peering up at him, meeting his challenging stare, encouraged by their support.

'How *clever* of you,' he sneered.

'Needs must!' she hissed, in retaliation of his ill-treatment of her. 'If I am to protect myself—and that which is rightfully *mine!*' she then added, to spite him.

Oran narrowed his eyes, confused by her statement, forcing him to question it.

'And what do you mean by that?'

The Dhampir's eyes travelled, having felt *its* presence, her knowing look answering the Warlock's inquisitiveness as she regarded Nepthys—the horse stomping the ground with her hoof.

*The book!* He panicked. He would deny having it, but … *How did she—*

'Please! Make her stop!' Rosalyn's desperate plea distracted Oran and Wareeshta back to Eleanor. Though still in the Samurai's hold, the young woman was convulsing again, her mother's hands shaking as they hovered over her daughter, helpless, afraid to touch her.

'It is all right!' cried Wareeshta, rushing to her side. 'Please, trust me.'

Hands still raised, Rosalyn looked and felt powerless until the one who had remained poised throughout the ordeal reassured her with his calming voice.

'You must trust Wareeshta,' said Kai. 'Her word *is* honourable.'

Rosalyn nodded.

'I know,' she said, placing her confidence in the Servitor's soothing words. 'And I *do* trust her.'

'Her body is reacting to my venom,' Wareeshta explained. 'It is part of the process; the movement of her body will increase the flow. We must let it do its work while my venom flushes out the badness—and it will.'

Rosalyn looked into the Dhampir's calm, deep-set eyes searching … until she saw it—her honesty. Now she did not know whether to laugh or cry; her mixed emotions were playing havoc with her own exhausted body.

Wareeshta gave her a warm smile. 'Eleanor shall be well again … but—' She quickly stopped herself, biting her lower lip, mimicking her friend's habit, then looked away.

'But—what?' said Rosalyn—the unwanted sense of dread starting to gnaw at her again as she took hold of the Dhampir's arm. 'Tell me.'

'She means our daughter will no longer be *mortal* … like *you!*' Oran remarked in a disparaging tone.

Hearing the bitterness in her husband's voice, Rosalyn's face stiffened at the insult and turned to him, while resisting the urge to take Eleanor's dirk from Gill and drive the dagger through Oran's heart. As she approached him, eyes fixed on his, Oran saw the loathing in his wife's look, his face falling as she glared up at him with disgust.

'She *lives!*' she growled through gritted teeth. '*That* is all that matters to me—whatever the cost. And should it be for eternity … then … so be it. At least, she will no longer be alone'—she clasped her hand across her heart—'after *this* mortal has gone.'

Oran lowered his eyes, unable to sustain the look of wrath from his wife's—the distinction between their colour—one blue, one green—prominent in her glare.

'Tell me … *husband!* Would you think the same of her if she were *yours?*'

A streak of silence divided husband and wife, her vengeful response stunning everyone. Gill was shocked; to think his mother could hurdle such cruelty like that at his father. And though Eleanor was not Oran's, he had been a father to her since she was a bairn. While his behaviour was uncalled for, he sympathised with his father but feared husband and wife would never forgive one another, leading him to wonder if his parents could survive all this.

Oran's heart sank to a depth so low it rendered him speechless; Rosalyn's retaliation had been hard to swallow, and as she turned her back on him, to be with her daughter, he felt numb inside from her dismissal of him. For a moment his anguish turned to guilt. But then he questioned it: *Why should I feel guilty?* he thought. He knew where the blame truly lay: *The Elliyan will pay for this.*

Dismissing Rosalyn's cutting remark, for now, he threw a glance at the three monoliths—the ever-changing emotions having a profound effect, keeping them in constant chaos, with their surfaces changing again and again. He clasped the object concealed beneath his shirt—the ever-constant reminder of their task. He looked down to where his daughter lay, motionless but alive, her mother watching over her like she used to when Eleanor was a bairn. He then looked at Gill, his son subconsciously stroking the beard he so proudly wore as he stared down at his sister, wondering how she would cope, knowing she would never be the same—*his Nori!*—again. It broke his heart, to see his family like this. *'Tis all my fault.*

He then looked to Kai—the two exchanging a look of concern; it was now early evening, and darkness was lurking, ready to pounce. They nodded to one another, knowing what had to be done if they were to stop the monoliths. As he moved to fore-warn the group, particularly Gill, he stopped dead, hearing the elated sound of his wife's voice.

'*Eleanor!*'

As Oran turned, he saw Eleanor's eyes flickering wildly beneath their closed lids, trying to open. The Warlock's mouth gaped as he watched the taint of pink flowing through her pallid skin. Gone was the sun-kissed glow, never to adorn her fair complexion again. Her long, fair hair gleamed like pale gold, lush and vibrant, beneath the dusky sky.

Her eyes continued to flicker as they adjusted to her awakening, and still danced as she listened to profound new sounds around her, trying to distinguish them—one, in particular, standing out: a single heartbeat, somewhere near. Smiling faces stared down at her, uttering words of relief to one another; she flinched, hearing their crowded conversation, though unable to make sense of it.

'Rest a moment,' the soft voice advised; Eleanor's eyes moved beneath their lids in response. 'It is your body adjusting to its new life. Your senses are heightened but will find their place, soon enough. But you must concentrate. Breathe.'

With her friend still in the Samurai's hold, Wareeshta continued to ease Eleanor into her new existence with her encouraging words, while gesturing to Reece, with her hand, urging him to resume his grip on the young woman's ankles, as a precaution.

Asai glanced up at Reece. The two colleagues nodded, sharing their approval—and silent agreement: Wareeshta would now live.

Eleanor groaned, then squirmed when her body began to writhe, distorting itself as though she had no control over it. The others made to rush to her side, to help, then stalled when Wareeshta motioned them to *wait!* Something was wrong; her friend's body should not react like that. Inside, she panicked, fearing some of Magia's venom remained. If so, Eleanor could end up like L'Ordana's creatures. *But I removed it all!* She was sure of it. But when she began to question herself, doubt seeped in. Her eyes darted to the Samurai.

Seeing the alarm on Wareeshta's face, Asai nodded, his instincts telling him not to let go of Eleanor, and when his eyes flashed to him, Reece took a deep breath, heeding his friend's silent warning, to tighten his grip, too …

# Chapter Twenty

Suddenly she jolted, wrenching herself from Asai's firm grip and hurdling Reece away. She leapt to her feet, hissing—the rush of adrenalin, like fire coursing through her veins, elevating her mind and body like never before. She was alert, her eyes scarlet and new, her heart pounding and echoing like a scream, almost deafening.

She looked up, sharp, then winced, now fully aware of the heightened sounds around her as they pierced and crowded her new senses. She heard another sound escaping the madness—a voice, crying; *"Wait! Leave her! It will settle."* She focused, seeing shapes, her keen eyes watching as they quickly formed, their outlines defined in the dusk. When a breeze stirred, her eyes darted up, catching the flicking of tiny leaves, their rustling like a melody as it sang to her from above; she tilted her head, lending an ear to its haunting song. Again, nature snatched her attention and she looked down sharply, towards the trees, catching fleeting movements between their narrow spaces; fascinated, she listened to the chorus of its residents—the anthem of their little hearts beating as they scurried through the foliage, their paws disturbing the leaves as they pattered over the damp ground. Her eyes widened and her mouth gaped at the wonder of it all. She felt new, strong, *alive!* She closed her eyes and lifted her head, filling her lungs, inhaling the newness of her awakening. Her eyes flashed open to something else when an uncontrollable urge came over her, filling her with an insatiable need to act on it. And yet, she was confused, her thoughts muddled, trying to recall things. She stalled when her nostrils twitched. Her eyes darted around, aware she was not alone—the overwhelming sense of being watched, calling out to her for recognition. Her nostrils flared when she caught *it*—the overpowering scent; it taunted her with a desperate "need".

She spun and stopped dead when her newborn, hungry eyes found them—the two mortals. She tilted her head low, eyes set, chest heaving as she leered at them, her throat parched. She tried to swallow but the dryness was unbearable, that "need" driving her to a frenzy of want. Her energy was boundless. She needed to release it.

They stood rooted, unsure, as she stared back at them. Her new eyes moved erratically between Daine and Rosalyn, making them uneasy, and when she looked directly at Daine, he froze. Though already disturbed by how Eleanor had regarded him before she fell victim to her attack, this was something entirely different; her crimson eyes had a certain look in them, one of intense interest, a wanton stare, like someone who had been starved of—

'*Food!*' he realised, with horror. He gasped—Rosalyn, too. 'She wants to—'

Asai and Wareeshta had grabbed Eleanor just in time before she could leap at Rosalyn and Daine—the two mortals now safe within the Servitor's protective shield; Kai had also pre-empted the attack, having sensed Wareeshta's concern. Eleanor's unusual "reaction" had been unanticipated.

'No!'

Eleanor jolted within their grip when she heard the voice whisper to her. Still, she kept her eyes set on Rosalyn and Daine, wanting, needing … Her strength was such, that it took both Wareeshta and Asai to control her. Grasping her shoulders, Asai looked to his beloved, begging for her to come back to him.

'See me.' His words were clear and defined. Her flaming eyes moved, following his voice; she inclined her head slightly at its familiarity. She liked his tone yet was uncertain.

Asai nodded and smiled at her, hoping she would recognise him.

'She will,' said Wareeshta. 'But you must keep talking to her.'

'You cannot harm them,' he went on. Eleanor shot another glance at Rosalyn and Daine, and flinched, now struggling to break free, but already the initial impact of her change was subsiding; the muscles in her heart were slowing to an unnatural beat—barely there, but there, nonetheless. Unlike before, when she lingered on the delicate threshold between life and death; she had passed through it briefly, her heart stopping before being wrenched back—the torturous pain reminding her.

The first phase was the deadliest, Wareeshta knew, should there be no intervention. Control was the key to a newborn—the one thing the Sorceress had forced Wareeshta to avoid when creating her legion of warriors. L'Ordana had wanted them that way, savage and murderous, killing without remorse. She would not let that happen to her friend.

'Keep going,' she urged Asai as she slowly released Eleanor, leaving her in the Samurai's capable hands—the calming effect of his loving hold taking over.

'You cannot harm them, Eleanor.' She froze, hearing him speak the name. It was familiar. 'No matter what you feel, Eleanor,' he persisted. She held his look, peering into the warmth of his unusual almond-shaped eyes.

He smiled again, then took her hand in his and placed it against his chest. She looked down, feeling the slow methodical beat, then released a short gasp when another—*hers*—matched his, bonding them once again. He nodded, feeling it, feeling her. 'I am your Asai … and now we are *one*.'

Then she saw *him*.

Guided by the *one* who would always be by her side, Eleanor stretched the rigidness from her body, feeling its departure as if ridding herself of an old enemy before embracing her newfound strength and vitality, like that of a new friend. Soon, the last trace of pain she had endured drifted away from her new physique, taking with it the affliction that had tried to drag her to the depths of hell. Also gone, were the remnants of the dark Warlock's poison, it finally flushed from her veins, along with the insatiable need to devour the two mortals. She felt invigorated.

Eleanor lifted her arms, inspecting them: the cuts and bruises inflicted on her throughout her ordeal—from her abduction to her escape—had all but gone, save for two. She reached for her neck—the puncture wounds, where Wareeshta had initially worked on her, had now reduced in size, and would soon close. She then looked down, aware of the other—the faded scar from the Dhampir's blade, now a shade of grey. These were the *stains* left by her transformation, marks she would carry into an unmarked future until time and events dictated her demise.

She looked skywards; the clouds began to part. As her new eyes widened with clarity, she gazed into the deepening turquoise sky and marvelled at the coming of the night, her face lighting up, seeing the distant flickering blue and red lights, emanating from the stars. Though immune to its late autumn chill, she closed her eyes and inhaled the night air, lavishing in its intoxicating scents, nature's glory filling her heightened senses with all its wonders. She lingered there a while, oblivious, at first, to those watching her, until insight compelled her to open her eyes again, aware of the constant figure next to her—the *one* who would die for her.

'You have been through quite an ordeal, my love,' he whispered to her. 'But this will be forgotten.'

Her blue eyes sparkled like pale sapphires, resting on *his* until they locked together in complete understanding of the unique bond they would always share. The Samurai's heart swelled with each matching beat, uniting them in perfect, timeless harmony. Now, fully aware of him, she placed *her* hand gently on his chest, feeling their connection, knowing nothing—and *no one*—could part them. And should that time come, she would gladly go with him—in life or death.

Asai stared down at Eleanor, spellbound by her. No words were needed to express his feelings; she *knew*. His life was complete, now that they shared the same affliction. But he no longer saw it as that—nor did he care. He would rather be locked in eternity with her than endure a mortal life without her—and should anyone try to separate them …

The two lovers smiled together as the group looked on, moved by their reunion yet feeling intrusive of their private moment as they shared awkward looks.

'What just—I don't understand,' said Daine. 'I thought she was going to attack us.' He looked to Rosalyn. Reluctant to admit that her daughter could do them any harm, she nodded in agreement. She had seen the look of hunger in Eleanor's eyes—the same look she had seen in Tam's when they had first met. She sighed when the Highlander came to mind; she missed him.

'Perhaps,' said Wareeshta, 'had she been alone and without the unique bond she shares with *him*,' she added, pointing to Asai with her chin. 'It is a rare thing to not …' Her words drifted, sparing the feelings of the mortals; her friend's mother did not need to hear how her daughter would have torn into them with her need to satiate her thirst, had a part of Magia Nera still flowed through Eleanor's veins. But the Samurai's timely intervention had, to say the least, saved their souls. They were no longer in danger, and Asai would show his immortal beloved the way. She looked up, hearing the silence as everyone waited for her to finish what she was saying. She glanced at Eleanor and smiled. 'Yes, it is a rare and beautiful thing, to see her and know that she is now … well.'

'But what if she ...?' Oran was glaring at Wareeshta.

'She will not,' said Reece, intervening. 'You have our word.' He looked at Wareeshta and nodded. She lowered her eyes and smiled faintly with a feeling that their "relationship" had shifted, and hoped that any conflict between them had ended. *Time will tell*, she thought.

Rosalyn eyed her daughter, trying to grip the reality of what had happened to her. She was no longer the same Eleanor she had given birth to, almost twenty years ago. While she looked like her, she was "different", and "changed" beyond recognition—in a way she could not fathom. *Cursed like the others*, she thought. She had no idea how to approach it, or *her*, for that matter; Eleanor seemed distant and detached from what was happening—save for the Samurai's constant presence. But Rosalyn understood why; they were the perfect match, inseparable, through the unexpected affinity the two had shared from the moment their eyes first met, it now sealing their union forever. *How long is forever, in their world?* she wondered.

Sensing another's enquiring look, Eleanor slowly turned from Asai, to meet her mother's gaze. Rosalyn managed a hesitant half-smile as they looked across at one another. It took several moments for it to register, Rosalyn blinking when her daughter returned a faint smile; though not the wide-eyed beam Eleanor always gave—*used to give*—it came across as one of recognition. And yet ... It would take some getting used to. But, despite her daughter's new ... *disposition*, she would always be *her* Eleanor—and still alive!

'Give her time,' said Wareeshta, having observed Rosalyn's awkwardness and uncertainty. 'He will help Eleanor to find her way. While a part of her has died'—she stopped when Rosalyn made a start at the statement—'she is *still* your daughter. It will be all right. I promise you.'

Reassured by the Dhampir's soft words of consolation, Rosalyn smiled at Wareeshta; it was a heartfelt one, of gratitude, for giving her back her precious daughter.

But the moment of acceptance was short-lived when Eleanor's

head snapped up, her new senses alert. She looked towards the forest, her eyes tapering as she looked up; something had distracted her, warning the group.

'I see five,' stated Asai. Eleanor remained rigid, staring, as he removed his weapons.

'Likewise!' said Reece, now wielding his broadsword.

Oran rushed to Gill and Rosalyn's side. Daine edged close to them; he did not want to be alone if they were attacked again. Sensing her mistress's instincts, Rave went to Eleanor, her hackles raised as she crouched beside her. She nudged her hand; prompted by a memory, Eleanor responded, by tipping the hound on the nose, silently telling her to *stay!* She obeyed.

A sudden, uncomfortable quietness gripped them while they waited, its sinister effect putting them on edge. Rave snarled.

'I see them, too.' They were her first words—strong and controlled. Her eyes darted, catching glimpses of swift movements, dancing erratically between the trees.

Daine narrowed his eyes, trying desperately to see what the young woman and the Dhampir were looking at. He then made a start, seeing them, too. 'Oh, my—there are so many!' he blurted.

'Do not be fooled,' said Asai. 'It is an illusion to trick the eye, to make it appear as if there are more. It is a tactic used in battle—one I was foolish to teach *them*.'

Daine inched closer to Rosalyn, who stood behind Oran and Gill; he knew who the Samurai was referring to when he said "them."

Reece's eyes flashed, following the Dhampir warriors' predictable movements as they built momentum before their attack. He was privy to their games; he had participated during his incarceration and knew what to expect.

Gill jolted when the dirk was abruptly snatched from his hand by its true owner. Sister and brother shared a look and he wondered if Eleanor remembered him, and when she smiled in a way he recognised, he cast aside his worry.

Reunited with her precious family heirloom, Eleanor grasped the hilt, becoming one with it. Then, turning on her heel, she swiftly took her place between Reece and Asai.

'Wait!' said Reece. 'I count six.'

'No,' she replied, with conviction. 'There are *more!*'

# Chapter Twenty-One

*The Ruins of Moyne*

Swiftly, and quietly, she slipped into the sepulchre, taking care to keep within its shadows, away from the entrance; insects, lurking between the crevices of its damp walls, scattered, aware of her ominous presence.

Kara looked around its emptiness, allowing her eyes to adjust to the dim light until she could see clearly; another advantage of her transformation. As she moved to inspect it, a slight movement on the sepulchre's threshold forced her to stall. Lifting her head, she searched for a scent, catching it, then smiled in recognition of the one who wore it.

'Have you missed me, Turloch?'

Turloch, the self-proclaimed ringleader of the remaining six Dhampir, glanced over his shoulder before stepping into Kara's presence. *Good*, he thought; the others were not watching him.

The Valkyrie smiled with contempt when Turloch entered the sepulchre. She had had the pleasure of his company—*once!*—and had almost destroyed him after, but decided against it; she was "fond" of him and, just like the Highlander, had decided to let him live, too. Turloch would be useful; only this time, she would make certain *he* would not betray her.

It had come to her attention, as she came to know them, the older—and more experienced—Dhampir had begun to question their existence; the longer they remained bonded to the Sorceress, their human side began to influence them, with fleeting reminders of their past, when they were once mortal. While it proved interesting, they were, nonetheless, still a threat. And because of that potential "inconvenience" she needed to dispatch some of them.

"Attack their weakness," she had once told the Sorceress, much to L'Ordana's distaste. However, as for the younger—*fresh*—ones ... they were senseless, like suppressed puppets made to dance under invisible strings. Their duty was to serve, fight and destroy. Nothing more. Nothing less.

Turloch's vivid blue eyes widened when she came into full view. She now stood head-to-head with him. He marvelled at her transformation as he eyed her from head to toe. Everything about her—apart from her crooked nose—was exaggerated: grandiose in stature, she stood before him in her armour, its colour now like graphite, where it was once silver; her physique was solid, displaying her power as she held the Obsidian in her grip; and her eyes—they peered at him with such intensity he thought he would weaken, even die, should they stab him with their cold-blooded wintery glare. When she lifted her chin, allowing him to admire her, his nose twitched, aware of *it*—her new scent. Gone was the aroma of sweet lemon oil, it now replaced by another; though pungent on the nose, it was its underlying taint of putrid that caught him, with its provocative allure. Yes, she was more powerful ... and dangerous.

Kara then lowered her head, her eyes still on him as he caressed her with his scrutiny, she relishing in the way he leered at her.

An image of *that* rendezvous then cast a pleasurable and unrefined expression on his face—the feeling gradually moving through his body.

The corner of her mouth twitched. 'I see you remember, Turloch,' she purred, teasing him.

He took a step closer, stimulating her heightened senses. She could almost feel him upon her. The temptation was great, but there was no time for that. She would have to resist ... for now.

'I want you to come with me.' Her voice was controlled and steady.

He hesitated, tilting his head to the side. 'She thinks you—'

'Dead?' she interrupted, in a matter-of-fact tone.

He slowly shook his head.

'She thinks you have betrayed her, by desertion,' he stated.

'How curious?' she said, frowning, trying to retrace her steps before her transformation. Fragments of images were still scattered in her head, coming and going as she tried to put more pieces together of what had happened, in the moments before. Though vague, they were gradually forming into pictures. Her eyes then dropped to her arm, seeing the scar. She studied it, realising it was the only visible one; all others she had received from great battles had gone. This one, however, was a stigma of an unwarranted act inflicted upon her.

Kara glanced over Turloch's shoulder, looking beyond the sepulchre's exit, then nodded to herself, reminded again of the perpetrator. *Magia Nera!* She glanced down at the scar again, her gut feeling prompting her to believe, the dark Warlock had not been alone in his scheme. *Wareeshta! She knew!*

She nodded again, her thoughts distracting her from Turloch's suspicions as they competed with his unquenchable want for her. It was all too obvious now as she called to mind Wareeshta's behaviour: the sideward glances; the subtle smirks towards her; the contradictions … *The blade!* Yes, Wareeshta knew all along and had said nothing.

*She left me to die!*

Kara, stone-faced, stepped towards Turloch and leaned in his ear, her gravelly voice low and vindictive.

'Side with me and you shall reap the rewards—all the rewards you seek.'

He knew what she wanted—*Revenge!*—but it would not be easy.

'What of my rival?' he replied, side-glancing her. 'What of *him?*'

'You have none,' she said, drawing back, understanding his meaning.

Turloch turned his head and faced her, their eyes within inches of each other.

She smirked. 'Tam is … no more.'

The Dhampir raised a brow. 'How can I be certain?'

'Because …'—she stroked the Obsidian—the grin still etched on her face—'it was by *my* hand.'

'And Asai and Reece? Did they not retaliate, for their comrade's demise?'

Kara released a deep-rooted grunt of self-satisfaction, then nodded.

'But they were unable to,' she revealed—the sneer in her tone hinting at the extent of her new powers, linked to her transformation. He would now re-think his loyalties. It seemed it would be more rewarding to side with the Valkyrie. It excited him. His eyes warmed, watching her with undisguised longing while she waited impatiently for his resolve. However, her mind was too caught up with thoughts of other pressing matters, to give him what he craved. *It would be a shame to destroy you*, she thought as their eyes clung to each other.

'You have my ear.'

*Wise choice, Turloch.* Content, Kara proceeded to indulge him with her plan, feigning her "need" for him, to help rid them of Asai and Reece … and the others. Yes, Turloch and the remaining Dhampir would buy her time.

After she had said her piece, a heated silence filled the sepulchre with their energy as they continued to hold one another's look. She hoped he would not keep her waiting while he made his decision. If he refused, she would dispatch him. She grasped the Obsidian tighter, feeling its charge as she waited, her patience running out while, in her mind, silently warning him:

*You have five seconds … One … Two … Three … Four—*

'You have my allegiance,' he quickly responded, as though he had read her narcissistic mind.

She grunted. 'I never doubted your loyalty to me,' she said, with a wry smile. 'And the others? They will follow you?'

His face twitched from the edge of his mouth. He was sure of it, though he had never commanded them before. It had not been his place. But he was confident the younger Dhampir would; though reckless and non-too-bright, they would likely do what he asked, especially if it involved a conflict; they hungered for it. But there was one he was wary of … the dark Warlock. Magia was clever and also unpredictable.

A thought then occurred to Kara: 'There is the small matter of a particular "obstacle" that stands in your way,' she said. 'If you are bonded to *her* … how can you follow *me?*'

Smiling with confidence, Turloch took great pleasure in reassuring his new ally. 'L'Ordana has freed us all from our bonds, for us to retaliate against the enemy—should we be required to venture farther than our restraints allow,' he revealed.

Her moist lips parted as her eyes widened. This was good news and it excited her to hear it. She leaned towards him, enveloping him in the sharpness of her heady, new musk.

'You have no idea how much this pleases me,' she whispered, stroking his long white hair.

He closed his eyes, feeling the warmth of her breath against the coldness of his pallid skin. At first, Turloch had had misgivings about the Valkyrie, but now there was something in her new appeal—something he could not resist. Knowing this, Kara slowly pressed her lips against his cheek; he groaned from their moistness. And when he felt the tip of her tongue touch his skin, he drew a quick breath, it intoxicating him, and casting away any doubts.

Feeling the surge of his energy, Kara recoiled; another second and he would have been upon her—and she, unable to resist.

Turloch made a start, his eyes flaring, angered by her rejection of him.

'There will be time enough for that—later,' she purred, lowering her head while keeping her eyes on him. 'You know what to do, now?'

Silence divided them and, for a moment, Kara thought he would change his mind. If so …

He then nodded.

'But the Warlock keeps a watchful eye on us,' he stated.

'Magia's eye has been diverted by something more urgent,' she returned. 'This, I can assure you … unquestionably!'

Yielding to her self-confidence, Turloch acknowledged it with reverence. 'Now that you have my loyalty,' he began, 'where will you lead us?'

Kara smirked and slowly nodded.

'Oh, you shall *know* it,' she said. 'For you shall *smell* it. Now go … before you are missed. Speak to them,' she added, glancing towards the entrance. 'Show them *you* are their leader.'

Now convinced, he grinned and turned from her, to exit.

'And Turloch …?'

The Dhampir paused in the stepwell, then looked over his shoulder at her, his eyes blue again—the hue of red barely visible now as they watched her with longing, still hoping …

'When you find them … destroy them! Except for the girl. She is mine!'

Turloch's departure went unheard, like a ghost, his tread silent and quick. His scent lingered on her nose, and she knew hers would stay with him, its potent effect spurring him on.

With the resumption of quietness, she resumed her observation of the sepulchre, keeping her wits about her.

Below her, on the stone ground, she noticed strands of hair strewn across the surface, near a blanket, like uneven fine lines of gold inlay. She moved closer, catching traces of the girl's scent on her nose.

*A great pity*, she told herself, reaching down to take a strand, then pausing when her attention was drawn to a dark yet notable stain in the stone floor. Disregarding the hair, she let her hands wander to it. She slid her fingers across the cold stone, touching it, feeling it, smelling it. She then grunted, remembering: it was the stale remains of the sleeping potion they had used on the girl. She frowned, momentarily frustrated, aware of something else, it niggling at her, urging her to look for *it.* Her eyes darted, searching, then stopped when the glint of a small object caught her attention.

Tossed away into a shadowy corner, by the hand that had last held it, she picked it up, her thumb flinching from the sharpness of the glass when it cut into her flesh. The deep, crimson blood poured from the wound; she inhaled the glorious smell of it before running her tongue over the flesh, indulging in its salty, metallic taste. She picked up the remnants of the shattered vile. As she inspected it, she subconsciously licked her thumb again, then drew back, frowning, when the blood flow had stopped; already, the cut was healing.

As her eyes slid back to the pieces of fine glass, it dawned on her: '*Wareeshta!*' she whispered, nodding.

It was now evident to Kara what had unfolded in the sepulchre: 'So, she *did* help you to escape, pretty one. I should have guessed.' It was likely the girl was reunited with her friends. *You will pay for that, too, Wareeshta.*

As Kara turned to leave, the sound of a raised voice outside stopped her.

'No! *I* am in control!'

Hearing the female voice—one she did not recognise—Kara dared to peep her head out of the entrance. On the far side, near the edge of the cemetery, she saw the Sorceress in a state of agitation. But who did that voice belong to? Beside her, Magia Nera attempted to calm and reassure her.

Fascinated, Kara maintained her curiosity, engrossing herself in the interesting conversation that followed, absorbing it. She grinned, relishing the revelations—the two ignorant of her presence. She wondered how Magia failed to detect her. She subtly lifted her head. *Ah, yes,*' she realised, catching the Dhampir's scent. *The wind is in my favour.*

'I fear I am losing control.'

Though confused about the mysterious voice, Kara recognised this one and continued her scrutiny, watching L'Ordana, with intent; her whole demeanour cried, "*weakness!*". Seeing her hunched over like an old woman, almost pleading to the Warlock, Kara concluded her "Mistress"—as she once called her—was losing her powers.

Kara's eyes then widened when L'Ordana's hood slipped from her face, revealing her diminishing features, just before Magia replaced it, concealing them again. She narrowed her eyes when she observed the dark Warlock dragging the Sorceress back to her holding, noting the reason: the remaining Dhampir and Turloch were watching them. She smirked, listening, grasping pieces of their wily conversation. *Well done, Turloch.* Magia and L'Ordana had failed to miss his brief absence.

Kara held on in the sepulchre, stalling until the time was right to leave. As she moved to go, she paused, distracted by something across the grounds, like a beam of yellow light, glinting at her. She caught her breath, catching a glimpse of an object, its brilliance magnetic as it was briefly held to the daylight by its master. It was the amulet. She gazed at it from where she stood, hoping Magia would not see her. But no, he was too distracted by it. She clenched her hand, conscious of the fading scar on her palm, from when she had tried to retrieve it for the Sorceress. It had burned the thick skin, preventing her from taking it. She resented L'Ordana for that; the Sorceress knew what she was doing when she had asked her to take it. And now, seeing it again, in its true glory, she wanted it. But when Magia turned away, disappearing from view, Kara's face fell, her features hardening. Things had now changed.

She cursed herself for thinking she could solely destroy the Sorceress while she was in Magia Nera's company. And with his amulet returned to him ... He would gladly send her to Valhalla, claiming to be the victor. It was now clear to Kara, the Sorceress and the Warlock were allies. And she knew where they were going.

Thoughts of a strategy ploughed through her mind as she hovered by the doorway, contemplating her next move. She would follow them … from above.

'Give it back to me!'

Kara looked sharp, then peeped out again. She saw L'Ordana standing at the entrance to her tent, her back to the clearing, yelling at the dark Warlock.

'Give it back!'

*And, also, her mind, it would seem*, Kara mused, grinning to herself. The thrill of killing the Sorceress now stimulated her senses. *How easy it would be—while she has her back to me.* She worked out the attack in her mind: with her new exceptional speed, she would rush L'Ordana—while they were oblivious—and drive the Obsidian into her failing body. It would pass through her with ease, unlike the Highlander, who had been built like an ox.

Kara looked again, her concentration pinned on her target. Now was the time to strike. *While she is vulnerable.*

As she stepped up to the stairwell, her hand gripping the Obsidian, Kara readied herself for the attack, then hesitated, hearing Magia's voice again.

'My amulet is of no use to you, L'Ordana …'

Kara raised a brow. *How interesting*, she mused, re-assessing the situation; if the Sorceress could not have it …

Slipping quietly back into the sepulchre, she pondered over this new revelation, her icy grey eyes travelling over the moss-ridden walls, trying to catch her thoughts—the sound of the little insects scurrying about, their loud scratching distracting her; she scrunched her face, their sweet musty odour also prominent. It disgusted her. Feeling the weight of the sepulchre's dank atmosphere, she knew she could not stay much longer.

'We must go.'

Having heard Magia's words, and with vengeance at the forefront of her mind, Kara resolved to leave.

Once more, she glanced out; Magia and L'Ordana were still out of sight, though not for long. With her mind filled with notions of power and triumph, Kara chose her moment to go and quietly crept out. And as she did, she caught Turloch's eye. With a final nod to him, she took flight.

# Chapter Twenty-Two

*The Paths of Lome*

'There are *more?* Are you—'

'Eight!' Eleanor snapped, her eyes flaring at her grandfather.

As Reece stared into his granddaughter's eyes—the whites coated with the familiar reddish hue from her transformation, he saw certainty in them. He believed her; as a newborn, her new elevated senses could detect things quicker.

As Eleanor turned her attention to the thicket of trees, the group followed her eyeline. Alert, she lifted her nose, catching *it* on a subtle breeze. *I can smell her!* 'It is Kara!' she blurted, drawing Asai to her. 'She has changed …' She stepped back, then looked up at him. 'She is *stronger!* I can feel it. But how?'

'Kara was also struck by one of their blades,' Wareeshta stated, 'like you were.'

'The venom?' said Eleanor, turning to her friend.

Wareeshta nodded.

'Unfortunately, she survived the transformation,' she said. 'And without my help,' she quickly added.

'Hence her alteration,' said Asai, 'it changing her to something beyond evil.'

'I wondered when she would show her face again,' sneered Reece.

'Nor is she alone,' said Asai.

An eerie stillness fell over the company—the ominous calm before the storm. Conscious of it, no one stirred, and no one spoke as they listened arduously for the slightest indication of an attack. But the threat had left as quickly as it had arrived. But for how long?

Taking advantage of their distraction, Wareeshta slipped behind Oran—the Warlock unaware of it until she murmured in his ear; 'I know you have it.'

Oran flicked his head, taken aback then looked down at her.

'I … don't know what you—'

'Do not insult me, Warlock!' she hissed, her eyes skimming back and forth, watching the others, hoping they did not hear her. 'What was once my father's, is now mine.'

'Your—'

'*Da!*' My *father's!*' she echoed, tilting her head towards Nepthys, eyeing the buckskin, leather satchel attached to the mare's saddle.

Oran's mind raced at the sudden revelation, that Wareeshta was the daughter of the Elliyan's old enemy, Vlad the Impaler. It seemed the Dhampir was steadfast in wanting to reclaim her legacy. However, as the amulet around his neck pressed against him—his constant reminder of their task—he was not ready to surrender the book.

'What fate awaits it?' he asked beneath his breath.

'I intend to destroy it.'

'No!' he snapped through gritted teeth, keeping his voice low. 'I *cannot* let you—at least—not until I am done with it. Allow me this *one* thing, then I shall return it to you. You must trust me.'

The Dhampir raised her brows, somewhat bewildered, then grunted. 'Trust *you?*' she sneered, 'when you would not do so for me?' she reminded him, glancing over at Eleanor. 'I saved her *life!*'

Oran's eyes travelled to Eleanor; he regarded his daughter as she stood proud and armed between Asai and Reece, undaunted by the impending conflict as it hid in the shadows, biding its time. Despite what she had become—despite him having to come to terms with it—Eleanor was still alive. He never thought of it that way, then realised, deep down, how grateful he was to Wareeshta for what she had done. As with Gill, Eleanor was equally precious to him.

'Forgive me.' The words fell softly from his mouth as he turned to acknowledge her. He hesitated, narrowing his eyes, confused by something. 'Why destroy what you claim to be rightfully yours?'

'*Claim?*' she returned. She shook her head. 'It belongs to *me*. Nevertheless, despite my … "claim" … I have always known of the evil attached to its cursed pages and what it is capable of, should it fall into the wrong hands. It must be destroyed.'

Oran held her look, then understood the determination in her deep-set brown eyes.

'On all that I love and cherish,' he began, 'I vow to return your book to you—but *not* until I am done with it. Trust in my vow; it is an honourable one—not a capitulation.' Wareeshta peered up into his hazel eyes, looking for the honesty in them. 'Only a true Warlock keeps his oath,' he stated, still feeling obliged to justify himself. 'I *am* that Warlock.'

An element of doubt niggled at Wareeshta, unsure of Oran's promise. But as he kept his eyes on hers, she rifled through his words for a hint of betrayal. Detecting none, she nodded, though maintained her guard.

'That remains to be seen … Warlock,' she returned. 'Use it, then—for your purpose.' She side-glanced him. 'But *only* for that.'

With a tilt of his head, a rare understanding passed between Warlock and Dhampir. It did not go unnoticed.

A tinge of jealousy appeared on Rosalyn's face when she eyed her husband and the Dhampir in their private conversation. Pan-faced, she pressed her lips together, trying to hold her tongue when the two held each other's gaze. *What stirs between you?* she thought. She considered their "relationship". After all, Oran had spent the last three years associated with the Dhampir. As she watched them, huddled together, her eyes narrowed, raising her suspicions when she saw Wareeshta smile warmly after Oran had whispered something in her ear.

Compelled to know what amused the "collaborators", Rosalyn

moved to confront them, then stopped, feeling a chill when the wind conjured itself, disturbing the stillness; autumn's withered leaves lifted off the ground—the shift in the wind transporting them into a myriad of orchestrated dance as they swirled about the groups' feet. It was unnatural, giving them cause to keep their guard. Then, as if on command, the leaves ceased, falling lightly, coating the ground again, their autumnal shades now grey beneath the gathering darkness.

The atmosphere returned to its uncanny quietness—along with the sense of unease—rising to apprehension, filling its void. Rave snarled and crouched low, her sharp, sixth sense fore-warning the group. The horses had sensed it, too—the stomping of their hooves, adding to their restlessness.

With a sharp nod from Oran, Kai glided over to Rosalyn, standing near the monoliths, and placed his protective aura around her. Servitor and Warlock nodded to one another with conviction; no matter what, Rosalyn was to be kept safe, and should it come to a worst-case scenario, the Servitor would know what to do.

'No, Kai,' she whispered—the tone in her voice insistent as he enveloped her within the safety of his shield. 'You must protect Gill.'

'He does not need it,' he replied, smiling at her, confident.

With the threat still looming over them, the company of seven grouped in silence, and waited …

Exploited by centuries of evil and immorality, the forest stared down, intimidating them, its ether more threatening than their encounter with the Picts, earlier—the lowering of the misty evening sky, adding to the sinister atmosphere.

Daine, the other mortal among them, subtly inched towards the Dhampir, keeping within their protection. If there were a time he longed for home—and a drink—it was now, though feared he would never see either again. His eyes wandered towards Oran; the Warlock was still hovering where the horses were tied, engaged in what looked like a cutting conversation with the female Dhampir. *How curious*, he thought, then stole a look at Rosalyn while her husband was distracted; catching it, she forced a smile, then slowly lifted her shoulders as though acknowledging what might have been … had her husband not appeared. In his mind, he hoped that had been the reasoning behind her silent response. *I should have left—when I had the chance*, he thought, regretting his decision while regretting not having her. But there was still "that moment". *That kiss* …

Oran glanced over his shoulder, catching the exchange between his wife and the guide. He narrowed his eyes, slowly shaking his head, his mind still awash with thoughts of them—

'Ready yourselves!'

Reece's warning snapped Oran from his suspicions.

'I will protect the horses!' Wareeshta called out to Reece.

Oran's face creased into a scowl as he stared down at Wareeshta.

She rolled her eyes. 'If we leave them unattended, the Dhampir will either take them'—Oran glanced at Nepthys, eyeing the satchel—'or kill them,' she said, removing the stiletto daggers from her boots. 'They will do anything to stop us.'

'Well, we cannot allow *that*,' he returned. With one final glance, to be sure his wife was under the Servitor's protection, Oran gripped the Albrecht.

Ignoring the erratic shifting of the pylons' surfaces, the group shuffled, preparing themselves. The nervous silence was broken, by the horses' increased agitation—the distant rustling and creaking of branches as the wind rose again, taking momentum, unnerving them as it advanced towards the clearing, forcing the trees to bend to its will.

It was announcing the arrival of their unwanted guests.

One by one, the creatures catapulted through the forest, their speed increasing as they weaved their way with expertise between the stagnant army of trees—the fevered desire to destroy ingrained in their making. But as they advanced, Kara and Turloch held back, keeping their distance, biding their time—planning their moment to strike.

'Remember the blades!' warned Wareeshta as she followed their silhouettes with keen eyes.

Though surrounded by his comrades, Daine felt alone and defenceless against their attackers' speed as he looked on, their constant activity casting flittering shadows against the ghostly light; it was confusing and dizzying. He staggered but was promptly steadied by Asai, who had taken it upon himself to protect the guide, by choosing to stay with him.

'Now is the time to remove your sword,' uttered the Samurai, indicating to Daine with the katana, then promptly showed the guide how it was done. 'Extend it so … and keep it there with all your strength, no matter *how* they attack. It will be soon. Keep your wits about you; they will pause briefly to avoid the blade. Watch for that. When you see it, seize the moment and use your weapon. Do *not* waver, otherwise …'

*Otherwise* … It was all he needed to hear, to convince him. And though the Samurai's advice was short and to the point, it renewed some of his confidence. Knowing he had Asai's protection, Daine, as instructed, reached for his sword.

Still armed with Tam's claymore, Gill cast aside his self-doubt and swiftly took his place beside Reece and Eleanor. He seemed to tower above them, with his strong and muscular physique.

Meanwhile, Wareeshta remained by Oran's side, near the horses, keeping an eye on her "interests". Until she had her book, she would ensure that the Warlock was steadfast in his promise.

'Here they come!' Reece's warning was final.

Out from the shadows, they leapt—the fire in their eyes and the hardness on their pallid features, warning the company of their purpose—and how they would be relentless in their attack. *"No survivors!"* It had been instilled in them from the beginning—to kill with no remorse. They were young and predictable; Reece, Asai and Wareeshta knew that, however, the company they protected did not, it compromising everything, should they stray.

Wielding their weapons, the creatures rushed straight into the clearing where their enemy waited. Within seconds, the clash of metal reigned over the stillness as the creatures rushed to and fro, ducking and diving, their aim to confuse. But Asai and Reece were privy to their methods.

Two skirted dangerously close to the horses, unnerving them, and threatening to strike them with their poisonous blades, their agility keeping Oran and Wareeshta occupied as they fought them off.

'Daine!' cried Rosalyn, catching a glimpse of one of the creatures near him. 'To me!'

A moment delayed in producing his weapon would have meant the guide's demise had he not heard her cry. Daine spun on his heel, narrowly avoiding the creature as it brushed by him. It swiftly turned and rushed him again. But when Daine's sword clashed with its double-edged—the two weapons ringing in song as they struck—the creature paused briefly, as if the high-pitched tone had stunned it for an instant, rendering it vulnerable. The creature's red eyes locked with Daine's—the guide's wide with astonishment, staring into their emotionless pits. Both were caught unawares. But the failure had been on the creature's part; Asai, having seen its brief hesitation, and conscious of how crucial timing was, cried out;

'To the ground!'

Sword in hand, Daine dropped to his knees. As he did so, the Samurai swung around. With katana and wakizashi united again in battle, he sliced the creature's torso, deep, its dark rancid blood staining the beauty of autumn's carpet.

'Finish it!' cried Asai when the creature's body dropped with a heavy thud beside Daine—the guide's stomach heaving when he saw the deep gashes pumping blood, it spreading out over the ground towards him. He stared, momentarily stunned by the gruesome sight.

'Do it!' He flinched at Asai's demand, then shook his head, confused, unaware of the Samurai's meaning. Daine looked up, his mouth gaping when he saw Asai resume his fight, setting his sights on the other attackers, with no thought or regard for what he had just done.

Daine panicked. 'Fi—finish what?'

'Through the heart!' Reece cried back as another creature leapt high. 'Until the tip of your sword connects with the earth,' he quickly added, raising his broadsword skywards before the creature fell on it—the weapon impaling it clean through before Reece flipped it over, pinning it to the ground. Wrenching his sword from its spasming body Reece brought the blade down, finishing it off, its head then rolling by Daine.

Spurred by survival instinct, Daine jumped up and, lifting his sword above his head, plunged the weapon down, driving it clean through the creature's heart. As it connected with the earth, he could feel the slow vibration of the doomed creature's heartbeat through his steel. It screeched and writhed, its bulging eyes staring up at the guide as it clawed at the blade, blood flowing from the deep gashes in its hands as it tried to reach for him—the black veins beneath its skin throbbing, desperately holding on to what remained of its pathetic life. Struggling against its immense strength, Daine threw his weight on the hilt of his sword, his grip shaking as he drove it further into the ground with all his strength, leaving only the hilt exposed. The creature ceased in its struggle.

Then silence.

Breathless, Daine recoiled, his chest tight and heaving as he stared down at his victim. He jolted, falling back when the creature's head was suddenly parted from its body, by the swiftness of the Samurai's katana—the curved, lethal weapon slicing clean through all the muscles, nerves, blood vessels and arteries, severing it from the cervical spine.

'What the—'

'It is necessary,' said Asai, hauling Daine to his feet. 'We must be sure they do not live because the others *will* return,' he warned.

A stream of sweat rolled down Daine's face as he looked up, still shaking inside from the ordeal. The other creatures had disappeared into the deep crevices of the forest, as quickly as they had appeared.

All except one.

Daine's mouth gaped. 'Watch out!'

Wild with rage while burning in a frenzy of want, aware of the two mortals within the group, the lone creature came from nowhere, careering around its targets, its eyes flashing between Daine and Rosalyn, working out how to get to them. It then fixed its hungry stare on Rosalyn. Though shielded within Kai's protection, her strong, female musk still reached the creature's senses; it emanated from her fear and adrenalin, driving its appetite to the point where, in its blind hunger, it overlooked the others.

Suddenly, it bolted through the gap between Reece and Asai.

Rosalyn froze.

In its frenzy to have her, the creature failed to notice the individual coming from its right, their immediate intervention preventing its charge.

When the creature had successfully bypassed Reece and Asai, the Samurai, in his attempt to stop it, had missed his target, by a fraction; his wakizashi had only sliced through its clothing, leaving the creature unharmed. It was in that vital moment, having pre-empted it, when Eleanor leapt into action, her movement so swift it caught the creature off-guard; it stumbled, losing its sword in the process. It hesitated, then looked sharp, caught between its weapon and Eleanor. But by the time it found its feet again, she had pinned the unarmed creature to a tree with one hand—the dirk in her left—ready to pierce its throat with her deadly weapon.

'Wait, Eleanor!'

Hearing Asai's voice, Eleanor stalled as she met with the creature's face; her nose twitched from the stench of his foul breath. Where once, she had recoiled with fear from the look in their killer-instinct eyes, she now matched them, prepared to do the same. She flinched when she found her grip replaced by that of the Samurai's.

'Release your hold on him,' said Asai, his voice calm yet firm; he did not want her parents, especially her mother, to witness the potential bloodbath their daughter was now capable of running.

Eleanor, her nostrils flaring for the want—the desire—to kill the creature that would threaten to do the same to her family, stood firm and reluctant, her eyes boring into her potential victim. She wanted to do it—to *kill* him—the urge so strong she found it difficult to tear herself from the irresistible craving inside her.

'Eleanor.'

Eyes still burning, she drew back, releasing her grip, leaving the creature in the capable—and controlled—hands of her Samurai.

Mindful of another likely attack, knowing their enemy was lurking somewhere in the dark, among the trees, the group remained alert while Reece and Asai dealt with their captive.

'*Where* is she?'

The creature lashed out under the Samurai's grip, refusing to answer.

'Where is the Sorceress?' hissed Reece, now holding his blood-stained broadsword across its throat. 'Tell us, or do you want to end up like *them?*' he added, nodding back to what remained of its fallen comrades.

The creature snorted and spat at him. 'I do not serve *her*.'

'*Who*, then?'

'You will know, soon enough … *traitor!* … when she *dispatches* you all!'

Tightening his hold on their captive, Asai leaned closer to say something, then looked sharp when another hand gripped the creature, lifting it off its feet and away from him.

'Your work here is done!'

The creature glowered up at Gill, unsure, stiffening within his hold as it was hauled away from Reece and Asai—towards the three monoliths.

On seeing this, Oran rushed forward—the weight of his amulet reacting to the sudden panic in his demeanour.

'Gill! No!' he yelled out, desperate to stop his son. Nor was he alone in his desperation; Kai was already making his way towards Gill, fearing the consequences of his next move—should he succeed in his unforeseen actions.

Gripped hard within its enemy's hold, the creature stared at the monoliths as they loomed quickly, confused by their ever-changing surfaces—the ancient structures aware of its evil presence. Without a second thought, and unaware of his father and the Servitor, in their urgent need to stop him, Gill charged forward, then briefly hesitated on the threshold of one of the passages.

'Don't do it, Gill! It could be the—'

By the time they reached him, it was too late. Blinded by anger, Gill had hurled the creature forward, and when it landed on its feet it took off, disappearing into the tunnel of darkness—oblivious to what lay ahead.

'What have you done, Gill?'

# Chapter Twenty-Three

As if wrenched from a nightmare, Gill flinched and stared at Oran—the trace of anger still visible in his eyes, it momentarily concealing the flecks of gold before they reappeared, glinting back at his father.

'What?' he said, squinting at Oran, somewhat confused. 'What do you mean?' Gill rubbed his eyes, then, feeling the creature's energy coursing through his hand, looked down. His eyes widened when he saw it again—the blackness of his unexpected actions creeping along the lines of his palm, like before, when he almost cast the guide into the cursed waters at the Cordhu Pass, it making its mark. He rubbed his hand against his cloak, repulsed by it, trying to rid himself of its stinging after-effect.

Then it was gone.

'Gill!' Oran persisted.

His son jolted.

'Have you lost your mind?!' he yelled, pointing towards the passage where Gill had sent the creature on its way. 'What if—that was the right one?'

'What is happening?' asked Rosalyn, promptly moving to Kai, making a point of staying close to him. But the Servitor, in complete understanding of what Gill had done, and the possible consequences attached to his thoughtless actions, kept his concentration on the monoliths; they were still in their chaotic and constant state of change, making it difficult to decipher them. 'Is someone going to tell me or—' She stopped when it dawned on her, seeing the look of disbelief and realisation appear on her son's face.

Now aware of his grave error, Gill peered back at his father, his mouth gaping. He turned towards the monoliths, unable to take his eyes from their surfaces when they began to slow, aware of their "intruder". He shook his head in denial, trying to grasp what he had done, fearing he had shown the creature the way to Elboru. If so … No, he refused to believe it. What were the chances? He had seen what lay in wait beyond two of the passages. And yet, it was possible the creature could have …

'Quiet!' said Eleanor, suddenly lifting her hand. She stepped forward, taking her place beside her brother.

'Oh, Nori, how could I have been so—'

'I hear something,' she whispered, interrupting him, then tilted her head towards the passage, where the creature had disappeared, her acute senses working.

'I hear nothing,' said Gill.

'Shh!' she hushed, narrowing her eyes.

The group exchanged wary looks as they waited; no one else, not even the Dhampir had heard it.

Then it came—the piercing shrill—echoing back at them from within the depths of the passage as they listened to the creature's final moments being played out through death's fatal grip. Rosalyn gasped—the chill of its demise reaching her, sending tremors down her spine. She stepped back, fearing it. She looked over at Daine, pitying him when she saw the strain of their predicament etched on his face; he looked drawn, a shadow of his former self as he stood rooted and alone. Inside, she battled between shame and longing, still unsure of her feelings.

The sharpness of the silence that followed wrenched her from her confusion. She looked towards the passage, no longer hearing it. Whatever *it* was—it had finally taken its victim, causing the monoliths to resume their constant motions of change.

'It seems luck was on our side,' said Reece.

'Luck had nothing to do with it,' snapped Oran. He then turned to his son; relieved, though guilt-ridden, Gill hung his head, avoiding his father's glare, conscious of his annoyance.

'*Timing* was the decider in this,' added Kai. 'But *this* cannot happen again,' he warned.

'I—' Gill raised his shoulders and lifted his hands, his silent plea for forgiveness having already been accepted.

'They will be back, though,' Asai stated.

Reece grunted. 'Where is your ghost army now?' he muttered.

Kai glanced at the Dhampir, then turned to Gill. 'You summoned the protectors of the monoliths?' he asked, taken aback by Reece's remark.

Oran looked sharp, equally surprised. 'Only the Magus has the power to do that!'

'They must have known *who* you are,' said Kai.

Gill shook his head.

'No! I did not summon them. It seems I have no command here until I am Magus. However, moments before the attack, instinct urged me to … speak with them; it was then, when I confronted them, they knew who I was destined to be. The clan chief recognised *this!*' He pointed to the brooch on his cloak, depicting their family name and crest.

'You—you spoke with him?' said Oran, stunned.

Gill nodded.

'And, he could converse with them in the ancient Gaelic,' Rosalyn proudly added.

'You could?' Oran raised his brows, a little amused, aware that his son was not quite fluent in the "modern" Gaelic.

'Aye. It seems we are descendants of his,' said Gill. 'He also informed me of my challenge—to test my willingness and to establish my true identity,' he went on, eyeing the monoliths.

'But why do they not show themselves now—with our enemy on our doorstep?' Reece persisted.

'When you disturbed the monoliths,' Kai began, 'the Picts were woken from their eternal rest. They are here for a reason—to stop the "intruder" from entering Elboru. And, despite the great challenge of having to unravel the enigma of the Paths, the "intruder" does not survive long enough to even *try* …' He turned back to Gill. 'But *you* are no "intruder". However, while their surfaces are still in motion, the ghost army will not appear now, assuming *you* are still here.'

'Even though …?' said Gill.

Kai nodded.

'Despite *who* you are.'

Reece grunted. 'How inconvenient.'

'And yet, how lucky for you,' said Kai, throwing the Dhampir a look, 'that the Picts knew who Gill was. Your grandson saved your life, Reece,' he then remarked before turning to Gill again. 'When you are Magus, instinct will always tell you which path to take. But, for now, you must choose. You cannot fail this test.'

'Which is why we should concentrate on getting out of here,' said Oran, eyeing Nepthys.

With a single sharp nod, Asai returned to where the fallen creatures lay, to ensure they were dead. Seeing the guide's sword still embedded in his victim, Asai removed Daine's weapon without effort. He looked down to where the slain Dhampir's de-capitated head had rolled—close to Daine's feet—and nodded, satisfied; the guide promptly stepped away, still shaking inside from his kill. He stared down into the lifeless eyes, now blackened by death, and shuddered; they seemed to be watching him, putting him on edge. He looked up, his eyes darting about, thinking everyone was staring at him. No one except Rosalyn took any interest. The deed was done, and that was it. The creature beneath his feet was dead, as was the other—the once-trained predators now worthless in death.

Rosalyn inched closer, unable to take her eyes off the corpse. As she stared down horrified, at first, her expression slowly changed; Daine saw a look of pity appear on her face as she tilted her head, her look of sympathy evident in her watering eyes.

'He *was* once mortal—someone's son,' she stated, feeling it necessary to remind the others of the life the creature had once lived before he was cursed. 'He, too, was a victim.'

'Your weapon.'

Daine swung round to see the Samurai handling his sword, its blade still fully drenched in the creature's blood.

'It is a fine, heavy weapon,' Asai remarked.

'It—it was my father's,' Daine muttered, grimacing, as the Samurai handed him the bloody sword; he could smell the foul stench of death on its steel—rancid and stagnant, where it no longer flowed through the creature's veins. 'Though … I know nothing of its genesis,' he added, turning his eyes away, looking for something to wipe it clean.

'Leave it,' said Reece, noting the look of disgust on the guide's face as he regarded his weapon. 'You are not finished with it yet, and a display of their colleagues' blood will mark a warning to the others. It is better to wait until they have all been destroyed, *then* you can cleanse it of their evil.'

Unimpressed, Daine threw a wry smile back at Reece, conscious of the stigma of destruction on his sword—and his hands. Though tempted to wipe it away, he thought better of it, not wanting to appear weak in their eyes.

Wareeshta promptly checked over the horses, taking advantage of the short reprieve before the next attack. Mindful of Oran's closeness and continuous eyes on her, she turned her attention to Nepthys and subtly patted the satchel attached to the mare's saddle, feeling the hardness of the book inside, assured of its ominous presence.

Oran grunted. 'Do you still not trust—' He stalled, distracted. He looked down—the constant presence of the object around his neck weighing notably heavier, demanding his attention. As he removed his amulet, the light radiating from its exquisite, centred stone drew their attention.

Oran exchanged glances with the Servitor. The urgency of their departure was now paramount.

'I see it!' blurted Gill as he gazed into its centre. 'The *Egress!*'

Oran looked at his son. 'We must leave for the portal, Gill,' he urged, then looked skywards, his eyes gliding over the tips of the trees as though he were searching for something. 'I had hoped …' His voice trailed. He then returned his attention to Gill. 'Time to choose one, son,' he said, pointing at the monoliths.

'But—but they're still changing,' said Gill. Oran looked into his son's pleading eyes, reminded of when he was a child, always giving that same look of helplessness when faced with a challenge yet knowing he would overcome it.

'Try again.'

The calmness in the Servitor's voice was confident and encouraging, and when Kai smiled, Gill was certain he caught a shrewd wink in his eye.

'But what if *they* come back?' he said, glancing around.

'*We* can deal with our enemy,' said Oran. 'You, however, need to leave. Reece and Kai will go with you—*and* your mother.'

Rosalyn spun. 'Go where?' she said, glaring at her husband.

'You must go with Gill, Rosalyn,' he said. 'While you remain here, you are vulnerable—an easy target for them.'

Rosalyn glanced over her shoulder, where Daine was still staring at the dead creatures, then back at her husband. 'And what about *him?*' she said, pointing at Daine. 'He is also vulnerable.'

'He is a *man*, Rosalyn,' he snapped. She frowned, taking a deep breath, ready to say her piece, but Oran was having none of it. 'And, as a man, certain things are expected of him.' But when he saw the glare in his wife's eyes as she narrowed them, and the clenching of her fists, he promptly cut in. 'But I …' He paused, sighing. 'I will stay by his side—protect him—if that *pleases* you.' He threw his eyes skywards, instantly regretting the remark when she side-glanced him with a look of disapproval. 'Besides,' he continued, 'we … *need* him.'

Rosalyn drew her head back at her husband's admission. What had changed his mind? She was dumbfounded at this sudden turnaround in his attitude towards Daine, while it was clear to her, he was envious of their "friendship". She never doubted her husband's ability to strike the guide down with a single blow, given the chance … She wanted to reassure him that nothing had happened—well, nothing serious—despite her feelings. As for *that* kiss … Perhaps it *had* been a moment of madness when she thought they were going to die at the hands of the Picts. But she knew—should she tell Oran—it would cause nothing but heartache. And what was the point in that—when there was nothing to be heartbroken over?

*Think what you will, Oran Shaw,*' she cried out to him in her mind as she stared at him. *Your jealousy will keep you on your toes, and attentive towards your wife.*

'No! You are coming with us, Oran,' Gill insisted, breaking the awkwardness between his parents.

Oran second-glanced Gill, still unable to accept his son's casual usage of his name. He shook his head.

'I cannot go with you. I betrayed the Elliyan to be here. And for that, I have yet to face the consequences of my actions.'

'When I am Magus,' said Gill, 'the Elliyan will no longer have a say.'

Oran smiled, placing a comforting hand on his son's shoulder, feeling the softness of the damask cloak he wore. 'Aye, it does fit you well,' he remarked beneath his breath, nodding, then looked Gill in the eye. 'I'm proud of you, son,' he added, then looked over at Eleanor. 'Proud of both of—' He stopped short, noting how his daughter was staring at Daine, her eyes tapering as she slowly leaned her head from side to side, surveying him from behind.

Eleanor slowly walked towards the guide, and as he turned to see what they were all looking at, he met with the young woman's intense curiosity.

*Not again! Why now?* he thought. Daine now felt confined and nervous by her as he looked into her eyes; they were still pale red from her transformation, her stare intimidating him. *She* intimidated him.

Eleanor took a step closer, raising her hand and, as she reached to touch his face, the moment was disrupted by the agonising cry of an animal.

They turned, then froze, seeing Rave being wrenched off the ground and into the air. It had happened so quickly. They had failed, yet again, to hear the Valkyrie's approach—the swiftness of her advance being masked by the brief relaxing of their guard, and Eleanor's untimely deep interest in the guide, distracting them from their surroundings.

Kara had swooped down from above, like a bird of prey, and snatched Rave without effort. Holding the dog by the scruff of the neck, her long nails piercing Rave's skin, the Valkyrie displayed her victim like a trophy—the hound's eyes bulging as she howled, struggling to break free.

The group looked to one another, now fearful for the dog's life.

'Do something!' cried Rosalyn.

'Stop it, *Dog!*' Kara snapped, shaking Rave like a piece of cloth.

'Let her go!'

Still, the hound resisted. Teeth exposed, Rave snarled and snapped at Kara as she tried to turn her head to bite her—the hound aware of the menace, telling her to fight back. Asai removed the wakizashi dagger, contemplating using it, then stalled, fearful of missing his main target while the dog thrashed out within the Valkyrie's grip. Frustrated by Rave's continuous skirmish, and refusal to bow to her whim, Kara's patience was wearing thin.

'Please—no!' cried Gill, aware of the Valkyrie's intentions.

'Payback—for *my* pet!' she casually stated, wielding the Obsidian.

Gill's eyes widened, then flashed to Asai.

'So, it was *you,* who destroyed Nakia, *Strange One,*' she said, following Gill's look.

'Let the dog go!' Asai returned.

As the familiar smirk crept across her mouth, Kara grunted, then slowly shook her head.

'I think not,' she hissed.

No sooner had she instigated her motive, Kara immediately took flight, with Rave still in her clutches. But as the Valkyrie rose, she seemed to struggle as the hound tried to free herself, continuously writhing within her grip and snapping at her.

Suddenly, Gill saw his window of opportunity. Overcome by hate, and with no thought for his mortality, he snatched the wakizashi from Asai and rushed forward. But as he gave chase, the Samurai, along with Reece and Oran, stopped him just as Kara lifted herself free from the potential attack.

'No, son.' Oran shook his head—the sombre look on his father's face telling Gill what he refused to believe.

'It is no use,' added Reece.

The young man glared at his grandfather, not wanting to hear it. 'But—I can't just let—'

'We need you here, Gill,' his father insisted.

Gill's mouth gaped as he looked from one to the other, then to the sky—the urge to pursue the Valkyrie etched on his face.

'Do not do it, Gill-san,' warned Asai, taking back his dagger. Gill never noticed.

'The dog will be *dead,* soon enough,' Reece stated.

Gill's eyes flashed to Reece—the bluntness of hearing the raw truth, stabbing him in the heart. But he knew they were right; no one knew the Valkyrie better than they. Kara would not spare his beloved Rave. Sentiment did not come into it. Heartbroken, and with eyes welling, he looked to his sister. But when he met with Eleanor, she was just staring at him, her brow furrowed, uncertain. She leaned her head to the side as if displaying her sympathy, and yet it was not the reaction he had expected—not like his Nori; she would have been by his side, weeping for their loss. But Gill knew she was no longer *his* Eleanor. No, she belonged to someone else now. But he did not resent her in any way for it; in fact, he sympathised with her as she, too, was trying to adapt to her new life.

Tears poured from Rosalyn's heartbroken eyes. Though she had rarely shown it in front of her children, inwardly she had loved the wretched hound and the joy it had brought to her family, after Gill rescued her when she was a pup, discarded and left to die, beneath the wheels of an abandoned cart. And in return, the dog had lavished them with nothing but unconditional love—a unique gift, only bestowed on those who knew little else—and a rarity among man, so seldom witnessed.

First his grandmother, then Tam, and now his beloved pet. Gill shook his head, trying to comprehend it.

'We cannot let her—'

'Finish this!' the raspy voice yelled.

The company looked up, catching the Valkyrie's departure before she disappeared, above the tree line, her large, black silhouette now barely visible against the darkened sky. With no time to retaliate, Gill took one last look skywards; he could see nothing now, only hear the pitiful howl of his loyal companion fading in the distance, his heart sinking with each cry as their bond was severed—the finality of their separation inevitable.

His heart stopped when he no longer heard her.

'They are coming!'

The rustling sound of sporadic, rapid movement, coming down from the forest, alerted them to the next onslaught.

The group eyed the creatures, catching flittering movements, unsure where and when precisely the attack would come.

Ever mindful of the timing of their task, Oran grew concerned, certain the Sorceress and Magia Nera would soon locate the Egress. It was within the dark Warlock's ability to do so. And if L'Ordana still had Magia's amulet … He was sure of it. He was also sure they were allies. *When had things become so complicated?* he thought. *None of this was meant to happen.* It was clear to Oran that things were now getting out of control.

He looked sharp when Reece, Gill and Asai rushed towards the forest. But the three had only made it a few yards when they were forced to stop.

# Chapter Twenty-Four

Gill, Reece and Asai found themselves face to face with four Dhampir warriors, Turloch taking centre stage and standing head and shoulders above the others—the three young warriors waiting impatiently for his orders. It was clear, by his poise, Turloch was the dominant one. Tall and lean, his shoulders were wide and set, his face square and chiselled, his colourless lips full while his most notable feature, his long, white mane, gave him the appearance of a spectre, within the gloom of night. A distinctive thick, pale scar crossed the temple of his left eye, weighing on it a little. Though unable to recall how he obtained it, Turloch displayed it with sinister pride, like a souvenir.

Before him, stood his opponent—Reece. The two had form, in that they disliked one another intensely—Turloch being jealous of his rival's skills.

As he lowered his head, glaring at his would-be challenger, Reece matched Turloch's stare, non-plussed by his presence. He had been aware of Turloch from their first meeting: when Kara made a point of introducing them, she showered Turloch with her attention, by ogling him and fingering his long, white hair, her pathetic attempt to make him jealous; it had failed miserably. But Reece quickly realised how shrewd the newcomer was when he occasionally caught his inquisitive and intrusive stare.

Turloch then glanced over Reece's shoulder, eyeing Rosalyn and Daine, their scent enhancing his senses and driving the ones by his side with a fevered hunger. Seeing this, Reece stepped closer, matching his rival's height with menace. Together, they stood statuesque-like, their eyes burning, fixed hard on one another, each trying to predict the others' next movement—a tactic they would persist in until one made that first, vital move.

'Do not divert your eyes from them, Gill,' muttered Asai, his eyes marking *his* two opponents. He had not seen them before but noticed something intriguing and familiar about them; they were twins—almost identical—save for one, who stood an inch or so taller than the other. Also, he surmised they were of similar origin as he, from the Realm of Saó, in the Far East; their hair was jet black and short, and their dark, almond-shaped eyes were similar to his. They seemed to stare back at him with the same interest.

Gill's mouth fell when his eyes locked with the creature in front of him; he was young—so much younger than he—*no more than thirteen*, he thought—the same age his friend Will Grant was, when he died from an infection in his blood.

'You're just a … *child?*' he said to him. The creature frowned back at Gill, uncertain.

'Do not be swayed by their youth, Gill-san,' said Asai. 'Remember, they are no longer mortal—and have only one thing on their mind. And do *not* turn your back on them,' he then warned, clenching his weapons.

Behind them, the remainder of the group watched and waited in anticipation. When Turloch looked at Rosalyn with purpose, she cowered behind Kai, grateful to be wrapped in the safety of the Servitor's protection.

'Your mistress has deserted you, Turloch,' said Reece, refusing to take his eyes from the Dhampir, his intention to keep him distracted, by goading him; he knew Turloch disliked being made a fool of, especially when in the company of young and imprudent warriors.

As Turloch stared into his foe's green eyes, he sensed the growing agitation of the three young Dhampir, beside him. Their senseless inability to be patient threatened their demise. But when he had heard the young man speak calmly to one, referring to him as a "child" it concerned him; any recollection of their past could prove difficult. They could flee, lost and confused, should the seed of memory be planted in their heads. And where would that leave him? He would have to act quickly.

'Do you think she cares about you?' Reece continued, mocking him. When the side of Turloch's mouth twitched, Reece knew he was getting into the warrior's mindset, and under his pallid skin. He casually shrugged. 'She is using you, Turloch … using all of you.'

Hearing this, Gill's young opponent let his eyes travel to Reece, then up to his leader. The other two Dhampir seemed oblivious, their eyes still fixed on the Samurai. Asai tilted his head forward, intimidating them, knowing he could easily take both—as did they. He could sense their inner turmoil, it obvious by the discouraging glances they shared with one other. They both looked up at Turloch, still awaiting instructions from their appointed leader.

'We have an understanding,' said Turloch to Reece, his voice thick with confidence.

Reece grunted at his ignorance and sneered back at him. Turloch tensed at the insult, then calmed himself; he could not give in to his opponent's mockery of him, despite resenting him for it. No. He was wise to Reece's plan; a sudden move of weakness on his part would catapult them into a premature, and unpredictable, battle. He needed his wits about him.

The tension mounted—the nervous shuffling of feet beside him, making Turloch edgy. His eyes flashed as he made a quick head count of their enemy; there were more than he anticipated. *A new addition, too,* he realised—the familiar sweet scent of a newborn, settling on his nose. Also, he had to consider Wareeshta's presence. Though small and svelte, he knew her capabilities and was mindful of the weapons inside her boots. Sharp and lethal, Turloch had seen her use the stiletto daggers like they were part of her making. She was swift and capable—and no longer alone. Despite the odds, he was undeterred.

'Join us!' urged Reece, sensing the unpredictable position their enemy now faced.

Turloch lifted a brow at the unexpected invite.

'You are *clearly* outnumbered,' added Reece as though he had read his foe's thoughts.

'Perhaps—but you are clearly *out-skilled*,' Turloch hit back.

Reece snorted at the incessant arrogance of his antagonist. As the two locked together in their mind games, Wareeshta discreetly stepped forward, her concern mounting, questioning Reece's precarious motives. *What are you playing at?* she thought, aware of how dangerous Turloch was. Catching her subtle advance, Turloch slid his eyes in her direction and cast her a disparaging smile. There was a time that *look* would have unsettled her. But now, as she stood alongside Reece and his companions, she was un-wavered by Turloch's attempt to browbeat her.

'It is a tempting offer, Reece,' he said, letting his eyes travel down her.

Still, Wareeshta remained unperturbed, her mouth curling as she smirked back at him. To taunt and remind him of her skill set, she tapped her foot on the ground, and then against one of her boots. His eyes shot up, meeting the warning in her deadpan stare.

As he stood beside Wareeshta, Reece felt an unusual sense of pride, satisfying his belief in her loyalty to Eleanor, it prompting him to say; 'Kara has no *loyalty* to you, Turloch,' he continued, 'or anyone, for that matter. I can only assume she has promised you a seat by her side, as her word of honour for your … *services*?'

Turloch lifted his head and raised his brow again, as though his place was assured.

Reece slowly shook his head.

'She *will* fail in this venture of hers. It is nothing more than a fantasy, conjured by her madness.'

Thrown by the conversation, the three young Dhampir looked to their superior. Feeling their eyes on him, Turloch slowly lowered his head at Reece. *Liar!* He was certain of it; the Valkyrie had promised him a place by her side and told him she "needed" him. He stepped back—the warriors mimicking his movements, eyes still focused on their challengers.

The tension was nearing its peak.

Reece, Asai and Wareeshta prepared themselves and waited for the pre-empted look that always came before the attack—the startled one—signalling the enemy was about to leap. For Gill, the wait was unbearable as he looked into the eyes of his young adversary—the *child!* He could see the reflection of his face in the blackness of his enemy's eyes, searching for an indication of the inevitable assault. Reminded again of his friend, Will, he wanted to reach out, place a hand on the *child's* shoulder, and help him. He contemplated it. Compelled to do so, he raised his hand. The *child's* eyes widened, then shifted slightly. Gill frowned, wary of it. Though insignificant, it had been a notable change, and when the *child* lifted his head and closed his eyes, he inhaled the intoxicating scent as it wafted over him and his comrades. His eyes flashed open, then moved like a predator's in the direction of the irresistible cause. That was when Gill saw it—the image that had snatched the *child's* attention.

Caught up in the suspense and fear of what was happening, Rosalyn had subconsciously stepped away from the Servitor's protection. It was then when the creature caught her eye, she realised her error and promptly returned to her safety net.

But it was all it took …

Drawn by her strong female scent, the *child* stepped forward—the bold move proving fatal.

'No, you don't!' Gill muttered through gritted teeth before plunging Tam's claymore into his heart—the distraction forcing Reece and Asai from their marks. The *child* screeched in pain, his high-pitched cry rising above the trees, scattering the forest's inhabitants.

Chaos erupted.

Gill stared at the claymore still embedded in the *child* as he gripped the hilt, trying desperately to remove it.

'The head!' came the voice from behind. 'Quick, Gill—before he withdraws it.'

Gill jolted and spun in time to see Daine tossing his blood-stained sword to him, his reflexes sharp as he caught it. It felt natural in his grip as he swung it around with the proficiency of a great warrior at one with his weapon. He knew what he had to do.

But the *child* had found his bearings again and was already removing the claymore. But as it left his body, he hesitated and looked up, his eyes wild with recognition as another sword was plunged right through him, with such force he knew he was incapable of stopping it as it pinned him to the ground. Aware of his impending doom, the *child* cast the claymore aside and grasped the hilt of the other weapon embedded in him. But despite his strength, he was unable to break free. Desperate, his bulging eyes darted between Gill and the claymore; the great sword was still on the ground and within his reach. Knowing his end was mere seconds away, he groped for the claymore, but as his fingers touched the hilt, the Highlander's weapon was snatched from him. With no more thought or sympathy for the *child*, Gill brought Tam's sword down on the creature.

Distracted by Gill, Reece had briefly taken his eyes from his challenger, but when he turned to battle with Turloch he made a start. There was no sign of his adversary. *I never took you for a coward, Turloch.*

The *twins*, having seen the brutal demise of their young colleague, stood armed and bewildered as the Samurai now wielded his swords in front of them. With Turloch gone, they were confused. Behind them, Wareeshta crept closer, brandishing her daggers.

When a branch snapped beneath her foot, one of them—the smaller—turned, eyes blazing. He hissed then lunged his sword at her. But Wareeshta, having anticipated his move, leapt high, avoiding his blade by inches. When the other saw this, he spun, so fast it disoriented him, making him lose sight of Wareeshta, for a moment.

When he glanced around, searching for her, the Samurai made his move. Holding his weapons across the creature's throat, Asai forced him to look and watch, at what was about to follow.

With her audience looking on, Wareeshta took the other *twin* from behind. He struggled to turn, to challenge her, waving his sword but could not. In an unexpected move, she grasped his chin and wrenched it sideways, snapping his neck. His body slumped. Despite it, she knew he would still be alive. As he fell to the ground, he lost his grip on his sword. Promptly, Wareeshta kicked the weapon away, then dropped to her knees, on top of him. Eyes on his, she raised her daggers high, then crossed her arms before bringing them down in one swift sweep across his neck, severing his head from his body, quick and clean.

Having witnessed the execution of his twin, the other lashed out within Asai's grip. Reece moved to assist, but stopped when the Samurai shook his head; he would deal with this one.

'You saw what happened to your … *brother*,' Asai whispered in his ear. Aware of the "connection" between twins, it compelled the Samurai to offer the remaining one a choice. 'Do you want the same?' His captive continued to writhe and squirm within his grip. Frustrated yet determined to try, Asai shoved his captive's face down towards the pool of blood as it slowly spread from his twin's torso. 'Look at him!' He leaned harder until his captive could smell the foul stench of his twin's blood—the damp, night air now turning it black and rancid. 'I am giving you a choice,' he stated, before wrenching him back on his feet.

The twin looked to where his other colleague lay, headless. His eyes darted, searching; the *child's* head was nowhere to be seen. Such was the impact instilled by Gill's strength, the head had been severed clean—the force catapulting it beyond the tree line. Regardless of it, he felt nothing but ignorance of what had happened.

'You have been abandoned,' said Asai, still trying to sway his train of thought as the twin's eyes danced erratically as if weighing up the odds. But when the wind shifted, his crimson eyes flashed towards Rosalyn—the lure of her scent driving him to a frenzy.

Then he was no more.

With the settling of the wind and chaos removed, Rosalyn stepped away from her protection. Maintaining caution, she slowly approached the place where the bodies of the dead creatures were scattered. She shook her head.

'So young and—'

'Not so innocent,' Reece interrupted, joining his daughter as she surveyed the scene. 'They would have killed you in a heartbeat, Rosalyn,' he added.

She nodded, swallowing the lump in her throat, then tilted her head in pity as she looked at the *child's* headless corpse.

'He was just a boy before they—' She stopped when her eyes fell on the weapon nearby, on the ground, and as she moved towards it, she paused when it was lifted and handed back to her, wiped clean of death's stain.

'Thank you, Gill!' she said, pressing down on her quivering lips.

'I know you want to return it to them,' he said.

'Aye, and I will,' she replied, determined to keep her vow, by returning the claymore to Tam's clan, when all was done. With the Highlander still in her thoughts, she went to Farrow, carefully placing the claymore into the sheath attached to the steed's saddle.

'Where is Turloch?' Wareeshta suddenly called out, anxious.

'That is what I would like to know,' said Reece as he approached the edge of the forest. She followed him. They both surveyed the trees, searching through the shadowy night, hoping to catch a glimpse of his white hair, any hint of his presence. Above them, an owl hooted, watching the trespassers. They looked up, their attention stolen by the constant motion of the nocturne's wide eyes within its large, broad head. Other than that, nothing unnatural stirred.

Turloch had fled.

'I have no doubt he is pursuing the Valkyrie,' said Reece. His tone was firm yet calm, surprising Wareeshta; it was the first time he had spoken to her, civilly, like an equal.

'We could hunt him down … between us?' she suggested.

He grunted. 'I will not risk separating the group. It is not—'

She turned to him. 'No! I did not mean—'

'I know what you meant,' he cut in, holding her gaze for an instant. 'No, myself and Asai will go, to be sure there is no sign of Turloch—or another attack.' As he moved to leave, Reece hesitated and looked back at Wareeshta, then nodded, and as he turned away she swore she detected a faint smile on his lips.

With a brief explanation of what they were doing, and asking the group to wait until they returned, Reece and Asai wasted no time—the Samurai assuring Eleanor they would not be long, his promise to return encouraging her to stay, to protect her mother.

Alone, and his sights set in the distance, where Kara had disappeared with Rave into the night, Gill felt as if someone had wrenched a piece of his heart from him. He needed no one to tell him his loyal companion was gone; he could feel it. He fought back the tears, determined not to show his emotions. It was not right; he was a man, soon to be a great leader. *I cannot show any weakness*, he thought. *Men don't cry!* But he knew he would have sobbed, had things been different, showing no shame in his sadness. And yet, it tortured him; he had not been able to mourn his grandmother, either. But he would, when the time was right, and in his own way. Yes, Onóir, Rave and Tam would be honoured.

'Gill?'

The young man closed his eyes, hearing the Servitor's voice. Kai was now facing him.

'You must let her go.'

Gill knew he had no choice but to. It was breaking his heart—the impact of the loss he had to endure, and in such a short space of time, too. It was beginning to take its toll. And though overwhelmed by grief, a longing for revenge was brewing inside him—and he would have it. Trying to stop the tears as he pressed his quivering lips together, Gill released a sigh and slowly nodded.

'She, along with the others, are with you—*here*,' Kai added, placing his hand on Gill's heart. 'Know that.'

Taking a deep breath, Gill looked up into the night, then released it. Rave was gone. He then turned away—the void in his heart from her absence prominent. *That whore will pay for this*, he silently vowed. *She'll pay for all of it.*

'Gill … are you all right?'

He turned to his mother as she moved to console him. 'I am,' he replied, meeting her sympathetic stare. They were all looking at him. He could no longer bear it. He wanted to yell, tell his father, the Elliyan—*everyone!*—he had had enough. Then young Meghan entered his mind, making matters worse. He missed her terribly; the image of their last night together was ingrained in his memory, with the overwhelming sensation of their entwined bodies lingering on him. He would carry the afterglow of their love with him, forever.

With so many gone, he suddenly felt utterly alone. Again, he looked to the night sky, now seeing its sliver of moonlight; it seemed to hang over him, marking the beginning of the end of the life he once knew, marking his unknown future—and the weight of an unwanted burden. As he closed his eyes, fighting his desperate need to leave it all behind, he flinched, feeling the warmth of a feathery touch on his cheek. His eyes shot open.

*Grandmaw!*

Renewed by the ongoing presence of Onóir's spirit, Gill realised he was not alone. He could now feel the weight of everyone's loss—not just his. They were all in this together.

'Son?' He looked up when Oran drew beside him. 'Gill, I know this is difficult for—'

'I am all right,' he said, with a half-hearted smile. 'We need to get out of here.'

Reminded of the guide's honourable deed, Gill turned from his father and looked to where the *child's* body lay, seeing Daine's sword still embedded in him. He marched over and, gripping the hilt, withdrew it, smoothly. He paused, narrowing his eyes; the sword's blade was clean—no blood. *Strange*, he thought.

'Thank you,' said Daine, reaching out to take it back. Gill, however, was reluctant to part with it.

When the guide moved to retrieve his sword, Gill subconsciously stepped back from him, his inquisitive eyes surveying the steel, his brow knitting, deepening his frown. 'How is it I can …?' He paused, then looked at Daine—the guide somewhat confused by Gill's enquiring look and intense interest in his weapon.

Stirred by its uniqueness, Gill drew the sword closer, and as he did so the moon's sliver of light penetrated the clouds and reached down; his brows lifted when its shaft of light enveloped the steel.

'Can you *see* it?' Eleanor remarked to Oran, joining her father. The Warlock stared down at his daughter, perplexed, then looked over to where Gill and Daine stood, facing one another, Gill's back to his father. Prompted by Eleanor's comment, Oran moved towards them, craning his neck as he tried to see. But as the Warlock drew near, Gill spun to meet his father, his arm extended, pointing the sword at him.

'I believe … this is *yours!*'

# Chapter Twenty-Five

As though reawakened from a millennium of dormancy, the ancient hieroglyphs, etched deep in the steel, appeared, glinting again with life. Gradually, they revealed the weapon's resounding past.

'Where did you get that?!'

As Daine reached out to take his sword back from Gill, Oran intervened and grabbed hold of the guide, wrenching him off his feet.

Daine could feel the threatening force of the Warlock's firm grip as Oran kept him suspended mid-air. Though seething inside as he glared down at his challenger, he did not retaliate; he would not give the Warlock the satisfaction.

With her heart in her mouth, Rosalyn rushed forward to stop the altercation, fully aware of her husband's capabilities when anger and jealousy struck.

'Oran, leave him—'

'I said, where did you get it—the sword?!' he demanded, his face crimson and twisted with anger.

As Rosalyn grasped Oran's arm, to tear her husband from Daine, he shrugged his wife away. Still, the guide felt no fear as he glowered into the Warlock's hardened face, keeping his silence, his daring look feeding Oran's rage.

'Just tell him what he wants to know, Daine!' she pleaded.

Ignoring Rosalyn, Oran repeated his words, his insistence now slow and clear as he spoke through gritted teeth, his intense stare penetrating Daine's unwavering look. 'Where – Did – You – Get—' Oran stopped dead when their eyes locked—the iris of time linking them, and momentarily blocking out the world around them. The past had found its way back into their lives, their fates colliding in an epiphany.

'*Now* you see it,' stated Eleanor.

Oran and Daine could not take their eyes from one another—the realisation of what was unfolding—the *unthinkable!*—rendering them silent.

'Oh, my—' Rosalyn hesitated, then drew closer, her mouth gaping as she looked back and forth between her husband and the guide. It was unbelievable yet there it was—the truth—staring them in the face, exposing what had been hidden behind the "mask" all along. There was no mistaking it.

'It—it was my father's,' Daine whispered, breathless, still suspended in mid-air.

Oran lifted his brows, his eyes widening, suddenly woken to his meaning. 'Your—' He shook his head, his mouth opening and closing, trying to catch the words on his tongue. Unable to tear his look from Daine, he carefully lowered him, returning him to *terra firma*, then stepped back, cupping a hand over his mouth in disbelief. 'My—' He shook his head again. He could scarcely believe it, let alone *say* it. He dropped his hand. 'You're my …' He could not get the word out.

'*Grandson!*'

Everyone turned and looked at Eleanor when she finished her father's sentence for him. She nodded in response, her eyes moving between her father and the guide.

'But—how can this be?' said Oran, still shaking his head in denial, his thoughts awash with inconceivable notions, and yet ... His hand twitched then moved, wanting to reach out to Daine, to touch him, to … He snatched it back, clenching his fist, afraid to—the shock of this new revelation holding him back.

'Is it possible?' said Daine, craning his head forward, searching the Warlock's features.

Gill, equally confused, moved to his sister's side and looked down at her.

'Nori? What do you mean … *Grandson?*'

She indicated to their father, then to the guide. 'Look at them!' she casually urged.

Gill's eyes flitted between Oran and Daine, then widened, seeing the resemblance, it hitting him like a bolt of lightning. He glanced at his mother, Rosalyn regarding them closely and nodding to herself, having made the startling connection, too.

The uncanny likeness gradually came to the fore the more Rosalyn stared at Oran and Daine; she shook her head, trying to grasp the reality of their exposure. *How could I have not seen it?* she thought, then realised why: she had been blinded, by her attraction to the guide. And now, here they were—Oran's eyes—looking back at her, through Daine's. It was obvious to her now—the truth appearing from her husband's past—and in the most unusual and unlikely circumstances. Even the shape of their mouths—the *Cupid's bow,* full and prominent—were similar. But when her eyes fell on Daine's lips, she tore her gaze from him; the idea that theirs had touched—and in a most wanting way, too—now sickened her to the pit of her stomach. She *had* been blinded, flattered by his attention, having been denied the wants and needs her body had craved for so long. For three long years, she had missed the love of her man, while for Oran—a Warlock—three years of his life were mere drops in the ocean. But for her—a mortal woman in the spring of middle age—three years marked an immense difference in the calendar of time; she would continue to age … unlike him, making her question the worth of her mortality—and the true worth of their relationship. *I'm only human*, she thought, trying to justify her "human" flaws. It made her resent her husband more. Angry and ashamed, she promptly stepped away from them both, trying to come to terms with her own truth.

'But—the sword?' said Oran, taking it from Gill—the hilt so familiar it was as if he had only held it the day before. '*How?*'

With a cautious eye on his weapon, Daine looked upon it with fondness, before he addressed Oran again. 'It was passed to me from my father—before his death—some years ago,' he replied, a little dazed but placing emphasis on his legacy.

As Oran gripped the sword, a nostalgic smile appeared on his face, welcoming it back like an old acquaintance, sensing the ghosts of his past, and recalling the history behind the heirloom.

He turned to address Daine, his hand still gripping the weapon. 'And how did my—your'—he pursed his lips—'*father* come by it?' Although he knew, he had to be sure.

'It was given to him by his … father …' Daine's words briefly trailed off as he maintained Oran's steady look. He wanted to say it, but could not; neither of them could, hoping the other would. '… when he was a boy, a long—'

'Aye, that it was—*given!*' Oran cut in, his excitement building.

Daine shook his head.

'No—not given, well, yes, in a way … It was … *left* to him,' he said, correcting himself, 'before they were driven from their home.'

*Triora!*' Oran looked down, mouthing the name of the place he would have rather forgotten. It had jumped into his mind as if someone had put it there, to remind him of the horrific events that took place in *that* house. The recollection of that night was then etched deeper in his memory when the image of his young servant's charred remains came back to haunt him again. *Lucia!*

Oran lifted his head, recalling it vividly—the devastation, the heartbreak and the cruelty as his eyes returned to Daine's. *My grandson!* There, he had finally claimed it. But, as he re-visited his past, something behind Daine's eyes altered; though slight, it was obvious in his expression—a brooding one—shifting the atmosphere as it gradually morphed into one of hostility. This new "relationship" would not be welcomed with open arms—not just yet.

Then it came.

'*You!* You deserted your own son … like a *coward!*' Daine blurted, his face hard and glowering as he pointed at Oran—the accusation driven by resentment. 'You left him with nothing but a purse of gold coins and a legacy to claim when he was older. He relied on you. And yet, when he needed you most you … up stakes!'

Oran recoiled, shocked, as his past continued to unravel. *Coward?* To be stamped with the scornful label—and in the presence of the rest of his family—added insult to the injury. He shook his head, his mind a storm of activity as more stark images returned, re-playing those last moments. He could still see the boy's innocent face; his eyes were filled with horror and tears as he said goodbye, before leaving him in the capable hands of people he had trusted.

*"Whatever became of your parents?"*

He knew only too well. His parents *had* deserted him—and Daine was right. Oran's heart sank as it occurred to him now, the bitterness Petrio—*my son!*—must have carried with him throughout his life—and, rightly so. Forgetting the eyes of curiosity as the others stared at the estranged pair, eager for answers, Oran's face fell, displaying a look of regret as he met with the resentment in Daine's eyes. 'I had no choice …' He sighed. 'I *had* to leave Petrio behind.'

And there it was—the admission—spoken outwardly, and witnessed by those he loved. No more denial. With no thought of when or where it might expose itself, he had selfishly locked away another element of his past, leaving it dormant—along with the memory of the son he had sired, with another, long before Rosalyn. Though gripped by shame, he was overwhelmed by the knowledge he had a grandson. Then, aware of her hovering beside him, he looked at his wife, at a loss, her downcast look of uncertainty now giving way to aggravation. What would he say to her?

Unanswered questions filled Rosalyn's thoughts as her face bore the weight of dismay and mistrust. Her eyes flashed to Daine—the guide now standing with his arms folded, his eyes glaring at her husband, waiting for him to justify the actions from his furtive past. 'Another detail you failed to mention, Oran Shaw?' she hit out.

'Another son? And a grandson?'

Oran moved towards his wife, his hands outstretched to her as though begging for forgiveness.

Raising a hand, she shook her head firmly, pressing down on her lips, her eyes fixed, warning him to keep his distance for now.

'For much of your life, Oran, you have coward from your duties and neglected your loved ones.' She threw another glance at Daine, still barely able to look at him, then pointed. 'Abandoning *them!* Abandoning us!'

Daine stood rooted and silent as the words Rosalyn hurdled at her husband echoed in his thoughts. An image of his father entered his mind as he continued to stare at Oran … *My … Grandfather?* It was only hitting him now—the truth of it. How did he not know, see it himself? But of course! The sword. Had the Warlock not recognised it …

The venom in Rosalyn's words injected Oran's soul as she continued to spit them at him. He would plead his case to them; after all, it was a long time ago. He had no choice, then. He had to do what he could, to save them—the boy and his cook, Sofia—after the devastation left behind by Petrio's mother. *Oh, Kristene!*

If his heart could sink any lower, he was sure the *Devil* himself would welcome it into the pits of hell, for his deceit. He had to explain—at least, *try!* 'Do you not understand?' he hit back, then turned to Daine. 'I simply had no choice! Time was against us, then … as it is now. Call me a "coward" if you will, but I *know* I did the right thing—at the time,' he persisted, wielding a clenched fist. 'They could have killed your—my—' He stopped, his heart pounding, pleading to be heard, begging for impunity, knowing he had failed them all.

Suddenly conscious of each other, in its untimely revelation, Daine and Gill shared awkward side-glances—the connection of their true identities slowly sinking in while sparking some confusion. *You're my … nephew?* thought Gill. He was unsure, as was Daine. *My uncle?*

Seeing the look of guilt and hurt appear on Oran's face, Daine's anger subsided, as Rosalyn continued to glare at her husband. An element of guilt ignited inside him, too; the feeling for her was still there, still real, but unobtainable now. She would never be his; nor would he steal another moment of pleasure from her. However, inside, years of resentment had made their home and, despite the Warlock's attempt to justify his actions, Daine struggled to forgive Oran—*my so-called grandfather*—for the neglect and personal suffering he had instilled on his son, Petrio—*my poor father*.

Daine's bitterness ate away at him each time he looked at Oran, and when he saw the Warlock try to explain to Rosalyn, the reasons for his past actions, Daine wanted to go to her, take her from him. When it came to it, and despite their lineage, Oran meant nothing to him. He was a stranger.

*You don't deserve her!* The more he thought about it, the more temptation picked at his wants. *You will regret your actions … Grandfather!* he told himself. *You denied my father. Therefore, in return … that is exactly what I will do to you.* Daine knew he had to be clever, should he proceed with his plan; while Oran exposed his vulnerability—by openly seeking forgiveness—he would play on it.

'My father returned to the great house, years after you …'

Oran spun, hearing Daine speak out. For an instant, his voice had sounded like Petrio's—the child beneath the man. He approached Daine, displaying a faint smile, his defences wide open, wanting to welcome this fine man—*my grandson!*—into his family. He wanted to make amends—if that were possible. Again, he felt the need to reach out and embrace him, but, still, the awkwardness prevented it. Instead, he looked him in the eye and, for an instant, saw a reflection of Daine's grandmother—*Kristene!*—staring back at him. He shook it away. 'Tell me, please?' he urged.

'He went to the *secret place*—in your quarters,' Daine continued. 'Behind the mirror?'

Oran nodded eagerly, trying to visualise Petrio's movements: his return to the abandoned house; stepping into the mirror; whispering his name—*"Oran!"*—and retrieving his legacy—just as he had instructed him to do.

'He took what was required.'

'Ah! This sword,' said Oran, indicating the one still in his hand.

'Yes, but—' Daine stopped, then shook his head slowly as he eyed the weapon.

'But what?'

Daine lowered his eyes, for effect, to add to the heartache, then slowly shook his head.

'He believed, in his heart and soul, you would return for him, but …' As his words faded, he shrugged.

Silence prevailed for several moments, waiting for someone—anyone—to respond, to break the delicacy of the situation; it was too much to take in.

'But I never did,' said Oran, admitting his failure to do so. 'A huge regret, on my part.' Daine was his proclaimed grandson. That was the truth of it. He could see it now. But it had never occurred to him that Petrio would grow up, marry and have a family of his own. From his memory, he could only see the face of a child, not wanting to be left alone—and in the most dangerous and tragic of circumstances. But it pleased him to know Petrio went on to have a life, under the guidance of Sophia and her husband, Gino. It made it all too real, how short the life of a mortal truly was. Despite his parentage—he regretted never telling him—Petrio had been mortal and was not the *Chosen One*. But there was something else he needed to know: 'How—' Oran cleared his throat. 'How did he—Petrio—die?' There was genuine sadness in his tone.

'So, *now* you take an interest in your family,' sneered Rosalyn, unable to hold her tongue. Oran shot his wife a dour look of protest. Daine concealed the smirk beneath his façade as Rosalyn remained steadfast in her argument, her hands firmly on her hips, a brow raised as she tilted her head forward, holding her glare.

Behind them, their son and daughter looked on—Gill rolling his eyes and shaking his head. *This has to stop!* he thought, eyeing the monoliths—their surfaces having resumed in their animated state of change, reacting against his parents' untimely "disputes". And Eleanor, still trying to exercise her emotions, hung her head to the side, observing the charged energy between her parents, fascinated by the feast of emotions on display. Though she could *feel* them, she could not quite fathom it. Then there was Wareeshta, who chose to stay where she was—by the horses—thinking it best not to interfere; their arguments were not her business.

Oran was having none of his wife's outbursts. 'Need I remind you, Rosalyn,' he began, in retaliation, 'that I have lived many lives before you were a mere thought in the universe, and I—' He momentarily stalled when his eyes darted to the horses, seeing Wareeshta there, coveting her "interests". He frowned—the lines between his brow emphasised when she smirked and nodded towards him; he still doubted her loyalty. If there were a perfect opportunity for her to take Nephtys and the book, it was *now*, while he was embroiled in yet another heated family "discussion". But a glance at Eleanor reminded her of the other reason for staying.

Catching the brief exchange, Rosalyn, dropping her hands to her side, drew back, shaking her head, her mouth slightly opened as she caught her breath, stunned by her husband's ability to be easily distracted—and by another woman, no less—while being abrupt towards her. *"I have lived many lives before you were a mere thought in the universe."* She felt the gravity of his words as they collided with her. Right now she wanted to strike out at him, deliver a few more home truths, and even admit to her temptations.

'Do you think I have walked upon this world of ours, through time, without the love of another woman?' he went on. He shook his head. 'No, I have not—and not just one!'

Her mouth dropped. More revelations. More hurt.

Hearing this, Gill moved to intervene.

'Oran—I think—'

'I have loved and lost more than you will *ever* know,' Oran continued, stopping his son in his tracks. 'And my life will remain so until time dictates. But I *will* outlive you, Rosalyn …' He paused, glancing at Daine. 'And *you*—and all those who shall follow, thereafter. Because of it, I chose to forget the heartache I have endured for so long, by leaving it behind, to search for happiness again. By trying to live a "normal" life, I have betrayed the Elliyan. I do not know what fate awaits me for my crime, but'—his face then softened as he tilted his head, his mouth curling slightly at the side, his words now calm and full of deep meaning—'I would willingly accept my punishment, for a life of simplicity with the woman I love, *now*. For the first time in—I cannot begin to imagine how long—I have felt true happiness and contentment with *you*, Rosalyn, *and* with my family, but …' He looked to Gill—the son he still hardly recognised as he stood near his sister, listening to his father's explanation. 'But this is the one thing I can no longer deny or change. The moment you were conceived, Gill, your fate was sealed. Nothing—or no one—can alter that now. *This*'—he tapped his amulet with his finger—'was your sanction, and is my priority.'

Feeling the tightness in her throat, Rosalyn's mouth quivered from her husband's declaration as it rang through, with honesty. Now she understood the reasoning behind his reluctance to share *all* his past with her; it had been to spare her jealousy of those he had loved and shared other lives with before her—and to spare the agony of the memories of those he had lost along the way. She had given little consideration to it. The sadness of her own personal loss—Eleanor's father, when she was a bairn, and Onóir—paled in comparison to what he must have endured, through the ages. The image of the small, ebony box, inlaid with mother of pearl—the one she had discovered in his coffer before she left Balloch—entered her thoughts: the lock of hair—the keepsake he still clearly cherished. And yet, she still had no idea to whom it belonged. But now was not the time to ask.

Racked with guilt, Rosalyn lowered her head in silence.

But her guilt was equally shared by her husband, who cursed himself for concealing certain aspects of his past from her. 'When this is all over, Rosalyn,' he said, his voice soft and low, 'I promise to tell you *everything!*—and promise to claim back the peaceful life we had.'

Gill strode over to his mother, placing a comforting arm around her. She clung to him as though her life depended on it, there and then.

'Don't leave us!' she pleaded, her eyes welling as she looked up at her son.

'He's right, Maw. I cannot—'

Rosalyn broke away from him, tears now streaming down her flushed cheeks. 'I beg of you, Gillis!' She shook her head—the reality finally taking its toll as they neared their destination—and their inevitable parting. 'I cannot bear to let you go.'

As Gill placed a tender hand on his mother's face, Rosalyn leaned into his touch. Gently, he stroked her cheek, wiping away the tears. 'I am bent to fly, Rosalyn,' he said. 'It is as it—'

'Consumption!'

All eyes turned on Daine as he looked to Oran. 'My father—*your son!*—died from the consumption,' he stated, referring back to Oran's enquiry, which, at that point, he felt had been dismissed.

'I—I am sorry for your …' Oran sighed, returning his attention to Daine. 'Did he—did you—have a good life?'

'The three of us wanted for nothing.'

*Three*, he thought. *No more grandchildren, then*. Oran managed a half-smile, thankful, at least, they had made good use of the gold he had provided for them. 'Was he … happy?'

'I like to think so,' said Daine. 'He loved my mother, dearly. But there were times he was distant with us—with life—losing himself to long periods of isolation and sometimes leaving us for months on end. Like you, he kept parts of his life secret. He let us believe he led the life of a travelling merchant. However, it seems his time away from us was spent searching for his father. It was during the final days of his life when the truth came to light … about *you*.' Daine stole a glance at Rosalyn as he spoke, seeing the pity in her eyes, while Oran listened, dumbfounded. 'I'll not lie when I say, beneath the hope there was deep resentment in my father, for your … desertion of him. After he died, I took it upon myself to continue that search; something I felt obliged to do.' He pointed at the sword in Oran's hand. 'He gave it to me the day he died, but I knew little or nothing about it, as did he. I spent years searching this world of ours. But it was when I landed here—in Scotland—that I felt I was … *close*, as though it were guiding me. And so, I stayed, to continue looking.'

'So near,' whispered Oran, overwhelmed.

'At first, I thought it inconceivable that you might be alive,' Daine continued. 'No doubt the woman who bore my father has long since departed this …' Daine paused when Oran quickly diverted his eyes, looking down, at the mention of *"the woman"*—the grandmother he never knew, giving rise to suspicion. His reaction had been obvious; he had seen it in *that* look—Oran's look of guilt. Daine looked at Rosalyn; she had noticed it, too.

'Is there something else, Oran?' she asked, her tone calm but firm. Oran grew restless, feeling he was being judged as all their faces peered at him, their suspicions rising the more he lingered on Rosalyn's question, maintaining his silence when she followed it up with another; 'When did she die?' she quizzed, subtly moving closer to Daine. 'Petrio's mother?'

On seeing them together, side by side, Oran felt another rush of jealousy, regardless of who Daine was. But his silence was questionable—and obvious—reeking of the guilt he could not shake off.

Rosalyn gasped, shaking her head in disbelief.

'Oh, my—she's still *alive!*' she realised, her jealousy simmering again. 'This just gets better!' If Rosalyn had not been aware of the true extent of her mortality, she was now, more than ever, as she stood among those in her company; it made her feel vulnerable, and out of place. But there was the one other exception, keeping her sanity: Daine. Despite everything, she was glad of his presence, their mortality uniting them, strengthening their human weakness', though still toying with their easily-led human emotions.

Oran looked towards the trees—anything to avoid eye contact with his determined wife, his eyes searching through the night, longing for Reece and Asai's swift return. *Where are you?* He needed a distraction.

'Well?' she persisted, noting another blatant avoidance of her enquiry. 'It is obvious that you know Petrio's mother is still alive, Oran. She must be—'

'True—she still lives,' a voice answered.

Oran breathed a sigh of relief when the Servitor intervened. Until then, Kai had removed himself from the tension, staying in the background, observing everything, and digesting every word. But he had sympathised with Oran, feeling it was his duty to mediate on the mounting pressure his friend faced, to provide answers.

'Aye, but she is not the woman you *think* she is,' Oran added, glad of the Servitor's support.

Baffled by the statement, Daine shook his head, confused.

'What do you mean, not the woman—'

'Her name was—*is*—Kristene,' Oran defended.

'*L'Ordana*.'

Daine spun and stared at Eleanor, hearing *that* name again. 'What did you say?!'

She slowly nodded, her expression lacking shame for saying it.

'The Sorceress.'

Reece and Asai stalled, weapons still in hand, and looked around them, uneased. It was much too quiet for their liking as they stood among the forests' silent sentinels. Accustomed to the dark, their eyes searched for any sign of Turloch, his ghostly-white mane a sure giveaway of his presence. But still, they saw and heard nothing. And yet, something was not right.

'I do not like this uncomfortable *silence*, Reece-san.'

'Likewise,' said Reece, his brow deepening, sharing his friend's discomfort.

A soft breeze raised itself, stirring the hairs on the back of their necks as it brushed by the two Dhampir; they lifted their noses, hoping to catch a lingering scent on its passing. But nothing stirred, save for the soft rustling of the sentinels' withering leaves, and the dampness of autumn's breath.

'I think he has gone—as is the Valkyrie,' Reece surmised. 'Turloch knows he is outnumbered. Even if he were to return to the Paths—regardless of Oran and Gill—he would have little chance against Wareeshta, alone.'

Asai raised a brow, eyeing his friend; he had spoken the female Dhampir's name with a softness he had not heard before. It seemed the anger and contempt Reece had harboured for Wareeshta was dissolving a little.

Having caught his friend's curious look, Reece frowned. 'She saved my granddaughter,' he snapped, obliged to justify his remark. 'We should be thankful to her for it,' he added. 'We cannot deny her loyalty to Eleanor. I …' He paused. 'I—*we*—cannot deny Wareeshta's right to live.'

Asai nodded, his mouth twitching.

Reece cast the Samurai a frustrated and deep-rooted frown. 'And … what is so amusing?'

'How things have changed so, in the last few days,' he remarked. Reece side-glanced his friend. 'I mean—since you were united with a family you never knew existed—and reunited with …' Asai paused, noting the sombre look on Reece's face—the two friends then sharing a direct look, each knowing what the other was thinking.

Nothing needed to be said between the colleagues about the great loss they had experienced, and the sadness of having no time to mourn them. It would have to wait.

'Whatever becomes of us, my friend, and however all this shall end,' said Reece—the feeling of foreboding niggling at him, 'it is comforting to know you will not be alone, and will take care of Eleanor.'

'With my life,' Asai returned, placing a hand on his heart, still feeling her inside him. He then bowed to his colleague, and as he rose, his eyes narrowed, looking beyond Reece's shoulder, prompting his friend to turn. 'It is not yet time for the sun to rise,' he remarked, confused. 'It is far too—'

They quickly diverted their eyes when a brilliant light shot up through the darkness, lighting the sky. As it continued to soar, a shroud of yellow light poured from it, showering the forest in its glow as it crept down the sentinels' long trunks before connecting with the earth. Then gradually it spread out, weaving its way through their narrow gaps before reaching the two Dhampir, bathing them in the false light of day.

As the light dimmed a little, the Dhampir turned to face it, blinking, letting their eyes readjust.

'What is that?' said Reece.

Asai took a step forward, staring up. 'I do not know—but it is not of this world.'

In a small, clearing in the forest, two horses jolted, almost throwing their riders to the ground, aware of something sinister lurking in the night air. Though urged to proceed, they refused, reluctant to go further.

Suddenly night turned into day, wrenching nature's residents from their slumber, their instincts telling them dawn had arrived in its brilliance—the sky spilling a dazzling light down on their abode, illuminating everything beneath it. And yet, dawn had not broken.

One of the two riders looked up, meeting its awakening, shading their sensitive eyes from it as it rose higher, breaking through the clouds, separating them, to reveal the wonders of the universe.

'There it is!' one whispered, taken aback by the beauty of its phenomenon.

The other, half-slumped in a stupor, tried to lift their head—the effort of it, like a weight, pressing down on their narrow shoulders.

'What?' they mumbled, slurring their response, somewhat disoriented.

'Look at it!' the other persisted, pointing, their dark eyes intense, dancing wildly at the sight.

The other, hearing their voice, groaned, straining to pull themselves up to see what *it* was. Exhausted by the mere exertion of their journey, they struggled at first to open their eyes. But when the brightness fell on their eyelids, they sprung open, then widened, seeing it—the light connecting them in mind and body, lifting them from the doldrums of their slow decline. As the light soared, it suddenly plunged itself down, finding them, bathing them in the splendour of its glow, and increasing their level of consciousness; lifting their body, they stretched their limbs, then spread their arms, welcoming its arrival, inhaling it as it breathed new life into their soul.

Seconds went by before the other spoke again.

'Would you like to know what—' They stopped, sensing an abrupt shift in the atmosphere. The horses were now more restless, their ears flicking, eyes darting, and hooves stomping the ground, aware of it, too. Taking control of their horse, they slowly turned, drawing back at the sight that beheld them.

*'Bella?!'*

# Chapter Twenty-Six

Daine recoiled in horror, recalling *that* meeting in the forest—two nights ago—when his life hung in the balance as he stared into death's facade.

'I—I have met this woman—this … *Sorceress*. But—how could she possibly be my …?' His words drifted, incapable of saying it. He shook his head, defiant. 'No!' He refused to believe it. 'Besides, she is too—' He stopped and ran his hand across his forehead, eyes scouring over the ground, thinking … Although the Sorceress had erased the events of what had happened to him that night, they had been gradually returning, since, when he had met the others at the *Ardgore Inn*, through snippets occasionally popping into his head. He frowned—the lines of concentration sculpted into his brow when something niggled at him—something she had done.

'Go on,' urged Rosalyn, seeing a vague look of recognition appear on his face.

'She … *saved* me!' he stated, lifting his eyes to look at her. 'I'm sure of it.'

'*Saved* you?' said Oran.

Daine nodded. He remembered it now: when the two *creatures* were sent to finish him off by that "devil", the Sorceress—*is she truly my grandmother?*—had stepped in, ordering her servants to destroy them … to save him. He shot a glance over at Wareeshta. He remembered her now; the female Dhampir had been one of them but had become an ally, since—through the girl. He nodded again then pointed.

'*You!*'

Wareeshta stared back at him, then at the others.

'You helped to fight off those creatures. You and the other one.' He let his tongue discreetly run over his bottom lip, feeling the lump where the "other one" had bit him, to entice the creatures. He shook the image of her away.

'The other one?' said Rosalyn.

Wareeshta sighed and nodded as she approached them.

'He means Kara.'

Reece grunted. 'I imagine the Valkyrie was none too pleased, being forced to let a mortal live.' Wareeshta gave him a sideward look, a faint smile appearing on her lips when she shook her head.

'Is this true?' said Oran, his interest deepening as he set aside his jealousy.

'I am certain now,' said Daine, 'had it not been for her intervention, that … *Devil* would have had his way.'

'Magia Nera?'

'That was his name!'

'How curious that she should save your soul,' said Oran. 'Perhaps her subconscious had something to do with it. She may have recognised something deep within you—to avert your death.'

'I somehow doubt it,' Daine hit back. 'I have witnessed her cruelty, at first hand.'

'But she is not …' Oran sighed. 'I *know* what she is really like. I was there when your father was con—'

'Spare us the details,' snapped Rosalyn.

Oran glared at his wife, then narrowed his eyes with suspicion; he was certain she had moved closer to Daine—the two mere inches from each other now. An image of them, entwined, momentarily jumped into his head, manipulating his ongoing reservations. He discarded it; he had to forget any notion of his wife enjoying the company of another man, let alone his … He shuddered at the mere idea of it.

'Listen to me, Daine,' he insisted. The look of disgust emanating from the guide told Oran he would have a difficult time convincing him. Then, if that were the case, there was only one thing to do: be blunt! 'Your … grandmother's name *is* Kristene,' he declared. Rosalyn grunted and stepped away, wanting nothing to do with it. 'And, yes'—he braced himself then turned his eyes skywards—'we had a full relationship, and from that union, your father—Petrio—was born. But Magia corrupted Kristene, and lured her away from me, to use her.'

'For what?' said Daine. 'Or does it speak for itself?' Rosalyn smirked at the guide's remark.

'As a *vessel*,' said Oran, trying to bite his tongue, 'to house the spirit of an ancient Sorceress, to make her live again, inside the form of a mortal.'

'That mortal being Kristene.'

'Aye, your father's—Petrio's—mother.'

'And your *whore!*' Rosalyn muttered, voicing what Daine had insinuated.

'She was no *whore!*' Oran retorted, defending the woman he had once shared a life with. Husband and wife glared at each other, Rosalyn standing her ground, seething with jealousy. Knowing her husband had bedded another woman—other *women!*—in the past was bad enough, but to know this particular one was still alive, enraged her. And then there was "their" son, to add to the mix. She had tried, with much grievance, to put his past to the back of her mind, but despite her efforts, she knew it was there, lurking inside her, as a reminder. She thought she had accepted the ghosts of his past, believing they were all dead. But now she had a rival from his past—a living, breathing rival. *Kristene!* To even utter this woman's name in her mind made her cringe. And, to make matters worse, she was not *mortal.*

*How can I compete with that?* she thought.

Conscious of Oran's eyes on her, she edged closer to Daine again, almost pressing against him now, as a show of unity in their vulnerability—and to antagonise her husband.

'So, Oran,' she started—the sharpness in her tone warning the Warlock of another verbal attack. 'What is your plan, now? To rekindle what you once had with … *Kristene?*' From the corner of her eye, she was aware of Daine watching her—and so persisted. 'Has this been your plan all along? Is that your intention, Oran? Do you—'

'Enough!' cried Gill, at his feuding parents. 'Stop this bickering and jealousy. It is not helping matters,' he added, pointing at the three monoliths, their surfaces still in constant turmoil. 'We are causing *that!* So little time left, and you have done nothing but bicker, in defence of your egos. Do you realise how childish you sound?'

His parents drew back at their son's outburst as shame consumed them. Gill stomped towards them, his heavy steps reverberating beneath his march. 'Forgive me, Rosalyn,' he said, looking down at his mother. 'I understand Oran's predicament. Have you not realised that I, too, am to lead a life of longevity? I will also outlive you. I have accepted his past. Now I beg you to do likewise.' He sighed a heavy sigh. 'It was a long time ago.'

With a sense of duty, Gill turned to Daine, to apologise for his parents' behaviour, but as he opened his mouth to speak, he stopped dead when he saw the guide's features altering; they were glowing, as though painted like the glory of a bright new dawn. Daine then lifted his eyes as if watching a bird take flight. Gill turned to follow his gaze. In the distance, beyond the *Paths of Lome*, the large funnel of light rose through the trees, pushing skywards. Higher it soared, dispersing the heavy clouds which had settled on the night, before stabbing the dark. Aware of something happening, the rest of the group turned, shielding their eyes from its initial intensity. The brilliant ray of yellow light continued to ascend into the black velvet night, with no sign of it ceasing, proclaiming to the world it had *"arrived!"*. No living soul could avoid its presence of beauty as it lit up the sky. Like a blazing sunrise, it blocked out the stars, illuminating everything below its grandeur before connecting with the moon's crescent, its curved rim now shining like gold, all lit up, pointing the way.

'What the …' Daine was stumped by what he was seeing.

'It is the *Portal!*' Gill stated.

'The what?' said Daine, throwing him a bewildered glance.

'The *Egress*,' said Kai

# Chapter Twenty-Seven

It seemed everything that had come to light was thrown by the wayside when the anticipated moment arrived. Oran had hoped it would manifest and was thankful it finally had. All Gill had to do now was choose the right Path.

With that, he promptly removed his amulet. It had now reached its full radiance, its intense colour matching that of the *Egress*. Now visible in its entirety, Oran knew how important it was Gill reached the portal before it began to fade, and before it returned from whence it came. The fear was—should they fail to do so—it would be too late, and then the window of time for Gill to bond with the Shenn would pass, making it *fair game* to another contender. On the other side, he also knew the *Assembly* would be waiting for his son's arrival at the Sanctuary of Armistice, for the transformation. And, despite his betrayal, Oran knew the Elliyan needed him—or, at least, his amulet—to complete the process. He also knew they required Magia Nera's. *"We need all five!"* He cringed, hearing Tuan's irritating voice in his head again. He promptly dismissed it.

Gripped by desperation, Oran looked to his son, then, without saying a word, turned on his heel and marched towards Nephtys—the horse stomping the ground on his approach, anticipating their impending departure. Oran's eyes flashed a look of warning at Wareeshta, then towards the trees; there was still no sign of Reece and Asai. He hoped they had not been led on a wild goose chase. *No, not them.* They were no fools.

Oran spoke softly to the mare while stroking her sleek mane, then lowered his hand, perusing over the leather satchel attached to her saddle. The book was still there, alongside the Playwright's work he had also taken, after growing attached to the story of the tragic Prince, having read it several times during his incarceration.

'Remember your vow.'

The Warlock flinched, hearing Wareeshta's voice in his ear, then drew back, on her sinister warning; 'I can take her life as swiftly as I gave it back.'

He turned and glared down into her lying eyes, seeing the truth behind them.

'You would no more harm my daughter, than—'

'If my father made a vow to you, Wareeshta, be assured, he will keep it.'

They turned to find Eleanor standing behind them; she had overheard their secret conversation.

Wareeshta lowered her eyes. 'Forgive me, my friend. But you know how it is'—she shook her head, her eyes begging to be understood—'I would *never* have …'

'I know,' said Eleanor. 'I would have done the same.' She then tilted her head slightly, a little unsure. 'Perhaps?'

Wareeshta smiled warmly at her friend, nodding.

'*Da!* You would have.'

'As my daughter is my witness,' said Oran, 'the book shall be yours, to do as you will—as with …' He paused when Wareeshta and Eleanor turned, having heard the rustling of trees—the approach of something heading their way, fast.

Eleanor looked sharp, her eyes lighting up as her heart beat in time with *his*. '*Asai*,' she blurted. The others turned, hearing her, then saw the Samurai as he broke through the thicket with Reece—the portal's light throwing their shadows against the trees, its sudden appearance prompting them to return to the Paths.

The two Dhampir shook their heads in frustration; without a scent to track, and though they had searched the area, thoroughly, there was no sign of Turloch or Kara.

With the portal now visible, Oran returned to Gill, with purpose. 'Kai will accompany you to the Egress, where it will take you to the Sanctuary of Armistice. He knows the way.'

Gill looked from his father to the three monoliths, his eyes lifting, following the Egress. 'But—'

'Asai and Eleanor are to go with you, also,' Oran then decided, interrupting his son.

Asai and Reece exchanged glances, realising they would have to part ways, indefinitely, not knowing the outcome—not knowing if they would meet again in their present life or the next. Reece's uneasy feeling returned, preying on his mind as he felt the pang of separation between himself and his true friend—not to mention his daughter and grandchildren. However, they were both aware of their duty and the great task at hand. Warriors in their own right, they were bound by that duty to those they loved, despite the potential risk and the possibility that some may not survive. The Samurai—with Eleanor by his side again—bowed to his comrade as a mark of respect, acknowledging the parting.

'But—what about you?' Gill asked his father.

'It is likely I will not be permitted entry into the Sanctuary. I have no doubt the Elliyan have a—' He grunted, smiling. 'Oh, do not concern yourself, Gill.' He then winked. 'They still need *this*,' he added, tapping his amulet. 'Besides, there is another way in.'

Gill frowned when Oran grinned at him.

'There is *always* another way, Gill,' he stated, sharing a knowing look with Kai. 'But *you*, as our future Magus, must prove yourself'—he glanced at the three monoliths—'before you can enter the Egress.'

Gill took a deep breath and sighed, feeling weary and tested to the limit. With the ultimate trial now facing him he began to second-guess his ability to succeed.

And then what?

*"You can do it."*

And there it was, his muse—his grandmother—dousing the flame of self-doubt.

'I have every faith in you, Gill,' said Oran, sensing his son's reservations. Gill looked at his father, his deep frown marked with apprehension and determination. 'We *all* do,' he championed, trying to reassure him like any father would. 'And … I *will* see you again.' As he looked his son in the eye, he saw the tiny flecks of gold glinting back at him. And yet, he detected something else … but could not place it. Resting his hand on Gill's broad shoulder, he vowed; 'You have my solemn word.'

'Look!' said Daine, pointing back at the three monoliths. 'They've stopped!' He marched towards them, followed by the others. They glanced over the plaquettes, their surfaces motionless before their eyes were drawn to the passage, on their left, where a stream of light appeared through the dim, then slowly expanded. It grew brighter by the second, its radiance then spilling out, crawling along the ground towards the pylon, then climbing onto its surface, lighting it up.

'This is it—the one!' Gill stated, pointing to the monolith, shimmering in all its wonder. He looked at Kai, his face a picture of certainty and excitement. But the Servitor was staring at the monolith with mixed feelings. While he knew about the Egress and its purpose—he briefly looked up, seeing it in the distance, then looked down again at the monolith—he knew nothing of this phenomenon. He looked at Oran. The Warlock shrugged and shook his head, equally baffled. Did the Elliyan know? *I am certain of it*, he thought as it dawned on him. It was clear to him they had chosen to keep it a close-guarded secret—even from Oran. And he understood why: they could not risk it being "common knowledge" beyond the walls of Elboru—the deterrent a necessity, to avoid any intrusion. And though they had been kept in the dark, Kai knew it was the right path, giving him a sense of relief; Gill would now be spared the dangerous task of having to choose. The timing, albeit limited, was perfect. He smiled and nodded.

'Indeed, it is,' he agreed.

Gill, with an open mind, approached the monolith. However, its surface now looked different; no longer did its white moonstone dazzle on its surface of black graphite, or glaze over like ice. But this did not deter him. He reached out, letting his hand hover over the plaquette; it was no longer cold, and the moon had now dimmed to a deep, midnight blue. But the one thing standing out was its final crescent; it was glinting like gold—the light from the Egress highlighting its curvature—and showing him the way.

'See here?' said Kai, pointing to it. Gill nodded. 'This is the moon in its current phase, letting us know how much time we have left.'

'How long?' said Reece, approaching the Servitor.

'When the light begins to recede, the Egress will eventually swallow it up, then …'

'Then what?' said Gill.

'… the portal will disappear.'

A look of fear and dread spread across Gill's face as he glanced between the Servitor and the passage.

'You have enough time, though,' Kai promptly reassured him. 'But do not waste it. Therefore, I suggest we go.'

'And what about us?' asked Rosalyn, referring to herself and Daine. She marched towards Oran, to challenge him. 'I want to see it—Elboru.'

Oran closed his eyes and sighed. 'You cannot go with him, Rosalyn.'

'Oh, really?' she retorted, making a stand by moving to her son's side, displaying her stubbornness; hands on hips, casting her husband that all-too-familiar look—the tilted head, the pursed lips, and when she began to tap her foot, his shoulders slumped in defeat, knowing he would have to surrender.

''Tis a great risk, Rosalyn,' he warned, moving towards her—the genuine look of concern, married with true love, set in his eyes. 'I'll not lie to you, my love.'

For a moment husband and wife looked deep into each other's

eyes, re-connecting—the tension that had separated them temporarily gone.

'Well, I am willing to risk it, Oran,' she stated, her voice now soft and low.

He shook his head, taking hold of her shoulders.

'I would not feel comfortable letting you go.'

'We have come this far,' she said, shrugging. 'And besides, should the Elliyan have anything to say about my presence …'

Oran laughed out. 'Then I pity them.' He held her gaze, her determined eyes refusing to leave his. In an unexpected move, Oran stabbed the Albrecht into the ground, then clutched his wife, pulling her closer to him. He grinned, then winked at her before drawing her up, to meet his lips. He kissed her with a tenderness—one filled with passion, as though it were their first … and last. And when they parted, she gave a small grunt, smirking from the side of her mouth. He side-glanced her, knowing *that* look. But through her determination, Oran saw the hint of dread stir in her eyes.

Taking his wife into the fullness of his embrace, Oran gently rested his chin on her crown. He closed his eyes and inhaled, languishing in the faint scent of lavender still lingering on the softness of her hair. He would remember it, savour the precious moment—savour the familiarity of her body, a feeling he had missed and longed for. He let his hand travel down her back, to the base of her spine, resting it in the arch. His hand tensed, pressing against her, not wanting to let her go. He sighed when she moved, tightening her hold on him. Gill was right; all the bickering and suspicions cast at each other had all been for nothing. What he would give right now to— He suddenly flinched when something dark shifted between them—the feeling of unease instantly separating the couple; she had felt it, too. They held one another's gaze—the look of mutual concern now evident. Forcing a smile, Oran drew his finger along the outline of his wife's face, tracing each line— noting new ones—knowing every flaw of it, seeing *only* her, for a moment. He then nodded, giving in to her desperate plea.

'All right, but you will go with Reece and Wareeshta,' he decided, '… and Daine.'

She nodded sharply in agreement. It was time to set aside their arguments and differences where their lives—both, past, and present— were concerned.

Gill was their priority now.

Standing in the wings, Daine looked on with new envy, his jealousy gradually fading. He knew, despite their disagreements, the bond between the husband and wife was armoured with true love, and it had been obvious in the way they had parted; when Rosalyn turned away from Oran, her hand still in her husband's, Daine saw the deep-rooted sadness in her eyes when her fingertips finally left his. He realised it was a parting the couple dreaded, unaware of how things would turn out. And as she turned from her husband, she glanced over at him with incurious eyes, then away—the look marking the end of something that had never begun. He then knew she would never be his. And so, discarding his plan to destroy the unbreakable bond, Daine swallowed his pride.

'You said there was another way?'

Everyone turned, hearing Asai.

'Aye,' said Oran. 'Unfortunately, it is only known to Warlocks. No other may use it. Though, I must assume *another* will—or already has.'

'Magia Nera,' Gill assumed.

Oran nodded, his brow drawn, creased in thought as he turned to his son.

'While he has been suspiciously too quiet,' he said, 'I know he is near.' He tapped his amulet again, nodding slowly. 'With the Shenn in its completion, each Warlock who bears an amulet can sense the other—the Egress bonding all and one,' he added. He now knew Magia had reclaimed his. 'Even Kara and her new "friend" have somewhat resorted to secrecy. It unnerves me.'

Oran looked down at the sword he had left in the earth, then retrieved it, clutching it in his hand—the matching Albrecht to his own. *My own!* He shot a glance towards Rosalyn. She gasped when it dawned on her—when it dawned on both of them.

'A moment, Gill!' she cried, and ran to Farrow, retrieving from his saddle the other Albrecht sword, opposite Tam's claymore—she closed her eyes briefly, touching the hilt of the Highlander's sword—before returning to Oran. 'I had almost forgotten!' she said, handing over the prized weapon.

Oran winked at his wife, then held the two identical swords up, feeling their boundless energy—united again. The black, shagreen, covering their grips, moulded into his hands and, as his eyes travelled down their steel, the tiny, gold inlays of hieroglyphs glinted from the light emanating from the Egress. Turning to their son, Oran held his heirloom out towards Gill.

'What was mine, is now your legacy. Use it wisely, son.'

Gill pressed his lips together as he stared down at the piece of family history being handed over to him. He reached out and, taking the Albrecht in his hand, felt its energy in the power of his grip, it stronger than Daine's. 'What has been given, cannot be taken,' Oran concluded, proud to see the heirloom finally wielded in his son's hand.

'Now, go!' he commanded. 'Your future awaits you, Gill. The title of Magus belongs to you, and no other.'

Gill, Asai and Eleanor made for the horses.

'We will not need them,' said Kai, turning towards the path.

'But—' Gill stalled when the Servitor looked back at him. He side-glanced Kai.

'Trust me,' said Kai.

Gill threw his father a look of concern, and when Oran smiled and nodded at him, he drew in a long breath and nodded back; who was he to question Kai?

There were no more goodbyes, no more parting displays of affection. Gill turned to his mother one more time and simply bowed to her. But as he made to leave, with those chosen to accompany him, he took one last look around. The remains of the dead creatures still lay on the ground. Nature would, in time, take them; already the flies had settled, laying their eggs on their rotting corpses. However, it was the disturbing and heart-breaking images of what had happened to Tam and Rave that would never leave him. *I'll make her pay.*

With nothing left to say, Gill, Kai, Asai and Eleanor walked towards the chosen monolith—the Egress still lighting the way. Together, and on foot, they moved by it, picking up pace as they approached the arch. Without stopping, they entered, disappearing into its unknown, towards the final leg of their journey.

Oran hesitated when something stole his attention. He looked up to where the forest met the sky, then beyond, seeing the moon's crescent shining like gold, its last phase connected to the funnel of light … *For all to see.* Then it would soon hand itself over to a new moon, where Gill and the Shenn would need to connect. *By then, Gill will be Magus.* Oran's heart swelled with pride.

'Now what?' said Daine. Gone was the tone of sarcasm in his voice; it was now replaced with genuine interest, though with underlying apprehension.

'Oran!'

The Warlock tore his look from Daine, hearing his wife's voice; she had remained by the monolith, still watching, feeling the pang of separation from her offspring when her son and daughter faded from view.

'Is it me … or is the light beginning to fade, already?' She pointed towards the passage.

The remainder of the group moved to her side, following her look of enquiry. They stared, narrowing their eyes while exchanging looks of uncertainty; a trick of the eye, perhaps? But as they observed the lengthy passage, from its monolith, it soon came to light as they watched its snail-like movement retreat into the passage.

'Aye, 'tis beginning to fade,' said Oran, staring through its arch—the urgency in his tone, alerting them. He glanced down at the pylons' surfaces; they had, so far, remained motionless. But, for how long? If the others did not leave quickly, the plaquettes would return to their state of disorder. Oran knew he had to act. Wasting no time, he turned to the remaining few.

Taking the sword he had bequeathed to Petrio, Oran handed it back to Daine—his grandson—advising him: 'Take it. It *is* rightfully yours. It will also gain you entry into the castle of Elboru, as it is a Warlock's sword. The one you seek—when you reach there—his name is *Lothian.* He is trustworthy. Tell him who you are'—he eyed the diminishing light then stepped closer to Daine, tempted to place his hand on his shoulder, but changed his mind—'who you *truly* are, and who your grandmother was—*is.*' Behind him, Rosalyn bit her tongue, keeping a fixed eye on the passage, aware of its fading light. 'Should Lothian inquire of my… situation,' Oran continued, 'inform him that I went to search for another. He will understand. But now, you must leave, through the same passage, but—' He stopped, at first distracted by the horses stomping the ground, on edge; the atmosphere had changed, stirring their fear as it took a sinister turn. Far behind, in the distance, beyond the narrow gorge that had led the group to the Paths of Lome, they heard a sound, like rolling thunder. And yet, the sky looked clear. They all turned to face it, lifting their gaze high.

'What is that?' said Reece.

'That,' said Oran, 'is the sound of *evil.*'

They could feel its looming presence, its oppressive threat filling the air with its charge. They could see its dark energy hovering in the sky, then spreading, like an infection, gradually blocking out the faint hue of a distant pale blue light, marking the dawn of a new day. Still, it crept across their divide, dousing the fading stars above with its bleakness.

'This cannot be happening,' Oran muttered. Suddenly he was conscious of his amulet pressing against him, causing him some discomfort.

'What's wrong?' said Rosalyn, her eyes lifting higher, seeing the blanket of doom move across the sky as though it were devouring the universe. She drew back when her husband spun on his heel—the look of trepidation etched on his face. He glanced back at the monoliths, now aware of the controlling presence, threatening to rouse them from their slumber and hurl their surfaces into chaos again.

'Take the horses and go. Now!' he stated, looking back at the group. Reece and Wareeshta, realising the urgency, nodded and, with Daine close behind them, took charge of their horses.

'But—why do we need the horses?' asked Rosalyn. 'When Gill—'

'Trust me—you *will*,' Oran blurted, eager to see them on their way.

With her husband's hand leading her briskly by the elbow, Rosalyn looked up at Oran, mouth open and eyes wide with concern. With no knowledge of what awaited them, she froze, her mouth opening and closing, indecisive. 'But—but—'

'Please!' Oran begged, gripping her shoulders, and wrenching her from her fear. He briefly held her gaze—the fear evident by his intense stare—the terror visible behind his eyes. He leaned closer, sharing one last kiss—quick, hard and passionate—then drew back. 'Please, my love. For once, do not question me.' Another glimpse back at the monolith, told him the light would soon be gone; he panicked when its surface suddenly flickered, threatening to change again. They needed to go through the same one as Gill and the others. 'There is no time.' Swallowing the words, she had wanted to say, Rosalyn nodded, placing all her trust in her husband. Hearing his sigh of relief, thankful to her for holding her sharp tongue, they promptly joined the others.

'Quick!' he insisted, clasping his hands together, for her to mount Farrow. Rosalyn did not hesitate. With moments to spare he ushered her towards the monolith, where Reece, Daine and Wareeshta—who had taken over the reins of Gill's horse—eagerly waited. He did a double-take when the plaquette flickered again. *Any moment now.*

'Look after her, Farrow,' he said—the steed, flicking its ears in response to its master's voice. 'Go! Before it changes.'

Husband and wife's eyes locked in a final moment of understanding as they parted. Within seconds, the four galloped through the arch—the light chasing after them, then diminishing the instant they leapt over the threshold, with Oran's voice echoing after them;

'Stick to the main path—no matter what!'

Oran looked down at the monolith's surface and gasped; it had already changed. He looked up towards the passage and jolted when it fell into a blackness, so dense it was as if its void had swallowed Rosalyn and the others, wiping them off the face of the earth.

Then silence …

He hoped they had heard his warning …

# Chapter Twenty-Eight

Save for the ghosts of his ancestors, lingering in the still of the night, Oran had an immediate sense of deep loneliness as he stood staring into what seemed like oblivion. He pondered on its disturbing effect until it passed, unaware of how long he had stood there. His eyes lifted, following the light emanating from the Egress, in the distance. There was still time before it diminished, closing the portal for good. He was confident Gill would make it now, especially with Kai by his side. It also woke him to the time they had spent here—wasting it on petty arguments. But he could not think about that now. 'What's done is done!' he mumbled. He jolted when his heart skipped a beat, like a warning, not to falter or stall—the dull feeling drowning his mood.

He looked around, suddenly drawn in by the unwavering stillness; nothing stirred, not even the wind. And yet, a charged silence clung. He stalled, aware of a heavy sound, its strong, rhythm rising and falling inside him; he held his breath, fearing he would bring attention to himself. His eyes moved around the residual silence, left by his family's departure. *It is like they were never here*, he thought. But he knew they had. He was sure he had sent them on their way through the right passage, just before the monolith's surface changed. But as he released his breath, an ember of doubt flickered inside him.

His eyes then flicked, catching something from the corner of his vision, an erratic movement, as if the universe had been disturbed. But without diverting his look, he knew all three monoliths had resumed their state of change. However, this time, he sensed something different—something out of place—coming from their surfaces. Though reluctant, his instinct told him to look. Slowly, his eyes lowered, then slid sideways. He then spun, staring at them, wide-eyed; they were being manipulated—not by emotions, but by another source, creating anarchy among them.

His attention moved from one to the next, seeing the black cloud of mist swirling above them, blocking out their markings. And though he could not see the *Sun*, the *Moon* and the *Universe*, he knew they were there, but were in constant turmoil beneath the blanket of darkness—the sinister threat sabotaging their behaviour.

Oran looked sharp; something was niggling at him—that underlying doubt—as he looked up towards the passage Rosalyn and the others had gone through. Stepping away from its monolith, a dreadful feeling came over him, like he had made a grave mistake. Eyes set forward, he rushed towards the void. He stopped dead when a force pressed against him, pushing him back, preventing him from following the others, to warn them. He tried again but failed. Chest heaving, he moved back and raised his hands, conjuring his powers to fight the force that held him. With each failed attempt, his amulet weighed heavier, like an unfamiliar burden on his person. Behind him, he could hear the remaining horses' distress; their senses had picked up on the threat. He looked to where they'd been tied, Nepthys being the dominant one, her behaviour spurring the other horses on in their desperate attempt to break free. Teeth bared, they reared, constantly whinnying loudly as if pleading with him to free them.

Feeling the constant, heavy tug of his amulet, Oran ran to the horses and released them—the sound of their hasty escape then evident, by the fading thud of their hooves as they galloped back towards the entrance to the clearing—the escarpments echoing their escape through the gorge. Only Nepthys remained—the Warlock's horse having been trained not to desert.

Promptly, Oran checked the mare, feeling the leather satchel attached to her saddle, assured of the book's presence. Suddenly he keeled over, his amulet pressing on him, demanding his attention. Breathless, from its persistent persecution of him, he grunted, muttering profanities at its untimely intervention. He wrenched it out, wincing when the heavy, gold chain pinched the skin on his neck. He raised it high—the reflection of the light emanating from the Egress, matching its intensity. He tilted his head, his brows knitting together as he narrowed his eyes, seeing something within its centre.

'What the—' He flinched when the light vanished. He looked up, mouth open. The Egress was gone. He hoped Gill and Kai had made it. Hoped? No. They *had* to, otherwise … Again, he lifted his amulet, squinting from beneath his brows, unable to see into the centre of the stone. What exactly had he seen? Then something stirred beneath his feet. He could feel the vibrations. He looked up, hearing it—the desperate charge of pounding hooves, coming from the passage—and straight for him. His eyes widened as it came into view.

*'Farrow?'*

*The Naoi – The Sacred Chamber: Elboru*

The lonely figure stood wrapped in the silence, hands grasped together, head tilted low and eyes closed in reverie—the wavering flames within the sanctum forming slow-moving shadows on their imposing features. Since its inception—beyond a millennia—he had stood before the hallowed shrine, watching over the precious item he had been chosen to protect until it was re-awakened from its dormancy, its *Light of Life* announcing, each time, the birth of a new Magus—and the dawn of a new era. And there its guardian remained until it was time for the precious item to bond with its new master—Lord of all Warlocks.

The Ushabti's eyes suddenly flickered beneath their lids, disturbed by an image—the same one he had shown Oran when the High Warlock was challenged by his superiors. The vivid image now flashed through his own mind, playing out its scene of death and devastation: faces, both strange and familiar to him, fought against a relentless and determined force. One by one, they fell in battle. He saw the *Chosen One* challenge the malevolent force, ready to strike it down. Another troubling picture entered his mind: clutched in the enemy's hand, for all to see, the Shenn amulet glowed in its true magnificence. But it was a warning—a display of power—letting everyone know who ruled. However, the face of the bearer was distorted. He went deeper into his subconscious, letting it guide him until a gradual sense of clarity began to unveil their features. But the image was severed from his mind as if someone had cut it down. A victory perhaps? Or …

The Ushabti's eyes shot open—the glow within the chamber highlighting the particles of gold glinting from his almond-shaped eyes, their colour—lapiz lazuli—intensified by what he had seen. Slowly he lowered his gaze to the shrine, sensing the restlessness coming from within; small, though prominent, he had felt it, too—the disturbing unbalance within the universe.

The Ushabti looked up, aware of more than one presence behind him. Only one Warlock was usually permitted entry at a time, where he could give devotions to—or ask forgiveness of—their Magus. But this was not the case.

Not now.

He turned to see Tuan, Lothian and Greer standing before him, decked out in their regalia. They had come for the Shenn, and to accompany him to the Sanctuary of Armistice, in readiness for the transformation.

Tuan, the self-proclaimed speaker of the Elliyan, bowed to the Ushabti.

It was time.

The Shenn's guardian moved to the shrine, and closing his eyes extended his hands over its surface before slipping into a quiet mantra.

He suddenly stopped.

His eyes flashed open, then moved sideways, still mindful of the Warlocks behind him, waiting—one, in particular, agitated. He could sense the sudden quickening of their heartbeat; then it slowed, back to its natural rhythm, prompting him to resume.

As his chant grew in momentum, its melodic tone hypnotising, the shrine's doors separated, opening out, to reveal the precious item inside, its intense light escaping into the chamber.

Carefully, the Ushabti reached in and, taking hold of it with both hands, lifted it out. As he did so, the Shenn's deep-yellow, radiant light, lit up the whole chamber, bringing the shrine's sunken reliefs to life as they flickered and danced, telling those who looked upon it the story of the first Magus—*Lumeri*. But as he held it to the level of his eye, the Ushabti saw something within its core. He leaned his head sideways, eyes tapering as he inspected it. Though small, it was there—a black mass—like a cloud, swirling in constant turmoil, its unexpected presence having a profound and troubling effect on him.

Again, something unsettling shifted behind him. With the Shenn still in his protective hands, the Ushabti turned and looked directly into the immoral eyes of another.

# Chapter Twenty-Nine

*The Paths of Lome – Muir Forest*

The sea of trees stretched up and out as far as the eye could see as she searched. Still, she was unsure. With her pursuit hampered by the forest's mass of ancient trees, she was forced to rise higher above their stature; they seemed to grow in height, occasionally obstructing her view as she advanced in her search. She also sensed she was losing speed. *The trees must be protecting something*, she thought, as her icy grey eyes darted through the thicket, still looking. *It must be here, somewhere!*

Eventually, she broke through the treetops, gulping the air, then lurched when she swallowed its foul, stinking breath—the presence of evil now taking precedence. It was nauseating yet she detected a familiarity about it.

Kara slowed, trying to combat the denseness in the air, eventually stopping in mid-flight, to find her bearings. She had headed east after escaping her enemy and could now see the great ragged crests of the Ardmanoth mountains, curving like the crescent of the moon. But as her sharp eyes followed the grandeur of their peaks, she suddenly became aware of her great, black wings, struggling to keep her in flight. She had felt the added weight of their burden the moment she broke the treeline. She failed to understand why, at first, then concluded that the forest's oppressiveness was the culprit; its atmosphere was pressing down on her, affecting her ability to heighten her speed. She had lost some of her feathers in her flight through the forest's dense shrubbery—the trees' thorn-like branches catching them as she tried to flee after taking *their* "pet". Also, the animal's bulk had almost hindered her ascent; as she distanced herself from *them*, the hound's weight seemed to slow her as it thrashed out, its sharp nails tearing at her skin—hence her finally ridding herself of the unnecessary load.

But it was gone now, and she was sure it was dead; she had heard its howls when she dropped it into a deep ravine. *An eye for an eye*, she told herself—then thought nothing more of it.

Despite the drag of her wings, she pressed on, though unsure of her direction. She was then aware of Turloch's presence far below, on the ground; she had spotted him at intervals, catching glimpses of his long, white hair as he flitted through the narrow spaces between the trees, to keep up with her.

Turloch, having witnessed her escape from a distance, had made it his business to track her, by scent; he had his own interests to protect and, with no more warriors by his side, knew he needed her.

She had contemplated ridding herself of his company, but he was her only ally. She thought of their "attachment" and knew he wanted more of her. A curl appeared at the edge of her mouth. *Perhaps I will spare him, and award his loyalty with a place by my side when I—* She stopped. Still suspended in mid-air, she was drawn to the sudden appearance of pale light; it looked like the dawn as it lifted and spread across the tips of the trees, moving over them like a blanket of pale gold. A murder of crows suddenly sprung from below the tree line, their loud, rambunctious cawing almost deafening, and their black silhouettes intimidating as nature's *Agents of Death* took flight towards the mountains, eventually fading into their shadows.

Kara's mouth slowly fell as the light made its way towards her. She lifted her brows, gasping when it touched and caressed her skin, spreading over her body, throwing a lustre on her black armour. She threw her head back in ecstasy, relishing in its unearthly effect.

'Can you see it?'

Jolted from her trance-like state, she looked down, seeing Turloch through a gap in the trees. He, too, had stopped and looked in the same direction, having seen it—the unexpected sunrise. But something was out of place.

Confused, she spun and looked around; though the dawn was looming, it was too early for sunrise. She drew back, seeing the cause: rising from the ground, in the distance, the funnel of intense, yellow light lifted itself from the depths, rising into the void above them, their eyes following it, with intrigue.

Turloch shielded his eyes as the brightness filled them with dazzling light.

Kara smiled at its magnificence. For a moment, there was no malice in her eyes as she looked upon the spectacle, overwhelmed by its splendour. It now had an unusual calming effect on her. Was this what she was looking for? She wanted to go to it, touch it, but drew back when tiny shards of light leapt from its core, melting into the atmosphere before they could reach her. Though in a quandary of the spectacle, she could not help but admire its allure as it absorbed her, almost casting a spell over her.

'Is it what you seek?' he called out again.

She grunted, frowning, put out by his insistence for a reply. She was reluctant to go to him; instead, she wanted to follow the light, to find its source, certain it was what she was searching for—like the others.

Finally, Kara resolved herself to the fact that she would need to keep Turloch on her side.

'Is *that* what you seek?' His voice was impatient as he glowered up at her, her eyes still fixed on the funnel. It radiated over everything within its perimeter—above and below—while casting a warm glow over their pale faces, giving them a human-like appearance.

Still, with no reply from the Valkyrie, Turloch struggled to vent his frustration as he continued to wait for her response. But Kara's mind was awash with thoughts of power and domination. Eventually, she descended, taking care not to lose any more of her foliage.

Lowering herself, she cast Turloch a quick mischievous eye, then smirked; it was written all over her face—her intentions—warning him, before her eyes returned to the light in the distance. But Turloch had already pre-empted the Valkyrie's next move; when Kara's feet touched the ground, she darted in the funnel's direction. He was quick on her heel.

The measure of distance between them and the beam of light was farther than anticipated. Nevertheless, Kara and Turloch made ground. But as they drew closer, they slowed, realising where they were—back at the Paths of Lome, facing the three pylons, their surfaces shrouded by swirling clouds of dust. There was no one around save for the dismal atmosphere, lingering within the heavy silence of the open space. Gone was autumn's palette, its carpet of red, yellow-and-gold, now blanketed by a mist of ashen grey—the veil between the living and the dead.

Kara looked sharp, towards the trees, her eyes steady as she scoured their surroundings, paying no heed to the outline of the rotting, headless corpses scattered on the ground. Something had stirred her wits.

Sensing it, too, Turloch removed his sword.

'There is something up there,' she stated, pointing with her chin, keeping her voice low. Turloch's eyes travelled up, then stopped, seeing a pale mist between the trees. Slowly, it began to meander, spreading out and wrapping itself around the tree trunks before making its descent. They followed its course, narrowing their eyes when it rose, dispersing into shapes.

'What are they?' he whispered.

'I do not—' Kara stopped short when the shapes materialised, into human-like forms. One by one they appeared, growing in number as they made their way towards them—the sound of their battle march now palpable, and getting louder with each tread. 'It is … an army!' As their numbers increased, drawing closer by the second, she discarded any notion of engaging in battle with this army of phantoms. She would lose.

She looked back towards the Paths. Tempted to flee into one of the three passages, something inside her—an instinct—told her not to. Beside her, she could sense Turloch's apprehension. She looked up, her eyes following the light, then back at the advancing army. There was only one way out of their situation now—if they were to survive. Taking hold of the Dhampir, she rose—the burden of his bulk a frustrating effort for her. She could have left him to the mercy of the phantom army, but as much as it pained her to admit it, to do *that* would have been a mistake; she needed him.

Drawn to the curious humming, emanating from its core, Kara flew high over the treetops, following the line of the passages; they seemed to merge into one, towards the funnel, then split again into three. She veered left, seeing it now. It was so close. She looked down, searching for a gap, and frowned; still nowhere to land. Her arms were now aching. She had the Obsidian in one hand, and Turloch cradled against her other shoulder, his eyes fixed on her with a constant look of suspicion.

'Be mindful of how you look at me, Turloch,' she warned. 'All I have to do is—' He jolted when she briefly released him. But before he fell from her, she grasped him again into her clutches but struggled to keep flight as their feet dragged through the treetops. This time, he held her tightly. She grunted; even if she wanted to discard him, she knew he would not let go of her, thus dragging them both into the shadows below.

Gradually, she gained height and speed; any slower, she would fall.

Then there it was, before them, in all its magnificence: the *Egress*. With the added weight of her load, Kara finally landed, hard, in a small clearing, nearly stumbling when their feet hit the ground.

Instantly, they removed their weapons, listening with caution. No sight nor sound of another living soul was near, save for the relentless humming. They turned to face the funnel; the noise was coming from inside. Pleasant to the ear—like the voice of a child humming a song—its haunting melody was surprisingly hypnotic. Kara and Turloch looked at one another, then back at the Egress, craning their necks as they followed its endless light, skywards—the sparks still sprinkling out over them, then rising again before dissolving into the universe.

'This is it!' she stated, finally answering his question. 'The portal I heard them speak of.'

He stared at her; her face was a glow of warmth, her plaited hair gleaming, and the gold band on her head, with its centred onyx stone, glinted in the light. It completely transformed her, momentarily softening her hardened features, only to be altered by the ugliness of her crooked nose and malicious thoughts. 'The portal?' he echoed.

She slowly nodded, her eyes locked to its secret.

'It holds the key to my sovereignty—and I shall have it!'

'But you must claim it first!' came a dominant voice from behind.

Turloch spun on his heel, swiftly raising his sword—the blade's tip stained black with venom.

Rolling her eyes at the inconvenient intrusion, Kara turned to find four determined faces staring at her. Her eyes glanced down; three were armed.

'And should you have it in your mind to crown yourself with that which belongs to *me*,' Gill continued, stepping forward, 'I would think again … *Valkyrie!*' He glared at her—the image of Rave ingrained in his memory, when she hauled his loyal companion away from him. It was clear she had discarded his beloved pet, since. Hate simmered inside him.

Turloch kept a watchful eye on Asai; the Samurai was wielding his sacred weapons, prepared to defend and protect. He would willingly draw *his* blood. His eyes flashed to the young woman beside him, then dropped briefly, distracted by the constant turning of the dagger in her left hand. She reeked of youth … and something else. He perceived her demise … *If it were not for him* … She would be easy to destroy. But then he noticed her features—the obvious *change*—just like him. His eyes then moved to the ghost-like creature who stood quietly and unarmed, its black eyes focused on him. Naïve to its ways and capabilities, its presence intimidated him.

Kara strode back and forth across the Egress, blocking their way as if marking her new domain, letting her eyes glide over them, then cautiously around. She detected no more than four as she calculated the possible outcome. Despite the hindrance of her wings, her strength on the ground, however, more than matched Turloch's as she contemplated dispatching her "guests".

She grunted. 'Your numbers seemed to have … dwindled,' she said, lifting her deep-throated voice above the constant humming behind her.

Her arrogance infuriated Gill. It simply oozed from her pores, and when he gripped the hilt of his newly-acquired sword his knuckles whitened as she smirked at him. As images of Tam and Rave continued to flash through his mind, he gradually lifted the Albrecht, his rage now visible from his battle stance. He was prepared to attack, to avenge the lives she had taken from them. He wanted to slay her, shed her blood, there and then.

Kai had been assessing the looming situation; the Valkyrie was taunting Gill—and only Gill—in her own evocative and depraved way, alerting the Servitor to her motives. It was possible she knew who Gill was and had no intention of letting him—or anyone else—pass through the Egress. It was also possible she knew about the Shenn and was prepared to do anything to take possession of it—and its power.

Sensing the Valkyrie's intentions towards her brother, Eleanor grew restless as she toyed with the dirk. She was finding it difficult to restrain herself from attacking, and with limited knowledge of her new skills, was uncertain of her ability to do so, risking her demise. If it were not for Asai's presence, and his calming words, she would lose control, spurring her into a frenzied attack.

'As have *your* numbers!' Kara's eyes found the Servitor's, hearing his statement. 'It is apparent your mistress has deserted you,' Kai added, gliding towards her without fear, his black eyes briefly eyeing the Egress, watching for signs of its diminishing light; he thought he had detected a flicker from within its core.

She snorted. 'I have no mistress—nor master.'

'Do you plan to rule, solely—and in isolation—a world you truly have no understanding of?'

The Valkyrie glowered at the Servitor, his calmness irritating her as she tried to fathom his meaning. Her eyes moved to Gill when he edged closer, too. His imposing features made her smile. She noted how striking in stature he was. Her eyes travelled up and down his impressive physique, his frame broad and muscles solid with strength. He *had* changed since their first encounter, when she abducted his sibling—a few days ago. *The sibling!* She lifted a curious brow, seeing Eleanor, aware of her altered state—the trace of her newborn scent tickling her senses. *No longer mortal, I see.* Her eyes flashed back to Gill; she narrowed them when they met his—the flecks of gold glinting back at her, driving her intuition. *Could he be the one?*

'Perhaps there will be no need for me to be burdened alone with such a task,' she purred, continuing to eye Gill. She inclined her head towards him. 'Join me!'

Eleanor took a step forward, then stopped, feeling Asai's grip on her arm.

'Wait!' the Samurai whispered to her, perceiving the rising conflict.

Gill was seething at Kara's narcissism, as was Turloch—the Dhampir's jealousy simmering beneath his cold exterior as she blatantly disregarded him. And, as she kept her tantalising look on Gill, Turloch, now consumed by envy, leapt between them, glaring at her, his eyes burning with anger. Her loyalty had been nothing but a ploy to use him. He knew that now.

'You gave your word to *me!*' he hissed, raising his sword against her, his back to the others. "A place by your side—together we will rule",' you said.

Kara rolled her eyes and sneered, ignoring Turloch's outburst, then looked over his shoulder, her dismissal of him infuriating him further. But as she continued to taunt them with her games, Kai noticed something behind her; the funnel was flickering, changing, beginning to lose its lustre. It was fading and would continue to do so until it disappeared. And once it was gone … The Servitor looked up. It was now beginning to diminish from the top. He had to warn them.

'Time is running—'

'Gill!'

Eleanor's raised voice snatched Kai's attention as she and Asai rushed by him, towards the funnel. The Servitor looked back at the Egress, in time to catch a glimpse of Gill; the young man, intent on attacking Kara, had bolted towards her, only to be enveloped by the portal's fading light.

He was gone.

Kai looked up; the funnel was now in its decline back to earth. For the first time since he had known Gill, the Servitor panicked. He looked around, frantically searching …

There was no sign of the Valkyrie either.

'She has gone, too,' said Asai, pointing at the Egress. He made for it, stopping when the Servitor blocked him, shaking his head.

*"You know what to do."*

'This is a duty—*my* duty,' Kai stated, recalling Onóir's parting words, to him.

In the final seconds before the light would cease to exist, the Egress glowed spectacularly, forcing the on-lookers to turn away. With moments to spare, the Servitor, loyal to his dear friend's honour, threw himself into the portal's last flicker of life, before throwing Eleanor, Asai and Turloch into temporary darkness.

Gradually as their eyes adjusted, after the intense glow of the Egress' departure, Eleanor and Asai glanced at one another. Through unspoken words, they knew what they had to do.

Deserted and betrayed by the Valkyrie, Turloch turned to face his foes. Armed with his poisonous sword, he reached inside his black coat and removed another weapon.

Asai's eyes widened, seeing the katar—the dagger, with its H-shaped hand grip, showed the blade sitting above Turloch's knuckles. Also known as a *Push* dagger, Asai knew Turloch was skilled in its use; he had seen him display it effortlessly, in his attempt to impress Kara when he was first imprisoned, by the Sorceress. Even in the dim light, the gold, H-shaped handle glinted as he wielded the foot-long blade in front of them, his sword gripped in his other hand. Turloch rose to his full height, emphasising his true physique, his chest expanding as he inhaled deeply, gripping his weapons. He would defend himself to the end.

He crossed his two weapons—the clash of blades ringing loudly, marking the start: the show of strength before the battle. As he slowly ran the katar's blade down the length of his sword, the sound of their steel screeched through Eleanor, right to her core. Then, in a display of utter conceit, Turloch extended his long, muscular arms towards his two foes before widening them to their full span, welcoming, inviting them to challenge him. It would be a glorious battle.

Gritting her teeth, Eleanor's impatience finally won her over. The temptation to accept Turloch's offer was too great to resist. Overwhelmed by her growing strength and urges, despite her lack of skill, the young woman leapt from Asai's side before he could stop her.

Pre-empting her first attack, Turloch snorted, then casually stepped aside, deflecting any potential contact. He grunted, side-glancing at her feeble attempt. She was a newborn; though fast, she lacked experience.

Eleanor stopped abruptly and turned, her eyes crimson, her face wild with aggression. But Turloch paid little attention, almost dismissing her; his focus was on the real threat standing before him, armed with their katana and wakizashi, his sacred weapons joined again, in *Daisho*. Conscious of her behind him—and anticipating Eleanor's next attack— Kara's discarded ally lowered his left arm to his side, ready to draw the push knife behind; he knew she would rush him, throwing herself in the path of the lethal blade. Once dispatched, he could indulge himself in single combat with the *Strange One*, without interruption.

But what Eleanor lacked in experience, she gained in perception—the one thing she had carried with her through life, from the old to the new. She rushed at Turloch, stopping within an inch of his lethal weapon. She looked down at its shining metal, seeing the distinct black stain dulling its edge; it, too, had been marked with the same toxic venom as his sword—the same poison which had almost taken her life. She was unsure if the deadly venom posed another threat to her. She had no intention of finding out.

'Have a care!' she called to Asai, quickly stepping away from its harm. Her warning momentarily distracted Turloch's concentration from the Samurai, his error spurring Asai forward.

Caught unawares, Turloch stumbled, but his swiftness of defence prevented him from falling. The force of their impact resonated throughout. Their attack and defence were relentless and predictable to one another as Eleanor looked on—the two matching in skill, a skill she was unfamiliar with. Promptly, she stepped back, keeping her distance from the conflict, her mind in deep thought.

Locked in combat, Asai and Turloch blocked out everything around them as the fight intensified and their speed accelerated. Even to her quick eye, Eleanor found it difficult to discern the difference between the two, save for the occasional glimpse of Turloch's long, snow-white hair, mingling with the blackness of Asai's. Only then, could she decipher who was who. They battled on—the clash of their blades ringing like a lament, getting louder, straining her sensitive ears. And yet, while she observed, she felt alone and vulnerable, expecting an attack from more Dhampir. On this thought, she momentarily turned, glancing about, alert and focused. Then something made her stop. It had gone quiet. She looked sharp, back to where they had been fighting.

Asai and Turloch were nowhere to be seen.

With the dirk grasped within her hold, Eleanor spun, searching for the small clearing where they had all stood, a short time ago. It was gone, vanished, along with the portal. She was now back in the long, winding passage. She listened. Nothing. Then heard it—the petering clash of blades ahead in the distance, where the fight had taken them deeper into the passage—the one they had followed, from the Paths. It had reappeared after the Egress vanished, but she had failed to notice it—too caught up in events.

She moved towards the clatter of steel, then hesitated, her lack of skills preventing her. A sudden rush of emotions overwhelmed and confused her. She turned, eyes searching, not knowing what to do without her soulmate by her side. What would she do, should Asai be defeated? The thought had never occurred to her, until now. She knew how they died: brutally stabbed through the heart, then beheaded. Should that happen, she would feel every ounce of his death. *Then I will be next!* If it came to that, there would only be one option for her—and she would not live without him.

She glanced back in the opposite direction from whence they initially came—the fading clash of their weapons echoing from behind. Frantic, and unsure, she glanced back and forth from one end to the other, indecisive. She could run, back to the Paths, and save herself; he would want her to. But when she looked again, towards the rhythmic sound of conflict coming from the darkness, she shook her head, defiant. *I am no coward.*

Steadfast in her decision, to face what could be thrown at her, she felt the vague presence of another inside her, influencing her train of thought. It puzzled her. A single emotion suddenly gripped her, dominating the others: *fear!* She could no longer feel Asai's vibrant energy—the bond which kept them in touch with one another's auras. She felt empty, as though he no longer existed.

Eleanor clutched her slow-beating heart, listening to the gloom; still nothing. Then, like a wild animal, she perked up, warned of a potential threat. Now, her instincts were not of concern but that of survival.

With her heart beating loudly, she tilted her head towards the steep bend in the dark passage, listening—the extended silence cautioning her defences, to something deep within its tunnel of trees. The waiting was intolerable. As she contemplated her next move, she jerked, hearing the rustling of leaves being pounded beneath hasty, heavy footsteps. With eyes locked ahead, she watched and waited, peering into its blackness, crouching as they grew closer—the thud of each step pounding in her head. But without seeing them, she already knew.

Eleanor gripped the dagger she so cherished with all her might, feeling the residual energy from the hands that had previously owned it as though they were passing their strength on to her. She briefly closed her eyes—'Wait for me, Asai!'—then rushed forward, to meet her assailant, head-on.

# Chapter Thirty

Plunged into sudden darkness, the horses reared and jolted, reluctant to go on. Eventually, their riders calmed them. A little hesitant, the group lingered—the dark temporarily hampering their vision. As their eyes adjusted to their surroundings, they slowly urged their horses on, treading carefully—the ground beneath them sodden, breaking their stride; the horses' hooves were sinking into the thick, heavy mud. Yet, even on horseback, the riders were aware of something beneath the uneven surface, it preying on their thoughts.

Tightening her control of Farrow's reins, Rosalyn looked down through the gloom, her eyes narrowing as she glanced over the ground, its black surface glistening wet—the thick, squelching sound of hooves, dominating the eerie silence. It unnerved her, having to take a slow pace. She looked up, seeing the canopy of trees bent over in submission, from the weight of the oppressiveness hanging in the air; they formed a continuous arch along the route, blocking out the sky, making it difficult to see, and heightening her uneasiness.

'Can you hear it?' said Daine. 'That … awful silence.' He shuddered, feeling its lingering presence wrap around him.

'We are all aware of it,' said Reece, his tone flat and sharp. 'Hence we must keep moving.'

As they rode on, the ground seemed to harden a little. Rosalyn looked down again when it crunched beneath the horses' hooves. Save for the rise and fall of the surface, she could see nothing, oblivious to what lay beneath its ancient layers as it paved the way. It now disturbed her, turning her unease to dread. She then flinched, as though someone—or *something*—had just walked over her grave. She shook the feeling away, keeping her mind focused on Farrow.

Riding close together, the group gradually increased the horses' speed to a canter, maintaining their silence. Rosalyn made a point of keeping alongside her father; she wanted to avoid further awkwardness with Daine after the public display of affection she and Oran had shown, back at the Paths. She was still aware of him though, as he and Wareeshta rode close behind. But in the end, she had made a choice—not that there had been one to make. Despite his faults, Oran would always be "the one" for her. She had been flattered by Daine's attention; it had turned her head briefly. She knew that, now. And then to discover he was her husband's grandson … That, in itself, had doused the embers of something that had temporarily stirred—not her heart, but her want of male company which had gone astray for three years. But Oran was back—she pressed her lips together, holding on to their parting kiss, it now replacing *that* other one—and his return had re-ignited the fire that had diminished between them. She welcomed it back with a burning passion.

Guiding their horses along the bleak and lengthy path, they held a steady pace, mindful of their grim surroundings, and taking care not to disturb what could be lurking in the darkness. There seemed to be a restlessness following them every step of the way. It was as if they instinctively knew something was out there, in the shadows, beyond the path's harsh and twisted route.

*"Stick to the main path!"*

Reece had heard Oran, just before they were consumed by darkness. *Why did he say that?* he wondered, then halted—the others following suit.

'Why are we stopping?' asked Daine, keeping his voice low—the growing, dismal atmosphere prompting him to do so.

Wareeshta came up the rear of Reece's horse. The two Dhampir exchanged a perceptive look, then turned their attention away from the path towards the mass of trees, on their right. Eyes wide and alert, they searched through the thicket, having sensed something skulking about deep within the unknown terrain. All around them, grey dominated, its dreariness depressing, weighing heavily on their mood. It was everywhere—and unavoidable.

Daine, feeling the dampness tighten his lungs, suddenly coughed.

'Shh!' Reece snapped back at him. But Daine could not suppress the effects of the dismal atmosphere; he could feel the cold air catch in his throat, before creeping into his chest. He caught his breath, making it worse, then exploded into a fit of coughing. Catching the obvious glare on Reece's face, he promptly removed a cloth from his coat pocket and wrapped it around his face, covering his nose and mouth. It seemed to help.

Staring out into the vastness, they could now make out the elongated shapes of the trees. It looked as though nature's *sentinels* had gathered closer, preventing their escape—should they be inclined to do so.

'Something is not right, here,' Reece stated, Oran's warning tormenting his mind. He looked back, surveying the path, its dark, relentless winding passage, making it difficult to gauge how long their journey would take. Also, there was a disturbing quietness about the place. There was no wildlife, he noticed; he would have heard it. The forest looked and felt *dead.* No. Nothing stirred or existed here, and yet … *something* did. Though cautioned by his instincts, Reece needed no warning to tell him something was afoot. It was obvious—not only to him but also to Wareeshta, her keen sense of hearing having heard Oran's warning, too.

'Is this not the same path the others took?' asked Rosalyn, also keeping her voice low, feeling the need to. 'I'm sure it—' She stopped when she saw her father's hand move to the hilt of his broadsword. She looked down, catching Wareeshta flexing her ankles; the Dhampir was checking the daggers inside her boots, giving her cause for alarm. She glanced at Daine, seeing him reach over his shoulder, his hand briefly resting on his sword. She swallowed, her concern mounting, knowing *she* was unarmed.

Reece leaned his head sideways to acknowledge his daughter but kept his eyes fixed on the trees. 'I am not sure …' he replied. 'The light disappeared the moment we crossed the path's threshold.' He frowned. 'It is possible—at that moment—they may have—'

'Look! There!' said Wareeshta, subconsciously placing a hand on Reece's shoulder—he flinched, feeling her gentle touch—swaying his gaze in the direction she was pointing, straight ahead.

'Where?' He narrowed his eyes then cast a side glance when she swiftly removed her hand.

'There it is—again. Can you—'

'I see it now,' he cut in, lifting himself in his saddle, to gain a better view.

'See what? Where?' asked Daine, his voice muffled, trying to stifle another coughing fit, while subconsciously touching his sword again.

In the distance, they saw a speckle of colour, blinking at them from the shadows—the unusual spectacle hovering, its vivid colour emphasised by the greyness.

'What do you suppose it could—' Rosalyn stopped when it moved, fluttering about like a giant moth. She blinked, straining her eyes when it faded into the murky shadows.

'I suggest we keep moving,' said Reece, sharing a look of unease with Wareeshta—the subtle nod in return, marking her agreement. But as they moved to continue their journey, the horses suddenly stalled. They shuffled nervously, chomping on the bits in their mouths, then stomped their hooves—the ground crunching loudly beneath them.

'On, Farrow!' Rosalyn coaxed the steed, tightening his reins again; the last thing she needed was to be thrown, risking injury. But Oran's horse, spooked by the cloak of darkness and intimidating trees, refused to go on, as did the other horses, their fear mounting as they fed off Farrow's agitation. ''Tis all right, Farrow,' she murmured, leaning into his ear while stroking him. Eyes drawn back, ears flicking, hearing her soothing voice, the steed calmed a little. Despite it, Farrow would not budge.

Frustrated by his mare's reluctance to move, Daine grunted and pressed his heels against Nahla. She refused to give in, her stubbornness matching that of any female. *Typical!* He clenched his teeth, wrapping the reins around his hands, to keep her in check. 'Why won't they—'

'Take control of her,' snapped Wareeshta. 'We need to keep moving,' she insisted, her sentiments matching Reece's. But as they began to make some headway—the horses fretting as they edged along the uneven path—the *thing* appeared again, now more clearly, its red, cone-like shape bobbing lazily and swaying from side to side.

'There's another one!' said Rosalyn, pointing directly into the woods. They were prominent now as though they had moved closer. Suddenly, another appeared, flittering about, like the others. Then they stopped. Motionless.

Still trying to control Farrow, Rosalyn edged closer to her father and Wareeshta, but the horse was increasingly agitated, its sixth sense at work, aware of a threat.

'I don't like this—one bit,' she said, gripping the reins.

Then more appeared, their numbers gradually increasing as if grouping—the red shapes congregating into a large cluster, lingering in the distance—the red standing out now, fresh and bright. Then …

'Are they getting closer?'

The group tightened their reins, feeling the horses' tension mount to a worrying level.

'They are,' Reece confirmed.

'And they are swarming in numbers,' added Wareeshta, pointing.

The horses were now stressed, whinnying and rearing, their eyes wide with fright, their whites bloodshot, sensing the oncoming danger.

'This is not good,' said Reece—the urgency in his tone warning them all. 'Do whatever it takes to move them. We need to go!'

The sudden sound of heavy stomping could now be heard, coming from all directions as the red shapes moved erratically, heading straight towards the group, darting in and out between the narrow gaps in the trees. And as they loomed, their small silhouettes emerged from the gloom.

Rosalyn gasped, unable to speak. She held her breath as they came into view; she knew precisely who—*No!*—*what* they were—from the descriptive tales Gill had teased Eleanor with, tales he had heard from Heckie Grant, their old neighbour. But this was no tale …

This was an unfolding nightmare.

She gasped again—the horror of what was about to unfold finally being unleashed through her fear.

'*Redcaps!*'

Reece, Wareeshta and Daine looked at her, momentarily bewildered. But there was no need to ask; they knew they were in trouble, by the look of cold terror on Rosalyn's face.

Recalling the grim tale of these gruesome, mythical creatures, Rosalyn could not understand how they had reached so far north. According to legend, they had been known to inhabit ruined castles, along the Anglo-Scottish border, where evil once reigned. But this "tale" of the Redcaps—this "legend"—was all too real, by the sight and sound of their deadly advance.

The stomping grew louder.

'Draw your weapons!' Reece called out. 'Rosalyn—stay with me.'

Rosalyn watched with horror as the Redcaps darted about, their movements swift and dizzying—despite the weight of their iron boots. *Weapons!* Tam's claymore flashed in her mind, but it was still attached to Farrow's saddle. And though its presence brought her some comfort, from the Highlander's loss, she knew she could not wield it; it was too heavy.

Overcome by fear, she failed to hear her father's voice and loosened her grip on Farrow. But before the steed could bolt Wareeshta grasped his reins, holding them tightly.

'You must control him!' she shouted, handing them back. Rosalyn jolted, then snatched the reins from her, gripping them until the whites of her knuckles showed, ignoring the pain of the hard leather digging into her palms.

The chilling sound of the creatures' blood-curdling attack brought with it a new terror as their numbers grew, surrounding the four riders. Reece recoiled, sickened by the mere stench of them, their foul breath clinging to him. They were everywhere. He assumed them to be both male and female, judging by their numbers, though it was hard to tell; their grubby rags covered their bodies, and they all looked alike—short, thickset, goblin-like creatures with colourless skin and grisly hair streaming down their bony shoulders. Right now, he did not care. The creatures bolted in and out, intimidating the trespassers as they circled them. This was the prelude to their gruesome attack.

The horses, now thrown into a frenzy of alarm, reared higher, trying to avoid the Redcap's weapons—the pikestaffs—their black, serrated metal tips, lethal.

There was no escaping them.

As long as they stayed mounted, Reece felt they had a chance; had they been on foot … Most likely the reason Oran insisted that they take the horses—in case of danger. But there was no time to think about that now.

The unexpected attack came out of the blue, from behind a nearby tree—one creature leaping forward, catching the group off-guard. Farrow reared high, his front legs thrashing out when the Redcap lunged at him, reaching for the latch of his throat, then grabbing his bridle. Finding her voice again, Rosalyn screamed and lashed out continuously with the heel of her boot until the creature let go. It fell back, momentarily dazed. Allowing it no time to think or recover, Wareeshta jumped from her horse and sliced its throat with one of her daggers.

Everything ceased.

The group looked around them, puzzled; the Redcaps had

vanished. Wasting no time, Wareeshta wiped her dagger on the creature's rags, then swiftly re-mounted. Inside, Rosalyn was shaking. *What now?* she thought, afraid to utter a word.

But, no sooner had Wareeshta settled back in her saddle, than the creatures returned in their droves—the stomping of their iron boots loud as thunder and their vibrations felt by the group.

'*Go!*' yelled Reece. On his command, the group forced their horses to bolt, trampling the dead Redcap, in the process.

'Look!' cried Daine, pointing ahead. 'There's a—'

When Daine was cut short, the others halted their horses and turned—the strangling sound of his voice alerting them to his plight. But the void between them was now swamped with Redcaps—the savage creatures scrambling over each other in their desperate bid to acquire the fresh blood of their fallen victim.

Rosalyn gasped, seeing the mob blocking their path. 'Oh, my—*Daine!*'

They were not done with the creatures yet.

Daine had fallen when Nahla reared and was now wrestling with one of the creatures on the ground as it held its weapon across his throat. He grasped the pikestaff, trying to push it away; the Redcap was stronger than it looked. But he could just about hold it back, keeping it inches from him. His eyes flashed round, unable to see his comrades through the gathering of iron-clad feet and crooked, scrawny legs. He then saw his sword from the corner of his eye; it was still in its sheath, where it had slipped from his hand when he fell—and inches from his reach … But his fight to survive prevented him from claiming it back.

The Redcap, its eyes blazing, leaned on the pikestaff. Daine could feel the creature's rancid breath on him, his hands shaking, holding the weapon as it was lowered, dangerously close, it now pressing against his throat. He struggled to breathe, feeling his strength wane as he tried to fight it off, desperate to avoid being either stabbed by the creature's talon-like nails, strangled or impaled by its pikestaff.

Frantic, he called on all his strength and, by some miracle, managed to push the Redcap away, it dropping its lethal weapon in the process and snatching the cloth from Daine's face as it fell. But as Daine struggled to his knees, the creature came back, and raising its claw-like hand, swept it across his victim's face, cutting his cheek. Daine winced, then felt the blood ooze from the wound—the sight of it driving the Redcap and its spectators into a frenzy. The hunger in their distorted faces was evident as they edged closer, ready to lunge forward, to soak up what might remain of the victim's blood. Daine gasped, realising what the Redcap was about to do.

Aware of its insatiate counterparts looking on, the Redcap quickly reached for its rustic-stained cap. But when it hesitated, running the back of its pinched hand across its mouth, Daine snatched his opportunity and grabbed the creature, holding it at arms-length, its cap dangling in its hand.

'No - You - Don't!' he yelled at it, grasping its scrawny arms, so tight the creature screeched in pain, letting its cap drop. Daine clenched his teeth, tightening his grip … until he heard it … *Snap!*

Consumed by excruciating pain, the Redcap recoiled, its high-pitched scream alerting the other creatures as it grasped its broken arm—the bone now protruding through its pallid skin. It glared at Daine, its vengeful stare warning its victim, he was still in mortal danger.

'Do it!' shouted Reece to Wareeshta, seeing her aim her dagger at the wounded creature. When two of its counterparts inched closer to it, the injured Redcap screeched back at them, baring its sharp teeth, saliva dripping from its twisted mouth, warning them off its kill, despite the pain inflicted on it.

'What if I—'

'You will not miss. Trust me. Now do it!'

Instantly, the dagger left Wareeshta's hand—the precision of her aim skimming by Daine's ear before finding its way into the Redcap's jugular. The creature drew up, stunned—the stiletto dagger lodged deep. It reached up, grasping the hilt, but could not remove it. It then clutched its throat, trying to stop the blood. Suddenly it froze, its eyes spasming before dropping dead against Daine—the two slumping to the ground, again.

'No, Wareeshta!' cried Rosalyn, seeing the Dhampir leap from her horse, to help Daine. Instantly, a creature was upon her, its comrades eagerly watching and waiting their turn. Lythe and swift though, she spun, removing the second dagger, and drew it across its throat. Dead. She turned to Daine, who had found his feet again, having shoved the dead Redcap away, and nodded to him, seeing his sword safely gripped in his hand. He returned his thanks with a single nod. With no time for words, Wareeshta retrieved her stiletto dagger from the other Redcap's throat, its blood spurting from the gaping wound. But their victory was brief; she and Daine were still grounded and at risk from the creatures.

A hollow silence followed when the Redcaps momentarily stalled and stared at their dead. However, within seconds they were whipping their caps from their heads, scrambling over one another, pushing and shoving in a desperate frenzy, competing to survive. Snorting and licking their lips loudly, they salivated over the two bodies as they drenched their caps in fresh blood. Sickened by the sight of it, Rosalyn's stomach lurched and she raised her hand to her mouth, trying not to heave.

'Quick!' shouted Reece, acknowledging their horses. The creature's distraction had bought them time albeit short. Wareeshta had already mounted, however, Daine, exhausted, struggled, feeling the onslaught of another imminent attack. He turned to raise his sword, but as he did so, Farrow reared high, throwing Rosalyn to the ground. Spurred by pure fear, the steed bolted back the way they had come.

'Farrow!' Rosalyn was beside herself when the steed disappeared from view.

Hearing her cry, the Redcaps turned their attention back to their potential prey. Determined to dip their caps again, some charged towards Daine and Rosalyn, while others leapt at Wareeshta and Reece, forcing the Dhampir to battle with their attackers. It was no use; there were too many.

'Forgive me!' cried Rosalyn as Daine pulled her behind him, between himself and his horse, to protect her.

'There's nothing to forgive,' he returned, removing his sword from its sheath before lifting it high, with both hands. They would fight to the end.

The Redcaps stopped dead.

The creatures' eyes widened when they saw the Albrecht gleam back at them, its steel radiant even in the bleakness. They recoiled, their deafening screeches of hysteria echoing, fearful of the weapon; they knew what it was—and what it stood for. Slaves to the Elliyan, they had been abducted from the borders and put in this place of desolation, to protect the passage, and prevent unworthy souls from reaching Elboru. Beneath their feet lay the littered remains of victims—innocent souls who had trespassed and then tried to flee from their campaign of terror. Rivers of blood had flowed from their killing sprees over the centuries yet they were unable, by the Elliyan's ruling, to attack a Warlock.

The Redcaps recognised Daine's ancient sword, its overpowering influence warning them to retreat. It had been made clear to them what would happen, should they harm a Warlock: they would be cursed—the curse forcing them to turn and kill one another until none were left alive. *That,* however, was something they needed to do, occasionally: select one of their own—the weakest—if they were to survive.

'Keep your sword high,' said Wareeshta, aware of its impact. Promptly she dismounted, to help them. Wary, and aided by the Dhampir, Rosalyn mounted her father's horse, holding on to him with all her might, while, beneath her breath, cursing Farrow for deserting her.

'Carefully,' Wareeshta urged Daine, their eyes fixed hard on the creatures. They could still see the desperation on their ragged features, wanting to attack, with the smell of Daine's blood taunting their senses. But the Redcaps feared the curse hovering over them—should they attack—the Warlock's sword marking that ongoing threat.

But desperation had spurred a few of the creatures, whose caps had turned brown, into attack—the decay of blood slowly squeezing the life out of them. Doomed to die, it made no difference to them; they would risk attacking their victims, regardless of the sword's presence and influence.

They would die trying to live.

Three desperate creatures, their caps rustic brown, lunged forward. But no sooner had they rushed the group, than they were promptly destroyed by Reece and Wareeshta, who had marked them with their weapons, driving them through as the Redcaps leapt at them.

When the three creatures slumped to the ground, dead, the other Redcaps did not hesitate, their need to stay alive driving them to survive on the blood of their fallen. That was how it was in their gruesome world; as one died, the others drew on its blood, dipping their caps.

Without hesitation—and while under the protection of Daine's precious sword—the group, now re-mounted, bolted, striking any creature blocking their way, leaving behind a trail of dying Redcaps to rot—along with the bones of their past victims.

# Chapter Thirty-One

Eleanor stared at Turloch, her eyes piercing his frozen look as he glared down at her. He had underestimated her abilities. And yet, he should have known—should have seen it coming.

The two stood within inches of one another, eyes locked. She could feel the slow beat of his heart vibrate through the steel and on through the palm of her hand, its measure weakening by the second. Revelling in the growing look of defeat on his hardened features, she leaned in, slow and steady. He clenched his teeth and balled his fists, shuddering as the blade was driven deeper, unaware he had dropped his push knife and sword.

Eleanor stretched up on her toes, and as she watched Turloch's pale blue eyes fade to grey as the dagger slowly drained the life from him, she drew closer to him, feeling his cold breath on hers, it shortening with each laboured effort.

'*An eye for an eye!*' she hissed through gritted teeth, then twisted the blade; he stiffened, feeling its steel rotate inside him.

She then stepped away from him, letting go of the dirk. But the moment her hand left the hilt, she jerked, as though woken from a fevered dream. She looked down, her mouth gaping, with no recollection of what she had done. She took another step back, staring at her empty hand, dumbfounded. Her eyes then travelled up to the dirk in Turloch's chest, wedged deep into his heart—the Dhampir now peering down at it in disbelief.

Turloch flinched when survival instinct kicked in, telling him to act. Time was against him—the passing seconds measuring how long he had left. His heart was failing, fast. He grasped the hilt; if he failed to remove it, it would reduce his chance of recovery. He could not—would not—allow a newborn to kill him, especially a female. He looked sharp, his paling eyes filled with intent.

Seeing the look of revenge in Turloch's eyes, Eleanor, on survival instinct, leapt forward.

'Keep your grubby hands off it!' she growled, pushing him away. He stumbled, his face etched with surprise, taken aback by her strength. Again, he reached for the dirk's handle. In an instant, she was upon him, scrambling to reclaim what was hers.

'No, Eleanor!' a voice called out. 'Do not!'

Weapons still in hand, Asai spun. He was alone. He then stalled, risking the precious transient of time, to look and listen. Caught up in the height of their duel, the path—unbeknown to them—had taken on an ominous appearance, shrouding them within a dank, sinister atmosphere, when it slowly crept up on them. They had briefly stopped when the grey mist began to thicken, its stinging sensation temporarily hindering their vision. Wary of its sudden arrival, Asai had subconsciously glanced away from his opponent. But it had been a moment lost; when he looked back to his challenger, he had caught a glimpse of Turloch's long, white hair vanishing into the mist, like a spectre—the echo of his low-grunted, guttural laugh dominating until it was lost.

A sense of dread consumed Asai at the thought of Eleanor and Turloch locked together in battle. *He will destroy her!*

Fearing for her safety, he made to pursue his enemy, but when the mist thickened, its damp cloud swirling about, disorienting him, he stopped, to find his bearings again.

Nothing but a dense silence screamed back at him.

His eyes shot down; he could not see the path, let alone his feet.

He looked sharp, his keen eyes searching.

Still nothing.

He froze when something struck; he could no longer *feel* Eleanor. Without that, without her inside him, he felt utterly lost—the unexpected feeling of desolation heightening his concern. It was an emotion he had not experienced since …

*"Ayumi!"*

His dead wife's name came to him in his moment of isolation. Though alone, he felt comforted, hearing it again in his thoughts. Then something soft brushed by his ear. He subconsciously waved it away with his dagger, almost killing it. Still, it came back; with each return, he tried to flick it away. But when he felt the slight tingle of its feathery touch, caressing his ear, he turned, convinced *it* had whispered something.

Asai drew back when he saw the butterfly, its silver wings, with their strands of gold glinting as they fluttered silently against the bleak background. He raised his brows as it continued to hover in front of him—the rhythm and beauty of its delicate wings captivating. He tilted his head, eyes fixed when its ethereal green aura appeared, wrapping him with her everlasting love and devotion.

'Ayumi!' he whispered—the spellbinding moment then severed, by the voice of another, in his head.

*"Wait for me, Asai!"*

He jolted when a coldness stabbed him in the heart, its impact directing his gaze back to the mist.

He froze.

'No, Eleanor! She must think me—' He stopped, his attention returned to the butterfly; it was now fluttering wildly around him, demanding his attention again. Steered by something deeper than instinct, Asai began to follow it when it suddenly took flight. It was guiding him back to her.

He ran.

It was too late.

Eleanor had removed her family heirloom from Turloch's heart. And as she drew back, she could already sense it resume its sinister beat before gradually steadying.

Having sensed it too, Asai rushed forward and pulled her back; if Turloch was not destroyed before he recovered ...

'What are you doing?' she hissed, her face contorted in anger as she cast away his grip. Asai turned and scowled at her, his look changing when her expression altered, her eyes widening, her mouth gaping as she pointed. He spun.

Turloch was already on his feet, grimacing as he wrenched the dirk from his chest—the blood on the steel changing to black as soon as it came into contact with the air. He threw it aside, retrieving his sword—the swiftness of it alerting Asai.

Head now lowered, brandishing his weapon, Turloch grinned at his opponent, confident of a victory.

'Let us finish this!' he said, then lunged at the Samurai.

Momentarily caught unawares, Asai stumbled, barely missing Turloch's blade, his attack sharp and defined. Turloch was getting stronger—and he knew it. Turloch stopped dead, reaching back and across with his sword, almost decapitating the Samurai. But Asai, having pre-empted the move, ducked, dropped to the ground and rolled away. Within seconds, the Samurai was back on his feet, still wielding the katana and wakizashi. But trapped in the narrow passage, Asai knew he had to be on his guard—should the mist fall upon them again.

Stirred by his new strength, Turloch could not help himself.

'Look at me now, *Strange One!*' he boasted, arms stretched wide, goading Asai into taking him on. 'Think you can outdo me? Ha! I think—'

Turloch's body stiffened—the strain on his face exposing the thick veins in his throat as they pulsated. His body twitched, then shuddered as his nervous system went into shock. His fingers and toes first tingled, then gradually became numb as paralysis took over, making him lose all control of his faculties, his ability to move, with all forms of physicality now gone. His bulging eyes moved down when he heard the heavy thud of steel hit the ground; he had dropped his sword—the numbness in his hands stealing his last remnants of power. No longer able to feel a thing, he dropped to his knees, his body jerking forward when Eleanor thrust the dirk further into his back, then across, severing the spinal cord, completely.

Asai looked on, unsure of Eleanor as she stood over Turloch, her chest heaving, glaring down at him. Then, grasping the hilt of her dagger, she placed her foot on the Dhampir's back, and kicked him away, withdrawing the dirk as he fell, face down, to the hard ground. His body jerked. Asai wanted to go to her, stop her, but he knew it was only a matter of time before she would have made her first kill; and Turloch had been her first within the privacy of where they stood, and not in front of her family. He was, at least, grateful for that.

She raised her hand, brandishing the dirk—the intense look of determination on her youthful face, warning Asai what she was about. But the dirk would not decapitate Turloch, he knew; it was not big enough. And if she did not finish him off … No, he would have to do it for her.

Asai did a double-take when Turloch's head unexpectedly rolled away from its body, clean and swift. He stared at Eleanor, taken aback by her actions; until that pivotal moment, she had been detached, oblivious. But now she appeared attentive, on guard, as if her actions had woken her to her reality, making her discover her new state, her new skills—and her new life. And as she stood over Turloch's corpse, nodding to herself, he was still unsure whether she was fully conscious of what she had just done.

And yet …

She had given no thought to the slaughter. Her new animal

instincts had … *instructed* her to do it; when an image of Reece, performing the same act, had stirred in her memory she acted on it, its influence having spurred her to do the same. Her eyes shifted to Asai, seeing the look of disbelief on his face as he rose to approach her.

'He talked too much,' she stated. She slid her eyes to where Turloch's push knife remained on the ground, unused; his arrogance had made him believe he did not need it. *Not so clever,* she thought as her eyes returned to her victim. 'And … he was evil,' she added, justifying her actions for Turloch's "execution". She flinched when something touched her hand. Though delicate, Asai's touch made her feel as if she'd been torn from her deed.

'He is no more, Eleanor,' he said, seeing the dirk still grasped in her tiny hand. It was hard to believe that someone like her—someone who would never have contemplated harming a living creature—could be capable of performing such an act. But she did—and, yes, it had been justified. 'Eleanor?'

Still, she could not take her eyes from Turloch's headless corpse. She glanced down at her dirk, its blade stained with his rancid blood. She cast it aside with disgust, then stepped back, shaking her head—the realisation of what she had done, hitting her now, awakening her to the gruesomeness of the act itself. Once again, her eyes slid to Turloch's remains, tapering as she peered at him; she did not know how to react.

'It is all right, my love,' said Asai, trying to soothe the mixed emotions running wildly through her mind and body; he could sense her inner turmoil.

Promptly, the Samurai picked up the dirk and stood before her, blocking the horrific scene from her innocent eyes. *Innocent?* She was no longer that. 'Listen to me,' he went on. Her eyes shot up, captivated by the smoothness of his voice, and when he cupped his hand over her soft cheek, smiling, she leaned into his gentle touch, her eyes still resting on his, reconnecting with him.

She then lifted her head, her intense look silently questioning, seeking answers.

'It *will* take time,' he told her. 'You have been through an immense change. But soon, you will *see* yourself, for—' He stopped himself, then smiled. 'For *whom* you have become—my enigmatic and beautiful Eleanor.'

'But—'

'Shh!' He removed his hand and gently placed his finger on her lips, silencing her. When her eyes widened, unsure of him, he took her into his embrace, smoothing her hair—the softness of it like silk.

*Hold me*, he silently pleaded, urging her with his thoughts; he needed her to react. *Find yourself.*

And she did.

Slowly, Eleanor lifted her arms, now willing to return the emotion and the feeling of his embrace. The seconds passed as they held one another, relishing each other's touch. Then it came—the rush of adrenalin—surging through her new body, prompting her to hold on to him tightly and never let him go.

Asai grunted. 'You must loosen your hold, my love.'

She pulled away, glaring at him, offended. 'You do not want me?' she asked, her brow furrowing, head tilting as her eyes held his.

A smile spread across the Samurai's face, lighting up his deep, almond-shaped eyes.

'Oh, I am sorry,' she realised, seeing him massage his arm.

He nodded, satisfied. It was a good start.

'In time, you shall control your strength—and emotions.' He moved towards her again, his stature overwhelming her as he looked down into her craving eyes. 'As for not wanting you …?' The edge of his mouth curled. 'We have a lifetime of that ahead of us. But, for now …' Her face dropped, disappointed. He raised a brow, side-glancing Turloch's body. He returned to it, eyeing the severed head; Turloch's lifeless eyes were staring into the void of everlasting death, and yet there was a peacefulness about his features, erasing the animalistic look he had worn while under L'Ordana's bond. Reminded that he was once mortal, it prompted Asai to close Turloch's eyes, in perpetual sleep. *Be at peace, Turloch*, he privately told the Dhampir.

His eyes moved to Eleanor's dirk; the dagger was still lying in the dirt beside Turloch's body, where she had flung it. Retrieving the weapon, Asai wiped the dead Dhampir's blood on his clothing, then rose, handing it—now cleansed of death—back to Eleanor, where it rightfully belonged.

'I will say it was I, who killed Turloch—if they should ask,' he stated. 'We cannot have your parents thinking you are a cold-blooded murderer.'

She gasped, stunned by his casual reference to her actions, then relaxed when he winked at her.

'One step at a time?'

She nodded, now understanding.

'Now'—he turned to find their bearings, looking from left to right, along the dark, winding passage—'we must go,' he said, pointing in the opposite direction they had come, hoping—assuming—it would take them to Elboru. And as they moved to leave, he caught a fluttering movement from the corner of his eye. When he turned to look for it, *she* was gone.

# Chapter Thirty-Two

Oran ran towards Farrow, then halted, hands raised high in a bid to stop his horse; it was evident—when the steed unexpectedly appeared from the passage—it was frightened as it galloped towards him, almost stampeding its master.

'*Whoa! Whoa!*' cried Oran, reaching for the reins. But the horse, still spooked, reared, snorting and rattling. 'Be still, my beauty,' he persisted, finally snatching the reins, gripping them tightly as he pulled them down towards him, trying to calm the steed.

Hearing his master's voice of encouragement, Farrow gradually came to a standstill. But Oran could still sense the steed's fear; it was trembling, on edge. Easing his grip, the Warlock cautiously moved around to face Farrow, to look him in the eye. Slowly, he raised his hand and ran it gently down along the horse's forehead, lulling him with soothing words.

'There, there. You are safe. Be still, my Farrow.'

Finally, the steed connected with its master as their eyes locked, bonding them again.

''Tis all right,' Oran whispered, reassuring him. The horse snorted then whinnied in response though was still trembling, beneath his master's familiar touch. His brow furrowed, Oran looked over towards the passage, his dread heightening, realising Farrow was alone; there was no sign of Rosalyn and the others. He waited, listening. Nothing. The hairs suddenly rose on the back of his neck when a chill ran down his spine, fearing something may have happened to them. He shook the notion away. *No.* He was sure they were all right. They had to be. He would know it if— He stared into the passage, its gloom peering back at him, thick and foreboding. *But—what if …?* Panicked, he rushed towards the chosen pylon and reached out. But it was useless when another attempt to pass through it failed—the ominous energy hovering above it still preventing him from going further. He looked at the other two monoliths; their surfaces were also shrouded in swirling clouds of dust, concealing their plaquettes. To search for Rosalyn and the others was out of the question. His thoughts ran riot, taunting his imagination, thinking all sorts.

He spun and looked towards the entrance to the gorge—between the escarpments—then turned and looked up into the trees where the *sentinels* dominated, quiet and still. The ghostly Pict army came to mind. But they would be of no help to him. No, their duty was to protect the Paths of Lome from trespassers—those who had no right to be there—or from innocent souls who had the misfortune of losing their way. Regardless, the stranger would be challenged—*forced*—to choose a path … or die. Either way, the odds were always stacked against them. But he was no stranger here, therefore, the Picts would not come. He then knew he had no choice, but to go to the portal he had hoped to never return to.

'Three leagues.' He nodded to himself, gauging the distance. It was not far, seeing as they would be approaching it from the opposite side, on this occasion. 'Aye, 'tis the only way,' he decided.

He was then roused by the remaining horses, stomping their hooves; they were still tied, and restless. He eyed Nepthys and marched towards her, his mind now on the item attached to her saddle. Quickly, he removed it. Its contents seemed heavier as though it had been mustering all the evil it could, in preparation for the coming of something universal—and sinister. He wondered if the book was aware of its counterpart—the dagger. *Perhaps it is*, he thought, and if so … Both items could not be reunited … *No matter what!* His only solace was knowing the dagger was kept in a safe place. Lothian had seen to that.

He could feel the burden of the book's odious presence, through the leather—the one earthly thing separating him from it. Though reluctant to touch the cursed item—let alone use it—he knew he would have to do so, sooner or later, if he were to rid Kristene of the spirit inside her.

'First things first,' he muttered, untying the horses; one instantly bolted on its release, leaving Nepthys and a large steed behind. He wondered who owned it, then realised when he noticed a torn piece of faded red plaid, knotted to its saddle. 'You belonged to Tam,' he stated, having recognised the Brodie Clan tartan; it had been tied there by the Highlander, to claim the horse as his own. Oran sighed then urged it to go; 'North! And I hope you find them.' With that, the steed took off.

Oran turned his attention to Nepthys. As a Warlock's horse, it was the Elliyan's ruling that no other could claim another's as his own. But Greer's mare had been influenced by the Servitor. When Kai came to "borrow" Nepthys for Oran, to aid his escape, she had shown no objection; the Servitor's aura had had a calming effect on her. Oran snorted, imagining the rage on Greer's face when his fellow High Warlock discovered his precious mare was missing.

'You too, Nepthys!' he told her. 'Go wherever the wind takes you—to freedom—or back to Greer.' The horse snorted, then stomped the ground. 'I do not blame you,' he said. To the naïve eye, Greer had possessed the mare like a precious jewel, taking pride in her, lavishing her with treats and endearments. But Oran knew there had been an underlying menace beneath Greer's false, display of affection towards the mare; he had occasionally witnessed his abrupt and unexpected mistreatment of Nepthys when she failed to do her master's bidding. Oran promptly removed the bridle, allowing the mare to enjoy her new freedom. And as he removed her saddle, his face hardened, seeing the deep-seared mark on her flank, there for her master's eyes only. The hidden black scar—an elaborate "g" with the tail wrapped around itself, like a noose—signified Greer's ownership of the mare. For Greer to have done that to his horse would, according to the Elliyan, be regarded with condemnation—and defacement of one's prized possessions. It was against their ruling to mistreat or "label" an animal, especially a Warlock's horse.

He shook his head with disgust.

'How you must have suffered,' he whispered to her, 'when he applied the red-hot branding iron, marking you, forever.' Oran met with the mare's eyes. 'But now you are free!' Nepthys moved away from him, then stalled. 'Go!' he insisted. The horse dipped her head to him, neighed, then bolted back through the clearing's entry passage, in the same direction as Tam's horse—the echo of her departure briefly trapped between the escarpment's walls before fading into oblivion.

Satisfied they would find their way, Oran returned to Farrow, then paused before mounting him, now seeing the hilt of the Highlander's claymore, where Rosalyn had attached the sword to the saddle. He touched it for a moment and nodded.

'Aye, you will be returned,' he promised, patting the hilt. 'But you will have to wait, my friend,' he added, mounting Farrow. 'I have more pressing matters to attend to.'

Roused by his master's encouragement, Farrow galloped on, taking them away from the Paths of Lome, avoiding oncoming trees and prickly shrubs—the steed's agility marking his knowledge of the forest's domain. There was no need for the Warlock to guide Farrow; he knew the way.

Oran's next hurdle was to avoid the Bullwark; the mercenaries would be swarming the grounds of Elboru by now, protecting it from the expected threat hanging in the air, its thick blanket of doom edging closer and spreading.

The desperate need to know what happened to Rosalyn and the others plagued his thoughts. As for Gill and Kai? He was confident his son and the Servitor had reached Elboru by now. He cast aside any niggling doubts. However, there was still no sign of L'Ordana and Magia Nera. But they were near, he knew. He could *feel* it and, what was more, had sensed a worrying shift in the atmosphere when the Egress appeared; his amulet had vibrated against his chest, warning him. The dark Warlock might have already found his way.

As they approached their destination, Oran could hear the distant roar of the waterfall and smell the dampness, coming from the little river. It gave him a sense of *déjà vu*. Had it really been three years since he had last trodden its path? Seeing it again, however, made it feel like it had only been days, since.

The familiar outline of the small, stone bridge came into view. Though barely visible now, it made his heart race with anticipation. He looked up and, for a moment, could not see the arched entrance to the little cave—the laws of nature having concealed it over those three years since the Elliyan summoned him. But, with the Elliyan now preoccupied with the arrival of the new Magus—and aware of the threat hovering over Elboru—they had probably disregarded the portal. He could almost hear Tuan's smug voice, saying to the other Warlocks;

"Lord Oran would not dare use it again."

Still, he could not presume. It was a bold risk—and one he had to take.

Despite nature's control over its domain, Oran was still conscious of the cave's existence and pleased that *Mother Nature* had hidden it from prying eyes.

He dismounted Farrow. Before heading to the bridge, he removed the leather satchel and threw it over his shoulder. Again, he locked eyes with his precious horse.

'You know where you are, my friend,' he said. 'Rather than risk losing you in battle, I order you to return home.' The horse flinched, acquainted with the word—*home!*—having heard it often enough. 'Home?' Farrow stomped the ground in response. Oran smiled. 'My clever boy! Now, off you go!'

Leaving the steed to find its way back to Balloch again, Oran turned to face the portal, his mind occupied by thoughts and deeds as he stepped over the stony link between the two worlds he was connected to.

Not yet halfway across, he could already feel the slight pull of gravity towards the concealed entrance and hear the faint hum. A few short steps and he would be back, inside the castle. If there was no one about, he could slip into the hidden passageways, between the walls. His first port of call would be Lothian's chamber. But first, he would have to wade through the overgrowth that had taken over the cave's entrance, since he had last stepped through it.

He gripped the overgrowth to prize it away, then stalled; something was amiss: the thick foliage was loose and came away without effort. Years of growth should have bound the ivy to the moss-ridden stone, making it tough to root out. He had done it often enough, in Balloch; removing the woody evergreen from their outhouse was tedious, frustrating and hard-going.

Oran drew back and tilted his head, musing over it. Again, he took hold of the overgrowth and removed it, completely, disturbing its tiny inhabitants, who scuttered away to escape the intruder.

Letting go of the foliage, he could now feel the pull of the portal's energy, and yet it was not as strong as before, where its power had snatched him without warning; now, there was little resistance. Something was wrong. When a feeling of dread returned, creeping back into his thoughts, he stared at the opening, his instincts forewarning him. 'Aye, something *is* wrong,' he muttered. He looked down, then kicked the thick ivy away from his feet. He drew back when he saw the fresh indentations of footprints embedded in the damp ground. They were not his. He looked closer, narrowing his curious eyes as something else revealed itself, in the dim morning light: *two* sets of footprints—one smaller than the other. It appeared his nemesis had a head start on him—and he was not alone.

A sudden rush of fear provoked him to take immediate action.

'I hope I'm not too late.' He stepped forward.

# Chapter Thirty-Three

Gill lifted his hand to his crown; his head was pounding. He then felt a wave of tiredness crash down on him, thinking it must have had something to do with the *Egress* when he entered it, in its final moments. As he was catapulted through the portal itself, he had felt as if his whole body had been stretched, to the point where it would be torn apart and his limbs cast into obscurity. But as his eyes adjusted to his new environment, the wrenching effect began to wane, giving him some relief in the knowledge that his body was still intact.

He looked around, eyes blinking through the dim light as his surroundings came into focus, to discover he was inside an unusual chamber, hemmed in by six, angled walls—each coated in sunken reliefs, skilfully created by the hands of times past. He narrowed his eyes as he approached one of the walls and reached out. Carefully, he ran his fingers over the ancient symbols, sensing the craftsmen's labour as though they were still there, toiling and grafting. And as he traced each relief, they seemed to open up, allowing him to explore their complex world; they tried to speak to him, tell him of their past—and his potential future. And yet, he could not make sense of them, his head still muddled by the "crossover". But as his mind began to clear, and his eyes beheld the words as they gradually whispered to him, a sense of peace rested on Gill in his seclusion, offering him a restfulness—something he welcomed at this moment, though unaware of how short-lived it would be.

'Beyond one of these walls—you so greatly admire—the Sanctuary of Armistice awaits you.'

Gill spun, hearing Kai's voice behind him. He sighed with relief when the Servitor stepped out from a shadowy corner and into his company, his presence adding to the serenity of the moment.

'Where are we, Kai?'

'We are in the anti-chamber.'

Gill drew his head back, his brows furrowing. 'But … why are we *here?* The Egress should have taken us to the Sanctuary—according to Oran.'

Kai knew Gill was right; they should be there, where the Elliyan and the Ushabti would be waiting. Something had gone wrong.

'I can only speculate … our chosen moment to enter the Egress must have determined the time and place of our arrival,' said Kai, musing over their situation. 'However, I am inclined to believe the Valkyrie's entrance may have influenced the portal,' he added. 'Perhaps, her sinister presence upset the balance, threw it off course … so to speak. It is a wonder I ended up *here*, with you, considering …'

Gill shot a glance at the Servitor, hearing him mention Kara. 'This is bad, Kai,' he muttered, shaking his head, his desperate eyes then scouring from one wall to the next. 'There appears to be no way out!' Gill hesitated when it occurred to him: Kara had vanished mere seconds before he leapt. 'The Valkyrie!' He turned and stared at Kai. 'Then … what has become of *her?* She must be here, *somewhere!*'

'It is unlikely,' said Kai.

'But—what if …? Could she perhaps have …?'

'While she may have *entered* the Egress, Gill, she would not have survived. The portal knows its own, and would have rejected her, for her evil presence, alone.'

The mere notion of the Valkyrie's demise struck a chord of victory with Gill; he would have given anything to be the one to "dispatch" her—for her murderous deeds. Still … 'One less problem to contend with, then,' he stated—the knowledge of Kara's demise giving him some confidence, despite their predicament.

Kai nodded.

Putting aside all thoughts of the Valkyrie—he hoped her death had been a horrific one—Gill returned his thoughts to the chamber, now more conscious of the walls staring back at him, vying for his attention; they seemed to know who he was as they encroached on his presence of mind. He blinked, suddenly feeling light-headed again as the walls began to spin. As dizziness took hold, he reached out to break his fall, his hands quickly finding the solidness of the chamber's walls.

'Gillis?'

Gill took a few moments to collect himself. 'I—I am well,' he stammered. 'It … seems the journey through the Egress … has taken its toll.' He sighed, rubbing a hand across his forehead, trying to wipe away the weariness of his mind and body. ''Tis nothing. And, besides, I have not eaten for a while. That's all! Nothing to worry about. It will pass, I'm sure.'

Concerned for his welfare, the Servitor changed to his human form and, reaching out, took hold of Gill, steadying him, fearing he would stumble again.

'Thank you, my friend, but I—' Gill stopped when Kai suddenly drew back, staring at him—the Servitor's solemn expression concerning him. 'What is it?'

An added burden of worry gripped Kai as he studied the look of exhaustion on the young man's face: Gill looked pale and drawn—the heavy black rims beneath his tiring eyes telling him, all was not as it seemed; also, the flecks of gold that had glinted each time Gill blinked, no longer did so.

'You should not feel … or *look* like this,' he stated, maintaining his hold.

'I am all right,' he said, dismissing it, feeling his strength gradually return. Gill rose to his full height and forced a smile. 'It seems to be passing,' he added, finding his ground, once more. 'Thank you, but there is no need for you—' He stopped short, noting a doubt in Kai's dark, hazel eyes. 'I know you, Kai—and I see it … *there!*' He pointed to Kai's eyes, nodding. 'You are keeping something from me.'

Kai continued to study him in silence.

Troubled by the Servitor's scrutiny of him, Gill drew closer to his friend. 'Kai?'

Still, Kai remained quiet, his eyes distant, thinking.

Frustrated by his lack of response, Gill gripped the Servitor by the shoulders and shook him hard, commanding his attention. Kai flinched. 'Tell me!' Gill demanded, through gritted teeth. 'For it is not "concern" I see in your eyes, now—but *fear!*' Kai knew he would have to tell Gill the truth.

'Before you entered the *Egress*,' he began, 'were you aware of this feeling of … *weakness?*'

Gill recoiled, releasing his grip, perplexed by the enquiry; it was *how* it had been put to him. He could see the perturbed look on Kai's face, it prominent while in his human form. Gill shook his head. It had been quite the opposite; before entering the Egress, he had noticed a sudden intensity in his body, an undefined power urging him on, giving him the courage to pass through the portal. But it had only been brief—the moment disappearing as quickly as it had arrived. He had thought nothing of it, at the time.

'Please, Kai!' he begged—the unsettling feeling gnawing at him. '*Is* there something I should know?'

Kai diverted his eyes, his human form now betraying him, by his reluctance to speak; nevertheless, he was bound to do so.

'I made a vow to your father—one I participated in. I swore never to divulge—'

'What vow?' Gill broke in, his aggravation evident as he glared at Kai, waiting impatiently for his explanation.

'We have found ourselves in a perilous situation, and … it is for this reason I can no longer keep it from you …'

Gill braced himself—the erratic rise and fall of his chest, displaying his anxiousness—and more—to the Servitor.

'I did not anticipate our present scenario,' Kai started. 'As things stand, we have no choice but to act quickly. We cannot—and you must listen to my every word, Gill—we *cannot* let another soul, whose interests also lie with the Shenn amulet, enter the Sanctuary, to claim it as their own. It is with regret that I tell you …' Kai paused, searching for the right words, and yet he knew there was no right or wrong way to tell the future Magus—except through his vow of honesty. 'If you do not claim what is rightfully yours …' He sighed. 'Then you will *die!*'

Gill, his face frozen with shock, stepped away from Kai as though the Servitor was about to complete the deed himself.

*"You will die!"*

Thrown by what he had just been told, Gill remained speechless, his mouth gaping, wanting, trying to release the words ... but nothing came.

*"You will die!"*

The words had fallen from Kai's tongue with great remorse. Gill's head pounded as the chimes of doom rang; he wished they would stop, then feared they would, marking his end. When one's life is at risk, it tends to flash before them as a reminder of what is at stake. Then, out of the blue, he saw the face of Meghan Downy—the girl he had promised to elope with, to Eddin—and wondered what she was doing at this moment in time; was she pining for him, or moving on with her life, while he was doing all he could to save her world, and the one he was about to enter—a world he had been fated to, since his conception? Had it only been a few days since they last spoke, touched and …? Already, it felt like a lifetime ago. But she would no longer be part of his world. *Should I live to see it*, he thought. It then struck him—the true gravity of what was at stake if he did not survive; nor would Meghan—or anyone else, for that matter—live to see it if—

*"You will die!"*

He reeled as the words sank in, making him recognise the truth behind Kai's grave statement.

'Your father—*we*—were simply trying to protect you, Gill. It never occurred to us that history might repeat itself—that *this* could happen, and force us to tell you. We could never have envisaged—'

'You mean—this has happened to others? In the past?'

Kai lowered his head, then nodded.

'And you never thought to mention it?'

'The Elliyan were sure they had mastered the Shenn's progress and the bond it shared with its previous Overlords. They were certain the mistakes of the past had been amended.'

'*Mistakes?*'

'Initially, little was known about the Shenn and its influence on its true bearer. Those who abused it saw a short reign.' Gill's eyes widened. 'However,' Kai promptly responded, noting Gill's look of dread, 'those who respected it lived a great and noble life—as will you.'

'How can you be sure, Kai? *Am* I truly—' Gill suddenly swayed, his head spinning again with weakness.

'Gill!' But as Kai reached out to him again, he hesitated when Gill abruptly turned his back on him.

'I am all right!' he snapped, feeling his strength return. Inside, he felt let down and deceived. He refused to give in to the Servitor's revelation. *But what am I to do?* He could not let his doubts control his mind; after all, his life was in jeopardy, and, as much as he wanted more answers, this was not the time nor the place. But there was *one* thing he had to know. *Time to face your fears, Gillis Shaw!* 'How long, Kai?'

Silence.

Gill spun, his face now contorted and red with anger. 'How long do I have?!'

'Until the last light of the waning moon—before it fades to a new moon.'

Gill's look of rage altered to utter dread—the shock of what he had learned now taking grip. The first light of dawn had already surfaced when they entered the Egress. However, the light of the moon still prevailed. But soon it would fade—and he with it. *I must survive!* With no time to wallow in his fate, he looked sharp at Kai.

'So—how do we get out of here?'

'Behind one of these walls is the Sanctuary, where the Elliyan and the Ushabti wait for you. But …'

'Well?'

'… there is only one doorway leading into it.'

Gill turned, eyes darting as he surveyed each of the six angled walls; they were identical.

'But …'

Gill sighed and rolled his eyes.

'… it is *you* who must find it, Gill.'

Again, he turned to the Servitor and, staring at him with pleading eyes, swallowed. 'And … if I …' No, there was no point in asking; he already knew.

'Time *will* be lost to us,' Kai assured him, 'and the Ushabti will return from whence he came, leaving the inner—and most sacred—portal wide open.'

'Making it free for all,' Gill stated.

Kai slowly nodded.

'… and *Lumeri* will no longer exist.'

'Lum—' Gill stopped short, on an instinct. He spun and let his eyes glide over the reliefs again, searching … then stalled … His mouth gaped when he saw *it*—the name he was destined to wear: *'Lumeri!'* He let his eyes travel over each wall, smiling as he shook his head in disbelief; the name was written *everywhere!* echoing in his mind like a scream! He had read it yet never *knew* it … until now. He reached up, letting his fingers trace its outline, woken to the connection.

'That is to be—'

'The name I will take,' he stated, interrupting the Servitor, '*when* I become Magus.'

But as he regarded the sacred name, the frightening image of a dark and sinister world, preyed upon by misery and wickedness, disrupted his thoughts. He could almost feel the threat encroach on him. *Not while I am around.* Encouraged by a new determination, he nodded to the Servitor.

'You are right, Kai! We will not let this happen.'

Without delay, Gill turned to face the walls, studying each with care and letting his hands skim over their surface, frantically searching for the exit. Behind him, Kai watched, unable to help. If Gill was to be a great ruler, he had to decipher it himself. It was expected of him, to prove his worth, and without the help of another; if he were to become reliant, especially on a servant in a time of need, he would be deemed unworthy.

But Kai, sensing Gill's heightening panic as it seeped in, clouding his judgement, could not look on without, somehow, influencing him. No matter what, Gill *had* to claim the precious amulet. And so, going against the grain of the Elliyan's strict ruling, he took a chance …

'Your right-of-way into the Sanctuary …' He hesitated, then changed back to his ghostly state—the transformation lighting up the chamber, illuminating the hieroglyphs, momentarily bringing them to life. Gill, his hands now resting on the wall, paused and drew a sharp breath, in awe of what he was seeing. And when the hieroglyphs ceased in their dance, settling back into their niches, he looked over his shoulder and stared at the Servitor, waiting. '… is written in the reliefs,' Kai went on. 'All you have to do is … *look* and *see*.'

Gill turned and eyed each wall with purpose, narrowing his eyes in concentration as he read their symbols. They crept in on him as the cryptic text reached out, begging to be unravelled—the pressure of another task now weighing on him. He stopped and stepped back, overwhelmed by the enormity of it, and caught his breath, fearing another wave of weakness.

'Look at me, Gill!'

The young man failed to respond to the Servitor, making Kai believe, Gill had not heard him, in his struggle to concentrate.

'Gill—look at me!'

Feeling the force of the Servitor's words, Gill felt compelled to turn and face him again. Kai lifted his hand gracefully, commanding his attention. Unable to divert his eyes from the blackness of the Servitor's, Gill felt the potency of his power as its warmth wrapped itself around him.

Kai's mouth moved yet no words were spoken—none Gill could detect, at first. However, it quickly occurred to him what the Servitor was doing: he was trying to help him while putting himself at great risk.

*"Empty your mind of all that surrounds you until you are ready to let it in again. You still have time, Gill. Use it wisely."*

As Kai's silent words flooded Gill's mind, a feeling of calm came over him, releasing the tension from his body, and returning the sense of peace to him. And as the seconds passed, Gill became aware of his mind opening up, enabling him to focus.

Kai stepped away, leaving Gill to his thoughts.

The weariness Gill had felt had now subsided. But time was against him. In his mind, he visualised the six surrounding walls as they stared back at him. Opening his eyes, he turned, once again, to face them, and as he took their ancient script in—one by one—they gradually unleashed their secrets to him, as clear as day.

A faint smile crossed his mouth as he read them aloud—the Servitor nodding in triumph. Suddenly Gill jolted. Eyes still fixed, he backed away from the wall—the brief image that had interrupted his train of thought, disturbing him.

'What is the matter?' asked Kai.

Gill turned to the Servitor, his eyes wild and anxious.

'She's here—in Elboru!'

The crossover had felt like an eternity—nor had it been a pleasant one, either; when she leapt into the portal's fading beam of light, it had gripped her, stabbing her with shards of colours as though it were protecting itself from her intrusion. And despite her newfound strength, she could not fight it, thinking she would have died and remained trapped within its hold, denying her the *Halls of Valhalla*; it was her right, to enjoy the delights of the afterlife. But when she felt the enormous gravity of its pull, the pain had momentarily subsided, then dragged and stretched her body to the point where she thought her limbs would be ripped apart. And just when she had given up all hope of surviving, she had felt the hard thud of the cold ground, then darkness.

She had no idea how long she had been unconscious, but when she finally opened her eyes, she realised she was still in the grip of darkness, unable to see. She moaned as she tried to move about, groping for the Obsidian; it had been yanked from her grip when she leapt into the Egress—the force of the portal's energy snatching the weapon from her. She grunted with frustration, having been reduced to searching for it on her hands and knees. It would have been humiliating—had anyone seen her.

Finally, her fingers felt the familiarity of her precious lance; it sparked briefly, recognising her touch, letting her know it was there, bonding with her again. Shapes began to appear. *Good.* Her eyes were adjusting to the dark. Now, to find her bearings. She reached out, letting her hands guide her until they connected to a wall; it was uneven, enabling her to latch onto its thick, rugged surface. She winced as she slowly pulled herself up, finding her feet again. She swayed, a sudden pounding in her head blinding as flashes of light hampered her vision again. She blinked hard in a bid to see, then decided to wait, hoping it would pass. Eventually, the effects of the crossover subsided, returning her sight and strength. As her eyes focused, she looked around.

'What is this place?' she muttered, frowning, now seeing the entrances to three passages. She moved towards their foreboding arches with care as she surveyed them. Each passage was sparsely lit by torches, lining the walls on each side, their large flickering flames throwing an eerie glow through their shadowy routes. She took a wary step forward over the threshold of one and narrowed her eyes, their sharpness staring into its abyss until she could see no farther; the light, such as it was, faded into blackness, giving her no indication of its distance, or where it might lead.

Kara moved from one entrance to the next, studying them further yet could see no distinction between them. She released a long-winded sigh, incensed by it. Then, relying on her enhanced hearing, she tilted her head sideways, and listened intently; nothing or no one stirred in the far reaches, not even a slight draught. The silence was intolerable.

*Much too quiet*, she thought, looking around. *Is this how it will be when I rule?* she wondered. *I will soon change that.* To hail from a world of mayhem to a peaceful one like this, would instil a madness in her—one she was not willing to endure. In her world, chaos reigned—and would continue to do so.

But time was running out, and she was certain she had been followed through the portal. *They could be anywhere*, she thought, glancing around. *Perhaps they are already in the Sanctuary …*

Driven by this notion, the Valkyrie put her thoughts into action. *Time to choose.* Another brief inspection of all three passages drew the small straw in her mind.

With the Obsidian grasped in her hand and eyes set on her task, Kara stepped forward into her chosen passage. Her pace gradually quickened the farther she ventured. As she passed the torches nestled in their sconces, their flames flickered, distorting her oversized shadow as it leapt to and fro. Along the route, hidden alcoves appeared out of nowhere. She stopped, letting her hand reach out into their deep hollows, only to be met with cold, damp solid walls. She mused over their purpose; they made her curious about what might be hidden behind their stonework. She would make a point of finding out … when she ruled.

Stepping back into the passage, she moved to continue her journey, then paused, certain she had heard a noise. She glanced left then right, her eyes still … listening. *There it is!* It was a faint sound—but a sound, nonetheless. What it was and where it came from, she could not determine; the castle's immense size threw out its sounds in all directions, confusing her.

She spun, looking back in the direction she had come. The sound she had heard seemed to be heading her way, like footsteps, echoing towards her, their approach hasty. It was difficult to say how many, but when they gained momentum she leapt into the alcove, letting its blackness conceal her. Perhaps the corridors were being guarded … She contemplated jumping out, taking them unawares and ridding herself of the threat. She could despatch them easily.

Aware of their approach, Kara, deciding against any altercation held her breath; she would not risk it, not while she was out of her domain. In the open, she had the advantage of flight; she then frowned when she felt the weight of her damaged wings. How far they would take her now was debatable. The knowledge of this—dare she admit it—*weakness*, aggravated her, making her feel like an encaged animal, with the threat of an unknown assailant, lurking in the dark.

She could distinguish the footsteps now; they were pronounced, and she quickly realised there was more than one set. She remained still, her body pressed hard against the alcove's wall.

The footsteps stopped, mere feet away, pausing for a moment. Did they know she was there, hiding in the shadows? She wished she could see them. Again, she considered taking them on, and as she made to step out from her hiding place, the footsteps proceeded on their journey.

Kara lingered for several moments, listening as the steps faded, until the silence found its way back to her. But the quietness was insufferable; she could almost hear it scream. Despite it, though, she was content in her isolation and, convinced it safe to do so, stepped out from the alcove. She looked up and down the passage—to be sure. Only darkness peered back at her; whoever had passed through had extinguished all the torches. *Now why did you do that?* she wondered. Glancing back from whence she came, she decided not to go further and turned on her heel—determined to find the Sanctuary.

Wary of time, Kara hurried back to where she had first found herself, but as she drew near the exit, an unexpected force stopped her in her tracks, propelling her back into the passageway, almost throwing her off her feet. Gripping the Obsidian, she steadied herself, eyes fixed as she stared beyond the exit, watching and listening. Nothing stirred. Vigilant, she attempted to approach it again but could not. Pacing back and forth, she calculated the distance between herself and the exit. *No more than ten feet.* Not much. However, it was hampering her ability to discover the source behind the power.

Curious, Kara lifted her hand and extended it, wanting to touch the force, holding her prisoner. But as she reached out, she felt the rise of its heat against her scarred palm, its burning influence nudging her back.

She surveyed the space between her and her potential escape. She frowned and pressed her lips together in concentration, glaring at it. Where did *it* come from? It had not been there when she came through the portal. She then grunted, smirking to herself. *The Obsidian!* She would use its energy against the barrier. Kara stepped back and lifted the great lance and, with all her strength, hurled it at the invisible force; when the Obsidian collided with it, it sparked, momentarily displaying its deep-emerald glass, then dropped to the ground, dull and lifeless. When she retrieved her weapon, she drew her hand up and down its length, feeling the fine cracks in the glass.

Another attempt was now out of the question; it would shatter the Obsidian. And though aware of the sword on her back and the dagger inside her bodice of black armour, she knew they would be useless against the force. There was no alternative, she would have to go back through the passage and follow its route, in the hope of finding the Sanctuary. *There must be a way out*, she thought.

Unperturbed by her temporary setback, Kara saw it as another stumbling block in her bid for supremacy. It was never going to be easy. She knew that and welcomed the challenge thrown at her.

*"Be the victor of every challenge you face and it will make you stronger."*

Words spoken to her when she was younger entered her thoughts, and yet she could not remember who had said them. Someone of less importance, no doubt, though they rang true. She grunted; not only would this challenge make her stronger, but it would also make her a powerful ruler. *No one will dare provoke me, then.*

Obsessed, she retrieved the Obsidian, and as she turned to make her way back down the long, dark passage, a movement caught her eye. She gripped the lance and waited. There it was—again! Slight, but an undisputed movement, no less.

She edged towards it, gripping the Obsidian, and raised her arm, ready to defend herself, should it reach her. She stopped, seeing it more clearly now; it was a shadow—a shadow growing, beyond her reach. But as she stood, armed and ready, she could still feel the pulsating force between *it* and her, then realised she could not penetrate it. Kara glanced over her shoulder into the blackness. Her instincts were telling her to go yet when she looked back, observing the shadow as it increased in size, her curiosity got the better of her.

She braved a determined step forward. As she did so, the barrier's heat subsided, allowing her to move closer. Another step. Then another. Her eyes widened when the shadow took on a shape, moulding itself into a form until it finally revealed itself to her …

# Chapter Thirty-Four

'Have you figured it out yet, Kara—which one it is?'

The Valkyrie raised her head, glaring at the familiar face grinning back at her, then lifted herself to her full stature, displaying her imposing new physique, in a vain attempt to threaten her antagonist.

Magia Nera's grin slipped from his face, his lips slightly parting as he took her in, studying her from head to toe. Kara smirked, revelling in his reaction.

'*Oh, magnifica!*' he declared. 'Truly, *magnifica!* Now I can admire you, fully.'

'I must thank you,' she sneered back, 'assuming *this*'—she raised her hand, indicating her body—'is *your* doing?'

The dark Warlock stretched his face and, looking up, tossed his head from side to side, musing over her assumption. 'Not quite,' he said—the sarcasm present in his velvet accent. He shook his head. 'You were simply … *careless!*'

Kara gripped the Obsidian so hard he could hear her knuckles crack beneath their thick skin, betraying her silent anger. He shook his head again, feigning his sympathy, then grunted, seeing the scar on her forearm—the inadvertent little vestige she acquired from the Dhampir's poisonous blade.

'I am *never* careless!' she retorted, subtly releasing her grip on her weapon, conscious of the cracks in its glass; should her precious Obsidian be destroyed …

'We shall beg to differ, then,' he said. 'But if you proceed—and alone—in your task … you will risk everything!'

'I have always relished the challenge while accepting the risk,' she boasted.

'Even if it means your demise?'

'*My* demise?' She threw her head back, releasing a deep-throated laugh, then discarded it, resuming her hardened stare. 'I have no intention of *losing* this battle,' she hit back. 'I will achieve what I came here to do.'

Magia glanced over the gap between them, then, clasping his hands behind his back, moved across it, slowly nodding in contemplation. He paused, eyes fixed on the space separating them, sniggering beneath his breath. 'But not without its difficulties, I should imagine.'

The sneer in his tone riled her as she realised his meaning; it was obvious who had placed the invisible barrier between them—the force of its shield keeping her prisoner, and stopping her from wanting to tear him asunder.

'Now I see.' She grunted, nodding. 'You want *it* for yourself.'

Magia recoiled as if caught off-guard and stared at her, eyes wide and mouth gaped, his hand on his heart, shaking his head, professing shock. 'No, no, my dear!' he returned, moving towards her. 'I am a Warlock and'—he nodded—'true, I *should* desire it, but … While I know *who* I am, Kara, I am also aware of *what* I am—what you and I are.'

She side-glanced him with uncertainty.

He rolled his eyes, releasing a short sigh. 'Even *I* am no fool, to risk taking the Shenn,' he stated.

She lifted her head, her brows knitting. 'Why not take it?'

'Because … it would destroy me, as it would you—or anyone else, for that matter, apart from the *Chosen One*—should we—or they—attempt to possess it.'

Kara narrowed her piercing, grey eyes, unconvinced. 'You are full of lies, Nera.'

Magia shrugged, then, stepping away, waved his hand across the void between them; at once, Kara felt the barrier's absence. She stepped back, her wary eyes still on him.

'*Per favore!*' he said, sweeping his hand across as he stepped aside. 'You are free to try for yourself, if you do not believe me.' He forged a smile. 'I shall even show you where it is, if you like?'

As doubt replaced anger, she regarded him with suspicion as his unwavering smile tried to lure her over the threshold; though enticed, she stalled. Why should she trust him? She had no reason to.

Holding his pretence, he raised his hand, then motioned her towards him. Despite her hesitation, he knew she would succumb to him, eventually; he had the upper hand, where her greed was concerned.

'You have my word,' he added, 'to show you the way—if you desire it.'

'I thought you did not know the way to Elboru,' she remarked.

'*This*,' he replied, lifting a finger in the air, 'is true. But I had the source to guide me, all along. It was just a matter of … reclaiming it,' he pointed out, patting his chest, where his amulet now rested, re-united with its master. 'The exterior of this … *Castillo*—castle—call it you will—is a façade, concealing the true nature of what lies behind the fortress of Elboru. But once inside—a difficult feat, I might add, unless one knows the way—each is identical. You, however, were fortunate, in that you discovered a way in, through the portal.' She smirked at him, pleased with herself, despite not knowing precisely where she was. Yet. 'But I am also here, Kara, and this is *my* territory. I know the rulings and laws where the Shenn and its true master are concerned. But'—he slowly lifted his shoulders—'if you doubt my word … then take the risk.' He hesitated, watching her face; her head was tilted low and her eyes narrowed, telling him she was unconvinced.

'Go on …' he urged her, his tone now soft and teasing. 'I *dare* you!'

For once, the Valkyrie felt something she had rarely experienced—an element of defeat. As the dark Warlock stood with his hands clasped behind his back, again, looking at her with the twitch of victory at the edge of his mouth, she felt confined, conquered. Even her damaged wings weighed heavier now, their burden prominent, and a hindrance, and with her trapped like a fly in the Warlock's web, they were dragging her down. She shifted, contorting her back; they were uncomfortable, too—no longer the natural extension of her body. She wished she could rid herself of them. With her new heightened powers, her legs were stronger—*faster!*—and would compensate for her damaged wings. *A minor inconvenience*, she convinced herself—a temporary setback, nothing more. She would overcome it and refuse to surrender to his taunts and lies.

Marking her discomfort, Magia sensed her inner frustration, regardless of her attempt to hide it. While amused by her predicament, he was also aware of her stubbornness and hunger for victory, and so persisted in needling her. 'But first'—he lifted his finger, then wagged it at her—'you must find the *Great Hall of Eminence.*'

She cocked her head. He had her attention.

'I should imagine it will be easy to find,' she said, with an edge of arrogance in her tone. 'Judging by its *name.*'

He snorted, relishing in his little games. 'Indeed.' He slid his eyes towards her, smirking. 'It is *there* you will find the *Sanctuary of Armistice.*' Kara arched a brow. 'But … be warned!' he added. 'By now, the Elliyan will occupy the Sanctuary, as they await the *Chosen One.* Should you succeed in penetrating their defences and can enter its inner sanctum, where the *transformation* will take place … then it will be there, waiting for—'

'You mean—the Shenn?' she broke in, edging closer and licking her lips as though it were already within her grasp.

A simple nod from him confirmed this.

Kara drew back, casting him another sideward look. 'But I thought you said, to attempt to overthrow it would mean death to anyone who would even *try*, except for the *Chosen One.*'

'Ah!' Magia exclaimed, throwing his hands up, at her moment of realisation. 'So, you *were* listening, then.'

Kara glared at him; his ongoing insults were wearing thin.

'However, there is one thing I overlooked.' He bowed. '*Mi scusi!*'

'Your apologies are wasted on me, Warlock,' she snapped. 'What is it you claim to have … *overlooked?*'

'Should the poor unfortunate soul—chosen to wear the Shenn and rule this world of ours—fail to claim it before this day diminishes, chaos will erupt, leaving the precious item there for the taking, by those who desire it.'

As Kara's eyes widened at this new information, she slowly raised her hands to her throat, caressing it, then guided them down, cupping them over her breasts, imagining the sacred amulet between them, touching her, bonding with her. She imagined it nestled there, adorning her as it hung for all to see—*and they will see it!*—telling those who would be loyal to her, who their new ruler was. A thought struck her: many would rebel against her. There would only be one solution to that … *Dispatch them!*

Observing the wanton glint in her eyes, Magia could almost hear her thoughts as the cogs turned, manipulating her into believing she could have it all. 'Think of it, Kara!' he went on. She shot him a glance, her eyes wild with excitement, listening, yearning … 'Think of the Shenn in your hand. It has everything you crave—the power of the universe, and more! All there, waiting for *you* to command. *Sì!* I can see you now, glorifying in the moment.'

A tortuous grin formed across her mouth—the greed now evident in her icy grey eyes as she visualised the sacred object, clutched in the palm of her hand. But as his words returned to her—*"I can see you now, glorifying in the moment"*—all notions of power began to fade from her deranged mind. Magia watched the hope he had given her now disintegrate as her face twitched—the anger inside her, rising.

'But alas!' he said, lifting his shoulders and hands and tilting his head to one side. 'That is all it would be—a *moment*—before it consumes you to the depths of hell!' Once more, he relished in watching her submit to defeat. She lowered her head, eyes melting with rage.

Still, he goaded her; he shook his head slowly, his eyes fixed, silently torturing her with their penetrating stare. 'You would then be cast into their dark underworld, and forced to journey against Gods, demonic creatures and gatekeepers, to reach the *Hall of Final Judgement*. But … that shall be of no concern to you.'

She shot him a wary look.

'You see, Kara, *you* shall never be offered the opportunity to take such a journey.'

*"Your demise shall not end in your Halls of Valhalla."*

Fear and doubt enveloped the Valkyrie—two emotions she had never envisaged; she *feared* being denied the privilege—the right—to enter the glorious halls of her forefathers. It had been her aspiration in death, to enjoy the bountiful riches Valhalla offered to those in the afterlife. To never reach them would be her ultimate failing, not only to herself but to her predecessors. It was the one risk she was determined not to take; she then *doubted* she would see the glory of it … It was, in all likelihood, probable, adding to that fear.

Seeing the surrender in her eyes as the fading light of promise was extinguished, Magia knew the Valkyrie was his—and a useful distraction, too, should the need arise. With the Sorceress creating mayhem, making things difficult for the Elliyan, and adding the Valkyrie to the mix, it would leave him free to seek out the book. And now that he knew L'Ordana no longer possessed it, a new niggling feeling inside convinced him it was now in the capable hands of another.

Promptly, he returned his attention to the Valkyrie, her eyes still lowered from her downfall. For a moment, he felt pity for her.

'But—I know someone who *can* take it.'

# Chapter Thirty-five

'I see nothing but an endless road ahead of us,' moaned Wareeshta as she peered through the time-worn stone arch with its imposing towers, flanking its sides. She looked from left to right, her eyes then travelling over them, studying the ancient structures; a parapet, lined with turrets, stretched across from one to the other, where armed guards once marched back and forth, watching, protecting … against something. Her eyes were next drawn to the mass of trees beside each tower, their thick, aged trunks leaning against the stone. *Impassable!* she thought. There was only one way to go—straight on, through the arch.

Aside from the enduring route facing them, the group could see little beyond the structure. Centuries of overgrowth draped heavily over the towers—the thick, ivy almost concealing their lancets, where once attentive eyes peered out, bearing the dark secrets of their past.

When they dismounted, Reece stepped up to survey one of the towers, his inquisitive eyes narrowing, seeing something behind the overgrowth. Removing his broadsword, he hacked away at its thickness, his brows lifting when unique carvings on the ancient stone revealed themselves; the hieroglyphs were deep and defined, their unusual drawings depicting shapes of various animals, birds, people and symbols unknown to him, with traces of faded colour still visible.

*Interesting!* he thought, curious of their meaning as he returned his sword to its scabbard. He reached out, letting his hand trace the unusual shapes, unable to decipher their archaic stories. He turned when he heard a short grunt from behind and saw Wareeshta, her attention still focused on the arch. He snorted, seeing the gathered lines of frustration etched between her brows. 'It appears you have already forgotten,' he remarked, his eyes flashing to the "view" beyond the arch, then back to her.

Detecting the smugness in his tone, she turned, ready to answer him back, with an equally smug remark.

'Your eyes fail you,' he continued before she could speak. He moved to her side. 'Look there'—he pointed—'can you not see?'

'I do not care for your mockery,' she retorted.

He sneered a sideward glance down at her, then grunted; at times he found it difficult to contain his frustration on Wareeshta. The vow made to Eleanor—not to destroy her "friend"—occasionally pecked at him as a reminder. He could still hear his granddaughter's voice inside his head;

*"She saved my life!"*

How could he forget—or ignore—Eleanor's plea, not to mention the determined look on her face? Without the presence of his granddaughter and the Samurai, keeping his anger at bay, he was struggling inside. The temptation to drive his sword through Wareeshta's slow-beating heart was sometimes irresistible; his fingers twitched by his side, feeling the broadsword pressing against his thigh as though it were urging him to act on his impulse. There was also the dagger—attached to his belt—perhaps he would use that? He clenched his fist, still aware of the scar it had left on the palm of his hand, when he had tried to kill the Sorceress, on their first encounter; she had turned his dagger to fiery steel, rendering him defenceless against her power. Reminded of it fed his desire for revenge. When his eyes flashed to Wareeshta, meeting hers, he tore his look away, having seen Eleanor's insistence through her look.

*"Promise me!"*

He sighed, rolled his eyes, then inched away from the Dhampir, relaxing his hands.

'What do you think you are doing?'

When Wareeshta and Reece turned, hearing Daine's exasperated voice from behind, they saw Rosalyn march towards them—the urgency to be reunited with her son evident, by the determined look on her face, it fixed hard with concentration, ignoring Daine's plea.

'According to Oran,' she began, glaring at them, 'Elboru is beyond this *illusion*.' Reece threw a—*now-do-you-see-it?*—glance at Wareeshta, who slid her eyes from him, irked by his arrogance. Despite their "allegiance", and occasional civil moments, she remained wary of his underlying urge to rid himself of her. Still, she knew she had him at an advantage and could keep him at arm's length, thanks to her friend.

When Rosalyn stomped by them without a backward glance and headed straight for the arch, Reece did a double-take when he realised her intention.

'No, Rosalyn! Wait!' he cried, removing his sword again as he pursued his daughter, with Daine and a reluctant Wareeshta following suit. Despite the *illusion*, he remained cautious.

At first, Rosalyn had also seen the long, relentless road in front of them, with nothing but an endless stream of trees skirting it, stretching farther than the eye could see. She stopped and glanced back from whence they came, then shuddered, still trying to discard the memory of the Redcaps' horrific attack. There was no sign of them now. Had they been an illusion, too? The experience had felt real. When her eyes flicked back to Daine, a chill ran down her spine, seeing the wound on his cheek, where the Redcap had cut him with its claw-like hand. *All too real*, she told herself, slowly nodding.

'I am not sure about this, Rosalyn,' Reece insisted, regardless of what Oran had said.

Rosalyn looked up at her father, seeing his furrowed brow and the intensity in his green eyes as they remained fixed, staring out at the unknown.

*"Do not be fooled by it!"*

Unlike Wareeshta, however, whose thoughts had been elsewhere—too focused on retrieving her father's book, to recall Oran's words—Rosalyn did not forget what her husband told her;

she was confident the castle was within their grasp. Head held high, she marched on. But the moment she stepped beyond the threshold she froze.

The four stood side by side as the ghostly mist swirled about them, its thick, white veil hampering their vision yet they sensed something within its core. Their eyes lifted as it dissolved, into a slow descent, letting the morning light fall on their anticipation. Slowly but surely, the great fortress of Elboru emerged through the haze; its elaborate round turrets seemed to reach up to greet the new day, rising high above their spectators before gradually exposing its grandeur: battlements stretched across its highest walls yet no one marched between the gaps behind their parapets; four huge round towers with their conical roofs adorned each corner of the immense structure, with smaller towers flanking its sides; but no banners or standards swayed in the breeze to identify its residents. And when nature's light caressed the pale limestone, distinct veins of gold glinted, mapping its rising façade. And as the morning glow spread, its splendour reflected off the latticed arched windows, illuminating the array of colours within their stained glass. But there was no movement from behind their panes, giving the impression that no one resided there. As it rose higher from its ghostly slumber, the fortress seemed to stare down at the four strangers, as if ready to pounce on their unwarranted presence as a warning, telling them to leave, and never return. And though intimidating in its semblance, the great fortress was not the real threat awaiting them …

As the mist gradually paled on its final descent, large shapes began to appear, crowding the space before them.

Daine gasped under his breath. 'What the …?'

In a grand display of armour and weaponry, a sentry of guards stood pride of place, its purpose: to defend the structure behind it.

Their numbers filled the courtyard, with each sentry rooted to his post, ready to strike at any moment. Loyal subjects of the Elliyan, these unwavering mercenaries of old were the Bullwark.

Reece quickly fell privy to the Bullwark's surveillance upon anything that moved within their eye-line as their sharp eyes darted about, in constant vigilance; when a small bird suddenly took flight, Reece saw their cunning eyes catch its fluttering movement with quick precision before swiftly returning their gaze upon the four strangers, casting aside any threat from the bird.

'I think it wise that we should remain still,' he stated, his voice low and steady.

It was evident, by the elaborate and luxurious state of their attire, the Bullwark were of immense importance, their intimidating presence dominating their surroundings. Their splendid physique was as impressive as their height; Reece surmised they stood taller than Tam. The thought of his friend brought with it an unusual ache inside him. He missed the Highlander, more than he realised, Tam's demise heightening his awareness of Asai's untimely absence. And yet, Reece sensed him near. *Where are you, my friend, when I need you?*

A striking, unique piece of head armour concealed the Bullwark's faces and the crown of their heads, leaving only their eyes, ears and mouth exposed. Other than that, there was nothing to distinguish their features, save for one thing: their striking eyes, their piercing colours set and determined.

All wore similar clothing; long, calf-length tunics, elaborately decorated with gold and silver fine thread, skilfully crafted into the material by unknown delicate hands. The tunics stood out in the beauty of late dawn, their menacing colour—blood-red—bold and threatening. Reece thought the sentries reminiscent of *Knights of Honour*—similar to ones he had seen on a great tapestry, once, though different in their inimitable way. The lengthy boots adorning their feet were of the finest black leather, and clung to their muscular legs like a second skin—the tips on the toes capped with yellow gold. But most impressive was the item each sentry held by his left side: his shield. Reece had seen nothing like it before.

Each shield graced its master's side, matching his height and width.

Its metal was anomalous and gleamed beneath the watery sun, its engravings highlighting the intricate and unknown design, similar to the hieroglyphics they had seen earlier on the towers, flanking the arch. Each shield was matched with a fine sword, held in place by a thick, leather baldric—the belt expertly crafted to house the great weapon which was worn over the shoulder, to rest on the opposite side of the other hip, giving the Bullwark quick and easy access to it.

The four companions braved glances from one to the other, each filled with uncertainty. Wareeshta felt particularly vulnerable; her only weapons were the two stiletto daggers concealed inside her boots. And, apart from the one she inherited from her father—the "gift", to take or renew life—she knew she could not take on the wall of mercenaries guarding the fortress. Unsettled by them, she looked at Reece.

Sensing her unease, Reece was then woken to his predicament. Should Wareeshta die, his mortality would be restored—something he had longed for. However, the irony in it would only seal his fate; he would no longer be capable of defending himself, let alone Rosalyn and Daine. For once, he was thankful for his affliction, and—as much as it irked him to admit—was now grateful for Wareeshta's presence. Therefore, he promptly discarded any prior sentiment against her and thoughts of her demise; he needed to safeguard her now, to gain any hope of survival.

With the Bullwark's numbers far surpassing theirs, the small group knew a battle would be swift and, with no notion, whatsoever, to the extent of the legions' skills ... Reece was not confident. While he and Wareeshta had, at least, an advantage, a chance of surviving—as little as it was—Rosalyn and Daine, being mortals, did not. With this concern preying on his mind, and aware she was unarmed, he slipped Rosalyn the dagger from his belt.

But Reece's sleight-of-hand did not go unnoticed; the swiftness at which the dagger had been passed alerted the Bullwark. Their eyes suddenly darted, turning directly on Reece. The tension in the atmosphere reared as the Bullwark regarded the Dhampir—the looming threat prompting the rest of the group to prepare themselves for the unexpected.

With Rosalyn now conscious of how fragile she and Daine were in their hostile state, in this new and hostile world, she realised there could only be one solution—one tactic—as her mind raced with desperate thoughts; *We'll throw down our arms—give ourselves up!* Anything to buy them time. They—*she*—needed to get inside the castle.

Decision made, she cautiously raised one hand in defence, while slowly laying down the dagger Reece had given her, with the other. With wary eyes fixed on the sentries she stepped over the weapon, both hands now raised above her head, signalling her "surrender".

Behind her, and feeling vulnerable under the weight of the Bullwark's scrutiny, Reece, Daine and Wareeshta looked on in disbelief, reluctant to act on Rosalyn's brave, but unnerving, strategy.

Rosalyn stopped. Swallowing her fear, she cleared her throat. 'I am Rosalyn,' she began, in a clear, definitive voice. 'Wife of Oran of Urquille, High Warlock of—'

'The *Traitor's* wife!' came a prominent voice.

Rosalyn gasped, hearing the allegation, her eyes searching, unable to see the accuser. Suddenly, one of the Bullwark stomped forward; she jolted from his threatening advance, her eyes lifting as he marched closer, making her stumble backwards. Reece rushed to his daughter's aid, but in doing so, he failed to notice the actions of another.

With no regard for his mortality, Daine had bolted forward, raising the great sword his father had given him as he rushed by Rosalyn, just as Reece had caught her. But the instant he had moved, charging towards the Bullwark, the mercenaries had already pulled their shields across them again, and drawn their swords before advancing towards their victims, their roaring march vibrating the ground beneath their feet.

The sentry at the forefront raised his weapon, ready to strike it down on the advancing mortal. Daine gripped his Albrecht with both hands and lifted it high across his head, in self-defence, hoping it would have the same commanding effect here, as it had on the Redcaps. He shut his eyes at the sound of the oncoming attack, ready for impact, while thinking; *should this be my end, then I am thankful for my companions and know I'll not die alone.*

The noise then ceased, replaced by a crushed, overbearing silence.

Daine waited a few moments before a familiar voice spoke in his ear.

'I think you may have just saved our lives,' Reece muttered. Aware Daine's eyes were shut tight, the Dhampir subtly nudged him. 'See for yourself.'

Face scrunched, Daine opened one eye, then both. He drew a breath; the sentry at the forefront had stopped dead, and now stood within mere feet of him, his eyes staring at the sword still raised above his potential victim's head. Still fearing the attack, Daine did not move or make a sound, save for his anxious breath.

'This sword you wield before us,' the sentry began, his voice, thick and low as though rising from the depths of *Hell*, 'is that of the Elliyan.' He leaned closer, glowering down at Daine, threatening him with his searing look. 'How did *you* come by it?'

Daine swallowed before speaking; the imposing figure, leaning over him with his piercing and enquiring eyes, filled him with panic. 'It—it was my father's,' he stated, 'and his father's before him—handed down to *me*,' he added through gritted teeth, trying to conquer his fear.

The sentry regarded the mortal's words with caution, searching deep within his dark-brown eyes, intimidating him, in the hope he would falter. But Daine, feeling the support of his colleagues behind him, held his own and returned his gaze. But the sentry's penetrating eyes were hypnotic, their colour wavering between sapphire and amethyst as they searched for the lie behind the stranger's challenging stare. And while the Bullwark probed, Daine knew he could not lie—

even if he tried.

Satisfied, the sentry drew back from the mortal and returned to his post. Once more, silence prevailed, and as the four comrades re-grouped, they waited, confused and blind to their fate.

Having regained her stance, Rosalyn boldly edged towards Reece, her eyes never leaving the lingering threat.

'I've never seen anything like them,' she voiced from the side of her mouth, eyeing the sentries. 'Who are they?'

'They are the Bullwark.'

The group jolted, hearing the voice, then looked at each other, thrown by it; it belonged to a child. The sentries promptly parted to make way for the young boy, who emerged from his place of concealment.

'They are protectors of Elboru and guardians of the Elliyan,' he continued, stepping out into their company.

Dwarfed by the Bullwark's impressive height, the barefoot, scruffy young boy approached them, scratching his pock-marked skin. Rosalyn gasped, recognising him as the boy who had visited Oran before her husband had been forced to leave his family. Then, to their surprise, the child transformed himself, revealing his true identity.

Rosalyn drew a sharp breath. 'Kai?' she subconsciously blurted, fooled for a moment by the ghostly form walking towards them.

'You are mistaken. I am not *he*.'

Rosalyn's heart sank. Of course, it wasn't Kai. She knew that.

'I am Lorne, of the Servitor. What is your purpose, here?'

She stepped forward, accompanied by the others.

'We seek the one you call … Lothian,' Reece broke in before Rosalyn could speak. 'I believe he is expecting us,' he added, lying. His eyes fixed on the Servitor, Reece sensed something about the *creature*—something in its persona he disliked; it was different from Kai's, warning him to take heed.

Lorne's eyes drifted from Reece to the weapon in Daine's hand, recognising the symbols on its hilt and steel—the true identity of its owner exposing itself to him: *Oran's!* But when he raised his eyes, meeting Daine's, he leaned his head to the side, taking him in until it dawned on him; there was no doubting the likeness. His curious black eyes then travelled to Rosalyn. He tilted his head, blatantly surveying her. *Surely not*, he thought. *Another son? Impossible!* he concluded as his eyes rested on Daine again. *This one is too old to be their son.*

'Lothian?' said Reece, in a firm and impatient voice, reminding him of the reason for their presence. The group looked at one another, shuffling with discomfort when Reece spoke the Great Warlock's name; the Bullwark had moved closer in response.

Lorne raised his hand, like a salute, silently telling the mercenaries to remain.

'Well?' added Rosalyn. 'Where is he?'

Lowering his hand, the Servitor stalled, prolonging his answer, to goad the trespassers. He could *feel* their frustration mingling between fear and doubt. 'I am not at liberty to say,' he returned, in a matter-of-fact tone. 'For his … *protection*.'

Rosalyn grunted, a flicker of anger stirring inside her upon hearing this. 'Surely, not against us?' she disputed, disregarding the Bullwark's threatening presence as she stepped by Reece while almost shoving Daine aside.

Rosalyn moved as close as she dared to the Servitor, resuming her stance; looking into the blackness of his large, almond-shaped eyes, she matched his stare, her hands now firmly on her hips.

'Enough of this!' she started.

Reece rolled his eyes and shook his head. In the few days since their first meeting, he had learned much about his daughter and witnessed how she reacted in certain situations. And now, faced with the possibility of death, he subtly stepped up behind her—should her fiery tongue get the better of her and threaten to drag them down, into deeper waters.

'If you failed to hear my name, the first time,' she persisted, unaware her father was standing right behind her—Reece measuring the odds stacked against them, in the event of an attack, 'then let me remind you. I am—'

'The beautiful Rosalyn, wife of Oran of Urquille, High Warlock to the Elliyan or … "traitor" as one of our sentries referred to him.'

The Servitor's eyes, still on Rosalyn, widened, hearing the booming voice behind him.

The small group exchanged curious looks as the distinguishable figure came into view; he was less than the average height of a man but ample in size; his frame was strong and compact and his muscle tone visible, through his clothing. He wore a long, silver-grey tunic—the luxurious material moving gracefully with him, on his measured approach. About his waist was a thick, black silk sash with elaborate embroidery—the symbols similar to those they had seen on the towers. And if he wore a weapon, it was concealed well. However, it was the gold band, sitting on his hairless crown that stood out; embellished with round lustrous sapphires, they highlighted his striking blue eyes, which seemed to dance as he eyed the strangers individually. He smiled at them, his look, at first, appearing kind and reassuring—the façade then momentarily slipping as he passed by Lorne, casting the Servitor a scathing glance.

The Servitor bowed and stepped aside, keeping his head lowered yet maintaining his focus as Greer neared the small group, his attentive eyes now on Rosalyn. The Warlock matched her height, making her feel less vulnerable among the overbearing mercenaries. And yet, he appeared unfazed by it, even when forced to lift his head to meet Reece's wary stare; when the Dhampir looked down at him, Greer dragged his eyes back to Rosalyn, with such self-assurance it was evident, beneath his impassive exterior, he was someone not to be trifled with.

The High Warlock slowed, his eyes still on Rosalyn. She squirmed, feeling his penetrative stare as he studied her with the deftness of a predator. He then subtly lowered his eyes, and when he paused, momentarily marking her with his uninvited look, her stomach tightened into a knot; she knew what he was doing … and thinking. She wanted to look to Reece and Daine for support, wondering if they had seen it, too. Surely, they would have responded? But the look had been so brief she assumed otherwise and so remained steadfast, not wanting to appear weak in this individual's intimidating eyes. She was grateful she was not alone.

She flinched, suddenly aware he had stopped and was standing before her. He bowed before taking her hand.

'I am Greer, High Warlock of Kah-luan, in the Western world,' he began. He flashed a smile at her, then lifted her hand to his lips, his eyes fixed on hers, dancing wildly as he studied her—the moistness of his breath foul against her skin, making her stomach lurch as he lingered there. She cringed when he slowly ran his thumb over her hand, caressing it, momentarily languishing in the softness of her skin—a woman's skin; it had been too long. He paused, his eyes resting on something.

'What an elegant brooch,' he remarked, admiring the blue stone, its colour matching his sapphire eyes.

Rosalyn tensed as he tilted his head to admire it, and when he lifted his eyes to meet hers, she swallowed, placing her free hand over the brooch as if protecting the heirloom. She lifted her head slightly, looking down her nose at him with distaste. Inwardly insulted by this, Greer released his hold and stepped back, his eyes still locked on hers. Though not tall for a Warlock, his intimidating presence and demeanour made up for what he lacked in stature.

'It—it was *he*—Oran—who sent us here,' she stated, moving her hands to her side, while subtly wiping away his touch on her clothing. She cleared her throat. 'And it was *Oran* who gave us the name—Lothian—the one we seek—the one who shall take me to see *our* son'—she lifted her chin with pride, a subtle smirk appearing on her lips—'*your* Magus. And while you are privy to the wrath of a Warlock, then let me warn you … it does not match that of his wife!'

Greer raised a brow, keeping it there for a moment. The corner of his mouth twitched, now amused by her.

Daine eyed Reece; the two shared a look of mutual concern, fearing Rosalyn may have just placed them in grave danger. And when his eyes moved to her, Daine saw Wareeshta grinning from ear to ear, in admiration of her strength of character; for Rosalyn to threaten someone more powerful than she was awe-inspiring, giving the Dhampir a new and welcomed respect for the mortal.

Lorne, silently hovering by Greer's side, drew his head back, lifting it high, astonished at the mortal's unexpected outburst—and courage; she seemed different now from when they first met—when he was sent to summon Oran to duty. Yes, there was something about her he liked, it urging him to help … to *warn* her. But when Rosalyn edged closer, Lorne moved aside as she spoke, his eyes subtly watching Greer, unsure of his response; the High Warlock was capable of anything.

Though temptation picked away at his conscience, Lorne knew he could not risk getting involved; should he even attempt to interfere, the repercussions were far too great for him.

*No, I am never going back to Purgatory.*

And yet, he wanted to turn and go to Lothian, tell him what Greer was doing, what Greer had … The enormity of what he knew had become a burden too great. But, where Lothian had once favoured him, by rescuing him from Purgatory, he had, of late, experienced a sense of detachment from the ancient Warlock. He knew why, though it had not been his fault. *My hand was forced.* Unlike Kai, he had no one to call "friend". Kai had warned him. He should have listened. *But I had no choice.* His eyes slowly lifted to see Greer glaring down at him, as though the High Warlock knew his thoughts. He flinched then looked away, knowing he could do nothing to help; he was in too deep, as it was. With an element of defeat, Lorne lowered his head.

'I swear it,' Rosalyn persisted through gritted teeth. 'On my son's life!'

Greer smirked, then, with a sharp nod, lifted his hand with intent. In response, the Bullwark promptly shielded themselves—the sound almost deafening, like the clash of thunder and lightning as they prepared themselves.

Rosalyn jolted, her eyes alert, darting, reawakened to the danger, and conscious of every eye focused on *her* as they anticipated her next move. She froze. But, for what little comfort it gave her, she could now feel the tension of her father's presence behind her.

'Stay still,' he whispered over her right shoulder, while behind them, Wareeshta gestured to Daine to do the same, having heard Reece's words of caution to his daughter. At this imminent point, the four knew they were in danger; one sign from this Warlock would no doubt determine their end. But Rosalyn remained resolute, her eyes returning to Greer, locked to his, silently challenging him.

Greer thought the woman admirable and brave in her stand against him—and the Bullwark. She reminded him of another from his past. But he resented her dominance. However, it was clear Oran's wife was not aware of the upper hand she possessed, in her call for the Great Warlock, Lothian.

'But, of course!' he finally responded, with an underlying air of humour that concerned the group; they eyed one another, suspicious of his possible motives. The High Warlock stepped aside, motioning them towards the fortress. 'I shall be more than happy to direct you to the one you seek,' he sneered, his hand stretching out, to lead the way. Lorne flinched, taken aback by this. He looked at Greer with distrust, then away when the High Warlock stared him down before returning his attention to the group. 'You are most welcome here,' he added, nodding, then looked sharp at the Servitor, his tone now short and hard. 'You are dismissed, Lorne.'

Rosalyn regarded the Servitor when he tilted his head to her as he passed by. She snorted, relishing in her moment of victory, though aware it could be short-lived. But right now, her priority was to see her son. She was confident Gill was safe in Kai's company, and that they had made it to the Sanctuary. As for the others …? She had no idea where Oran, Eleanor and Asai were. Her concern for her daughter had seemed to lift a little, now that she and the Samurai were joined as *one*, though it had yet to sink in—what had happened to Eleanor. But it relieved her to know—when she herself was long gone—the two lovers would still be together. *As it should be*, she thought.

As they cautiously moved towards him, Greer held Rosalyn with a startling look; she did a double-take, seeing something behind his stunning blue eyes, something secretive, suggestive—and disturbing. As she walked by, she caught a faint curl at the edge of his mouth and frowned. Uneased by it, she tore her eyes from him, though still conscious of his sinister look lingering after her.

When Daine moved to follow as the Bullwark parted, their heads turning, eyes lowered, watching the outlanders' every move, he slowed, looking around.

'And what of our horses?' he enquired, searching for his precious Nahla, now unable to see her, or the other horses, among the throng.

'Do not concern yourself for their welfare,' Greer called back, determined not to linger. 'They shall be well cared for. You have my word.'

*Somehow, I doubt that*, thought Daine, feeling the sudden pang of separation from his mare, unsettled by it.

Amid Greer's unsettling "promise" to Daine, concerning their horses, Reece had stalled behind; something had diverted his attention away from their surroundings. He glanced behind him towards the trees, then back to the mercenaries; the Bullwark were too preoccupied with the fiery, outspoken female mortal, to notice him. Acting on it, he edged away.

Reece looked sharp, taking heed of a distant sound, it gradually finding its way to him. It was a familiar sound—one he was acquainted with. His eyes darted, searching for its location … until …

*There!*

As Rosalyn, Daine and Wareeshta approached the entrance to the castle, Rosalyn began to have her reservations as its entrance loomed. Her eyes travelled over the great oak doors as they opened wide, like the mouth of a lion, ready to snare them. It troubled her—the sense of foreboding, compelling her to look to the one who would reassure them.

When she turned to do so, Reece was nowhere to be seen …

# Chapter Thirty-Six

The lingering smell of dampness mingled with the faint scent of the unique odour as it wafted, tingling his nose while he kept his deep-set eyes fixed on Kara's now curious gaze; when the Valkyrie's nostrils flinched, he knew she had sensed it.

He could almost read Kara's thoughts as his words still teased her. *"I know someone who can take it."* She was contemplating it, he knew. Then, in true theatrical fashion, Magia stretched his hand into the darkness, out of the Valkyrie's sight. She narrowed her eyes and tilted her head, unsettled, yet inquisitive of his loitering; it was evident, by his keen and piercing stare that he was up to something.

When the slender hand reached out from the shadows to meet his—the gracefulness of its movement, having an air of authority about it—he took it with care; it was more precious now than ever.

The Valkyrie recoiled, mouth gaping when L'Ordana was led from her concealment, her scent now flooding Kara's senses; where she had once carried the pleasant aroma of sweet almond oil, a musky, earthy, flowery scent with undertones of pepper now drifted from the Sorceress—strong and present as its bearer.

The Sorceress turned and lifted her head slightly to meet the look of shock on Kara's face, then smirked. Speechless, Kara briefly shifted her gaze to Magia, but when she saw the smug grin on his mouth, she knew the upper hand belonged to the dark Warlock.

The Valkyrie looked back at L'Ordana, her brows knitting together when the Sorceress stepped closer. She gasped, seeing it: L'Ordana's features had been renewed; gone were the early markings of age, along with the pale, liver spots that had begun to plague her face and hands when she was her "Mistress". Once again, the vibrant glow of youth flushed her cheeks, returning the suppleness to her unblemished skin. But there was something else: her eyes; they now brimmed with a new lustre Kara had not seen before—like agate—only there was a rarity about them: the tiny flecks of gold.

Kara continued to stare at L'Ordana. She knew it was *her* yet there was *still* something ... *That's it!* she thought, seeing the slight, though noticeable, alteration to her features. *Two faces in one?* Kara then frowned when she saw L'Ordana's mouth opening and closing, though no words spilt out. She leaned forward to hear as L'Ordana whispered something to her. But as she drew closer, turning her head sideways to listen, the Valkyrie was suddenly forced back against the hardness of the uneven wall.

Slumped on the ground, and eyes closed, she grunted and moaned from the impact. She lifted her head, seeing the Obsidian; they were separated again. But as she reached out for it, her eyes shot open, feeling the sudden grip on her throat. It tightened as she was hauled to her feet, and as she was hoisted higher, Kara struggled, fighting to breathe—the desperate and pathetic guttural sounds coming from her throat, making the Sorceress smirk.

'Would you see me *dead?*' L'Ordana spat the words into the Valkyrie's face as she held her in mid-air, languishing in her renewed strength. 'The thought of it allures you, Valkyrie,' she persisted, then squeezed harder; Kara's bloodshot eyes bulged, feeling the ferocious grip of L'Ordana's long fingers as they added pressure to her wind-pipe, severing the sounds of her fight for survival as they clung to her throat like the *Grim Reaper*. If the Sorceress did not let go, soon enough, Kara knew her time would run out, denying her the bounties of Valhalla—should she die this way, and not on the battlefield. It was not how she envisioned her demise.

Desperate, her eyes searched for Magia Nera as her mouth opened and closed, trying to speak, wanting him to intervene. But the dark Warlock kept his silence as he stood, arms folded, behind L'Ordana, with a sneer on his face—one she would gladly remove, for good, given the opportunity. He was revelling in her weakness—and L'Ordana's transformation.

'Look at me—while I speak to you!' L'Ordana insisted, her voice slow and demanding. Kara's pleading eyes moved back to meet hers. '*Would* you—see me dead? No—wait—let me answer that. Of course, you would—now more than ever. Am I right, Kara?'

In her bid to stay alive, Kara grasped L'Ordana's hand with both of hers. But it was hopeless; she was unable to release her tightening hold, and as she sensed the veil of death begin to cloud over her icy-grey eyes, she felt the sudden impact of the hard surface beneath her, again.

Kara's chest heaved as she gasped for air, holding her throat, stroking, protecting it, expecting another assault.

'Remove any thoughts of my demise, Kara,' L'Ordana warned, leering down at her servant. 'For I shall see *you* dead, long before *I* am ready to leave this world.'

Kara tried to clear her throat, wincing through the pain. 'For—' She coughed, spluttering her response. 'Forgive me ...'

The Sorceress hovered over the Valkyrie, like a predator about to devour its prey. 'I did not hear you,' she taunted.

Kara turned her head and looked up, then jolted as L'Ordana's piercing eyes stabbed her with menace.

The Sorceress leaned closer and lowered her head, with added effect. 'Do not make me—'

'Forgive me …'

'Yes?'

Kara swallowed and cleared her throat again. '… my lady.'

Releasing a small grunt of pleasure, L'Ordana rose with Kara's eyes following her and smirked to herself.

'But—but my thoughts were—*are*—only of concern for—'

'Yourself, my dear, Kara,' she cut in. 'However, it is *you* who should be concerned.'

Convinced by her threat, the Valkyrie bent her eyes from L'Ordana's hardened stare, though, inside, was seething with hate and revenge. Having sensed this, the Sorceress grunted and shook her head, bemused by it.

As L'Ordana turned her attention back to Magia, she hesitated, her brows lifting as her eyes travelled over the arched roof above them, distant yet fixed in concentration. She listened. All was quiet. Nothing more stirred, since the voice inside her had ceased—the one that had been battling against her. She felt new, invigorated—the entity within more dominant, taking control, its sights set on one thing only—to seek revenge.

*"I will make them pay for what they did to me,"* she heard it tell her. L'Ordana nodded in response, feeling the spirit guiding her as it swiftly took control. It knew what to do, and she welcomed it, knowing it would help her take the Shenn amulet—and more! *So much more!* she thought, then heard its reply—the soft, whimsical laugh, making her smirk.

L'Ordana's eyes then fell on Magia, their tiny flecks of gold glinting at him. He narrowed his with suspicion then drew back when she suddenly stated;

'It is not far, now,' she told him; her voice was stronger, brimming with certainty.

*How could she know that?* 'No …' he slowly returned, feeling the pull of his amulet against his chest, it strong, like that of another beating heart, guiding him to the Sanctuary. 'No—Sorceress,' he promptly added, seeing her glare, 'it is not far.'

'Good. I cannot endure the wait,' she said, exasperated. 'But I know it will not be long; I *feel* it near. I cannot fail, Magia. I simply cannot!' she insisted, gritting her teeth. 'Nor will I!'

He held her stare for a moment, then nodded.

'Nor shall you,' he said.

The Sorceress turned and looked down at the Valkyrie, her features now softening, staring at Kara like a wounded beast. An image came to her of the Valkyrie—half-dead and tied to a tree in the pouring rain. She then had a recollection of herself—and another—untying her, saving her from the brink of death. She thought of the other individual who had stayed by her side. Another loyal servant? *Loyal?* she thought, wondering where *she* was, now. She grunted and shrugged, discarding the memory; it no longer mattered. She was in complete control now, and knew her mind—and that of the spirit's. They were "one"—and together would dominate.

As she stared down at the pitiful creature at her feet, she felt an element of sympathy towards the Valkyrie. And though she had no use of her, L'Ordana knew Kara *could* be of some worth—should the need arise. The curve of a faint smile appeared on her lips. Then, in an unprecedented move, L'Ordana extended her hand towards Kara—the same hand she had tried to destroy her with.

'Come with us!' she urged, her demeanour now calm.

Wary, Kara stared at the hand of death as it was offered to her. She looked to Magia, who had been observing her reaction at seeing her mistress again while indulging in their "reunion"; the "conversation" had proven quite entertaining.

'The Sorceress was … *unwell*,' he began. 'But, as you can see, she has been restored to her former glory … along with so much more,' he added, his suspicions now confirmed; the spirit he had placed inside Kristene now *owned* and controlled its host. He had witnessed it when the Egress appeared, bathing her in its energy while in the bosom of its possession, restoring her, once again. And now, she was hell-bent on having her revenge on the Elliyan, for their wrong-doing.

'You will be rewarded well,' added L'Ordana, her hand still extended. But Kara chose to ignore the offer of assistance, still feeling the overwhelming effect of its grip around her throat.

Gradually finding her feet again, Kara made to step forward, then stopped when L'Ordana snatched her hand back and subtly tilted her head, her eyes warning her against any advance or provocation.

Kara shot Magia a scathing look when it sank in—L'Ordana's

bribe: *"You will be rewarded well."*

'*She* plans to take the Shenn?' she argued to him, pointing at the Sorceress.

'Why not?' he replied, self-assured. 'She has as much claim to it as the Magus.'

'*Magus?!*' Kara grunted. 'She is not even a Warlock.'

'Ah!' he broke in, raising his finger. '*That* is where you are mistaken.'

Perplexed by this, Kara frowned as her wary eyes darted back and forth between the dark Warlock and the Sorceress. 'Meaning?'

'You see …' He hesitated and looked at L'Ordana, then second-glanced her, noting her eyes had glazed over; she appeared lost in reminiscence. 'L'Ordana was once known by another name, many centuries ago,' he went on, withholding it. 'She surpassed all others of her kind with her unique knowledge of *Necromancy*. And, because of it, she was invited to join a great *Council*—a rare honour bestowed upon any female, in an assembly of ruling males. She more than proved her worth and soon became a valued member. But …' He lingered on the memory, recalling the events of the time. 'She made a grave error'—he tutted and slowly shook his head—'a weakness of the heart, no less—the act going against the Orders' governing.'

Kara grunted. 'Love's "curse". Typical!'

'And, much to her misfortune,' said Magia. '*They* demanded she end the affair. She refused, of course, therefore severing her commitment to them. But, in doing so, she signed her death warrant.'

'What became of her lover? Does *he* still live?'

He stalled again, his eyes darting to L'Ordana, then back to Kara. He shrugged. 'I … cannot say.' Kara detected caution in his voice. 'Because of her refusal, and betrayal, she was condemned to a witch's death,' he resumed, pre-empting the Valkyrie's further enquiry. 'She was a risk to them. But her lover could not bear to lose her forever, and so asked a favour of me—knowing my knowledge of the *Black Arts*.'

'And this … *favour?*'

Magia perked up and, momentarily gazing at L'Ordana, smiled at his once prized possession. 'I stole his lover's soul,' he revealed.

Kara snorted. '*Stole* it?'

'*Sí!*' he said, throwing a disgruntled look at the Valkyrie, insulted that she would even doubt or question his ability to do so. 'As her body fought the flames when they tied her to the stake …' He paused and rolled his eyes, then sighed, recalling the barbaric penalty inflicted on her, by his then superiors. There had been other methods of punishment; they could have removed her powers and banished her. But the Elliyan wanted her gone—wiped from the annals of their history. '… I discreetly removed her soul, then kept it, until I found the perfect candidate to host it, vowing, in time, to reunite the lovers.' He glanced at L'Ordana again, then released a deep-rooted laugh from the pit of his stomach.

'Which, of course, you *conveniently* neglected to do,' said Kara.

He sighed. 'Vows are not my … *forte*. Neglected? No. I would be inclined to say, "decided against." You see, I could not bear to part from that which I created—and one so "gifted", too. The fact that they sentenced her to death, convinced me that *they* feared her true potential.'

'Do they know she … *lives?*'

He looked sharp at her as if she had insulted him again. 'No!' he snapped. 'The Elliyan do not know *who* truly lurks inside this woman's form. They are only aware of the Sorceress known as "L'Ordana".'

'For now, at least.' Kara and Magia looked sharp; L'Ordana was fully alert again—the mere mention of the Elliyan, wrenching her from her reverie. 'However, by the time I claim what is rightfully mine,' she continued, 'they will *know* it. But it will be too late, by then.'

'This … revenge you seek,' said Kara, 'is *your* battle, not mine. And if the Shenn is beyond *my* reach … then why should I help *you?*'

L'Ordana broke away from Magia.

'Side with us, Kara,' she said, 'and, I will grant you a place by my side—not as a servant—but as my loyal aide. Let us cast aside our past indiscretions and start anew. You will want for nothing.' She inclined her head towards her. 'You have my word.'

Kara frowned and pressed down on her lips as she mulled over the pledge being offered to her; it was a tempting one. Looking back on her recent time, alone, her exposure to its advantages now paled in comparison to its disadvantages. While she had relished in the idea of dominance, the lack of it, however, had done nothing to drive her; in fact, it had driven her to boredom, making her face the reality of knowing she could never achieve what she desired, on her own. But now, to be offered a privilege such as this … it simply intoxicated her.

'Now do you believe me?' Magia continued, his voice now soft and alluring. 'I told you that neither you nor I shall ever possess the sacred amulet …' He paused. 'Is it not better to help the one'—he motioned to L'Ordana—'who *truly* deserves it?'

Silence.

*You have no choice!* Magia held his tongue, preventing himself from uttering the truth, out loud. Kara's situation was bleak; he could tell, by the emerging look of defeat on her face, that she was already aware of it. She *would* be a useful distraction, should there be some retaliation from certain quarters, which was likely. *Useful, indeed*, he reminded himself. Yes, he would happily leave Kara to help L'Ordana to claim the Shenn, while he searched for his book. And once he had that … However, he was now wise to Kara's unpredictable nature. But while his venom flowed through her veins, he was sure she would make the right decision. Then again, it was possible she would refuse, and if that were to happen, he would have no choice but to destroy her. No, he could not risk the liability of her interference, not with time ticking away. *One last chance, Valkyrie.* 'Take it, Kara,' he prompted, ready to do what was necessary, should she rebel. 'Think of the glory, the imposition you will have over those under your command—not to mention the privileges.'

The three stood in contemplative silence for several moments, eyeing one another. Then, taking her stance, Kara reached for the Obsidian and stabbed the ground beneath her feet with it. The weapon's deep-emerald glass sparked to life. Filled with aspirations of power once again, she lowered her head, her eyes brimming with determination and malice.

'Lead the way!'

'A wise choice!' Magia returned, under his breath, as he led the Sorceress past Kara's confused look, grinning to himself.

Kara watched the smirk on the dark Warlock's face as he and L'Ordana brushed by her, making their way down the passage she had attempted earlier, their silhouettes gradually dissolving into the shadows.

'Surely … *this* is the wrong way?' she called after them, bewildered.

'As I said,' came the distinctive voice from the blackness, echoing back to her. 'A wise choice!'

# Chapter Thirty-Seven

He reached out into the dark as it enveloped him, and felt the cold, damp walls on each side, their closeness giving him a sense of entrapment; the last time he had passed through the portal, he had found himself in the Hall of Eminence—and confronted by the Elliyan.

This felt different.

Oran cupped a hand over his mouth.

'Light my way,' he whispered into his palm, then held it out. A flame ignited, and as it hovered in the hollow of his hand, shedding some light on his whereabouts, he took stock of his location.

The mundane passageway stretched beyond his guiding light as he looked from left to right, frowning and indecisive. *How did I end up here?* he thought, then was relieved he had. *A stroke of luck*; the mere idea of having to face the Elliyan right now … and then there was the Bullwark to consider … He rechecked the passage, trying to find his bearings, aware of the complex network of corridors within the fortress. During his brief time there—before being forced to leave, to search for the Sorceress—he had made a point of acquainting himself with Elboru, with some encouragement from Lothian, having been ignorant of its existence within the Realm of Urquille—*his* Realm, no less. It seemed—as was pointed out to him, by Tuan—the arrogance of his wayward past had made him blind to what truly existed, when all the while it was there, right under his nose. And, as much as it irked him to admit, he only had himself to blame. Then again, perhaps, subconsciously, he had known it all along and simply refused to "believe" for what it symbolised. But there was no point in lingering on something he should have done or should have known about. *'Tis the here and now that matters*, he told himself.

Time, for now, was still on their side; the sun had just risen before he had entered the portal, giving them a full day. But the threat still dominated, and Oran knew the night *would* come again and, with it, the last light of the moon, which would then be devoured by the glory of another new day—and, hopefully, *Victory!* But there would be nothing to glorify if Gill failed to secure the Shenn. It was vital that the sacred amulet bonded with its rightful master—and not their enemy.

He stalled, sensing Gill's presence somewhere within the castle, along with a sense of dread, it rising from the pit of his stomach. It reminded him of that Warlock and his son, during the Shenn's infancy: the struggle—not to mention the mystery—surrounding the sacred amulet, and how it could influence its master—should he let it. Each Magus had bonded with it in his unique way. He put that down to the *Chosen One* and the influence his character had on the amulet. But Oran had great faith in his son; Gill was a good boy—no, a good *man*—with good morals, and was pure of heart. He shook the feeling of doubt away, relieved to know Gill was with Kai. He was confident the Servitor would guide his son safely to the Sanctuary of Armistice, for the transformation.

Rest assured by this, Oran pressed on with his task, to retrieve the dagger from its hidden place, and destroy it. It was risky leaving it where it was—*too tempting for thieving hands*— and with no knowledge of Magia Nera's whereabouts … Then, as though it knew his thoughts, he felt the weight of the book in his satchel; it seemed to sense where he was going.

'Do you know your counterpart is here?' he muttered to it with distaste, as if it were listening. The satchel seemed to drag and pull as though the book was responding to his question, and protesting against his intentions. He grunted. 'You will *never* be re-united,' he stated, checking the tie, to make sure it was secure. 'Not while I'm—

' He stopped, detecting the muffled sounds of indistinctive echoes above, somewhere in the vast reaches of the castle. He looked up, listening hard, in an attempt to distinguish their source, but was now aware of the castles' deception; nothing was as it seemed.

The flame flickered when a cold draught brushed by him, carrying with it the heavy stench of dampness. It lingered on his senses, forcing him to cover his nose and mouth, and as it passed he looked sharp, to his right, detecting another odour—the distinctive smell beckoning him towards his destination. Oran now knew where he was going.

With Gillis at the forefront of his mind, Oran, carrying the familiar scent on his nose, quickened his pace—the faint echoes above continuing to murmur as he pressed on, occasionally ducking to avoid hitting his head off the uneven roof. The flame cupped in his hand urged him on; though dim, it was sufficient for him to advance, with ease. At times, the echoes seemed to follow his movements, forcing him to stop at intervals to ensure no one was privy to his presence. It was unlikely; the fortress would now be crawling with other Warlocks who had travelled from the far reaches of each Realm, to see their new Magus—some having never witnessed the "coming" before. They would be indulging themselves by now, he knew, in the sumptuous banquet provided for them. His stomach rumbled. *No time to think about food, Oran.* And then there was the Bullwark—the mercenaries of old who were loyal to the Elliyan. They had been gathered from each Realm for the special event, to protect the *Chosen One* and the *Council.* They were a force to contend with, their domineering presence intimidating, in every aspect. But with Magia Nera in allegiance with L'Ordana … He mused over her state of mind, and if her powers had weakened, or … *What if …?* A dreadful thought entered his mind, something that had not occurred to him, until now; if L'Ordana was already in Elboru, would the effects of its past influence the spirit inside her? If that were so, he then questioned the Bullwark's ability to stand up to the challenge of this dark, ancient power, should it reawaken. The possibility was great … and unsettling.

Oran soon felt a subtle incline, and as he rose with it, the powerful aroma grew heavier, alerting him; he was nearing his destination. He glanced down to check his footing, then halted. Lowering the flame, he noticed something beneath its pale, amber glow, on the limestone paving beneath his feet. When he crouched for a closer look, he saw it—the dark, heavy smudge—evidence of their presence, marked by the soles of the owner's boots. He ran his hand over the surface, then rubbed his fingers together; they were damp. Raising the flame, he looked up and narrowed his eyes, able to distinguish their outline along the passage. He rose then moved on, following them, quickly observing their steady pace before stalling again; their pattern had faltered a few paces before continuing, then stretched out ahead with a sense of urgency—the measure of their hasty steps, raising his concern. Had someone else been *there* before him?

He ran.

When the footprints halted in their tracks, Oran stopped and looked down the passage as far as his light would allow him. Beyond its glow, he saw only darkness; nothing stirred within it. He turned his attention to the wall, where the footprints stopped; they were pointing towards it. He lifted his hand, his eyes widening when the flame revealed the seared outline of an arch—the telltale indentation scarring its edge, suggesting its hidden doorway had already been exposed.

'Aye, someone else has been here,' he muttered, nodding, certain of it—the footprints and burnt outline, marking the "concealed" doorway, suggesting the intruder. Wary, he ran his hand over his jaw and contemplated his next move as he eyed it.

'I am going in,' he said as though addressing the flame, then paused. What if the intruder was still in there? 'All the more reason to enter.' Oran let the light travel over the arch for several moments. With lips pressed together and brows drawn tightly, he carefully followed its outline with the flame. As the stone gradually vanished, revealing the hidden door, he drew back, promptly covering his nose when the odour from its priceless agarwood attacked his nostrils. And when he coughed from the pungent resin, he covered his mouth; the smell of the mould emanating from its infected wood was toxic if inhaled too long. But he endured it, knowing it would not linger.

With the door fully exposed, Oran gently leaned against it; it failed to open. He stepped back, surveying it briefly, then, with some carefully-applied force, pushed it, disregarding the risk of disturbing the intruder, should they be loitering inside.

Still, the door refused to budge.

He scratched his head. 'Why do you not open for me?' he mumbled, frustrated. It was as if it had been tampered with. Chewing on his lip, his eyes narrowing, Oran knew he had only one option if he were to enter the chamber—and that would mean damaging the door. He sighed. 'Needs must!' He snatched his hand closed, extinguishing the flame.

Thrown into temporary darkness again, he placed his palms on the dense, dark wood, its touch ice-cold as he moved them about, feeling for its weakness. He stopped, having found it, at its core. Pressing hard, with all his might, he felt the heat of his hands burn into the rare and precious wood, expanding it. As the resin melted, he held his breath from its poisonous fumes and turned his head away from its overpowering stench. He hoped it would not be detected, above. Unlikely; the draughts along the passages would pick it up and carry it away through their crevices, where it would eventually disperse.

As he came to the point of extreme heat, where it became almost unbearable, he recoiled and waited. Oran winced when he looked at the damage he had caused, then sighed. 'Forgive me,' he mumbled as though the chamber's resident was standing beside him. 'I had no choice.'

With one last glance, up and down the passage, Oran, now satisfied there was no threat, or intruder, stepped over the threshold and into the quietness of the chamber, blocking out the sounds above.

Two lanterns still burned, their flames quivering upon his entry. Despite his "permit of entrance" Oran felt like the intruder; after all, this was not his domain. Each Warlock insisted on private quarters, to indulge in his secret passions. Each, also possessed a unique and arcane method of entry, known only to him, unless consent was granted by him, to another. But Oran had been made privy to its access, in the event that something untoward should happen to its resident. However, something *had* been altered, preventing *his* entry. His concerns mounted as he began to doubt his henchman; had he betrayed him? Oran knew, only too well, the outcome, should this be the case: banishment or, worse still, *death!* Or had his confidant been found out, and his whereabouts forced from them? If so, Oran knew the Bullwark would descend at any moment, and haul him away. He threw a glance at the chamber's entrance, then released a sigh of relief, discarding any notion of treachery; his confidant would never betray his presence or trust. Regardless.

Oran's eyes looked over the walls, adorned with the history of its owner's past. Memories of old were displayed for their pleasure, until such time, when they would be parted from them—the treasured items then living on as nothing but a visual reminder of the long and glorious life their owner once led.

Oran could not help but admire the décor; it was filled with souvenirs and tokens of a productive, though turbulent, past—each, more impressive than the other. Some he recognised, others he did not. Curious, he drew closer to inspect their peculiarities, stalling when he heard a soft crunch beneath his feet.

He knelt to pick up the item he stepped on; it was a quill, of the finest quality—the swan's snow-white feather much sought after for its excellence. He mused over its tip; it was caked with dry ink, where its owner forgot to clean it—*no, you would never have neglected it*—or, perhaps, did not have the time to, it hinting at a hasty departure. Oran then let his eyes glide over the chamber. The bed was unkempt; the owner was usually particular about their neatness. *Something made you leave abruptly*, he concluded.

As he picked up the fractured quill, his eyes were drawn to the small, writing table in the corner, beneath one of the lanterns; it was overflowing with parchments—a mix of documents and letters—some of which had broken seals. They looked as if they had been tampered with. His eyes fell to the floor, where some had fallen. *Most unusual*, he thought again of its occupant as he gathered them up, before putting them back on the table. He reached across the clutter, returning the broken quill to its gold inkwell—the little ornate pot stained with dry, black ink.

As Oran's eyes travelled over the chaotic mess, he paused, drawn back to the letters, their words quivering beneath the lantern's flame. None were recent. He could tell by the quality of the documents; they were yellow with age and worn, having been read countless times. However, it was the calibre of the handwriting that grasped his attention.

Moments before being aware of his intrusiveness, Oran took one of the letters in his hand. But as he observed the sender's seal, he felt the tinge of guilt rising inside him, sensing it was of a personal nature. Staring down at the parchment, his devilish guilt began its battle with his spirit of enquiry, along with his suspicions. He continued to toy with the personal item, carefully turning it over, indecisive, as to whether he *should* delve into the private, and intimate, affairs of someone he admired and respected.

But, as with all living creatures, his inquisitive mind promptly won him over. 'To hell with it!' he uttered, then unfolded it.

Oran glanced over the words; they were meaningless—at first—the peculiarity of the writers' language confusing him. He assumed them to be cryptic, to fool the prying eye. *Or a decoy?* He frowned as he studied them.

*"Talk of life … Talk of war…"*

Still at sea over their meaning, he went to cast the letter aside when he noticed a shift in the handwriting. The meaningless script began to flow into the finest calligraphy, opening its secrets to him. As the letters collaborated into words, they began to make sense, and it was clear by the script they had been written by the hand of someone deeply in love. Suddenly, the words leapt out at him: terms of endearment and affection now adorned the page, filling it with the beauty of their poetic voice.

Enamoured by their exquisiteness, Oran let his eyes and fingers caress each word. An element of shame seeped over him as he thought of Rosalyn. Although he knew he would lay down his life for her, he had never shared endearments towards his wife, like the ones lavished upon the bearer of the scroll he held in his hand. Guilt-ridden, he shook his head.

'No—this is wrong,' he admitted. 'I should not be—' He then stopped, his shame pushed aside when he noticed another shift in the writing; it was now erratic and heavy with the weight of anger and betrayal, where the writer had spat words of revenge on the page, with unsettling revelations. He read on … Now fixated, he subconsciously read them out, his eyes then widening in disbelief as he slowly recited the writer's last lines;

'"I will see to it. The flames will not vanquish our love. For I have found a way. I will not let them obliterate you, Eryian. I am yours, forever more …"'

As the letter slipped from his hand, Oran stepped back, shaking his head, stumped by the revelation.

'So, now you know, Oran.'

# Chapter Thirty-Eight

The methodical, heavy beat of regimented footsteps reverberated throughout the castle walls, its echo meandering through its corridors and vast spaces, marking the Bullwark's occupancy.

'Where are you taking us?'

Greer stopped, then hesitated before turning to meet Rosalyn's staunch and enquiring look. He smiled wryly at her before answering; 'Why … to see Lothian—and your son—of course.'

Rosalyn lifted her brows, her face brightening. 'Gill is here?' she asked, a smile appearing on her face.

Greer paused a moment and stared at her, enamoured by her smile and the flush in her cheeks, highlighting her feminine beauty, despite her unwomanly attire; his eyes subtly travelled down her body, undressing her in his mind, then back up, meeting her impatient look. He doubted she had noticed his inclination. 'Indeed,' he said, wearing his smile of deceit again. But when he turned abruptly, making his way deeper into the Great Hall, her smile fell. She knew he was lying; she had caught it in his feigned look as he turned away. His whole demeanour screamed, *liar!* But not only that … her instincts had warned her, too.

*But why would he lie?* she asked herself. A part of her hoped she was wrong and that Gill was safe within the castle walls and being prepared for his new role. But doubt gnawed at her; her intuition seldom let her down. She tried to convince herself she was wrong, grasping onto that ray of hope … but whenever Greer looked back, casting her *that* ominous smile—the one she longed to wipe from his face—she grew uneasy, her instincts persistent in their forewarning. No, she did not trust him—one bit.

Beside her, Daine sensed her restlessness. 'I'll not let them harm you,' he whispered to her.

As though he had heard him, Greer looked back over his shoulder again and smirked, only to have it returned with a sardonic grin from Rosalyn.

Behind them, Wareeshta marched in step with the Bullwark, keeping a close eye on their movements, not that it mattered; she knew they could not take on the mercenaries, despite Daine's brave efforts in the courtyard.

Though armed with the sword that had seemed to buy them time, Daine could not shake off the near-death experience he had felt beneath the Bullwark's threat, their dead-pan stare ever-present in his mind. He cast subtle glances around, keeping his head tilted, searching … He could see no gaps between the Bullwark as they were marched through the hall, their towering size and constant movement limiting his view, and giving him a sense of imprisonment. Any attempt to leave would be impossible.

That was when he knew …

*We are prisoners!*

When Wareeshta drew alongside her colleagues, Daine bent his head sideways, towards her. 'Where's Reece?' he snarled from the side of his mouth, furious at the Dhampir's sudden—and unexpected—departure.

She glared up at him, signalling him to be quiet. She knew Reece was near but did not intend to share that information with their overbearing company.

'It seems your friend has deserted you,' Greer called back. He snorted. 'More's the pity!'

'And what do you mean by that?' snapped Daine, trying to maintain his bravado, though, beneath it, was deeply concerned by the Warlock's cutting remark.

Greer raised his hand, halting the Bullwark, then turned.

Rosalyn's eyes slid towards Daine, throwing him a disparaging look; if he was trying to antagonise the Warlock, too, he was doing a good job of it while risking their lives; one antagonist was enough.

As the High Warlock sauntered towards the guide with a fixed coercive stare, his inquisitive eyes moved to the object sticking out from behind Daine's shoulder.

'How interesting,' he said, indicating with his chin, to the sword nestled on Daine's back—the unusual hilt having snatched his attention. As Greer reached out, extending his hand towards it, Daine stepped back, then jolted, hearing the Bullwark's sudden movement as their attention returned to him. Keeping his hand extended, Greer clicked his fingers and then flicked them, silently telling Daine to hand the weapon over.

*"This sword cannot be taken from its owner; it must be given."*

The words his father—Petrio—had passed on to him, which had come from *his* father, Oran, came to mind. He sneered at Greer and shook his head. With a subtle nod, Greer signalled to one of the mercenaries to step forward. Daine, Rosalyn and Wareeshta's eyes lifted as the Bullwark approached, looming over them.

'May I?' asked Greer, with an air of sarcasm in his tone; he, too, was aware he could not take the weapon, but knew Daine had no choice but to pass it over, his predicament forcing him to.

Daine looked up as the ominous figure staring down at him leaned closer. With great lament for the treasured possession, he reluctantly gave up his sword, his eyes boring into Greer as the Warlock motioned to the mercenary to retreat.

The instant the Albrecht met with Greer's hand, the High Warlock became aware of its origins. He removed it from its leather sheath and lifted it effortlessly. He nodded.

'An impressive piece,' he stated, raising the weapon to the level of his sapphire-blue eyes, admiring its detail for the first time, envious of it. And though his solid hand and thick fingers did not fit the worn, shagreen grip, Greer knew to whom it truly belonged—the fine, gold inlays of sunken reliefs etched in its anomalous steel, bearing the owner's *nomen*; *Oran!* And yet … He glanced at Daine, then back to the sword. 'Quite rare, indeed,' he remarked. 'And unique to its owner. So how did *you* come by it?'

'*Where* are you taking us?!' Daine insisted, disregarding the question he did not want to answer.

Ignoring the feeble demand, Greer's learned eyes slid towards Daine, dancing with enquiry as they searched for clarification. 'And there it is—the *answer!*—staring back at me. It is like looking directly into the eyes of someone I already know.' Rosalyn chewed on her lip and glanced at Daine—the two exchanging their look of worry. 'There is only one way to acquire a sword of this magnitude,' Greer went on. 'So, tell me … What is Oran Shaw to you?' Daine looked sharp. 'Your father, perhaps?' Greer sneered and grunted, amused by his own joke. 'How obtuse of me! Of course, Oran is not your *father*; you are too young.' Greer held Daine's stare, his eyes still dancing wildly as he persisted in his study of the mortal. 'Ah, but yes!' he exclaimed, having worked it out on an existing suspicion. 'You are his *grandson!*' He leaned closer, then slowly nodded. 'You even *look* like him.'

Rosalyn drew a sharp breath; it was how Greer had said it—*"You even look like him"*—with envy and resentment in his tone. *He's jealous!* she realised. It was obvious, by his manner, and the way he occasionally looked at her, with that unsettling wanton stare. And, because of it—she concluded—their situation was becoming ever more threatening as she stared at the sword in the Warlock's hand, her instincts telling her he had no intention of giving it back. Now and then, Greer glanced at her, each sinister and disturbing look making her flesh crawl. She swallowed, silently calling out to her husband. *Where are you, Oran?* He would know what to do. But as things stood, it was evident Greer was doing his utmost to provoke Daine, hoping he would retaliate and try to take back his weapon. An image of the sword—the match to the Albrecht—being thrust into Daine, almost made her heart stop. And when she looked into Greer's eyes, she swore she saw temptation in them, to do just that. She had to do something.

'Take us to Lothian … And my son!' she demanded, stepping in front of Daine, her voice ringing through the Great Hall. She stood staunch, but inside was shaking, fearing she had just signed their death warrants; the Bullwark had regrouped and closed in on them again. But when she felt the presence of Wareeshta beside her, it gave her a sense of solidarity, adding to her strength.

Greer, casting a searing glance at the brave woman, tightened his grip on the great sword, and turned his attention back to Rosalyn; he did not appreciate being told what to do, especially by a woman. *Just like the other one*, he thought.

'Yes!' she returned, nodding, her eyes widening, challenging him with her wild stare. '*My* son, *your* Magus! And you would be wise to be mindful of it,' she added. No, she would not give him the upper hand. As Daine pressed his lips together, trying to contain his smugness, he saw Greer shift—the High Warlock suddenly uneased by Rosalyn's blatant reminder as her sharp tongue continued to spit words of venom, while pointing her finger of authority at him.

During Rosalyn's rant, Wareeshta's keen eyes flicked about looking for a way to escape. The Great Hall was vast. She glanced up; its ceiling seemed to disappear into the rafters, above the great lanterns, overhead. Huge beams stretched across the wide space. Her eyes lowered subtly, drifting along the walls, then moved across the huge pylons lining the hall. She noted small scattered arches cut deep into the stone, between them. *Exists?* she wondered. Could she risk it? Speed was her ally. She contemplated it, despite not knowing where they would lead, regardless. But how could she tell Rosalyn and Daine she was not deserting them, either? She knew where Reece had gone. She had heard it, too—the faint and familiar sound of clashing blades.

She had to find him—and the others.

Her decision was made. It would only take seconds. That was all she needed.

With one last glance, to be sure, Wareeshta took her bold risk and ran, darting through the small spaces between the mercenaries, who were too preoccupied with another of Rosalyn's distractions to notice.

Save for one.

'Find her!' Greer bellowed, throwing the Great Hall into a storm of chaos as the Bullwark acted on his order; he had pre-empted Wareeshta's intentions, his vigilant eyes catching a glimpse of her as she disappeared behind one of the pylons and into its shadow. The mercenaries changed positions—some remaining, some in pursuit of Wareeshta, their departure brisk and as sudden as the Dhampir's.

Rosalyn and Daine spun, their eyes darting about, caught up in the confusion as the remaining mercenaries fell into a constant and confusing march about the hall.

'I have a bad feeling about—'

'Where's Warees—' Rosalyn gasped, feeling a sudden hard shove, it momentarily disorienting her. When she found her bearings again, she frantically searched through the mayhem for Daine, but could not see him. Had he followed Wareeshta, leaving her behind? *No*, she thought. *He would never…* It was when some of the mercenaries left in pursuit of the Dhampir—and with no sign of Daine—Rosalyn realised what had occurred.

Feeling abandoned, yet again, and left to the mercy of Greer and the other Bullwark, Rosalyn's bravado fell by the wayside as her emotions took over, disrupting her self-control. As her mouth slowly opened to call after Wareeshta, she cried out in pain, feeling the tight grip on her wrist. She reeled as it was twisted and yanked in a bid to drag her away. She looked sharp over her shoulder, her mouth gaping, then opening and closing, unable to speak, seeing their hungry eyes staring back at her. As Greer pulled her towards him, Rosalyn glanced down at the Albrecht, still in his grip. She shook her head, eyes wide with fear.

'You are coming with me,' he sneered.

Unable to find her voice, Rosalyn shook her head again, defiant. His grip tightened. Desperate, she looked back, searching for Daine through the chaos; he was still nowhere to be seen. Taking a deep breath, she opened her mouth to call him but was left breathless when she was wrenched off her feet and into Greer's clutches. Trying to catch her breath, she stared at the High Warlock. He grinned and slowly shook his head at her.

Finally, her words came …

'I'm going *nowhere* with you!' she retaliated, gritting her teeth as she tried to wrench her wrist from his steady hold. But seeing the madness behind the striking blue eyes, she feared Greer's intentions. When survival instinct kicked in, Rosalyn struck out and, tearing at the hand that would do her harm, she dug her nails deep, puncturing his skin until she drew blood. Greer winced and let go of her, dropping the Albrecht in the process. Seeing this, Rosalyn dropped to her knees and pushed the sword away from them into the eye of the chaos, hoping it would find its master again.

'*You!*'

Rosalyn looked up, hearing the rage in Greer's voice. His face was crimson, matching the blood on his mouth, where he had licked the wound she inflicted on him.

This was her opportunity to flee; she scrambled to her feet, almost stumbling when his voice roared again.

'*Take her!*' he yelled, pointing at his target.

Rosalyn drew her breath. Without looking back, she knew. *Run!* her inner voice screamed. Her eyes flashed about, looking for somewhere—*anywhere!*—to flee, from what had now become a fight for survival.

Then she spotted it—*a gap!*—her flicker of hope. *Now Rosalyn!* Wrist still throbbing from Greer's hold, she made for it, her breath exasperated and her heart thumping wildly as she sought her freedom.

Rosalyn's sudden high-pitched cry echoed as the pain shot up her right arm. She had heard it first—the clean snap, then the crunch of bone before the assault of severe pain—the Bullwark's grip being stronger than Greer's. Instantly, she knew her wrist was broken, shattered, and marking the seriousness of her evolving situation. She was now in trouble—more than she realised—with the long finger of death beckoning. Once again, she cried out through the searing pain.

On hearing the trauma in her voice, Daine craned his neck, desperately searching for her through the Bullwark's intense march.

He froze, seeing her.

'Oh, God! No! Rosalyn!'

But he could not reach her.

Daine panicked, his heart then skipping a beat when she slumped, lifeless, into the arms of the mercenary as he carried her away, out of sight … with Greer close behind.

# Chapter Thirty-Nine

Gill's concentration was disturbed by the faint, haunting echo of a woman's distressful cry. Forced back from the wall, which he now knew would take him to the Sanctuary of Armistice, he spun and faced the direction from where the cry came … beyond his reach. He approached the wall again, tilting his head. Had he imagined it? He cocked his ear to listen, his brows then knitting, hearing a dull, heavy rhythmic beat; he touched the wall, feeling its slight vibration.

'What is that?' he muttered. Kai followed his gaze, having heard it, too. 'Can you—' Gill jolted, hearing it again—the cry, like a lament, as if it were trying to reach out to him. He drew back, eyes wide, staring at the wall when he recognised it. 'Rosalyn!' Gill turned to meet the Servitor's look of concern. 'Maw is here, Kai! Somewhere! She's in danger!'

But the Servitor continued to stare at Gill, his mind full of worrying thoughts; with them so close to the Sanctuary—and on the brink of gaining entry—they were now faced with this new dilemma, not to mention their predicament: the sway of the pendulum was slowing and would take Gill with it, should they delay.

Kai shook his head. He had to make Gill understand.

'I know what you are thinking,' said Gill. 'I feel the same; behind me lies the Sanctuary, while there'—he pointed—'behind you—beyond *that* wall—my mother needs help. I—I cannot ignore her, despite the risk. If—' He stopped. 'If I—' Gill stumbled, reaching out again for something to support him. The dizziness and weakness had returned, ten-fold, bringing him to his knees, and with it, deep-rooted nausea. He heaved—the taste of bile rising, coating his mouth; he drew his hand over it and swallowed, almost heaving again.

Anxious, Kai moved towards Gill, and as he stared down at their would-be ruler, seeing his drooping lids and waxen skin, the Servitor realised the seriousness of their dilemma; if they did not get out, the future Magus would soon lose consciousness, and might even … He refused to think *that!* At least, not yet. He prayed Gill's life-threatening symptoms would pass, like before.

Kai looked up at the wall, where they had heard Rosalyn's cry from the other side, then back to Gill. Given the choice of who would live and who would die, the Servitor knew there would be none to make, in these final hours. For all that he felt for Rosalyn and her family, in the end, Gill had to live if mankind was to survive.

'Gill, my duty is to protect the true Magus—*you!* I made a vow. As long as I am in his company—*yours*—I am bound by it, but …'

Gill, panting with exhaustion and sickness, looked up at the Servitor through his leaden eyes; Kai noted the tiny flecks of gold in his irises, their glint now tarnished and slowly diminishing. Was this the beginning of his gradual decline? Intuition told Kai so—along with the obvious sense of foreboding. It was inevitable. Gill was going to die, unless … Torn between the head's logic and the heart's deep-rooted love, Kai knew he had to act on his inner dread.

'As a *Servitor*, I cannot interfere with your decisions.' Gill released a long-winded groan, feeling the pull on his destiny—and what was rightfully his—gradually loosen. 'However,' Kai went on, transforming himself again. 'I can help you in the *human* form you grew up with. *They* never said anything about *that*.'

Gill forced a half-hearted, lopsided smile when the Kai he knew so well now beamed down at him, winking.

Aided by his close friend, Gill struggled to his feet once again—the two then facing the wall where they had heard Rosalyn's cry.

'Where … does it lead?' he mumbled, holding on to Kai while trying to steady his breathing—the tightness in his chest temporarily restricting him. He gulped for air, then winced, feeling a crushing pain across his chest as though the castle walls were closing in, suffocating him, rendering him incapable. He coughed, hoping it would help. 'Where—' He coughed again, grasping his chest.

'To the Great Hall of Eminence,' said Kai, his concern deepening, sensed by Gill's dependency on him. 'It is adjacent to the Sanctuary. Fight it, Gill! You *must* fight it!'

Hastened by the desperation in Kai's voice, Gill nodded; he knew he had to focus and connect with the wall and its inscriptions if they were to reach his mother.

Gradually, the pain and nausea subsided. But his head still spun; he shook it, trying to cast the recurring dizziness away. Taking a deep, steady breath, he went to work. Letting his eyes roam over the ancient text, he took it in. Once again, the words leapt out; his head jerked back as they attacked him, with such velocity he found it challenging to decipher them.

'Find it, Gill,' Kai urged, bearing the weight of his friend's weakening body.

But still, the dizziness plagued him, bringing with it frustration as he struggled to take control of the words. 'Damn you!' he snarled, clenching his fists and shoving Kai away. Gill drew back his arms, preparing to pound the wall's hard surface with the last of his strength. Suddenly, he stopped. Lowering his hands to his side, he drew another deep breath, his eyes widening, mesmerised. Floating before him, in full view, he could now read the text—the words appearing to him in their most simplistic form.

*"Enter Stealthily."*

'I found it!' he whispered as if to keep it their secret.

'Then let us not waste time,' said Kai—the clamour in his voice prominent.

Now, fully reliant on the support of his friend, Gill placed his hands against the point of pressure where the text had guided him … and then pushed.

Nothing happened.

'My—my strength, Kai … I can't …'

Still holding on to Gill, Kai placed his free hand over his friend's and, together, with his added strength, they pushed.

The wall groaned in protest as though being forced into oblivion, releasing a musty smell into the chamber as a gap appeared, and with each shove it widened, giving enough space to release its two prisoners.

'Let's find her, Kai,' said Gill, ready to plough on, regardless.

'Not without *this*.'

Gill's face fell when he turned and saw his Albrecht in the Servitor's grip. 'How did I …? How could I have …?' He shook his head.

'You dropped it when we entered the chamber.'

'I don't remember,' said Gill, stumped.

'All that matters is that you have it,' said Kai, handing it back. 'Now, let us not delay.'

The passage, which ran parallel to the Great Hall, stretched out ahead, allowing them to move abreast of one another. It was unusual in that they could see clearly in front of them. Where the light came from, they did not know—nor did they care. Their progress, however, was slow; despite his broad physique, Gill's weakened body felt heavy and lethargic, as if the castle's weight had shifted, pressing down on him, challenging him in the final leg of his journey.

As Gill clung to the Servitor, Kai stretched his arm around his friend's waist, to bear the brunt of his burden. But as they moved further into the passage, they felt an unexpected rise in its route and along with it a sudden, overwhelming sense of euphoria, as though they were ascending to an ethereal plane. It lifted their spirits, particularly Gill's; he felt his strength return, injecting energy into every fibre of his body, driving him on. He gripped the Albrecht.

With no knowledge of how long it would last, Gill and Kai took advantage of the reprieve and made for the Great Hall of Eminence.

# Chapter Forty

'Is this true?!' Oran demanded, pointing to the letter he dropped, still reeling from the words he had read—and what they had revealed. 'That it was *you* who stole her spirit, and not—'

'No!' Lothian retorted, bending to retrieve his letter, his eyes momentarily resting on the precious parchment as he rose, drawing it to his chest. He then looked up at Oran, shaking his head. 'It *was* Magia Nera who stole it, after. Not I!'

'But—but this … *Sorceress* … here in your—'

'Eryian,' Lothian snapped, correcting Oran as though the High Warlock had insulted him.

'*You* were her secret lover?'

'Something I am not ashamed of,' Lothian hit back. 'Nor shall I …' He paused, seeing the leather satchel, hanging from Oran's side. 'You still have it!' He moved towards him, his hand extended, expecting Oran to hand it over.

Shaking his head, Oran stepped away from Lothian's sluggish advance but was forced to stop—the table behind, obstructing him.

'It stays with *me*,' he stated, warning his superior off with a sideward look. 'In the meantime,' he continued, '*you* have some explaining to do, Lord Lothian.'

The Great Warlock released a long sigh before starting. 'Eryian was'—Lothian smiled to himself—'*unique*, amongst her kind,' he said. 'Her powers surpassed those of many a Great Warlock and, because of it, the Elliyan invited her into their *Council*—a great honour indeed, for a Sorceress. She was the first female to enter the consortium'—he then released a heavy sigh of regret—'and the last. Because of her sex, we were all warned: a relationship between a Sorceress and a Warlock was forbidden. It was thought it would … dull our senses—taint our powers—so to speak.

'I was assigned to teach her our ways …' He lingered on a private memory, then continued; 'I found her … captivating, and, in return for my tutoring, she secretly taught me much about her—equally unique—spells, some of which were—and still are—frowned upon, by the Elliyan. 'Over time, we grew … close.' He shrugged. 'It was inevitable that we would become lovers, developing a deep love and respect for one another. It was unbearable—the burden of our secret—but imperative it remained so; we were aware of the consequences, should we be found out.' He paused, closing his eyes. 'But, despite our efforts to hide our secret, we were betrayed.'

'By whom?'

Lothian lifted his narrow shoulders and opened his eyes, their unique colour now almost lost in the shallow light of his chamber. He tightly grasped the letter in his hand; it had been his last one to her—the one she never received. His heart still ached from her loss and their separation, despite the passage of time.

'I can only assume it was Magia, however, I had no proof against his denial, at the time. Regardless, it signalled the end for us. She was condemned to death, while I …' He shook his head slowly. 'Her punishment was senseless and unnecessary, whereas mine … well … my *exemption* was to be my burden—my sentence—to remind me of our "crime" as it was put. So unjust.'

'What did you do?'

'I pleaded with them to let her live. I suggested banishment as her penalty and striping her of her powers … But alas! I, too, committed a "crime". I had disobeyed the rules. But I was desperate; sometimes one's desperation feeds another's greed. That was when Magia Nera approached me. He took advantage of my vulnerability, by proposing something bold and daring. It was a huge risk—one, I was, at first, unwilling to participate. But Magia, whose interests are purely self-serving, is, as you know, persuasive when an enticing opportunity arises. However, through my desperation, I failed to see his sinister motive and went along with his plan.'

'I'm confused,' said Oran. 'This happened before *my* time. How could Magia Nera have possibly…?'

'With his in-depth knowledge of the *Black Arts*, Oran—and with that kind of power—Magia is capable of anything. Oh, yes, your fellow Warlock has been around longer than you realise.'

Oran shook his head in disbelief.

'How long have you known it was *her?*'

Lothian lowered his eyes in shame. 'I realised when … you were summoned here.'

Oran drew his head back, his eyes wide. 'But you were *there*—when I told the Elliyan what Magia had done to Kristene. You *knew* your lover's spirit resided inside her, then? And yet, you said nothing.' Oran, his anger rising, glared at the Great Warlock. 'You should have told me, Lothian!'

'And for that, I am truly sorry, Oran. But the risk was too great. Far too great. You must understand the reason for my silence; had I admitted knowing that it was Eryian's spirit inside the woman you call, *Kristene*—they would have punished me for withholding that information and conspiring against them.'

Oran shook his head.

'What were you thinking of?'

'I was thinking of *her*. Would you not have done the same?'

'I—' Oran stopped himself, then sighed, nodding his admission; had it been Rosalyn … yes, he would have done the same. 'What happened, then?'

'As she burned, like a common witch, Magia used a spell to remove her spirit before she reached the point of death. I did not know if it would work.' He hesitated and closed his eyes, still seeing the image of the pyre as it took Eryian. 'They forced me to watch, you know—as another form of punishment.'

'I am sorry,' said Oran, his voice low and sympathetic.

'I threw myself on my knees and buried my head in my hands as the stench of her burning flesh filled the air. That smell has clung to my senses ever since, as a constant reminder—not that I need it. When it was over, I locked myself away in my chamber to mourn her loss, thinking we had failed in our conspiracy. But when her spirit came to me that night, I was overwhelmed. But I knew the Elliyan could never find out. Therefore, Magia sent her to *Purgatory* for … shall we say… safe-keeping? Each night, after that, she visited me in my dreams—and so vividly, too—where we spoke and planned a future together.'

Oran stared at the Great Warlock, stumped by what he was hearing. 'And, naturally, Magia wanted something in return,' he stated. 'I somehow doubt he did it from the goodness of his black heart. Not his style.'

Lothian released a short grunt. 'But, of course! Knowing Eryian was … "safe" … *I* had to honour my part of the bargain.'

'Which was …?'

'To convince the Elliyan to release him from *Council*.'

'Which they refused.'

Lothian nodded.

'And, because of that refusal, Magia denied me more visits from Eryian until he was granted "leave", as he casually put it. He had full control of her spirit, whereas I had none. And yet, somehow, I continued to sense her presence lingering, and so kept it to myself. It was better than nothing. Knowing she was still with me, in a sense, I continued to make my pleas to the Elliyan—to release Magia—telling them he could not be trusted, and that we were better off without his influential ways. But, when my pleas were met with dismissals and suspicions, I ceased asking.'

'When did he take her from you?'

'After the battle of Wallachia—when we presumed him dead. I must admit … I was, to my shame … relieved; my secret was then mine to keep—and mine only. Or so I thought. With Magia gone, I made it my mission to find a way to free Eryian.'

'Could *you* not have done so—released her from Purgatory—like you can with the Servitor?'

'Oh, I tried, Oran. But remember, we were dealing with the *Black Arts*—and still are. Also, we did not bank on Tepés' intervention.'

'I, too, was convinced Magia had been killed,' said Oran, nodding. 'I saw for myself how he fell. I was sure Vlad Tepés had destroyed him. I never expected him to indulge Magia with eternal life, though.'

'Therefore, allowing him to walk among the dead,' added Lothian. 'It gave him access to their world and their secrets—and *her*. It was *then* he decided to steal her spirit, by plucking it from Purgatory, for himself. I knew something had happened when I no longer felt her presence. The void was unbearable. When you were summoned to Elboru, with the unexpected revelation that Magia was—*is*—alive, nor alone—I knew it was her.'

Oran hummed in thought, nodding to himself, his eyes fixed, thinking …

Lothian probed into the High Warlock's contemplative stare. He opened his mouth to speak, but hesitated—the words hanging from his tongue … He *had* to know. 'Is—is she—Kristene …?'

'No—she—*L'Ordana*—is not dead,' Oran blurted, still trying to detach himself from their tumultuous past.

Lothian closed his eyes and nodded with relief. For a moment he saw Eryian's face, and with such clarity, it was as if she were there in front of him; her thick, long hair still shone like pale gold and was tied back, emphasising her heart-shaped face; and her eyes, the colour of teal, smiled at him with the warmth only he knew, and had never forgotten. And when she smiled, his heart swelled with joy and an overwhelming ache. *Oh, my love.* He yearned for the moment to last, not wanting to open his eyes, hoping against all hope they could be together again.

His eyes flashed open when the image was cruelly snatched from him. He looked sharp at Oran, his eager face now bright and filled with enquiry.

'Aye,' said Oran, nodding, seeing the Great Warlock's look. 'She is also *here*.'

Lothian gasped, his mind fevered with expectation as Oran's words echoed inside him:

*"She is here! She is here!"*

Eryian was no longer a thought or memory.

# Chapter Forty-One

A glint appeared in Lothian's amethyst eyes at the thought of her presence, her nearness. He stared at Oran, his eyes alive with renewed youth … and hope.

'Remember … L'Ordana is not alone,' Oran stated, anticipating more questions; he needed to remind the Great Warlock of the grim reality, and seriousness of their unfolding situation.

Lothian slowly nodded in understanding, more than aware of it. But he had allowed himself to briefly forget, letting the weakness from his past dull his mind, to relive the memory of a love that had been doomed from the start, despite his feelings.

'I think, by now, it is obvious who her travelling companion is,' he said. He grunted, a slight smirk appearing on his mouth.

'What amuses you?' said Oran.

'Did you know the name "L'Ordana" was his mother's?'

Oran lifted a brow, hearing this; it was difficult to imagine Magia Nera possessing any sentiment, let alone having a mother, or visualising him as a bairn, nestled in her bosom. He shook his head at the irony of it.

'A clever decoy—using his mother's name—to conceal the true identity of the spirit inside your *Kristene*. It seems Magia has purloined something belonging to us, Oran.'

'And has complete control of it, too.'

'But for how long?' Lothian returned. 'Eryian was powerful and knew the history behind the Shenn. She may be trying to gain control. Should that happen, I can assure you she will come seeking revenge against the Elliyan, for her wrongful death. Also, we do not know the extent of her powers, whether they are weakening or growing, the closer she—*L'Ordana*—gets.'

'Which is why I need the dagger,' said Oran. 'Merely as a precaution,' he added.

'We can, at least, be thankful you still have the book,' said Lothian with some relief, eyeing the satchel.

Oran smiled, nodding. Though tempted to share it with the Great Warlock, he decided to withhold his vow to Wareeshta; if the Elliyan knew he had promised to return the book to the Dhampir, they would take it from him. *That's not going to happen*, he thought. 'With their combined powers they could be useful, should we need them.'

Oran moved aside when Lothian brushed by him towards the table. The Great Warlock surveyed the mess, with no recollection of leaving it in such disorder. But with his mind on upcoming events, he shrugged off his untidiness, blaming the torrent of his years; even *he* was prone to thoughtless moments, as rare as they were. His eyes filled with sadness, then resentment as he stared down at the emotions he had poured onto the pages, a lifetime ago, now laid bare for probing eyes.

'I am as much to blame as *they* are—for her hatred,' he mumbled. He sighed before anger consumed him. In a rare moment of rage, Lothian tore to shreds the last letter he had written to her before Oran's startled eyes, then looked up at him. 'Do you know where they are?' he urged.

Oran shook his head.

'But I know they are somewhere within these walls.'

Lothian looked away in a moment of thought, then slowly nodded.

'We do have an advantage over Magia,' he stated, throwing him a mischievous wink. Oran second-glanced him, raising a brow. 'While the inner portal remains wide open, time is not quite on our side. However …' He paused, raising his hand, his finger pointing up as he waited for his mind to retrieve an undisclosed secret.

'Our advantage?' Oran prompted, his curious eyes following

Lothian as he slowly paced back and forth, treading on the torn pieces of parchment scattered on the floor.

Lothian stopped and grinned. 'This castle is immense, Oran. Do not let its façade fool you.' The old Warlock then turned and faced the fine weaponry adorning his walls, recalling, with pride, the many battles he had fought—and won—using them. 'You see, years of confinement nurtured my curiosity,' he went on. 'With time on my hands, that same curiosity evoked my interest further. And, in doing so, the castle was kind enough to give up its secrets to me. It is riddled with passageways above and below us …' He hesitated, this time casting Oran a cunning eye. '… more than you can know. There are secret corridors I never knew existed. I imagine one could spend a lifetime here without knowing all its mysteries.' When his eyes fell to the floor, he tapped it with his foot. 'Even beneath us, there are endless catacombs.'

'Have you—' Lothian returned a sly look to his friend. Oran's mouth widened to a grin, and he nodded. 'But of course, you have!'

'I have cleverly mapped out the ones I discovered—their length and destination—' He stopped, a curl appearing at the side of his mouth. 'There is one in particular which bypasses the Great Hall, leading back to the Cordhu Pass, and beyond it.'

Oran's eyes widened. 'There is?'

'Oh, yes. Granted, it is not for the faint-hearted; its width is confining and the ground unsteady. Someone of your height and stature would have difficulty pursuing it, though … it is not entirely impossible. It runs deep, beneath our feet, through the catacombs—so deep it runs in line with the great forest and the Ardmanoth mountains. It is a long and arduous journey but manageable. I have undertaken it.'

Oran stared at the frail Warlock with astonishment, trying to visualise his expedition, then with a sudden realisation said, 'Perhaps you should have kept going.'

Lothian lifted his shoulders, stretching his face. 'Oh, I

contemplated leaving this place, but … Look at me, Oran; I am too old, and my powers are not what they were. But as I stood with Elboru at my back, and freedom before me, beckoning, I saw nothing to entice me. I am ingrained in these walls and shall eventually die, where my ashes will then be interred within one of the Great Hall's pylons. No, it is too late for me, Oran … but not for you. Should you and your family survive all this, I want you to use this specific passage—to gain your freedom. I will entrust this secret to you—and *only* you.'

'But … I thought there was only one way to avoid the Cordhu Pass—through the mountains—until nature intervened, destroying it.'

'Nature?' Lothian shook his head. 'I question its interference.'

'You do?'

The Great Warlock nodded.

'The timing of its destruction was rather convenient, I would say.'

'Sabotage, you think?' said Oran.

'Call it a … *hunch?* Ah, but Oran, my friend … regardless of it, there is *always* another way; you just have to know where and how to find it.'

'So, where is it—this passage?'

Lothian approached the wall of weapons and placed his hand on a small, blunt dagger, purposely placed among the array of magnificent weapons, as a decoy; unappealing in design, he knew it would go unnoticed. Carefully, he removed it. A tiny, well-camouflaged notch, barely visible to the naked eye, revealed itself on the Great Warlock's command when his voice dropped to a near whisper; Oran heard the word *"Eryian"* sigh from Lothian's mouth as he waved his palm across its surface.

For a moment, nothing happened. But when he heard the scratching, grinding sound of stone against stone, Lothian stepped back as the wall inched away, to reveal what waited behind.

'This passage bypasses the Great Hall. However, you cannot gain entrance to the hall itself. Thankfully. It is impenetrable; its walls are so thick that they blanket any sound, travelling between the castle walls. It aligns with our chambers before descending into a long, steep passage, below the ground. Its route is perhaps a day's journey, at most, but distance enough to take you from here. Remember it, Oran … you may need it.'

'I'll not forget it, my friend, nor *her* name,' he vowed as he stared into its dead blackness, his mind an array of thoughts and deeds as he pondered its lengthy route. 'We had a child, you know,' he blurted as he hovered at the entrance, feeling the draught pinch his skin.

'A *child?*' said Lothian—the unexpected revelation evident by his heightened tone.

Oran turned and nodded.

'Aye—Kristene and I,' he confessed.

'You are full of surprises, my friend.'

'As are you,' Oran returned; he glanced at the parchments, then looked down to where the scattered remnants of Lothian's torn past were strewn on the floor, like dead rose petals. The two friends held each other's look of mutual understanding. 'However, to our shame ... we abandoned him. But Kristene was not who she was, then,' he quickly added, in her defence. 'Whereas, I'—he sighed with regret, slowly shaking his head—'should never have left our son in Triora. But I had no choice. To take him with me would have been ludicrous, given the treacherous circumstances!'

'You mean—the boy I saw with your servant—when they fled the great house …?' asked Lothian, somewhat taken aback, recalling the events, when he and Kai kept an eye on Oran. '*He* was your son?'

Oran nodded, seeing in his mind Petrio's little tear-stained face as his old cook, Sofia, comforted him with the promise of new puppies after his dogs were slain, by L'Ordana.

'All these revelations and secrets,' said Lothian, 'will suffocate us, should we allow them.'

'Aye, you are right. And look where they have brought us—to the here and now—forcing us to face them … along with the consequences, which must be put to right.'

'Indeed,' said Lothian. 'But tell me, what became of him—Petrio?'

'He became a man. I made certain he wanted for nothing. I knew I could trust Sofia and her husband to care for him. But it seems Petrio spent his adult life searching for *me*, neglecting his own family. It was after his death, that the search continued, through his son—my *grandson!*—who now stands with his newfound family, prepared to defend them. And, it is because of this, I must make amends and do all I can to protect them. Gillis has accepted his fate, and will make us proud as our Magus.'

Lothian stared at Oran with regret. 'It is our hope he does. Only …' He hesitated, his tone warning Oran of dread. 'We cannot seem to locate Gillis.'

'But I *know* he is here,' insisted Oran. He placed a hand over his heart. 'I can *feel* him—sense his presence. With Kai by his side, I know he reached the portal in time. It is inconceivable to think he should not have made it.'

'And he did, but—'

'Then, where is he? Where is my son, Lothian?'

'We know he entered the portal … However, it was moments before it closed.' Oran looked at him, with unease. 'When this occurred, due to the timing, he would not have entered the Sanctuary of Armistice.'

'What?!' cried Oran, his eyes glaring at the Great Warlock as he tried to grasp his meaning.

'For Gill to have passed through, to enter, the portal should have been static. The timing was wrong—mere seconds too late—and as it began to disperse, it revolved … thus casting him …' His words trailed.

'Where?' Oran persisted.

'We do not know—and we have searched. But the castle is so vast. If he is lost or trapped, Gillis must find his own way.'

'His *own* way?!' cried Oran, his anger rising again. 'And where are the Elliyan?'

'Locked away in *Conclave*, where they must remain, awaiting—'

'Their fate,' Oran interrupted. 'You mean to tell me—they have no knowledge of what is happening beyond the doors that protect them?'

Lothian hung his head in shame.

Oran grunted. 'How presumptuous and ignorant of—' He stopped short and stared at Lothian, his brows drawn. 'Why are *you* not there, with them?'

'I finally told the Elliyan of Eryian's likely return and her possible motive—to seek revenge. I even went further, suggesting she may want to claim the title of Overlord for herself. But they refused to believe such "nonsense" as Lord Tuan put it. For my protests, and for speaking her name, I have been shunned from *Conclave* until your son appears.'

'Then we have no choice, Lothian. We must go to the Great Hall and try to gain entry to the Sanctuary, to warn them.'

A foreboding look cast its shadow over Lothian's weary face as he turned and stared over at his chamber's threshold, out into unknown danger. 'If it is not already too late.'

'We have to *try!*' insisted Oran. 'But first—the dagger. We need to do something about it now, more than ever.'

Lothian, nodding in agreement, turned and made for the wall with its pale, buff-coloured sandstone, then straight for the single block peeping out, with its variable dark, wispy markings. With his delicate touch, it slipped into the crevice of the wall, drawing back. Lothian quickly slid his long, slim hand into the gap. When his fingers touched the plain, silver box, he gasped and recoiled, staring at the gap, grasping his hand; it was ice-cold.

'Lothian?' Oran looked over his shoulder, eyeing the orifice.

Lothian's silence sent a warning to Oran. Acting on fear and instinct, he ushered the Great Warlock aside and, reaching in, pulled out the tin box, shuddering at its icy touch. He flipped the lid open.

Oran drew back in disbelief as he stared into the box, seeing the deep indentation in the salt, which had kept the sinister item at bay.

'It was stolen!'

Oran and Lothian turned to see Lorne—the *boy*; he was scratching his skin, and nervously glancing over his shoulder.

'*You?!*'

'There—there is something I must tell you,' he stammered, casting another cautious look behind him, then back to Oran, his eyes wild with panic when the High Warlock seized him, his enraged eyes boring down into the child's terrified look.

'Start talking!' he demanded. 'Or so help me, Lorne, I will—'

'He—*he* has it.'

Oran drew back, drawing his brows together. '*He?*'

As Lorne shifted nervously under Oran's grip, his eyes darted between the Warlocks before settling on Lothian. He shook his head, silently pleading with the Great Warlock for guidance.

'Answer him,' said Lothian, his tone calm yet firm.

Lorne swallowed, then looked up at Oran.

'And … he also has your wife!'

# Chapter Forty-Two

Rosalyn jolted and sat up, then bent over in agony, cradling her hand against her chest, trying to support her wrist. She looked down, saw it, and winced; it was swollen and bruising—the veins beneath the tightening skin burst and bleeding. She touched it, inhaling sharply and whimpered; the skin was on fire, her face, too, with growing fever. If she did not have the wrist seen to … Her good friend, Blair, entered her mind. If Blair were here, she would fix it. She would know what to do. She would—

'Does it hurt?'

Wrenched from her racing thoughts, Rosalyn looked sharp, then gasped as she met with his searing eyes. She pressed down hard on her lips, fighting against the intense throbbing, her breathing quick and short. Her eyes flashed about the chamber, her mouth gaping, seeing the array of lethal weapons on display—and it smelled, too, of pure masculinity, its mix of deep musk, dry earthy woods and pungent spice, overpowering her female senses. *Where the hell am I?* she thought, then doubled up, grimacing from the pain. Trying to suppress her tears, she closed her eyes tight, then opened them again when she heard his contemptuous grunt.

'It does, doesn't it,' he sneered.

Unable to combat her agony, the tears finally came. Determined, Rosalyn wiped them away with her other hand and glared up at him.

'What'—she winced again, drawing her breath through gritted teeth as she held her arm against her, protecting it from him—'what do you want from me?'

Her captor lifted his brows. 'A fighter, I see—just like *her*.'

Rosalyn shook her head, her deep frown displaying her confusion. 'What? Who do you—'

'His other wife,' Greer cut in, bringing his hand to his mouth. 'I will forgive you this time—for *this!*' he added, licking his wounds, his eyes still on her.

'*Whose* other—' Rosalyn stopped short.

Greer smirked, seeing the realisation in her eyes. 'Did he not tell you?' he taunted. Rosalyn swallowed, staying quiet. 'I thought not. Very secretive, your husband. I wonder what else he has kept from you … lovely Rosalyn.' He moved towards her; she recoiled, her face hardening with hate and disgust at the mere sight of him.

'Oran's past is *his* business, not mine,' she snapped, attempting to show some bravado!

'Sahraya was beautiful, too,' he muttered, reaching to stroke her face.

Rosalyn leaned away to avoid his nauseating touch. 'Sah— Who?'

'You may not look like her'—he pulled back a little, tilting his head while fingering his beard, his eyes undressing her again—'in fact, you are quite the opposite—but you have her same fighting spirit. No doubt it is what attracted him to you, also.'

'Oran is expecting me,' she quickly stated, dismissing his ramblings. 'He will come looking …'

Greer rolled his eyes, then let them rest on her with a dead, sardonic look, telling her otherwise. He grinned and snorted. 'What is there to come looking for, when one is not aware of it?' His face slowly changed, now devoid of emotion, but his wanton look remained on her, filled with menace, it matching his tone. 'I doubt it very much.'

'What do you want from me?' she demanded again.

'Everything *he* has ever had,' Greer retorted. 'As long as I have known your … *husband*, he has had quite the privileged life. Oh, yes, Oran Shaw always got what he wanted. As for me …? I have done nothing but give a life of servitude to the Elliyan—and without asking for much, in return. But they always denied me. And why? Because *your* husband was prioritised over *me!* It was no secret they favoured Oran.'

Rosalyn stared up at Greer, her face mixed with expressions of fear, shock and utter confusion. What had this Warlock's past grievance with Oran got to do with her? It was puzzling, and yet at the same time disturbing.

'Then I suggest you take up your petty grievance with *him!*' she hit back.

Greer's face burned with rage. He leaned towards her again, so close she could smell his breath; it was stale from smoke and bitter fruit, from the wine he had been drinking, earlier—the stain of its burgundy tannins still on his lips. '*Petty?!*' he snarled. 'She was *mine*, and he took her from me.'

When Rosalyn stiffened, he slowly nodded at her—the movement of his head emphasising his striking blue eyes, set off by the sapphire-embedded gold band above them, on his bald head. But as his eyes glowered at her, the beauty of their uniqueness was discarded.

'Yes. Sahraya was truly mine!'

'His—his other wife?'

'She wanted me,' he continued, 'as much as I wanted her. You see, Oran often neglected his wife … Sound familiar? He would leave her for long periods, to go on campaigns. And, while away, he would entrust her into my care, where she received the attention she so rightly deserved. Unlike Oran … I looked after Sahraya.'

*Oh, I bet you did*, Rosalyn thought, eyes narrowing with suspicion.

'We grew close over time and, eventually, I asked her to leave him, to come away with me. *I* would never have neglected her.' He inhaled deeply through his nose, recalling the torment it had caused him. 'But she refused, and then …' He hesitated, his eyes drifting before sliding back to his captive. '… she lied to me—said the child was *his!*'

Rosalyn did a double-take. '*Child?*'

Greer gave her a sideward look. 'But I knew different.'

Rosalyn was struck dumb by this revelation, this other part of her husband's past she knew nothing about. *Another child? Since when?* The image of the lock of hair she had found in the little box, inside Oran's coffer, came back to her. Had it belonged to the child in question, or …? She blinked, woken to something stark, finding herself wanting—*needing*—to ask.

'You say, you *knew* different? In what way did you—' She stopped dead when he stared down his hawk-like nose at her, his blatant look of arrogance unravelling the truth behind his statement. She swallowed. 'You mean—you—' She could not say it, his silent and unnerving admission, momentarily rendering her speechless.

He said nothing. He didn't have to; his guilt was written all over his face.

She slowly nodded as the shock of it sank in.

'Aye, you did,' she stated, then found the courage to speak it. 'You *raped* her!'

*Rape?!*

Greer's initial reaction was one of horror, upon hearing *that* word. But when he recalled the reaction, in the aftermath of his "seduction", his expression changed to smugness, as if to say; "What of it?" 'I can still see how she looked at me, after—with disgust—as if she abhorred my existence.'

'She had every right to—'

'She had no right!' he snapped. 'How do you think it made me feel, seeing *my* daughter grow beneath the wings of another man?'

'You honestly think the child was *yours?*' she persisted, as though it were unspeakable—the mere notion of it!

'Yes!' he roared, his sour, heavy breath, making her want to retch. 'Raya was mine!'

Rosalyn swallowed hard, hearing him speak the child's name; it seemed to bring her back to life, making her *real.* 'And o*nce* makes you think you can claim ownership?' she hurled back at him, suddenly feeling protective of the child. 'Assuming it *was* once?'

'Is *once* not enough?' he retorted, adding further confirmation of his savage actions.

Rosalyn threw her head back, filling his chamber with her scornful laugh—the insult fuelling his anger.

'If I could not have them,' he retaliated, enraged, 'then why should Oran?'

Rosalyn's face dropped at the unthinkable, her mouth gaping. And yet, as much as he repulsed her, she needed to hear it from the offender. 'What—what did you do?' she asked, fearing what her intuition was trying to tell her; as the ominous, crooked grin spread across Greer's face, she instinctively knew ...

'You … *murdered* them!'

'Poor Oran,' he said, tilting his head, feigning sympathy for his fellow Warlock. 'Even to this day, he thinks it was a boating accident—as do the Elliyan.'

Rosalyn, still in shock, slowly shook her head.

'Why you unimaginable bastard!' she lashed out. He glared back at her. 'Had the child been truly yours, you never would have harmed her, let alone …' Rosalyn kept shaking her head, her face fixed, sickened by him. 'Such is the bond a parent has with their child, that they would *die* for them. No, you were *never* her father,' she stated, bending over in agony again as though in mourning for the wrongful deaths.

Reeling from her statement, Greer leaned closer to Rosalyn. 'The pain of it when someone hurts you, eh?' he growled, his eyes almost upon hers.

Rosalyn scowled, shaking her head at him.

'You're insane! Disillusioned! What woman would have *you?*' Then, to add insult to injury, she looked him up and down with distaste before challenging him with her steely gaze. Greer held it, his breathing quick and heavy with loathing; she was glaring at him—the same way Sahraya had after he had had his way with her.

He leaned into Rosalyn's ear; she side-glanced him, repelled by his clammy breath on her skin.

'But *I* would have them,' he replied, his tone dark and menacing. He pulled back, taking in her look, making her see deep within his eyes, and though she tried to divert from his hypnotic stare, she could not. Her breath quivered with fear, and as she tried to swallow her throat tightened.

Rosalyn flinched when Greer suddenly loomed closer, his hands now resting on each side of her. It was then she saw it—the disturbing truth—exposing itself behind his deadpan eyes: she saw the trauma of a woman with skin like copper, and hair like jet—a beauty whose face was contorted with fear. She saw the terror in her bulging eyes as she struggled, shaking her head, trying to cry out. Rosalyn now found herself witnessing it all, through the madness of Greer's hungry eyes—what the woman had endured—and though she could not hear her voice, there was no doubting his victim's words:

*"No! Stop!"*

And there it was—the truth of it—staring back at her. Despite the insanity of it all, Rosalyn now understood—and realised Greer's intentions.

Panic struck.

She would never be able to fight him off with a broken wrist. She felt weak from the pain, from the whole ordeal. And it was not over yet. Her stomach heaved as an image of him …

She shook her head and, as if woken from a nightmare and dragged into the reality of another—the one now facing her—she looked down, suddenly conscious of where she was sitting:

*His bed!*

'No, I won't let you—'

He pushed her back with such force, it momentarily knocked the wind from her. Her eyes slowly widened as he grinned, glancing down at his hand. He nodded, almost amused by it.

'Just like Sahraya.' His eyes travelled down her body. *A minor inconvenience*, he thought, seeing her buckskin trousers, their tightness showing off her shapely thighs. He wanted to see them, let his fingers touch her flesh and … Desperate for her, he yanked away the silk sash from his waist and opened his tunic, his eyes leering at her and his mouth open, wanting to taste her.

Rosalyn's instincts were now screaming, telling her to fight, to survive. She could not let him take her. She would rather die than let *that* happen. But his overbearing and intimidating presence had her trapped. She tried to lean away from him, wincing as she pulled her heavy shawl across her body; he sneered at her pathetic attempt to shield herself.

*"Wait for me, Maw!"*

The last words she had spoken to Onóir returned. If this was to be her end, so be it, but she would not die without a fight. Without another thought, Rosalyn thrust her leg out and kicked Greer hard, between his legs—the heel of her mother's leather boot connecting with his wanting.

Greer doubled over, then looked up at her, his rage evident by the fire in his eyes and the bulging veins in his neck. Rosalyn recoiled, eyes wide, then glanced down to where his hands were cupped. In her moment of nervous victory, she grunted and smirked at him. But her grin of satisfaction was wiped from her face when he shot her a vengeful look.

'Not hard enough, my sweet,' he snarled, humiliated. He contemplated punching her. But, no, he wanted her conscious, wanted her to feel every moment of it, and wanted her to see him as he looked down into her pretty face—not her bloody one—when he took her. The thought of making her cry out through his ecstasy aroused him further. He would make it last. He would make her pay.

Desperate, Rosalyn's eyes darted about the chamber, looking for a way out.

'*You* are going nowhere,' he sneered, then reached for her throat.

# Chapter Forty-Three

It had been brief though sympathetic—the earth-shattering news. But Lothian knew it would have been only a matter of time before Oran found out. However, there was a time and place for everything—and this tragic news could not have come at a worse moment … for everyone involved.

'How long have you known?!' yelled Oran, trying to comprehend what he had just been told. The thought of Greer … He kept asking himself how his fellow High Warlock could have been capable of the heinous crime. Surely, he would have seen the signs, yet … *Too caught up in my selfishness to notice*, he thought—the weight of self-reproach now burdening itself on him. He then caught Lothian and Lorne sharing another ominous glance. 'Stop it!' he snapped at them—the young Servitor jolting at his anger. 'Stop looking at one another, when you know you have no choice but to tell me. How long?!'

'Shortly after you left Elboru—after I had given you the book, in the sacred chamber,' said Lothian, maintaining his air of sympathy. 'I discovered Lorne skulking about. I thought he was spying on us, for Lord Tuan'—he looked at the young Servitor, tilting his head in pity, for the predicament placed upon him—'but, no, he feared for his life. Lorne knew what Greer had done, and had been threatened by him, should he talk.'

Oran glared down at the Servitor. 'My heart *bleeds* for you,' he snarled, through gritted teeth.

Lorne shook his head, wanting—*trying*—to justify his actions and silence.

'I—I could no longer keep it a—'

'Where are they?' Oran snapped, no longer interested in what the Servitor had to say, his concern for Rosalyn now at the forefront of his mind. And as for that murdering …? *I will deal with you myself, Greer.* 'Where did he take my wife? I warn you, Lorne'—he shot a glance at Lothian—'warn *both* of you: if anything happens to—'

'His chamber,' Lorne quickly revealed. 'He took her there.'

'Oran! No!' begged Lothian. 'You must not—'

But Oran had already left.

'What are we to do, Lord Lothian?'

The Great Warlock looked down into the young Servitor's look of anguish, his eyes thinking and head battling against his heart as Lorne waited for his response. Lothian released a long sigh of regret, his eyes now on Oran's desperate—and anger-infused—exit. 'We must alert the Elliyan,' he said. 'Lord Oran must be stopped; despite what has happened Lord Greer *must* be present for the transformation, otherwise …' He turned to the anxious Servitor. 'Go to the Sanctuary. General Ankur Seth of the Bullwark guards the Elliyan, with five others, while they are in *Conclave*. Tell him what has happened. He will inform Tuan.'

Though frail, Lothian, in his desperate bid to stop Oran, found his inner strength to pursue the High Warlock, leaving Lorne to deliver his message. *Let us hope we are not too late.*

His heavy, urgent breathing filled the chamber as he lifted his other leg onto the bed, straddling her as he pinned her to it—one threatening hand balled into a fist, the other on her throat—glaring down at her, his face mottled with anger, jealousy … and lust. He *would* have her—no matter what.

Struggling to breathe under his weight, Rosalyn's eyes widened with terror when Greer's free hand gripped her shawl, ready to tear it from her trembling body. She clung to it with all the strength she could muster up with her left hand, while trying to blank out the burning agony of her broken wrist, fearing she would pass out.

But as he yanked at her shawl, he suddenly flinched and let go of her, drawing his hand away in pain; the thick pin from her brooch had opened and become embedded in his palm, right through. Her mouth gaped as she gulped for air, staring at the precious piece of jewellery, in a moment of joy as if her mother had intervened. *Oh, thank you, Maw!*

But her ordeal was not over …

Greer tensed, staring at the brooch dangling from the pin, swinging loosely before him. And then she saw it—the weapon inside his opened tunic. This was her opportunity. Inwardly she thanked her mother again and her ancestors, for the family trait: of being left-handed. Acting on instinct—and with survival taking precedence—she reached up and snatched the dagger, paying no heed to its sinister design; the dragon had already begun to wrap itself around the unorthodox cross, in a frenzy. She held it out in front of him, her intentions clear.

'You think *that* will kill me?' He snorted, then slowly withdrew the pin from his hand before throwing it aside, his casual discarding of the heirloom infuriating her.

'Only one way to find out!' she stated. She jerked the dagger towards him.

He grunted, then laughed, unconvinced by her. 'It will take more than—' Greer stopped dead—the smug look on his face quickly replaced by one of disbelief. His sapphire-blue eyes turned glassy, then slowly travelled down, seeing the exposed blade; the tip of the dragon's tail had now fully wrapped itself around the unorthodox cross, ready to embrace death, excited by it. Greer jerked, feeling the blade as it turned red-hot inside him. He reached down to grab the hilt, but was too slow; Rosalyn had driven the weapon as deep as she could, holding it there with all her strength, teeth clenched, chest heaving and hand shaking from the sheer effort of it.

They stared at one another for what seemed like an age—the weight of his body measured by the gradual release of life as it slowly drained away. The High Warlock looked down; her hand was still grasped over the hilt as she maintained her grip. He looked up at her, his face contorting—the veins in his throat bulging, feeling the weapon wedged inside him. He opened his mouth to speak, then …

'This is for *her*,' she snarled into his face, 'and *Oran's* child!' With another intake of breath, she braced herself, then shoved the dagger deeper, manipulating it until she felt the warmth of his blood spill out over her hand, staining her skin; she grimaced from its metallic smell.

Rosalyn, her hand now soaked with Greer's impending death, watched as he began to fade, his breath slowing, heavy, foundering. She would wait until it was over, make sure he was dead.

As the remnants of life began to slip from Greer, his body finally slumped against her, forcing her back onto the bed, their eyes still locked on one another. His body was now on top of hers, lifeless, restricting her breathing. She had to break free, before … But as she desperately tried to squirm her way from under him, the unexpected happened …

Greer's eyes flashed open with life and realisation. He drew in a long breath, retrieving what she had tried to take. Rosalyn opened her mouth to call out for help, but the words had lodged in her throat. He began to move, his breathing taking momentum, once again. Now, fully aware of the dagger inside him, and her hand still clamped around the hilt, Greer's eyes bored into hers. She could feel his stale, heavy breath within an inch of her mouth and the coarseness of his beard against her skin. But that was the least of her concerns; what she feared now—what she *knew*—was evident, by the notable shift in his eyes.

He intended to kill her.

Fuelled by madness—and the newfound knowledge that Greer had murdered his first wife and child—Oran, at that moment, could think of nothing else but returning the favour, hell-bent on revenge. His mind raced with images of Sahraya and Raya, imagining their desperate struggle to survive as they tried to fight against the "storm" that was Greer before it took them to their watery grave. In his initial shock, he had questioned it: *Why kill them?* But now he knew, in the way it had been put to him, with heartfelt compassion.

"Jealousy, Oran," Lothian had said. "It was Jealousy that drove Greer to murder them."

His pace quickened as he made his way towards Greer's chamber—the gruesome image still in his mind of Sarahya and Raya, their senseless deaths dragging up the memory of their loss. Two beautiful lives destroyed, by the foulness of two deadly sins: lust and envy. But when another figure entered his head—*Rosalyn!*—he stopped, briefly. Though he still mourned their passing, he knew it was the here and now that mattered; the mere thought of Greer touching his wife … Having learned of the fate of Sahraya and Raya, there was no doubt in Oran's mind that Greer could do the same to Rosalyn.

He ran.

Oran could already feel Greer's on-coming presence, as he neared his chamber, it sickening him to the pit of his stomach. He would kill him—an eye for an eye.

From the minefield of his thoughts, as though he could reach her, Oran muttered through his anxious breath; 'Fight him, Rosalyn! You must fight him!'

The instant he spoke her name, Oran found himself at the entrance to Greer's quarters. He knew they were there, inside, behind its wall. He looked up, his heart racing, his mind in a frenzy as his eyes surveyed the entrance. He had to get to her. Then something clicked inside him, something dreadful: Greer *would* do it. He would kill her to spite him. No, he could not bear the thought of life without

Rosalyn.

He reached out and touched the hard, cold stone and, guiding his hands over its rugged surface, called on the help of his forbears: 'Tekkian, my friend, if you are here with me, in my time of need, *please*, I beg of you, let me enter this place of immorality.'

Oran closed his eyes and concentrated, throwing all his thoughts and energy into saving Rosalyn, knowing she was within feet of him, on the other side. He pressed hard until his fingertips hurt, to the point where he thought they would snap, such was his frantic need to reach her. But the pain eased when he felt the invisible touch of another's on his—the added pressure making his task easier. Finally, it gave way. The stone began to crumble.

'Thank you, my friend,' he whispered as the door fell away.

It took seconds.

Oran stopped dead, stunned, unable to fathom the scene before him. There was no movement as his eyes stared in disbelief at the two figures pinned to the four-poster bed; nor was there a sound. Were they …? Was she …? Had he …?

But when a flicker of movement caught his eye as Rosalyn gasped, struggling for air, he cried out, '*Rosalyn!*'

Her eyes darted, searching for his voice. But as hard as she tried, she could not respond—the weight of Greer's body on top of hers, preventing it. And then it was gone—the power of love, hate and revenge tearing it from her, in an instant.

Dazed, and with eyes still closed, she sobbed—the pain in her wrist now unbearable. She jolted, then froze when their hands gripped her shoulders and eased her up.

'Rosalyn?' She tried to catch her breath. 'Rosalyn!' Oran persisted, his voice guiding her back from her trauma. Trembling from the shock of what had happened she tried to cry, though could not bring on the tears. 'Did he—' He stopped, afraid to ask yet still had to know. 'Did he—'

She shook her head, sparing him the agony of saying it. He sighed with relief and briefly closed his eyes, then took her gently in his arms, holding her, not wanting to let go. She winced again. He could feel her body shudder against his, even though she felt hot to touch. Shock. Fever. He drew back, looking her over, reeling from her dishevelled state and the ordeal she had been put through.

'Oh, Rosalyn, forgive me for involving you in all this,' he begged, seeing the distress on her face, wanting to bear the brunt of her pain—of everything *he* had put her through. He would never forgive himself. When she winced, again, he looked down.

'We need to get that seen-to,' he said, meeting her look.

'Oh, Oran,' she whimpered, 'he did a dreadful thing. He—he murdered …'

'I know,' he said. 'Which is why he deserved to …' He stalled, his brows knitting together when her eyes moved away from his, distracted. And when they widened, he knew why.

Oran spun, quickly pouncing on Greer before he could find his footing; he knew Greer was stronger, given the opportunity. Already, he had begun to remove the dagger from where Rosalyn had embedded it.

Greer fell back against his attacker's weight, his hands now around Oran's throat, in defence.

'You *need* me,' he hissed.

'You think?' Oran replied, his voice hoarse, almost strangled by his aggressor's hold.

Greer sneered up at him. Oran's face twisted with rage as he tried to fight against his antagonist's strength; though smaller in stature, Greer was thick-set, his muscles compact and hard. His hold was getting tighter by the second. Behind them, Rosalyn looked on in horror but was unable to assist her husband, too worn and bent in agony. Both Warlocks rolled and grunted as each fought for their lives.

'Oran!' cried Rosalyn, finding her voice. 'The dagger!'

He heard her.

But as he released his grip to reach for the weapon, it enabled Greer to press harder on his windpipe. Oran, now straining against his hold, could feel his neck stretch and tighten; he could barely breathe now and began to feel his strength wane against Greer's. Should his aggressor get the better of him … Desperate, he reached down again, his fingers groping for the hilt of the dagger. But still, he could not grasp it, feeling the growing numbness in his hand. The situation was looking grim. Behind him, he could hear Rosalyn's voice as she urged him on, it growing weaker to his ears as he began to lose the struggle, his windpipe almost cut off by Greer's tightening grip. *Help me!* he cried in his head, then felt it, once again, Tekkian's intervention. Greer froze, loosening his hold.

Oran drew back, gasping for breath, his mind momentarily clouded. When he heard a voice cry out to him, he found his strength again and glanced down. With no time to lose, he dislodged the dagger from Greer's torso, then lunged it into him again; this time into the centre of his enemy's heart. In an instant, he was freed from Greer's hold—the High Warlock's arms dropping away in dead weight.

But Greer was not quite dead …

Oran hovered over his antagonist, blocking out everything around him as their eyes locked on each other, Greer's mouth opening and closing, trying to speak.

'Need *you?*' Oran grunted. 'I think not, you murderous bastard!' he scorned. 'I *know* what you did …' He leaned closer. 'Nor shall you ever do it again.'

'Oran!' the voice cried out again. 'No!'

'What have you done?'

Oran had driven the dagger so deep that little of the hilt remained visible. Chest heaving, he drew back and stared down at the blood on his hands; it momentarily reminded him of Lucia—his once servant—when he had tried to save her in Triora, many years ago. Again, he had blood on his hands, drawn from the same weapon that had killed the young, innocent woman, and many more. But there was a difference here …

Greer deserved to die.

No one stirred within the chamber. Oran lifted his head and looked back towards the bed where his wife was staring down at him, her face an effigy of pain and disbelief. He rose and went to her, taking her in his arms again, momentarily unaware they were no longer alone.

'What have you done, Oran?'

Lothian stood aghast.

Oran looked sharp at the Great Warlock. 'I have rid ourselves of that'—he pointed to Greer's lifeless body—'*Monster!*'

Lothian shook his head, his hands reaching out to Oran, trying to make him understand the gravity of what he had done in his moment of madness, and what Greer's death would mean to them all—and his son.

'He was going to rape my wife!' Oran yelled, rising from Rosalyn. He marched towards Lothian—the hurt and rage visible on his face. 'What did you think I was going to do, Lothian? Allow him?' Oran shook his head, seething as he breathed heavily through his nose.

'Greer was right,' said Lothian. Oran drew his head back, speechless, his eyes widening. 'We need—*needed*—him for the—'

Oran turned, dismissing Lothian mid-sentence with a grunt, and went to Greer's body. He stood over his corpse, staring down at it with no remorse; it was already showing signs of decay—the dagger's effect doing its work. He was dead all right. His eyes moved to the item near Greer's head, where it had come off when he hit the ground. The gold headband—once, his statement of vanity—now looked tarnished, leaving only an indentation on the dead Warlock's forehead; even its sapphires, which had emphasised Greer's intense blue eyes, had lost their lustre. Oran grunted then yanked Greer's amulet from his neck—the thick chain tearing the skin, leaving it bloody and marked. He turned to Lothian and held it up, like a victor's trophy.

'Tuan said we need all *five!*' he stated. 'All we need now is Magia's.'

Lothian stared at the amulet as it swayed before him—the gold chain stained with Greer's death. He sighed then slowly lifted his eyes, meeting Oran's rage.

'Well?' Oran persisted. 'I assume Lord Tuan was referring to all five amulets, and not—' He stopped dead when he saw Lothian's face—the Great Warlock's grim look and marked silence, telling him all he needed to know as it registered—the consequences of Greer's demise—and what it now meant.

# Chapter Forty-Four

*"I give you this place—this haven—the heart of Elboru, and I shall call it, The Great Hall of Eminence. It is the ethos of who we are and will remain so, for as long as the universe exists. Here, only peace shall dwell alongside the spirits of the great ones who, when time dictates, will glorify within the sanctity of its solitude, for eternity. Together, they will silently reign inside its grandeur while quietly watching those who will follow after, and carry on our traditions. But take heed: do not let the stain of evil mark this sacred place—for sacred it is … and shall remain so, henceforth."*

*Lumeri*

They followed the thunderous sound of constant heavy footfall, along the passageway, it drowning out their voices at first, forcing them into silence until they reached the Great Hall—where it gradually dropped, sustaining a low regimented beat.

Gill and Kai stood dumbfounded by what they were witnessing, as they kept to the shadows behind the pylon where Tekkian's ashes were interred.

The Great Hall had initially been thrown into disorder by Wareeshta's abrupt departure. She had been gone for what seemed like moments, only to return as quickly—and she was not alone. Now, with the return of Reece, Asai and Eleanor, Gill's heart leapt when he saw them, especially his sister, thankful they had found the way to Elboru.

The four, armed Dhampir had entered the castle with such speed that they went unnoticed, weaving their way between and around the

Bullwark's continuous march. Despite their stature, hampering their pace, the Bullwark's skilled precision, however, was flawless.

'Why do they march so?' said Gill, leaning into Kai's ear.

'I believe it is a tactic they use, to confuse the enemy before …' He hesitated.

'Before what?'

'… they attack.'

'Gill stared at the Servitor. '*Attack?*'

Kai nodded.

'It is what they do—to protect this place—should they detect a threat. It seems they are in sync with one another and know when precisely to make their move.' He shrugged. 'This is what I have been led to believe, and yet…' His words trailed, mingling with his thoughts.

'Well?' said Gill, prompting him to continue.

'The Bullwark should be *outside*—in the courtyard—guarding the fortress—not *here*. They are forbidden in the Great Hall. I can only assume they are under orders by … someone … and may have been *sent* here.'

'You believe so?'

Kai nodded.

'But I fail to understand *why*. In my mind …' Kai paused and looked up at the pylon containing the cartouche with Tekkian's name embossed in gold relief, then bent his head slightly towards it. He sensed nothing; it was usual for him to feel the late Warlock's residual energy each time he passed his place of eternal rest. 'It seems to be the only logical reason for their presence here, but …' He shook his head. 'No … Something has happened.'

'If so, then where are the Elliyan? Surely, they must be aware of it.'

'The Elliyan are locked in the Sanctuary of Armistice, in *Conclave*, awaiting your arrival. They would be oblivious to this.'

Gill glanced out at the Bullwark. 'Perhaps *I* should intervene,' he suggested, ready to take action, wanting to step into his impending role and take control.

'Do not even *think* it, Gill,' the Servitor snapped. 'Your present status means nothing to the Bullwark until you are Magus. As it stands, you have no power over them.'

'This is not good,' said Gill. Frantic, he peeped out again, looking through the Hall, his eager eyes now searching for his mother. He took a deep breath; he would chance calling her name.

'Do not,' warned Kai. Gill stalled, watching the Servitor as he assessed the scene. 'She is not here.'

'Then, *where* is she? I heard her—we both heard her and know—' Gill stopped and looked sharp, drawn back into the Hall. He narrowed his eyes, convinced the Bullwark had subtly shifted their formation but was then distracted by something unexpected; someone was waving at him from across the wall of mercenaries, on the other side, while trying to keep themselves concealed, occasionally ducking in and out from behind one of the pylons.

'Look!' said Gill, pointing. It was Daine and he was alone, and reluctant to move from where he was.

'I see him,' said Kai, catching a glimpse of Daine before he dipped from sight again.

'If what you say is true—about an imminent attack,' said Gill, removing his sword, 'then we need to get to *him*—and the others.' But as he made to move from their hiding place, he felt a strong grip on his arm and looked up to see Kai shaking his head, eyes set.

'You cannot take part.'

Gill frowned, drawing his head back. 'What do you mean, I can't—'

'If you are to be Magus, you must enter the Sanctuary pure of heart. You cannot submit yourself with blood on your hands—no matter what happens here.'

Gill stared at the Servitor, perplexed, his eyes then widening, recalling *that* incident with the Samurai and Eleanor's dirk. He gasped.

'Asai! But—did I not …?'

Kai shook his head, as though he had read Gill's thoughts.

'Asai lived … thankfully! It does not count. But whatever happens, Gill, you cannot—as much as you feel the need to do your duty—participate in this.'

Denied the right to fight alongside his family, and protect what was to be rightfully his, Gill slumped with a feeling of defeat and uselessness. He was to be a great Overlord, and yet could not interfere. He looked towards the centre of the Hall where the Dhampir, including his sister, were now circling the Bullwark, both parties eyeing one another; it was reminiscent of the calm before a great storm, with little knowledge of what was yet to come.

The Hall of Eminence was a mass of confusion and dizzying movement. Everything was happening so quickly, Gill's head spun. He lifted his hand and drew it across his forehead, wiping away the prominent beads of sweat.

'Gill?'

'I am all right, Kai,' he insisted, determined to see things through. But Kai was not convinced. 'I wish I knew where Rosalyn was, though.' Gill was still looking, craning his neck from where they remained, hoping to see his mother, but with no sign of her, it caused him concern, knowing she had already been in the Great Hall. And yet, he did not want her to witness what he sensed was about to unfold.

'Perhaps, she is with Oran,' said Kai, offering some reassurance, sensing his unease; he, too, shared Gill's sentiments. Yes, something was wrong—the Bullwark's unlawful presence within the Great Hall, marking its violation, and driving his suspicions.

'Aye, she *must* be,' said Gill, nodding to himself.

'I am certain of it. But, for now, we must think of you, and make our way to the Sanctuary of Armistice.'

'And how are we meant to do that?' said Gill, gesturing towards the centre of the Hall.

'Come with me,' urged Kai, motioning him back into the shadows, so as not to alert the Bullwark to their proximity.

'What about the others?' He caught a glimpse of Eleanor, on the other side; she was pacing about, dirk in hand and eyes set on the mercenaries. His heart skipped a beat, watching her, aware of her eagerness to fight.

'Cast aside your concerns, Gill, *they* are more than capable. Now, come with me.'

They made their way through the Hall's side passage, behind the pylons, keeping to the shadows, pausing at intervals to check their position.

The Bullwark suddenly began to clash their swords against their shields, their perfectly timed rhythm slow and methodical, like a tribal chant, in preparation for something … or perhaps, to send a warning to its enemy.

Relieved to see Gill and Kai, Daine rushed towards them, but as he opened his mouth to speak, he was interrupted by Gill—the young man's concern marked by his adamant approach towards Daine, stealing him of his opportunity to speak first.

'Where is she?' Gill demanded, his eyes flicking back and forth, catching fleeting glimpses of Reece and Wareeshta as they snaked around the Bullwark, who had now come to a standstill—the clash of their armour gradually mounting. 'Where is my mother?' he persisted, raising his voice against the thrumming.

'Taken!' said Daine, stepping back, a little exasperated.

'*Taken?*' Gill's eyes fixed hard on Daine's. 'By whom?'

'One of the Warlocks. Greer.'

'*Greer?*' echoed Kai.

Daine nodded to the Servitor.

'And I fear for her safety.'

Gill leaned towards Daine, his eyes boring into him, waiting for him to elaborate.

'He—he hurt her—broke her wrist, from what I could see.'

Gill recoiled, his face hardening, eyes wide with rage.

'And where were *you* when this happened?' he argued.

'I tried to reach her, but'—he pointed towards the mayhem—'as you can see ...'

Adamant to find his mother—and the Warlock who abducted her—Gill stared out, calculating the risk, should he attempt to brave the Bullwark. He had to risk it. He needed to see her. But as he raised his sword, he stumbled and fell into Daine's embrace. Daine jolted, then steadied himself as he held on to Gill.

'I … I must try … to save her …' Gill's words were slurred and his eyelids heavy.

'No—not now,' said Kai, reaching out to intervene.

'What's happening?' said Daine, almost buckling under Gill's weight.

'He is weakening, and if we do not get him to the Sanctuary on time …' His eyes met Daine's, alerting him to the gravity of their situation. Daine nodded, then looked down when Gill moaned.

'I am … all right,' he mumbled. Though his head was still light, he felt a little of his strength gradually return. But with each relapse, Gill knew he was growing weaker.

'This way,' said Kai, taking hold of his friend.

# Chapter Forty-Five

As they arrived at their temporary haven, Kai transformed himself back to his ghostly form, momentarily illuminating where they now stood, in the deep hollow of an arch.

Kai waved his hand in an upward motion, revealing an opening as the stone melted from them. Then, keeping a watchful eye, the Servitor implored Gill and Daine to cross its threshold. 'It will take us to the Sanctuary's annexe. Let us hope someone is there.' Inside, Kai was deeply concerned; with the Elliyan in *Conclave*—and no sign of their guests, who had travelled for the transformation—his concerns were growing. The *Assembly* and its festivities would have ended by now. Where was everyone? He turned to Daine. 'Do *not* leave Gill's side.'

Together, they followed the Servitor into the darkness, ready to press on when Daine stopped and glanced back over his shoulder, reluctant to continue; there was something he could not—and *would* not—leave behind.

'This way!' urged Kai, beckoning him.

Daine threw an uncertain look at the Servitor then back towards the Great Hall, his brows knitted tightly together, defiant. An icy chill travelled down his spine with a sudden and notable shift in the atmosphere; he could feel its charge, sensing something imminent. Ignoring the Servitor's pleas to follow them, he promptly turned back, then lingered at one of the pylons, focusing, as he surveyed the situation. The energy within the Hall was accelerating. Something big *was* inevitable. Spurred by its charge, he desperately looked for *it*.

'Where are you?' he muttered, his eyes lowering, gliding over the stone floor.

As if in response to his call, the heirloom which was rightfully his—and which rightfully belonged to his family line—glinted as it lay on the ground among the Hall's disorder, waiting for its master to rescue it. He leered at the weapon, anxious to have it back. Wiping his mouth with the back of his hand, he decided …

'Don't be absurd!' snapped Gill, having followed him, pre-empting his intentions, his face crimson. ''Tis madness to even contemplate it!'

'Perhaps I am *Non-Compos Mentis*,' Daine retorted, 'but I will not leave it.'

As Gill reached out to grab hold of him, to make him come to his senses, Daine leapt out right into the core of the Hall, his sudden, brash action instantly alerting the Bullwark.

Chaos erupted, throwing the Great Hall of Eminence into a battle arena.

Daine stooped, avoiding being stomped on by two Bullwark who were now being fought off by Asai—the Samurai displaying his skills in all their glory as he brandished the katana and wakizashi—the two precious weapons glorious together as one, in *Daisho*. Asai glanced down, seeing Daine from the corner of his eye. When he saw the Albrecht sword and realised what he was about, the Samurai swayed his opponents away, giving Daine enough space and time to manoeuvre towards the weapon.

Grateful to Asai for the reprieve, Daine kept low, stopping and starting in his attempt to avoid further clashes. To have come this far—and after experiencing so much—he was not ready to die, just yet.

He looked sharp—the glint of his sword catching his attention again, its influence guiding him closer. He ducked when Wareeshta and Reece fought off their challengers, on each side of him. If he did not move, he would be trampled to death, beneath the Bullwark's heavy footfall. Taking a bold risk, he clambered away, his heart beating loudly when two swords clashed dangerously near; he kept moving, narrowly avoiding their sharp steel, then stalled briefly when his sword was within reach of him.

Now, mere feet from the Albrecht, he scrambled towards it, on all fours. The timing was crucial, and as the fight took momentum—the Dhampir increasing their speed to enhance the Bullwark's confusion—Daine knew he had to act.

*"Do it!"* his instincts yelled at him. *"Now!"*

Daine quickly drew himself up and, leaping forward, reached for his weapon …

But the instant his fingers brushed off the sword's hilt, it was snatched from his grasp. He made a start, hearing the crash of heavy steel on the flagstones—the sparks from the impact, flying up towards his face. As he brushed them away, avoiding their contact, he looked up to see one of the Bullwark peering down at him, dead-eyed and shaking his head slowly, his towering presence making him look and feel like a vulnerable child about to be chastised. But his resistance was unyielding; he refused to be sentenced to death by his own sword, or another's, for that matter.

Daine jumped to his feet. He would make a stand against the sentry, who was now armed with both swords, his Albrecht and its own. As the sentry raised the weapons, ready to strike down his defenceless victim, Daine realised there would be no mercy in this battle; the Bullwark had been trained that way. But in his haste to snatch Daine's sword, the sentry's great shield had fallen to the ground, revealing a small, exposed area of flesh, inches beneath his armpit—their *Achilles Heel!*—and Daine had seen it. For a moment, the lone sentry stalled and looked at the two weapons in his hands, then down at his shield, momentarily indecisive.

*"Strike it!"*

Daine flinched, hearing the voice in his head—his instincts—screaming at him to do so.

'*Now!*'

Acting on it, he reached down and removed the small hunting knife from inside his boot, then plunged it into the exposed area. But the skin was tough like thick leather.

The Bullwark stalled before lifting his arm, then stared down at the dagger hanging loosely from his flesh, somewhat bewildered. Then, to Daine's horror, he removed it with ease and looked down at him with the same blank expression in his eyes, tilting his head at his victim as if questioning their feeble attempt to cause him harm.

*Oh, no! It didn't work!* Convinced he had failed, and fearing his end, Daine scrambled to escape the sentry but stumbled when something knocked against him—the blow hard and disorienting. Everything around him spun. His mind became a minefield of distorted sounds, and among their disorder, he thought he had heard a female voice calling out as he fell.

'*Reece!*'

Wareeshta's cry alerted Reece to the danger; he was closer to Daine at that moment, however, it was she who had seen what had happened. The Dhampir tore himself away in time to catch Daine while snatching the Albrecht from the confused Bullwark, leaving him staring at his empty hand.

'While I admire your courage,' said Reece, hauling Daine away, 'that was a foolish thing you did,' he added, returning his sword to him. 'Remember, you are still *mortal!*'

The brutal reminder struck Daine, hard. Reece was right; his recklessness had instigated the battle. What made him think he was invincible? Being the bearer of a Warlock's sword? And yet, a Warlock's blood ran through his veins. He was a Warlock's grandson. Not only was he aware of it, but he also *felt* it, and its driving effect.

Now safely returned to the shadows—along with stern looks from Kai and Gill—Daine raised his hands in a plea of defence. 'I know,' he said. 'Reece already had his say on the matter.'

Reece turned to Kai.

'Why do they fight us?' he asked, glancing back, checking on Asai, Eleanor and Wareeshta, who were still in combat. 'Their persistence is relentless. We seem to be going round in circles, with ill effect. Are they not duty-bound to Gill?'

'Not until he is Magus,' Kai stated.

'If that is so,' said Reece, 'then *who* controls them?'

'No doubt the influence of another,' he replied. 'This Great Hall is a peaceful place. What is happening here is sacrilege!'

'We cannot seem to penetrate their defences,' Reece admitted. 'We could go on like this, indefinitely, chasing one another's tails. It is as though their clothing protects them, not their shield. I have struck their armour—*hard*—but still they persist. Why is that?'

Kai shook his head.

'My knowledge of the Bullwark is … rather limited,' he said. 'I cannot—'

'They have a weakness!' Daine blurted, still catching his breath. Reece frowned, unsure. 'Behind their shield—beneath the armpit—there is a small opening. It exposes their flesh. I tried but failed to—'

*'Eleanor!'*

Oran's voice erupted from the far side of the Great Hall, desperately calling out to his daughter. The High Warlock had just entered the "arena" with Rosalyn and Lothian close behind. They stared, appalled by the spectacle as Wareeshta, Asai and Eleanor battled against the Bullwark.

'Maw!' cried Gill, seeing her.

Rosalyn, still cradling her arm, it now in a make-shift sling, courtesy of Lothian—the Great Warlock having had the sense and knowledge to bind it, to ease her pain—stepped forward, catching a glimpse of her son, but was then hauled back when four of the Bullwark stomped by, missing her by inches. She recoiled, then resumed her search for Gill, waving at him when she saw his hand in the air, letting him know she was all right.

'*Eleanor!*'

Once again, Oran shouted out to his daughter, but Eleanor was too preoccupied, her sights now set on the sentry who had challenged Daine; she had seen him plunge the dagger into the exposed area. She lunged towards the lone Bullwark, her speed lofty and without haste. It was a bold move on the young woman's part, her actions so quick and instinctive, they went unnoticed. As the sentry reached down for his shield, she saw her opportunity … and took it.

Clenching the dirk in her small, but dominant, left hand, Eleanor rushed the sentry and thrust her dagger deep into his exposed flesh. Not once did she flinch from her violent act.

Gill punched the air, brimming with pride for his sister's actions.

A shocking, high-pitched screech echoed throughout the Great Hall. The sentry jerked, then straightened, releasing his sword and shield as he emitted the deafening and agonising wail; she had pierced the target, with precision.

Eleanor winced then threw her hands over her ears, from the penetrating sound the Bullwark produced as the life was gradually sucked from him. His comrades halted and stared as he dropped to his knees—the impact like a clap of thunder before he collapsed.

A momentary pause and silence dropped on the Bullwark, as though the Great Hall of Eminence had commanded it.

Eleanor opened her eyes and lowered her hands, peering down at the corpse, her dagger still embedded in its body. As she retrieved it, she narrowed her eyes; there was no blood. Was it dead?

Feeling the glare of the other Bullwark pressing down on her, she glanced up. On the outside, she looked small and exposed against their menacing stature, however, inside, she was not intimidated. Her eyes slid from them, meeting another's; Asai was staring at her, armed and ready to resume the fight.

Close by, Wareeshta smirked, proud of her friend. She, too, was willing to fight to the end. It filled her with pride, despite everything, despite the fact she may never reclaim her book. Her task, her goal, seemed to be drifting from her; she was too involved now, and if she were to die, here, it would be a fitting death, knowing she was in the company of friends.

'What is happening?' whispered Daine. 'They look … *frozen!*'

No one moved, and no one spoke as the seconds passed. The tension was mounting again as if the Great Hall was regaining its energy and about to burst at its seams. Everyone present could feel its charge, along with the expanding silence. They were at a loss, uncertain of an outcome—should there be one. There had to be. But who would be the victor? It was overwhelming—the anticipation of not knowing. Still, the energy soared. Something had to give—sooner or later. Was this the herald of a bloody battle?

A distant rhythmic thud altered the mood again within the Hall, its crescendo drawing their curious attention to one another as it made its way towards them, from outside.

'What is that?' said Rosalyn to her husband. As it mounted, she looked down, feeling its vibration beneath her feet. 'Oran!' she called again, daring to lift her voice a little, but Oran's eyes were already searching for it, and when his look of concern met with Lothian's, both Warlocks stared at one another with growing dread.

Everyone turned when more of the Bullwark suddenly poured into the Hall's grand space, their pounding footsteps growing louder on their entrance, throwing the group into a state of turmoil.

And then they heard it—the heavy boom—as the massive doors of the Great Hall collided—the echo travelling across the expanse.

'They have locked us in!' stated Lothian.

'Then do something!' implored Rosalyn as the Bullwark took formation, filling the Great Hall with their formidable presence. Any hope of a victory was now fading quickly.

'If only I could,' said Lothian. 'But something else is controlling them.' He turned to Oran. 'Can you feel it—the grave atmosphere—and how it dominates the conflict here?'

'Aye, I do,' said Oran. 'And where are the other Warlocks—who have gathered for the *Assembly?* They would have banded together at the mere hint of bloodshed.' But the sounds of the festivities had long ceased into a dead and bleary silence, it now obvious and giving cause for alarm.

'Everything about the Bullwark's presence here screams a sinister obtrusion,' said Lothian. 'What they are doing is against everything the great Overlord, Lumeri, believed—that only peace shall reign here. Something terrible *has*—' The Great Warlock stopped when the slow, methodical beat of the Bullwark's shields resumed with their warning.

Eleanor flinched when an image entered her mind: it was that of a young woman. It confused her, but when the image became clear, she recognised the young woman as herself, frightened of the thunder, and then realised it had been a memory.

A voice spoke to her in her thoughts; *"I will protect you, Nori. I will always protect you."*

She knew that voice from the past; it had been Gill's. Her brother had been the one to protect her through the dark times as he got older when she became anxious, and when her father had not been there to hold her hand.

As the sound of the Bullwark's shields rose, it snatched her back to reality. She was no longer that young, innocent woman. No longer afraid. No longer mortal. Now everything had changed, and with that metamorphosis came happiness. Her eyes flashed to Asai, their look always meeting at the same time. They were *one.* They exchanged a brief nod, ready. Now it was her turn to protect her brother; the lives of others depended on him. Also by her side was her friend; Wareeshta remained stalwart in her defence, no longer feeling like an outsider. She drew on every movement encompassing her, anticipating the impending attack. Where once she had been tempted to flee, she, too, had chosen to stay and fight, despite her motive. She would not leave them … unless—

The sound of a great sword being removed from its sheath finally broke the heavy stillness.

All heads turned as Oran broke away from his group with strict orders to his wife to remain. He failed to hear Rosalyn call after him as he rushed towards Eleanor. But as Rosalyn moved to follow her husband, an unexpected voice spoke in her ear;

'Do as he says,' Kai urged her, with an underlying warning in his tone. Rosalyn spun and stared back at him, wondering where the Servitor had come from. 'I heard the last words you spoke to her …'

Rosalyn gasped, then swallowed. 'I—don't know what you—'

'Do not risk your life to save Gill—no matter what you promised Onóir.' Her mouth gaped, opening and closing, speechless. The Servitor slowly shook his head. 'No matter what happens, Rosalyn.'

Having snatched one of Greer's swords before leaving the dead Warlock's chambers, Oran marched towards the Bullwark, his sudden approach wrenching them from their trance-like state. They glanced from one to another, unsure, seeing the High Warlock's advance; nor was he alone. Within seconds, Oran was by Eleanor's side, along with the full support of her fighting comrades. United, once again. Together, they surveyed their opponents. The suspense of the prolonged pause began to show the unbearable strain on the small group as they shifted nervously in their places, eyes locked on their foe.

Trapped, besieged and outnumbered, like a flock of sheep about to be slaughtered, Oran, Daine, Eleanor, Asai, Reece and Wareeshta found themselves grouped within the centre of the Great Hall—and surrounded.

The group shuffled and eyed one another, readying themselves as the anticipated moment crept closer. It was almost suffocating—the wait—and only a matter of time before the Bullwark's imminent attack. And without the Elliyan's intervention, it appeared hopeless. But they would do what was necessary to save Gill, and should it mean sacrificing their lives for his … then they would have succeeded.

Weapons at the ready, they formed a circle, facing the Bullwark as the mercenaries swelled and encroached on them—the sound of their march now deafening. Daine could almost feel their heavy breath, its black veil ready to shroud them in death. *Keep your eyes open and fixed, Daine*, he told himself.

It was time …

*"You cannot submit yourself with blood on your hands."*

Kai's words taunted Gill as he stood on the sideline, now reunited with his mother—the grim warning reminding him not to interfere. And with the battle now fully resumed, all he could do was wait, be the spectator of something he had no control over. It was too much to bear, and when the familiar feeling returned—the one he had dreaded—it gripped him, stealing his strength.

His mind became clouded, his head dizzy as the heaviness leaned on him. *Not now*, he thought, trying to cast it away. *Please, not now. I need more time.* Determined it would not overthrow him, Gill fought against it, but despite his attempt, he felt the drag on his legs and began to sway. Panic hit when his hearing began to fail him, with a feeling that he was underwater, unable to hear the muffled cries and clash of steel above the surface.

Rosalyn jolted, then winced when Gill slumped against her. But Kai, having pre-empted Gill's deterioration, promptly changed back to his human form and took hold of her son before she lost her footing. Kai looked into Gill's eyes; the flecks of gold had now turned to bronze and were fading.

'What's wrong with him?' she cried out over the crash of steel—the look of horror evident on her face as she stared into her son's paling features.

'Gill has little time left,' he confessed.

Momentarily struck dumb, Rosalyn stared at Kai, then back to Gill, his eyes slowly closing on her. 'Gill?' She shook him lightly, then hard, and when he failed to respond it registered with her—what Kai had meant. She shook her head.

'No! He can't—'

'Help me!' Gill's voice was weakening. 'I don't know … how much longer … I can …' He slumped again.

Driven by her desperate need to help her son, Rosalyn, still cradling her broken wrist, looked out into the Great Hall, frantically searching for Oran. But when she could no longer see or hear her husband through the Bullwark's wall of sound, their constant march a rush of mass confusion as they battled the enemy, she panicked and yelled out, her voice lifting towards the rafters; '*Oran!*'

Everything ceased.

# Chapter Forty-Six

The Great Hall of Eminence was plunged into an unexpected and insufferable quietness. The small group looked at one another, hands still gripped on their weapons. They could not assume anything. Without warning, the Bullwark retreated. Obedient and regimental they formed a circle, leaving no gaps between them as they moved back, making certain their prisoners could not escape, their eyes focused, watching them. And when they stopped—the group still confused as their glances swept across their enemy, unsure of their next move—the Bullwark turned their heads sharply, attentive to the furtive command that had been made upon them.

'What is happening?' Rosalyn asked Kai as she clung to Gill. When Kai kept his silence, she looked to Lothian, her eyes imploring. The Great Warlock did not respond either; instead, Lothian discreetly moved away from where they had been hiding and stepped out into the Hall.

Though the Bullwark blocked his view, there was no doubting the reason for their orderly retreat; Lothian had sensed *their* presence, and when the voice he had not heard for centuries suddenly spoke to him, he stopped dead, his heart skipping a beat.

*"Come, Lothian,"* it enticed, through his thoughts. *"Let me see you."*

'Lothian!' Rosalyn hissed after him. 'What are you doing?' But the Great Warlock failed to hear her, his mind consumed by another as he drifted towards them.

'It is *her*,' stated Kai. 'She is calling to him.'

'Who? I hear no one.' Rosalyn gasped when it dawned on her. 'The

Sorceress!'

Kai nodded.

'But not as *we* know her.'

Oran did a double-take when Lothian brushed by him in a transient state, his amethyst eyes sparkling and fixed ahead. And as the Bullwark began to move aside, allowing the Great Warlock to pass, Oran and the others dared to edge closer, to see what was luring him.

'Has he lost his senses?' muttered Daine from the side of his mouth.

Oran shook his head.

'Something—or *someone*—is influencing him.' He called after the Great Warlock. 'Lothian!'

But Lothian continued to veer towards *her* voice; as he did so, the Bullwark separated—the space between them widening, revealing a sight the others did not expect.

There, on the Throne of Council sat the Sorceress, holding court. She lifted her head and stared down her nose at them, wanting—*allowing*—them all to see her.

Oran's mouth slowly fell. 'Kristene!' he whispered yet her features had altered again. No longer did he see the young, vibrant Kristene he once knew—and loved—but instead a woman whose years had advanced.

'It has been a long time, Lothian,' she began, her voice now clear and refined, and filled with authority.

The aged Warlock stalled—the look from her teal eyes intense, stopping him in his tracks.

Lothian narrowed his eyes when hers glinted back at him—the flecks of gold prominent, his fears heightening when he no longer sensed the presence of the spirits within the Great Hall, like before, when they would often welcome him. He would feel their peace, knowing they were at rest within the sanctity of their domain. But now, he sensed only turmoil, like tortured souls trapped within the depths of Purgatory. Was it possible, she had done that—sent them *there?* He glared at her.

'Why do you look at me so, Lothian? Have I changed much?' Lothian dared to let his eyes wander over her; she allowed him. Her long, hair cascaded over her bosom and gleamed like silver, and had one notable feature: a single thick strand of copper, plaited from root to tip, on the left. Though simple and archaic in design, her clothing was sumptuous: her long, shift was made of fine silk, its colour matching that of the single strand of hair, and its sleeves draped over the armrests as her hands rested casually on them. The neckline of the garment was high and almost covered her slender neck; when she sensed his scrutiny of her, she purposely tilted her head to the right and side-glanced Asai; the scar he had placed upon her, on their first meeting—beneath her left ear—was gone.

Beside her, sat the individual who kept his eyes set on Oran, their grin smug and oozing victory. Oran slowly shook his head at Magia in disgust; the dark Warlock returned it with a subtle nod of acknowledgement while still wearing his smugness. Magia then reached up, and gently patted the item hanging about his neck, teasing his adversary. Oran's face turned crimson, seeing the amulet they so desperately needed, to complete Gill's transformation. But when Magia's eyes dropped, along with his smirk, his brows arching high, Oran knew what his nemesis was staring at. Oran's mouth curled into a sneer, seeing Magia's reaction when he saw the satchel hanging at his side. In return for his antagonism, Oran subtly patted the satchel and slowly shook his head, silently letting his nemesis know, he had no intention of parting with it. Wareeshta, noting the muted exchange between the two rivals, also kept a keen eye until her attention was drawn from the item, she desperately sought, distracted by another individual stepping out into view.

Taking her place beside Eryian, in a feeble display of loyalty, the Valkyrie—looking somewhat dishevelled from the last time Wareeshta had seen her—flaunted the Obsidian lance with her usual stroking of the weapon, and lifted her chin, in a bid to maintain her self-importance. But it was clear by her demeanour that Kara had been reduced to the role of "slave" and not a loyal servant; when the Sorceress cast her a sideward glance, for merely moving, Wareeshta had seen the Valkyrie flinch and recoil slightly.

Their eyes met.

Wareeshta held Kara's look, staring her down, and when Kara's eyes, now dull grey, lowered, the Dhampir felt a new level of triumph and sneered at her. The Valkyrie had weakened. Yes, where Kara had never feared her mistress—or anyone—it was evident she did now, this "weakness" imparting an element of power to Wareeshta.

As Lothian and Eryian regarded one other with silent taunts, the Great Warlock found himself tormented by disturbing images of Purgatory, fearing Eryian had banished the Great Hall's spirits to that place. He now feared for Lorne. It was likely the young Servitor had not delivered his message; the Elliyan would have been here by now with reinforcements. But what if Lorne had suffered the same fate—the one he had dreaded most—and the guardian of the Shenn, too … and their guests … and ...? His eyes flashed to her.

'What have you done with them?!' he yelled, his hand balled into a threatening, wielding fist, demanding answers. 'And where are our guests?'

'Oh, I am sure they are … content … after their fill of food—particularly the wine; quite characteristic and a little … *potent*—judging by the aftereffect. I can only assume they are … shall we say … "sleeping it off?"' She paused, seeing Lothian's eyes widen—the Great Warlock having grasped her meaning. '… and, no doubt, will continue to dwell in their slumber until—'

'You decide,' Oran cut in.

A devious smirk crawled across her face. 'They may feel a little worse for wear when they eventually wake, but when they do—and they will—it will be to the dawning of a new day …' Her expression then dropped, a shadow of perversion appearing as her emotionless eyes stared down at them, defiant. '… and a new world.'

'Where is it, Eryian?' Lothian insisted.

She lifted her hands and slowly drew them up towards her. As if indulging in its power, she briefly closed her eyes and smiled to herself in a moment of ecstasy, as she lay them across her breast.

Lothian and Oran drew back, horrified. Adorned on each index finger, Eryian now flaunted the gold rings the Ushabti had worn, both bearing the name of the Magus:

*Lumeri.*

'What have you—' Lothian stopped and gasped when she carefully parted the neckline of her gown and lifted her hands away, to reveal what he had been dreading. 'No!' he implored, seeing the Shenn amulet around her neck. Knowing the gravity of her actions, he attempted another step towards her. She smiled and shook her head, then looked sharp when Oran's voice rang out from behind.

'You cannot do this to him—you *would* not! It is not yours to own!' he yelled.

Eryian threw her head back, releasing a deep-throated laugh, then paused when her eyes fell on Oran and his companions as they advanced towards her. Alerted to their attack, the Bullwark shifted, ready to defend, but a flick of her hand stopped them from engaging in combat; she would deal with Oran herself. Besides, it would amuse her.

Oran and the others suddenly jolted.

'Try as you may,' she began, lifting her voice to address them. 'But you cannot challenge me.' They looked at one another, then recoiled, feeling a surge of immense heat forcing them back, disabling them from their pursuit. 'Any attempt to do so shall be in vain.' She smirked, then grunted. As she dragged her eyes back to Lothian she paused, her gaze moving to the pylons, catching the movements of silhouettes among their elongated shadows. 'I know you are there,' she stated. 'Come out, where I can see you—not hear you skulking about in the dim, like nervous mice.'

Despite their desperate attempt to resist her "invitation", Gill, Rosalyn and Kai—feeling the pull of her effortless summons—were hauled before her.

The moment their eyes locked, Eryian threw her hand out, instantly obstructing Kai—the Servitor, still in his human form, now unable to move.

'What are you doing?!'

Eryian ignored Gill, her sights momentarily set on Kai, knowing who—*what*—he was. Yet, she was dubious of his capabilities, therefore, could not risk him changing back to his ethereal form.

Kai then felt it—the unbodied claw-like grip around his throat, his guttural sounds of desperation causing the others alarm as her grasp tightened.

'Please—don't harm him!' cried Rosalyn.

'*Harm* him?' L'Ordana threw back her head and laughed at the irony of it. 'Although I am aware you cannot kill *that* which is already dead,' she went on, then veered her scornful look back to Kai, 'I can, however, make you suffer in your "mortal" form.' When she flexed her hand, he jerked. 'Tell me, *Servitor*,' she persisted, taunting him, 'does it still hurt, like it did when your condemners sentenced you with their rope?' When Kai's eyes bored into her, she shook her head. 'Oh, no, I cannot risk it—letting you return to your true form. So, make your choice, Servitor, if you wish no harm to come to your friends'—she cast a lazy look at Rosalyn and Gill—'then you will remain as you are, like one of them … well, almost.' She released a short laugh. 'What is it to be?'

Made to physically relive the memory of his traumatic death, Kai's tormented eyes met with Rosalyn's. She shook her head, distressed, having to witness it. Eryian squeezed again. 'Well? Do make up your mind.'

'Do as she says, Kai!' urged Gill.

'I would suggest you listen to your friend,' she warned.

When Kai blinked, his silent decision was made: he would not interfere, in any way.

'Good,' she said, loosening her grip.

Overthrown and coerced into an unwavering silent inertia, Kai lowered his head, defeated.

At first, Magia watched with amusement as they were forced, against their will, to do Eryian's bidding, and yet, inside, he was wary of her powers and unsure of the extent of them. Now that she wore the Shenn she could own Elboru, the Elliyan and both worlds—the mortals', as well as their own. When a premonition entered his mind, of what their world would truly look like, should she have complete reign, a fragment of guilt niggled at him. It forced him to question it; *Can I allow this to happen?* It would also affect him. He glanced again at the satchel; he knew she needed the book and was set on having that, too. His face hardened as he took hold of his thoughts in what was becoming a race against time. *What to do …?* He had played his part and was ready to leave. *Not without my book, though.* It would not be easy, he knew, regardless.

'Why, Eryian?' Lothian begged.

She tilted her head slightly as if pitying him. 'Why not?' she returned.

'I am pleading with you,' he pressed. 'Do *not* do this. He'—he pointed to Gill, who was hunched over, weak and drawn—'is the rightful heir to *that* seat of *Council. He*—Gillis Shaw—is the true Magus.'

Her eyes slid over to Gill; when she saw him leaning on his sword, for support, she released a short laugh. '*Him?* Magus, you say?' She shook her head at the poor pathetic excuse for the individual they claimed to be their rightful Overlord.

'No good will come of this,' Lothian warned. 'Please, Eryian, I implore you,' he added, his hands still extended, trying to reach out to her. 'Revenge is not the way.'

'*Revenge?*' she retorted. 'Oh, I have had my revenge, Lothian.' Her eyes travelled back to another. 'As have *you* … Lord Oran.'

Oran's eyes widened. *How the hell did she—*

'Greer would have been the perfect ally,' she claimed, to his horror, 'had you not …' Beside her, Magia was slowly shaking his head, his lips puckered, tutting at Oran, in disapproval of Greer's brutal demise—not that he cared. Eryian slowly wagged her finger at Oran, as if scolding a disobedient child. 'You should not have done *that.* No matter,' she went on, dismissing the inconvenience with a casual flick of her hand. 'I will have one of my mercenaries claim the dagger from his corpse.'

On hearing this, Magia looked sharply at her, and when her eyes flashed to the satchel hanging at Oran's side, panic set in. *The dagger!* Her intentions were clear: she wanted it *all.* The reality of it now struck. No, he could not allow it. He looked at Wareeshta. She was glaring up at him; she had grasped Eryian's motives, too—as had Oran. While there was little they could do, about the dagger, there was—where the book was concerned—an opportunity to act. Someone had to stop her. But who would be the willing candidate?

'Where is Lord Tuan?' Lothian demanded.

When her eyes crossed back to the Great Warlock, she frowned—the lines across her forehead deepening in feigned thought before delivering her scoffing remark; 'I am certain Lord Tuan will eventually see reason. But until then, he and that … grubby little "child" shall remain within the *Naoi,* where I have given my persecutor time to reflect on the actions of his past.' She laughed. 'Oh, Lothian, to have seen his face when he realised it was *me!*—returned from the pyre to "haunt" him.'

'And the guardian of the Shenn?'

'The Ushabti is a willing acolyte, who will *always* serve his Master … or, should I say … *Mistress.* The guardian of this'—she took the sacred stone in her hand, the *Light of Life* glinting down at them like a glorious sunrise, new and powerful—'knows who their Ruler is. And he will also serve me.'

'Serve *you?!*' cried Oran, wanting to yank the Shenn from her slender neck, and wring his hands around it. She smirked. Furious and insulted by her mockery of him, he dared to take a step forward, brandishing his sword but was again forced back by the barrier's heat. 'My son is the true ruler of—'

Eryian's brows shot up. 'Ah, yes!' she broke in, then glanced at Gill. 'Your son …'

Oran hesitated and looked over at Gill and Rosalyn, his instincts warning him.

'… and his mother,' she teased. 'What a quaint family you have. Tell me, Oran of Urquille … would you do anything for them?'

Oran inclined his head low, eyes burning, sensing her underlying malice. It unnerved him. What was she playing at?

'Shall I give you more time to think about—'

'Of course, I would,' he retorted. '*Anything!*'

She slowly nodded, intrigued, then turned her attention to Rosalyn.

'And what about *you?*'

'I would *die* for them!' Rosalyn stated, still cradling her broken wrist while trying to suppress her physical and emotional agony.

'No, Rosalyn!' cried Oran, desperately wanting to go to his wife and son but could not. He turned to Eryian. 'Whatever your intentions are, leave my wife out of this. She is just a mortal.' Rosalyn clenched her jaw, having felt the sting of his statement yet she knew the necessity of it.

'That may be so,' Eryian returned. 'But she gave birth to *him*,' she added, glancing at Gill. 'His presence alone threatens my vision. No, I cannot—' She stopped when sudden movements caught her attention; Reece and the others had banded closer together. She laughed. 'I commend your loyalty to one another,' she called out. 'It is rather touching.' Her face then darkened and her eyes glared, boring into them, and their attempt to interfere—not that they would achieve anything. She had more pressing matters to attend to. *Time to finish this*, she thought, disenchanted by their feeble efforts.

The world of Warlocks and mortals awaited her.

Eryian regarded Rosalyn again, her eyes briefly resting on her broken limb. 'I do admire your valour, *mortal*, however—'

'Stop this!' voiced Lothian. 'You and I once loved one another, Eryian. Remember?' Reece and the others shared confused glances; this was news to them. 'If that love meant anything to you … you would listen to me, hear my plea.'

'Plea? You mean—to *save* them?'

Lothian nodded, holding her stare.

'Did our love mean anything to you?' he persisted, trying to reach into her mind to show her his thoughts, to relive what they had once shared, as a reminder of their most intimate and intense moments together. He wanted her to know his touch again; within seconds, Eryian found herself engaging with Lothian in unspoken sentiments, their marked silence captivating their anxious audience.

As the once lovers lost themselves again, embraced in their thoughts, Oran realised what Lothian was trying to do: distract her, hoping it would buy them time if the others were to escape. It was their only chance, while he and Lothian struggled to find a solution. Gill had to be crowned Overlord and sit in her place, where *he* belonged.

Oran promptly turned and silently signalled to the others to go, but when he pointed, marking a way—the captives acting on it—the Bullwark raised their shields and made their advance. The thunderous sound jolted Eryian from her memories, alerting her to their escape, and igniting her anger.

'*Gill!*' yelled Oran. His son swiftly turned to see his father pointing to Rosalyn, still by his side. 'Take her from here,' he urged. 'Now!'

Gill wasted no time. 'Maw, this way!' Still holding on to one other, mother and son turned and scrambled towards the pylons—the effort of their escape then thwarted when Gill jolted; something had seized him from behind, threatening to haul him from her. Fearing their separation, Rosalyn took hold of Gill's arm as he struggled against the invisible force. But the strain was too much for her; she could no longer maintain her grip with one hand. Gradually, she felt the pull. In their bid to stay together, they clasped hands, their knuckles white from the strain as their fingers entwined, desperate to hold on yet fully aware. And when their hands slipped, they clamped their fingertips together. But their parting was imminent. Conscious of it, and the precious moments they had left, Rosalyn mouthed something to her son just as he was wrenched from her …

# Chapter Forty-Seven

When the day is done and its light diminished, night moves in. But as the darkness settles, an ominous shift stirs the restless spirits; for the fragile *Veil of Night* between two worlds has drawn back. It sighs, announcing something. And it is there, from behind the murmur of its veneer, the spirits watch and wait. But they are not alone in their vigil … For the *Dorkdòer* are watching, too …

Denied the right to respond to what he had been told, Gill found himself silenced and on his knees before Eryian, head lowered and eyes downcast, worn and weary and hemmed in by the Bullwark. On the ground before him, and out of reach, lay the Albrecht sword; he had failed to hear it drop from his grip, in his struggle to stay with his mother. Despite his diminishing state of mind and body, he had tried with all his might to hold on to the heirloom, its presence now having no bearing on his status—the avenger's powerful hold on the Great Hall, dismissing the sword's true worth.

Trapped within the Bullwarks' "menagerie", and parted from his friends and family, an insufferable loneliness crept over Gill, along with an overwhelming sense of failure. Suddenly, his head snapped up, forced to look upon Eryian, her emotionless stare holding him for a moment before she released it. Gill dragged his eyes to each side of her, conscious of Magia and Kara—the malice in their scrutiny of him, shrouding him with dread.

Rosalyn froze when she could no longer see her son. '*Gill!*' she cried out, wanting to go to him—protect him—but knew, to even attempt to break through the Bullwark would be impossible; worse still, a death wish. Frantic, she turned and looked back at Oran.

'We must do something,' she begged. 'We have to try …' Her voice trailed when her husband's eyes held her, his look then altering to one of dread, sensing another notable change in the atmosphere. 'What is it?' she cried, attempting to go to him.

'Back, Rosalyn!' the chorus of voices shouted. She stopped, her mouth gaping, having felt the intense heat separating them. When the familiar sound of the Bullwarks' march resumed, she spun, seeing the mercenaries part.

Their mouths gaped when they saw Gill on his knees in submission before Eryian, and when she slowly pointed at him, Oran shook his head, fearing what she may do to his son. When her eyes glanced down at the Warlock—the edge of her mouth twitching with intent—an unsettling rush of adrenalin ran down Oran's spine when Gill was suddenly hoisted off his feet and suspended before her, helpless and vulnerable … as was he.

Tilting her head towards Gill, Eryian curled her finger, silently beckoning him; unable to resist her implicit command, he glided towards her.

'No, Eleanor,' whispered Asai, gently placing a hand on her shoulder when she made to challenge the Sorceress—the dirk continuously revolving in her hand; she would not hesitate to use it again. 'You cannot!' Eleanor looked up at him, but the Samurai could only shake his head—the despair on his face telling her what she now knew; for all their skills and abilities, they stood no chance against this malignant force. Nor would there be any bartering of lives. And with her brother's fate now resting with the "Gods" … Eleanor stepped back and resumed her place, beside Asai.

'A wise decision,' stated Eryian. 'You would never have—'

'Release my son!' Oran cried, then jolted when he, too, was wrenched off the ground. The others stared up at the Warlock, dumbfounded. Oran looked down, then back up at Eryian, shaking his head. 'Do not do this, *Kristene!*' She flinched. 'Please, Kristene!' he begged, trying to jog her memory, any flicker of their past that might help.

But when her eyes glazed over—the flecks of gold glinting—Oran knew Kristene was lost, gone forever; all that remained of her was an ageing body—the once vessel for the spirit that had finally taken control.

Eryian now dominated.

She peered up at him and smirked, and when her eyes dropped, his widened, seeing her wanton stare. He tried to strike out as she beckoned *it* but could not stop her. As the weight of its evil was lifted from him, he was forced to watch it go to her, like a loyal dog to its master—the book passing through the fatal barrier without a char. But when his feet were returned to solid ground, Oran knew the book was hers.

All hope was fading.

Eryian grunted then cast a disparaging smile at Oran. 'I told you it would be mine. As will *all* of it.' Prompted by her statement, Oran looked over at the pylons, his eyes set on the one where his old friend was interred. *Tekkian, help us!* Her deep-rooted laugh made him look back into her hollow eyes. 'Tekkian cannot help you now, Oran,' she sneered. Her eyes moved to Lothian, confirming his worst nightmare. 'None of them can,' she added, sweeping a hand across the Great Hall, indicating the pylons. She had banished their souls to Purgatory.

'What have you—'

Eryian returned her attention to Rosalyn, cutting Oran from his constant enquiries. 'So,' she started, lifting her head, curious of the mortal. 'You claim that you would *die* for them.' Rosalyn held her malevolent gaze and swallowed. 'But if forced to choose …?'

'What?' said Rosalyn, taken aback, her voice barely a whisper. 'Forced to …' Half-dazed, she looked around, her eyes meeting the others as they looked on, powerless. Her mouth opened and closed as she shook her head at the thought of the impossible task. *No, I can't!* And yet, deep down, she knew she would have to; the look of evil staring down at her was not asking—it was *telling* her to choose.

'I—I can't,' she whimpered. 'Please, don't make me …'

'I suggest you do,' warned Eryian.

'What—what do you mean?'

'Eryian!' Lothian called out. 'You are better than this.' But it was a despairing situation, rendering him defenceless against her, and though he had tried again, he could no longer communicate with her through his thoughts.

'You will not succeed!' yelled Oran, fearful for his wife and the choice about to be forced upon her.

By now, Eryian had had enough of their demands and pleas, their voices like a cacophony of pathetic whining inside her head. Lifting her hands she gathered her thoughts and conjured up a shield of silence, blocking out the uproar of their protests; namely Oran's.

She sighed. 'Much better.'

With her sights now set on Rosalyn—and for purpose—Eryian regarded the mortal and beckoned her towards her.

Rosalyn's eyes darted between Eryian, Magia Nera and Kara. She glanced back over her shoulder at the others, her eyes then widening in despair realising she could no longer hear their silenced cries as they tried, in desperation, to call out to her—and so near, too.

Now unable to communicate with the others and Gill, and with Kai rendered immobile and speechless, Rosalyn and Lothian felt utterly alone and vulnerable against the unmeasurable force staring down at them. Helpless and unarmed, the two looked to one another. Taking a deep breath, Rosalyn pressed her lips together and, nodding to Lothian, turned to face their enemy. Chest heaving, she finally released her quivering breath and spoke:

'What are you going to do?' While her tone was hard and defensive, inside, Rosalyn was terrified—and unwell; her body felt on fire from the fever of her broken limb and the pain was making her dizzy. But she had to stand up to them. 'Let my son go!' she demanded, her eyes briefly dropping, seeing the Albrecht. Would she dare risk it? 'Take me, instead,' she blurted, biting her lower lip, thinking, thinking … A strange calm came over her as she contemplated using the sword, her survival instincts driving her on. *You must try, Rosalyn!* But Eryian, having pre-empted her intentions, cast the great sword away from her with a mere glance. Rosalyn gasped as she watched the weapon being torn from her reach.

Eryian slowly nodded, then rose.

'I commend your bravery,' she stated, snatching Rosalyn's attention back to her. 'It is something to be proud of,' she added, subconsciously setting the book down on the Throne of Council, impressed by the measure of Rosalyn's virtue, in her bid to overthrow her, to save her son. 'Therefore, I will make it swift. This, I—'

'You told the Servitor you would not harm them,' Lothian reminded her, stepping in front of Rosalyn.

'And I lied,' said Eryian.

Lothian shook his head, his eyes blazing, then turned when he felt the gentle tug on his sleeve.

'It is all right,' said Rosalyn.

'You see, Lothian?' Eryian persisted. 'Only a mother would sacrifice it all for the love of her child. How endearing. Now, let her!'

Rosalyn swallowed hard and stepped out in front of Lothian, his tormented sigh following her as she approached Eryian, her eyes lifting, seeing Gill suspended in silence, only feet from her. To see him like this broke her heart. Closing her eyes, she inhaled deeply, and as she slowly let it go, whispered to herself, 'Wait for me, Maw.'

She was ready. Now was the time. She would give her life for her son.

Swallowing her fear, she waited …

Eryian stepped closer to Gill and lifted her eyes, meeting his dazed look. His eyes widened when a curl appeared at the side of her mouth. He opened his, about to call out, but was silenced when she placed a finger on his lips and shook her head. Holding his look, she stepped back and extended her arms; she then spread her long fingers wide before curling them into talons, pointing them down towards the floor. Her eyes darted behind Gill for an instant, seeing his companions as they continued in their vain and silenced struggle.

Rosalyn's eyes flashed open when the floor began to move and quiver. She glanced at Lothian, then followed his look when she saw him staring at the ground; she gasped as the black river seeped up through the Hall's flagstones and spread out. It grew thicker, expanding, then lifted into a menacing cloud before parting into human-like shapes, their elongated hands stretching and groping as they reached out.

'Who—*what*—are they?' begged Rosalyn.

Lothian shook his head, muttering to himself.

'This is impossible! I never …'

'Tell me, Lothian!' she demanded through gritted teeth, grabbing hold of him.

'They are the *Dorkdòer*—the *Dark Slaves*—servants of Purgatory.' He shook his head. 'We must stop them before—' But when Lothian moved to intercept the creatures before they could do their sinister deed, knowing what would happen if they were not stopped, the Great Warlock found himself rooted and forced into silence. When the six demon-like creatures paused and bowed before Eryian, she lowered her head, acknowledging their presence.

Still trapped behind the barrier and unable to intervene, Oran and the others looked on in horror when the creatures appeared. They looked to one another, stumped, then to Oran, searching for answers.

'What on earth are they?' said Daine.

'The *Dark Slaves* of Purgatory,' Oran whispered, unable to comprehend it; he had only heard of the *Dorkdòer* yet never witnessed their presence.

'What is she doing, Oran?' Reece demanded, fearing for his

daughter and grandson. A long pause came before Oran's response—the Warlock now dreading the worst as it dawned on him.

'She is controlling them with her thoughts. I fear she will …' His words trailed off when the creatures bowed.

'Fear what?' said Eleanor.

When Oran looked down at his daughter, her eyes darting back and forth between her father and Gill, he swallowed; how could he tell her? His mouth was bone dry. He simply could not get the words out. And when he looked back through the cause of their separation, his eyes widened when Lothian turned to face him—the terror in the Great Warlock's look telling him all he needed to know.

'Oh, my—' Oran stopped dead when the *Dorkdòer* turned and looked up, their sights on Gill. 'No, no, no!' he cried. 'They cannot!'

Gill flinched, feeling the cold sharpness of the spectres' grip as they tugged at him; he jerked and writhed, fighting desperately to free himself from their deathly clutches.

Helpless and disabled, Oran yelled as he and Lothian tried everything with their combined powers to break down the barrier between them. But when he saw the *Dorkdòer* dragging his son away, he stopped and cried out—the pain of their inevitable parting, bringing him to his knees.

There was nothing they could do except look on in horror at what was unravelling. But what happened next, no one saw coming …

Rosalyn's eyes shot open when she heard the high-pitched scream, like that of the *Banshee,* it grinding on her teeth and then travelling down her spine. Her heart sank to the depths of despair as she witnessed her son being taken from her. The muscles in her stomach tightened and spasmed—the immense feeling of her pregnancy with Gill, where he had been safe and protected, coming back to her. Then the feeling of his birth came, haunting her, his entrance into the world marking a separation where she knew he would be in constant danger—like now. She had been fooled into thinking she would be making the sacrifice.

Gill, now desperate, reached out to his mother, just as he had done when he was a child, wanting her to take him in her arms again, to protect him. Rosalyn shook her head, shocked by what was happening. As each precious second rushed by, Gill was being dragged farther from her—the agony on his face evident as he held her look, his eyes wild with fear.

As her maternal instincts urged her to go to him, she looked back at the others again, seeing their desperate, silent protests, knowing they were calling out to her and Gill—the strain of unrest and frustration written on their faces. Even her daughter, Eleanor; her dread was visible, despite battling with her emotions. She was trying to reach out to her mother, mouthing her name. But the only one rooted in disbelief was Oran, his look of torment fixed on her. When their eyes locked in a moment of precious time, images flashed through Rosalyn's mind; their first meeting at Eddin Castle; their smiles; their wedding; their love-making and their children—a lifetime of unforgettable moments gone in seconds. She could feel their hearts breaking together. The tears quickly emerged, cascading down her grief-stricken face as she struggled with her choice—with Kai's words still echoing in her mind; *"Do not risk your life to save Gill's, no matter what you promised Onóir."* Her frantic eyes darted between her son and her husband. Then, placing her hand over her heart, Rosalyn made her decision and nodded to them— once.

Oran froze, his eyes widening as he realised her intentions. Promptly he joined the others in their chorus of muted pleas, their cries lost to their silent restraint.

Oran shook his head frantically, yelling out her name. And though she could not hear him she saw him mouth the words; *'I love you!'*

Closing her eyes, Rosalyn turned from her husband, and in the seconds before the spectres melted into the void that would take her son to Purgatory, she leapt …

# Chapter Forty-Eight

*When devastation and rage collide, there is no consolation to be had.*

Oran jumped to his feet, his face marbled with anger and grief. As he fought back the tears his chest heaved as he stared down at the place where Rosalyn and Gill had disappeared, his eyes dead. No, he would not cry, show weakness, or give in to the whore who had banished his wife and son to the place he called *Hell!*

'What just happened?' cried Daine, dumbfounded, though aware of what he had witnessed. And yet …

'Where are they?!' Reece yelled, demanding answers.

'Gone,' Oran muttered, barely able to accept what he had just said—the simplicity of the word, having left a gaping hole in his heart.

*Gone!*

The others drew back, sharing looks of utter disbelief.

'*Gone?!* Where?!' Reece persisted, eyes fired with anger.

Too crushed and broken to respond again, Oran readied himself, his rage now taking over, spurring him on into a battle against the Bullwark, with no regard for his own life. 'Leave this place … if you want to live,' he then told the others, his eyes now displaying his anguish as they met the stark look on his daughter's. Confounded, and still struggling to express her true feelings, having seen what happened to her mother and Gill, Eleanor could only stare at her father, and yet she understood that they were gone. 'And you, Nori,' he went on, his eyes welling. 'Go with Asai.' He looked to the Samurai, who bowed to him, Asai's determined gaze telling the

Warlock he would always be by his daughter's side. Oran was grateful they, at least, had each other.

'And leave you?' She shook her head, defiant, her dirk gripped firmly in her small hand.

Oran looked down at this daughter, his mouth twitching, trying to force a smile; he was proud of her.

'They were—*are*—my family, too,' added Daine, joining Eleanor's stand. 'I'm staying.'

Oran's eyes flashed to his grandson's; for an instant, he saw Petrio staring back at him—the son he and Kristene had created—and now regretted abandoning him in Triora on *that* fateful night. He nodded, pleased they had found one another … despite everything.

Oran looked to the others, his heart a little lighter as they stood their ground, letting him know they, too, were going nowhere.

'Now that *that* has been established,' said Reece, 'How do we get them—'

'Leave us!'

The group turned, hearing Lothian's voice; it was loud and filled with authority. They stood, silenced, staring in disbelief when the Bullwark obeyed his command, and abruptly left the Great Hall—the echo of their retreat diminishing along with their threat.

'Now!' Oran's call was that of a battle cry. Aware they were no longer restricted—the barrier having unexpectedly been removed—Oran made his move. As he rushed forward, he spotted the Albrecht on the ground; discarding Greer's sword, he snatched it into his grip, his heart skipping a beat when he felt Gill's residual energy on the hilt.

Alerted to the Warlock's intentions, Reece and Asai leapt into action, quickly followed by the rest of the group. Together, they advanced towards the Throne of Council, their eyes fixed on Eryian. But as they closed in, she made no attempt to flee.

Oran stopped dead and raised a hand, his sudden action prompting the others to stop, too, when Lothian took charge and leaned over Eryian, his motions slow and attentive. Heart pounding, Oran edged closer and looked over the Great Warlock's shoulder; he drew back for a moment, then straightened up, his eyes boring into the pathetic form now slumped over the Magus' throne. Tightening his grip on the Albrecht, he shoved by Lothian—the Great Warlock almost stumbling—and reached for the Sorceress. He would destroy her, there and then.

Eryian did not respond when he shook her weakening body.

'Bring them back!' he seethed through gritted teeth. 'Damn you, *She-Devil!* Bring my wife and son—'

'Oran, stop!' pleaded Lothian, shaking his head as he reached out to his fellow Warlock.

'Why should he?' said Reece, intervening. By now, the others had grouped around them.

'Because'—Lothian paused and pressed his quivering lips together—'she cannot bring them back.'

'*What?!*' cried Daine.

'Look at it!' he urged Oran, pointing to the Shenn; the sacred amulet was now limp and dull around her neck. 'Look at *her!* I knew something had altered when I could control the Bullwark.'

The two Warlocks stared at one another, and as Oran opened his mouth to question Lothian, the Great Warlock's eyes travelled down.

'Look at them, Oran!' he insisted, indicating their amulets.

Silence again—a dull, unspeakable, intolerable silence that gathered the group into a defiant unit. And yet, within the quiescence, they could feel it, like the quivering of a flame before it diminishes.

'It is fading—the Shenn,' Lothian stated.

They all stared at the Great Warlock, his mournful eyes returning to Eryian as he felt her energy waver.

Now separated from its Magus, the Shenn was changing, its spectacular diamond slowly beginning to lose its lustre; no more did it glow like the sunrise, with the promise of a new dawn, a new day—and a new Ruler. It was diminishing—as were the Warlocks'—

signalling the end of something else. What had once been the glorious *Light of Life* was dying; the intensity of its sunrise had now waned to pale yellow, then white, then grey and was gradually weakening, save for a tiny ember of light still lingering within its centre as it continued to burn, instilling hope inside them. Oran kept his eyes fixed on it, praying it would not extinguish.

Lothian moved back towards Eryian, his arms outstretched towards her when she struggled to breathe, her efforts momentarily dragging Oran back from the brink of despair.

'What are you doing?' he snapped, grasping Lothian by the arm, stopping him in his tracks. But the Great Warlock could only look at his friend with pity.

He shrugged. 'I must … stay with her.'

'Why?' Oran pressed, his tone harsh with resentment.

'Because … she is dying,' came the unexpected reply.

'Then let her rot,' voiced Reece. Behind him, Daine looked on and, despite knowing who she once was—his grandmother, Kristene—knew Reece was right. He never knew her, and never would, her looming death now dousing any feelings he may have potentially felt for her.

Lothian shook his head.

'I need to say goodbye to her.' He closed his eyes and reached for his amulet, feeling the life draining from it. 'I never had the chance to … before.'

'Just as *I* never had the chance to say goodbye to my wife and son,' Oran hit back—the hate still prominent in his hard-bitten voice.

'But Gill and Rosalyn are not *dead*, Oran,' Lothian assured him, his hands raised, pleading with his fellow Warlock.

'Then *save* them!' he snarled, pointing the Albrecht directly at his friend. 'Save them from that place.'

'I—I—' Lothian shook his head, his mouth open, trying to find the words.

'You cannot.' Oran grunted. His eyes slid back to Eryian. He drew back when he saw her features; her skin was shrivelling and shrinking back, like parched leather, worn with the sudden swift passing of time that had finally caught up with her. Eryian slumped again, her body finally giving in to the ravages of time as it took back her beauty and strength. Then something happened, something that struck Oran when he saw it; her skin now looked scorched, and her hair was limp and wet. He grimaced—the signs now evident as the past stared back at him, telling him what they should have done, all those years ago: he should have let Kristene drown just as Lothian should have let Eryian burn.

When she drew in a sudden gasp, gulping for air, Lothian's eyes flashed to Oran, wide with desperation. But the High Warlock, anticipating his thoughts, shook his head, devoid of emotion.

'Say your goodbyes, Lothian.'

'But—but there is a chance we might be able to save her,' he stated, glancing around, his frantic eyes searching for something. 'To save them both,' he urged, hoping to sway Oran's opinion.

But regardless of Lothian's attempts to toy with his sentiments—the Great Warlock thinking he might sympathise with Kristene and spare her—Oran stood his ground and stared Lothian down, hard-faced, despite knowing he still harboured deep feelings for Eryian.

'I—*we*—must try,' Lothian persisted.

As Oran's cold eyes moved to Eryian's, he now accepted what he had, deep down, chosen to ignore, back then: his intuition. Yes, she—*Kristene*—always had an evil streak within her. He had sensed it from their first meeting—after he had sent the kelpie to save her, all those years ago. But he had been captivated by her charm, just as Lothian had, by Eryian. Undeterred by their power and status, these two women had used their influence on the Warlocks; they knew they could win them over. For it had been the age-old weakness of man; enamoured and bewitched by a woman who would steal his heart … amongst other things.

But Oran's decision was made. 'Let them *die!* As we should have done, then.'

Eryian opened her eyes—the mere effort of it weakening her further. She had heard what Oran had said—Lothian, too. Oran's words were clear and, despite his feelings, Lothian knew his friend was right. As he leaned back, dragging himself away from her, Lothian rested his ageing hands on his knees and hung his head in shame and despair. From the corner of his eye he could see Eryian's plea, through her pain and anguish. But he had to let her go. He shook his head—the tears building as he, too, accepted their fate; they were never destined to be together—then or now.

Eryian then stopped, seeing the lucidity in Lothian's eyes, its silence clear, telling her it was the end, for both of them. The Shenn was dragging her down with the weight of its demise as it began to slip back into its dormancy. It had not bonded with her; it had been aware of its true master's presence until they were separated by the evil that had threatened to steal it. It was never hers to own, from the start. It was over. And in that moment of clarity, she welcomed death and the peacefulness she hoped that would come with it. With a single, heavy nod, Eryian closed her eyes for the last time.

No more was the name L'Ordana spoken; it had been nothing more than that—a name—one they had come to know along their treacherous journey. A name that had slipped back to the relic of time from whence Magia Nera had used it, in a bid to keep alive the memory of a mother he had barely known. As with Kristene … L'Ordana no longer existed.

When the last trace of life left the decaying ruin that was once her body—one of seductive beauty he had often explored—Oran grimaced, then yanked the amulet from her neck, while glaring at Lothian as a silent warning, telling the Great Warlock not to intervene. He froze when the tiny light within the darkening stone began to flicker. He swallowed and held his breath. Then it was gone.

His heart stopped when the precious stone turned to coal, taking all hope with it. Suddenly the world around him began to dissolve, leaving him with a sense of utter loneliness and despair. Like a worthless piece of costume jewellery, he cast it away—the clash of its precious metal against stone, ringing throughout the Great Hall. For a few moments, he stood staring down at the decaying corpse of the old woman he no longer recognised. He watched as Lothian took over and cradled her in his arms, rocking back and forth, his remorse played out like a scene from his Playwright's book—the one he still carried with him in his satchel. Why he should think of it at a time like this, he knew not, then realised what connected them: *Death.*

'Look!' Daine blurted, pointing. The rest of the group spun and looked up.

Realising she was outnumbered and aware of the eyes of revenge on her, Kara lifted herself from behind the Throne of Council, where she had been hiding after the turn of events, and slowly spread her wings.

'The Valkyrie is mine!' Asai stated, moving away from the group, his katana and wakizashi gripped in his hands. He then stopped, his eyes rising with her as she made to escape, her damaged wings slowing her ascent.

Higher and higher Kara rose, her eyes on the shadows above the huge lanterns. Once there, she could disappear into the void above the rafters, and find a way out. She would be safe then, and they would no longer see her, especially the *Strange One.* He wanted revenge. They all did. It was her only chance. But as she sought her refuge, her dishevelled wings flapped hard, in her strained and desperate bid to escape.

The Samurai's eyes narrowed in concentration as the Valkyrie gradually blended into the darkness above them; but he could still see her outline, his sight sharp and defined, as long as he kept his eyes fixed on where she had left the dim light. As he raised the wakizashi, a sweet voice made him stall.

*"Not yet,"* it told him. He did not question it. He waited …

Asai drew back when he saw something fall, through the shadows; it was the Obsidian. Down it fell, hurtling towards him. He caught it, feeling the remnants of Kara's presence smeared all over it. He hesitated, wondering why she had dropped her precious lance.

*"Now!"* It was all he needed to hear.

Delivered by the hand of revenge, the Obsidian was hurled high. Higher it soared in pursuit of its mistress—the strength of its delivery sent with such force, it found its target within seconds.

Once again, an eerie silence fell, settling everywhere, for what felt like hours. Had the Valkyrie escaped? Had the great Samurai missed his target?

Asai never missed.

Then it came—the high-pitched wail of death as the Obsidian did its work, claiming the life of the individual it would have never sought. A streak of light suddenly flashed across the shadows above before burning embers appeared, falling like speckles of fiery snowflakes towards those watching below. And as they rained down, they grew larger, carrying the stench of burning flesh, with them.

Then it stopped.

As Kara's remains gradually turned to ash, it silently carpeted the ancient flagstones of the Great Hall of Eminence. And as it settled, the Hall seemed to breathe again, its breath then subtly picking up the ash and removing the stain of the Valkyrie's evil, lifting and casting it away into oblivion.

A bleakness enveloped the Great Hall as Lothian felt the absence of its residents; where their souls had rested in peace within the sanctity of its domain, he now sensed their torment, knowing what they were—prisoners caught in perpetual limbo.

'Where is it?!'

They turned, hearing the panic in Wareeshta's raised voice. They looked at one another as she scoured the Hall in desperation. With all that had happened, they had failed to witness the sleight of hand of another, who stole his opportunity while they had fought hard against the evil that had distracted them.

'It is *gone!*' she then stated.

Lothian, still cradling his lost love—he would give Eryian a proper burial, after—slowly looked up at Wareeshta. The Dhampir glared down at him, demanding answers. 'Where is it?' He shook his head; he could not find it either, when he had searched, in the hope that he could use it, to save Eryian.

'You *know* Magia has taken my book!' she yelled at him, then drew back, frowning when a faint smile appeared on his face. 'What is so amusing, *Warlock?*' she hissed.

'There is hope,' he told her. She tilted her head, momentarily confused. 'The dagger?' Wareeshta's face altered, her eyes widening, her mouth opening as she realised his meaning: the book and dagger were a pair. 'If the dagger is still where Oran left it …' Wareeshta nodded; Lothian was right, assuming it had not been taken from Greer's body.

Amid their discussion of the whereabouts of Magia Nera and the book, Eleanor took herself away from Asai for a few moments and walked out into the centre of the Hall, to the place where Rosalyn and Gill had vanished. She looked down at the flagstones, seeing the inscriptions of those interred beneath her, knowing they, too, were gone. The Hall now felt *empty*. She looked around her, observing the others; Reece was now engrossed in conversation with Wareeshta—no doubt conjuring a plan of sorts; while Daine looked like a lost child with nowhere to call home. What he would do now, she did not know. Then there was Kai—their friend and protector—who, now freed from his muted restraint and back in his ghostly form, was in deep conversation with Lothian, nodding, listening with intent. And then her eyes met with her soul, Asai, the one she would never be separated from. She smiled at him. But when the sudden absence of someone else—someone who had protected her throughout her childhood—dawned on her, her keen eyes searched for him.

'Where is my father?'

The lone figure stepped out into the light of the new day. And yet, they saw only darkness, its dismal atmosphere lingering, weighing on their thoughts and failings, with a quietness—the solemn kind that follows in the aftermath of tragedy. As they hung their head, feeling its burden on their slumped shoulders, a sliver of silver light appeared on the ground, marking the significance of an event that should have taken place. It moved towards them. Reluctant to follow it, they dragged their eyes up, then higher, seeing it—the moon's fading crescent. And they knew. But still, they watched. And as the new day gradually stole the last light of hope, they held their breath until it was snatched from them. And then it was gone—vanquished—the bleakness of its untimely loss, prompting the figure to act. Left with nothing but a shattering emptiness inside, they turned and walked away …

*Balloch, Scotland: 1631 – the following year – Midsummer*

The night remained still and balmy after the sun had disappeared behind the horizon, its lazy descent bringing with it a spectacular fiery sunset; it stretched out into the longest day, then gradually faded into the dusk, leaving behind the evocative atmosphere of *Litha* … before the shortening of days.

A female fox foraged for food while teaching her growing cubs how to survive the brutality nature would inevitably throw at them, now that they were weaned from her. Nearby, a buck observed them, but with no intent. It suddenly stopped and lifted its head, alert, its ears flicking, hearing an unusual cry, echo through the dark. Ignoring the fox and her juveniles, the buck lifted its nose with added interest, listening.

The strange sound grew louder—the stillness of the night carrying its prominent wail up and out into the world, as though heralding the arrival of something new. The fox looked at her young, unsure. Threatened, she promptly voiced them to "Come!" and nudged them away. But the buck stayed.

'That's it, lass! You can do it! One more!'

Then silence.

The buck stirred, lifting its ears again, hearing another cry—a new one. It looked over its shoulder from whence it came and raised one of its front legs. It was not the sound that disturbed it now but something else, as if time had shifted.

'Oh, ye have a wee, strong bonnie lass.'

The new mother looked up, her face flushed with exhaustion. Gone was the strain of her labour, it now replaced with a glow of overwhelming joy, married with relief. As the beads of sweat were dabbed away from her forehead, she soon settled. She caught her breath when the bairn was gently handed to her, clean and wrapped in its swaddle, to soothe and protect it after the trauma of its entrance into its new world.

'Well done, lass!'

The young woman looked deep into her baby's new eyes, wondering if she could see her mother as she fidgeted against her bosom. Her heart squeezed with unrequited love for the child, then ached, missing her father. She released a long-winded sigh; still, she would no longer be alone.

'Well, what will ye be calling her?' said the spaewife as she leaned over the new mother, propping her pillow.

The young woman looked up when she heard the sudden whisper

of old Gaelic behind her.

'What is that?' she then asked, eyeing something in the spaewife's hand.

'Oh, just the leftovers of the bannock you never finished—when you went into labour. 'Tis quite a prophetic symbol, you know.' When the young woman frowned up at her, the spaewife smiled and winked back. 'It means … that you may glimpse your future when you sleep. So, keep it under your pillow, aye?'

As the girl nodded with hope, her lower lip quivered.

'Now, lass … dinna fash … you have the wee'un to look after. So, what'll you be naming her?' she went on, distracting the girl from her inner thoughts. 'You must give her a name—and on this special night, too.'

Lifting her weary head, the new mother mused over her choice of names; she had chosen three yet was unsure. And when one unexpectedly came to her, her eyes lit up. Smiling through her emerging tears of renewed joy, she nodded.

'Aye! I shall call her—'

The spaewife raised a hand, cutting her off. 'Shh, lass!' Her eyes moved to the door, narrowing. Acting on instinct, she reached down and removed a weapon, from under the bed.

The young woman's eyes widened with fear, seeing the great sword. 'What—what is it?' she whispered, clutching her bairn as tight as she dared, her eyes darting between the spaewife and the door.

The spaewife hesitated, her eyes fixed and sword raised. 'I heard a noise out—'

Both women jumped when the door flew open, their eyes widening, stunned into silence before the spaewife cried out;

*'You?!'*

**To Be Continued …**

## Acknowledgements

While writing is a solitary undertaking between the author and their laptop—or pen and paper (or both!)—it is quite the opposite, when it comes to the publishing bit. Therefore, I would like to thank the following people for their help, along the way: Diana Toledo Calcado – from *Triumph Book Covers* – for working her magic, yet again! Tegan Sommers (artist) – for her amazing illustration of the butterfly for *A Flutter on the Wind*. Becky Wright (author) – of *Platform House* – for her wonderful formatting skills. Lewis Hickson – *Fantasy Maps* – for creating the maps for these novels. Jake Warren Black – my 'Wee Master of the Web'. Geraldine O'Malley (artist). James Dallin Taylor – the talented voice behind my poor suffering characters, on the Audiobooks. Eileen Budd – friend, author and Bard, who is passionate about keeping Scotland's myths & legends alive – a huge thanks to her for her help with the Scottish Gaelic. Jenn Campus, who helped me out with Magia Nera's Italian. Friend and author, Gavin (Gav) Gardiner, for the *Foreward*: cheers, guys! I owe you one! K. Summons-Walsh – my faithful critic (this one was a bitch, Kev!). And, of course, I can't forget my other great author pals: Julie Embleton – for all her help and patience; Linda Ganzini; my Scottish Bro, Stephen Mills (remembering Ellie); Graeme (and Molly!); and David Pelletier. To my dear friends – Ciara, Billy & Megan Aitken; Brenda, Aileen, Mary B, Mary (remembering Coco), Loui and Laura. The O'Shea Clan: Ruth, Ken, Naomi, Rachel, Adam, Jake & Belle (remembering Cooper). Your support means the world to me. And, finally, to all my fellow authors, readers and followers on social media, for your ongoing support. Thank you! If I have forgotten you, please forgive me and know your support is also hugely appreciated – more than you know X.

**PS:** I'll not lie, this one was a bitch to write. I blame my "muse" – for constantly bombarding me with those "extras". May it continue to do so …

## Typos & Errors (It's a fact!)

Every writer will admit, even after their books are put through the rigorous editing process—and with many eyes having scanned through the words and pages—that sometimes the human eye misses something. Even famous writers and authors will admit to this. And there's no shame in it. I get excited if/when I spot a typo in an author's work, especially if they're famous! It happens occasionally. After all, we are all just human.

*"Don't compare your Chapter 1 to someone else's Chapter 20."*
Unknown.

# About the Author

Asking an Irish person to write a 'few' words about themselves is, putting it mildly, almost impossible! But, here goes … My name is Miriam and I was born and raised in Dublin, Ireland.

Having dabbled in other "interests" over the years (I won't bore you), in the background, however, I was always an avid reader, with words constantly floating around in my mind yet doing nothing about them—in a literary sense. I always said I'd write a book, but never seemed to get around to it. I think the mere thought of putting those words—along with my imagination—to literary use, was daunting, therefore, I was always putting it off. That is, until 2011. After doing several writing courses, I finally took the plunge and picked up that pen and notebook (still have them, too!). I began to string those words into sentences, which evolved into paragraphs, eventually filling the pages of, what would become, my first novel—*The Sixth Amulet – Book One.*

Everyone has a story to tell—a potential book tucked away inside them, just dying to get out. All that's needed to create it is a simple recipe: a pen and a notebook. So, open your mind and let your imagination roam through the endless possibilities it has … then write!

I hope you enjoyed *A Flutter on the Wind* and I promise to start on book four (untitled) soon. But big books do take time to write, especially when "life" gets in the way. So, bear with me. In the meantime, and if you're inclined, the Audiobook of *The Sixth Amulet* is out now, with the Audiobook of *The Moon Chasers* (Book Two) due out, in early 2025.

Feel free to check me out on the following:

http://www.mamaddockauthor.ie
Instagram: ma.maddock_author
Twitter (X): @mamaddock1_a
Facebook: M.A. Maddock @thesixthamuletseries
https://shepherd.com/best-books/blood-curdling-time-travelling-adventures

Printed in Dunstable, United Kingdom

75458013R00296